IKE'S JOURNEY

A Novel of World War II

ROBERT KOFMAN

LION VALLEY
PUBLISHING

This is a work of historical fiction.

Published by Lion Valley Publishing, a Florida LLC
Miami, Florida

Edited and designed by Girl Friday Productions
www.girlfridayproductions.com

Cover design: Megan Katsanevakis
Project management: Emilie Sandoz-Voyer
Editorial production: Jaye Whitney Debber
Image credits: cover © USHMM

ISBN (paperback): 978-1-7329910-2-6
ISBN (ebook): 978-1-7329910-3-3

Library of Congress Control Number: 2022910476

This novel is dedicated to my wonderful, supportive, and understanding wife, Rosa; our beautiful daughters, Jenny, Abby, Miriam, and Becca; and our grandchildren, Jordie, Spencer, Jacob, Aaron, Emma, and Madison.

LIST OF MAPS

CHAPTER 1

The chief of staff for the US Third Army, Dwight Eisenhower, strode toward his Fort Sam Houston office in San Antonio, Texas, on a chilly Sunday morning. The crack of thunder from distant artillery practice rolled over the sprawling base as he reached the enclosed quadrangle housing Third Army headquarters.

In the center of the Quad stood the solid symbol of Fort Sam, a ninety-foot-high stone clock tower. A grassy green park surrounded the tower. Peacocks, deer, and other animals populated the park. Legend had it the animals were introduced when Apache chief Geronimo was held prisoner in the Quad. Before entering the stone headquarters building, Eisenhower tossed a red apple to a white-tailed deer that waited in the same spot every morning for its treat.

On the way to his office, he saw his boss, General Walter Krueger, coming out of the break room with a mug of coffee.

Eisenhower flashed a wide grin. "Good morning, General."

"Ike, grab some coffee and come into my office," Krueger said with a trace of a German accent.

In a few minutes, Eisenhower was sitting comfortably in Krueger's office, a steaming mug of black coffee cradled in his hands.

Krueger's shrewd eyes studied Eisenhower. "You look tired."

"I'll admit I'm a little worn down. The last few months have been pretty intense, beginning with the Louisiana war games."

"Those maneuvers proved what I feared—most of our officers

don't know their ass from first base when it comes to commanding men!"

Eisenhower nodded in agreement. The Third Army had participated in the war games and bested its opponent, the US Second Army. One conclusion to be drawn from the actions in sultry Louisiana was crystal clear: the hastily expanded army, fueled by a peacetime draft, was not ready to fight a war.

Krueger picked up his coffee mug. "You've served in the Far East. How much of a threat are the Japs?"

Eisenhower thought about his four years in Manila as General Douglas MacArthur's chief of staff. He had closely followed Japan's growing militarism. Its invasion of China showed a thirst for conquest. "The fact Japan signed the Tripartite Pact with Hitler and Mussolini has everyone in East Asia on edge. My major duty in the Philippines was training the Filipino army to resist a Japanese invasion."

Krueger grunted. "Yesterday I spoke with a friend who is well connected in Washington. He told me Roosevelt is really putting the screws to the Japs by freezing their assets in the US and imposing an oil embargo. I was surprised to learn we supply most of Japan's oil. He thinks the President is going to provoke a war with Japan."

"I doubt FDR wants a war with Japan," replied Eisenhower. "If anything, he wants to fight Germany."

An aide holding a sheaf of papers knocked on the open door. Krueger waved him in.

While the general reviewed the documents, Eisenhower thought about how dangerous the world had become. World War II had been raging for more than two years. The Nazis controlled most of continental Europe, including northern France, with the Nazi-collaborating Vichy government in control of southern France. Mussolini's Italy had sided with Hitler. Only Churchill's England had held out against the German onslaught, saved by the Royal Air Force's victory in the Battle of Britain and Hitler's decision to invade the Soviet Union. Now in December 1941, the German army was near Moscow—and Russia appeared on the verge of collapse.

Krueger finished reviewing the documents and returned his attention to Eisenhower. "What keeps me up at night is we're not ready to fight either the Japs or the Nazis! Roosevelt and those worthless politicians in Washington had their heads in the sand the entire decade of the thirties, stupidly cutting the army's budget while Germany and Japan built up their war machines!" Krueger stared out the window at the Stars and Stripes flapping in the breeze. He took a deep breath and exhaled. "Look, I've ranted enough. You've got work to do. But I want you to knock off at lunchtime. Take the afternoon off and get some rest."

A surprised Eisenhower asked, "Is that an order, sir?"

"It is indeed. You're no good to me if you end up in the hospital suffering from exhaustion."

He stood and with a crisp nod took his leave.

After calling his wife with the news he had the afternoon off, Eisenhower worked steadily, the occasional peacock shriek failing to break his concentration. At precisely 12:30 p.m., he headed home, looking forward to a restful afternoon.

As he walked across Fort Sam, he thought about that day in 1915 when he had been officer of the day, responsible for patrolling the large base. When he'd passed through the officers' quarters, he had spotted a visiting family with several attractive daughters sitting on a front porch. A friend waved Eisenhower over and introduced him to the Douds. After five minutes of small talk, he took his leave to continue the patrol. Mamie, the youngest daughter at age nineteen, stood up and asked if she could accompany him. Eisenhower said yes, and thus began their courtship. She must have been really smitten, because he later learned she hated long walks—and did not care much for short walks either!

He smiled at the memory from all those years ago as he reached his assigned house, Quarters 221. The two-story home had redbrick walls, a Spanish tile roof, and a wraparound porch. The home faced the parade ground, where recently arrived draftees were being drilled by a loud and shrill master sergeant.

His beloved Mamie, a petite woman with a round face, high cheekbones, and alert blue eyes, greeted him in the foyer. Pushing her bangs off her forehead, she beamed up at her blue-eyed, broad-shouldered husband. "I'm excited you're taking the afternoon off!"

Eisenhower leaned down to kiss her cheek. "So am I. I'm looking forward to taking a nap."

"Would you like a cup of coffee before lunch?" asked Mamie in a silvery voice.

"That would be great."

He headed to the living room, where Mamie's prized green Oriental rug covered the center of the wood floor. The room had a decorator's feel, with an ornamental Chinese folding screen angled in a corner. Mamie took pride in setting up her household. After each of the couple's sixteen moves, she ensured their new home's walls were quickly painted, drapes hung, rugs laid, and furniture deployed. She kept a stick of wood painted with her favorite colors—pink, green, and cream—to aid the painters in selecting the right hues.

Mamie returned to the living room with two cups of coffee in brightly painted blue china saucers and sat beside her husband on a green camelback sofa.

Before he took his first sip, Eisenhower asked, "Are you enjoying being a general's wife?"

"I'm still getting used to you finally getting your first star. A few of my friends seem put out you got promoted over their husbands. You know how rank-conscious army wives are."

"It's no different with the officers." As he drank his coffee, Eisenhower asked, "How did you spend your morning?"

"I wrote a letter to Johnny. I miss our son so much."

"Please tell me you didn't write you're worried about him."

Mamie's face flushed a deep pink. The death of their firstborn to scarlet fever and the loss of two sisters had turned her into a habitual worrier. Her husband knew her well.

Eisenhower felt his anger rising, tried to control it but failed. "Goddamnit, how many times have we been over this! You were an overly protective mother hen when he lived at home. You must quit imposing your fears on Johnny! He won't survive his plebe year at West Point if you continue undermining his self-confidence."

Mamie sprang up from the sofa and fled to the kitchen. She wrapped her arms around her chest and kept her back to her husband.

Eisenhower followed her into the kitchen to apologize for his short fuse. When he touched her shoulder, she flinched.

"Honey, I'm so sorry," he said, keeping his voice low and gentle. "I shouldn't have snapped at you. I never want to cause you pain. You'll always have my love and support."

Hearing his compassionate words, she turned, tears welling in her eyes. "I know you don't intend to be mean. But when you're angry, your voice has a rough edge that cuts through me."

Eisenhower took her hands in his. "I know you'll never stop worrying about Johnny, but for his sake, you need to hide your fears. He's nineteen and becoming a soldier. He needs to be strong and self-reliant."

"You're right. I shouldn't burden Johnny with my worries." Mamie gave her husband a searching look. "You'll love me forever?"

"Of course, honey. You're my one true love!"

He pulled her into his arms and gave her a reassuring hug. When they parted, they walked, hand in hand, back to the living room.

After lunch, Eisenhower walked upstairs to their bedroom, which bore Mamie's touch: cream-colored walls, green drapes, and a pink bedspread. He undressed and got into bed.

He was in a deep sleep when the ground began to shake. *An earthquake?* The shaking intensified. Disoriented, Eisenhower opened his eyes to see Mamie staring at him with her hand on his shoulder. Her face was pale, and her body was trembling.

He sat up, a knot forming in his stomach. "What's happened?"

In a faint voice she replied, "Japan attacked Pearl Harbor."

Eisenhower scrambled out of bed. "Pearl Harbor? Are you sure you heard 'Pearl Harbor'?"

"Yes, I'm certain the radio announcer said Pearl Harbor."

He reached for his clothes. *How brazen, how audacious the Japanese are to attack Hawaii.* He shook his head. *Japan is four thousand miles from Hawaii.*

"We're at war with Japan; I need to go to the office."

As her husband dressed, Mamie controlled her trembling and set her lips in a firm line.

Once in his uniform, Eisenhower took his wife's hand.

"I'm sure you're worried about your husband and son becoming embroiled in a war. Remember you're not alone. Every wife and mother who has men in the armed forces feels the same anxieties. We all have our duties to perform in war. Your first duty is to be supportive of me and Johnny. We need you to be our Rock of Gibraltar."

Mamie took a deep breath and straightened her back. "I've been an army wife for twenty-five years. I know my role. You and Johnny can always count on me."

"That's my gal!"

They kissed and he left the house.

As he walked across the base, Eisenhower thought about the fight ahead. The price in blood to defend American freedom was sure to be high. He hoped the army would find commanders worthy of leading brave soldiers in battle. Precious few leaders had emerged from the bayous of Louisiana.

Five days had passed since the Japanese attack on Pearl Harbor. The President gave a stirring speech, saying that day—December 7, 1941—was a date that would live in infamy. Congress declared war on Japan, and Germany declared war on the United States.

Third Army headquarters was abuzz in activity. Orders flooded in from the War Department. Fear of enemy saboteurs was great, and troops were dispatched to secure vital US infrastructure, including the Hoover Dam and the Golden Gate Bridge.

Soldiers and antiaircraft batteries were rushed to the West Coast to defend against possible Japanese attacks. Vital military aircraft factories in Los Angeles and Seattle were put under army protection. Troops were dispatched to the Mexican border to prevent the entry of spies and to the Gulf of Mexico ports to secure them from possible enemy attack.

Eisenhower was working at his desk and on his third cup of morning coffee when his phone rang. He answered the call and heard a familiar gruff voice.

"Is that you, Ike?"

It was his old friend of twenty years, General Walter Bedell "Beetle" Smith, assistant to the army's chief of staff, General George Marshall.

"Beetle, how are you?"

"Drowning in work. Listen, I don't have time for small talk. The chief says you should get your tail to Washington ASAP. Tell Krueger the paperwork will come through later."

"Why?"

"I don't fucking know! Just get your butt up here as soon as you can."

The line went dead. Eisenhower stared at the phone in his hand before slowly putting it back in its cradle. *What the hell is going on?* He didn't want a desk job in Washington. He craved action commanding troops in combat.

Mamie was startled when her husband arrived home in the middle of the morning.

"Ike, is something wrong?" she asked him in the foyer.

"I've been called to Washington."

"What are you going to do there?"

"I don't know."

"Should I plan on coming too?" she asked.

"Not yet; it could just be a temporary assignment. I'll send for you if it turns out I'm going to be there for a while. I need to pack. I'm leaving in two hours."

Mamie helped with the packing. When they finished, she asked, "We're going to win this war, aren't we?"

Eisenhower was silent for a moment. He knew wars were ugly, grotesque affairs without preordained winners. But he didn't want his wife, or anyone else, to doubt the outcome. Support on the home front was critical to an army's morale. Everyone needed to have confidence America would prevail over its enemies.

"We're in for a long and bloody struggle, but America is going to win this war!" He balled his hand into a fist and shook it for emphasis. "We're going to whip the Japs and the Nazis!"

A thin smile appeared on Mamie's face. "Thanks for the pep talk, Ike."

"I love you, honey," Eisenhower said before giving her a crushing hug. "I'll call you after I'm situated in Washington."

They kissed a long farewell, and then he was gone.

CHAPTER 2

Eisenhower reached the capital's Union Station on Sunday morning, December 14. The station's Great Hall was filled with travelers, mostly people in uniform. He worked his way through the crowd, occasionally glancing upward to admire the impressive vaulted ceiling.

He took a cab to the Munitions Building on Constitution Avenue. Erected as a temporary structure during World War I, the building took up a large swath of the National Mall, backing up to the Lincoln Memorial Reflecting Pool.

At 9:30 a.m., he was in the office of the army's chief of staff, General George Marshall. Pictures of George Washington, Abraham Lincoln, and Robert E. Lee hung on Union-blue walls. Light filtered in through a window that faced the reflecting pool.

Marshall had deep-set, penetrating blue eyes, a granite jaw, and a commanding presence that didn't invite intimacy. "Eisenhower, can you guess why I called you to Washington?"

He had thought hard about that question on his journey from Texas. "Sir, because I've had recent experience in the Philippines?"

"That's correct. You'll work in War Plans as deputy chief in charge of the Pacific theater. I'll give you an overview on where we stand in the Pacific. It's not a pretty picture. Pearl Harbor took a terrific beating. Casualties are over thirty-five hundred, with more than two thousand dead."

Eisenhower gasped. While the papers had reported many deaths, the enormity of the carnage was a shock.

Marshall stared at him without blinking. "The number of deaths is likely to rise. Many of the wounded are unlikely to survive."

Eisenhower urged himself to be calm; he didn't want the chief to think he rattled easily. "What's the situation in the Philippines?" he asked in a steady voice.

"They were bombed a few hours after Pearl Harbor. The Japanese caught the Army Air Forces on the ground at Clark Field and destroyed a large portion of it, including most of the B-17s."

Eisenhower felt like he had been punched in the gut. Losing the big bombers was a devasting blow. They had been an integral part of the plan to defeat a Japanese invasion. "And the naval base at Cavite Bay?"

Marshall delivered more bad news. "It was bombed and suffered heavy damage. Given Japan's control of the air, the navy has moved most of its ships south to the Dutch island of Borneo. There will be no air or naval opposition to the imminent Japanese invasion."

The military situation in the Pacific was far more desperate than Eisenhower imagined. "Can the navy get reinforcements and supplies to the Philippines?"

"The navy has refused to take any risks to provide relief to the Philippines."

Eisenhower was silent as he absorbed the tidal wave of bad news.

"How should we deal with the situation we're facing in the Pacific?" asked Marshall.

Eisenhower knew he was being tested. The chief must know what actions he wanted to take. "Sir, could I have a few hours to think things through?"

"All right."

Marshall returned his eyes to the work on his desk as Eisenhower got up and left the office.

Eisenhower knew his way around the Munitions Building, having worked there in the 1930s for Douglas MacArthur when MacArthur had been the army's chief of staff. He quickly found the office of his close friend Brigadier General Leonard "Gee" Gerow, who headed War Plans.

Gerow, a short, thin man, stood and warmly shook Eisenhower's hand. "It's great having an old friend on board."

"I guess you're my boss now," Eisenhower said with an easy grin.

"Maybe on paper. Your real boss is Marshall."

"How's Marshall to work for?"

"Demanding as hell. He expects his subordinates to work long hours, show initiative, and take responsibility." Gerow paused. "I'll show you where your office is. It's been set up with all the supplies you need."

"Does it have maps of the Pacific?"

"No."

"I'll need every map we have of the Pacific Ocean."

"Of course. I'll see you get them immediately," Gerow promised.

Eisenhower's office faced a tree-filled inner courtyard. That was fortunate, since the room's only decoration was an Ansel Adams print of the Grand Teton Mountains. Eisenhower sat down at the gray metal desk, thinking about a way to save the Philippines.

The US had received the 7,640-island archipelago from Spain following the Spanish-American War, and thirty thousand American soldiers were stationed there. Eisenhower's task in Manila had been to train a Filipino army to defend its homeland when the Philippines became an independent country in 1946. Now the American and Filipino soldiers he knew intimately faced desperate odds.

When the maps arrived, Eisenhower took down the Adams print. He taped Pacific maps to every square inch of wall space. He paced the office, studying the maps and paying particular attention to the islands between Hawaii and Australia.

After three hours of map study and intense thought, Eisenhower knew what strategy should be adopted. It was time to give Marshall an answer.

It was a make-or-break moment. If he failed to impress, his time in Washington likely would be short-lived. That might not be so bad;

failure here could lead to a field command. But Eisenhower was a born competitor. He didn't want to fail! While he was rarely nervous, he felt a tingling sensation in his hands as he entered the chief's office.

After Eisenhower was seated, Marshall asked, "What should our Pacific strategy be?"

"Given the navy's attitude, it will be a long time before we can get reinforcements and critical supplies to the Philippines. Probably longer than the American and Filipino soldiers can hold out." Eisenhower leaned forward, and his voice rose. "But we cannot turn our back and give them up as lost! Not only the Filipinos, but all those threatened by the Japanese, including the Australians, New Zealanders, and Chinese, will be closely monitoring our actions. Those people may forgive failure, but they'd never condone abandonment! We must do everything humanly possible to save the Philippines, even if those efforts are likely to fail."

"Do you have any other points?"

"Australia must be saved at all costs, and it should serve as the army's principal base of operations in the Pacific. We must establish a supply line between Hawaii and Australia by securing three key islands: Fiji, New Zealand, and New Caledonia."

"All right," the chief agreed, his eyes never leaving Eisenhower's. "Try and save the Philippines, and secure a lifeline to Australia."

Eisenhower felt a surge of pride. *I passed Marshall's test!*

As he stood to leave, Marshall motioned him back down.

"Your efforts will be impacted by our 'Germany first' strategy. This winter there was a meeting in Washington between the general staff and our British counterparts. The US agreed if it found itself at war with both Germany and Japan, it would make Germany the priority and fight a defensive battle against Japan."

"What's the rationale behind 'Germany first'?"

"If the Nazis were to take out Russia and England, the US would have no allies," replied Marshall. "Without our having England as a base from which to attack the European continent, Hitler would be secure and could take his time in planning attacks on America. The Germans could build up a fleet and attack the Western Hemisphere, probably first in Latin America. Once they had bases in this hemisphere, the Nazis could launch attacks against us. The thinking is we can hold off Japan in the Pacific while we build up forces to take on the Germans."

While Eisenhower understood the logic of making the Pacific a secondary theater, knowing his resources would be limited was a tough pill to swallow. "Is that 'Germany first' policy set in stone?"

"Not yet, but Winston Churchill and his military advisers are on their way to Washington. I expect the President will reaffirm it when he meets with Churchill."

Eisenhower left Marshall's office focused on getting men and supplies to Australia. He found Gerow in a small kitchen area, pouring himself a cup of coffee.

"Give me some insight into Brehon Somervell, the supply chief."

"Somervell's a doer; he gets things done. He built LaGuardia Airport when the army loaned him to the Works Progress Administration." Gerow sipped his coffee. "But he can be downright nasty when he is pushing to get something accomplished. Do you want me to introduce you?"

"That would be great."

Gerow led Eisenhower to Somervell's office. When Gerow knocked on the open door, Somervell looked up and growled, "What in the hell do you want from me now, Gee?"

"I want to introduce you to the man General Marshall has tasked with saving the Philippines, Ike Eisenhower."

Somervell stood up and walked around his desk to shake Eisenhower's hand, all the while appraising him with intense brown eyes. "Good to meet you, Ike, and please call me Bill. I hate to break it to you, but there is no way in hell that you're going to save those god-forsaken islands. The navy's abandoned MacArthur and the army, and without the navy, you've been given an impossible mission."

Eisenhower knew Somervell was speaking the harsh truth, but the words still angered him.

"Goddamnit," he roared, his neck turning crimson, "I'm not giving up before I even start! Bill, I need you to provide me with troop transports and supplies of rifles, machine guns, artillery, fighter planes, and bombers. And that's just the beginning of my shopping list! Are you going to help me here or what?"

Somervell laughed heartily. "Of course I'll help. You and I should get along just fine. You're passionate and have a temper. Reminds me of myself."

For the next few hours, Eisenhower and Somervell discussed every possible avenue of getting troops and supplies first to Australia and from there to the Philippines. When they finished, Eisenhower went back to his desk.

At 9:30 p.m., he called it a day. He found his assigned driver, who took him to his brother's house in Falls Church, Virginia. Milton had graciously offered to host him when Eisenhower called with news of his Washington assignment.

Eisenhower told the driver to pick him up at 4:30 a.m. He had made it only partway up the driveway of the redbrick center-hall colonial when the front door opened and his brother stepped out onto the stoop.

"Milt, it's wonderful to see you. Your hospitality is most appreciated!"

"Of course, Ike, you're family. Come in. Helen has supper waiting for you."

The balding Milton wore thick horn-rimmed glasses and was nine years younger than the fifty-one-year-old Eisenhower. The brothers and their wives had become close in the 1930s when they both worked in Washington. Milton was a government employee who survived the transition from the Hoover to the Roosevelt White House. He was one of FDR's go-to people for tough assignments.

When they reached the kitchen, Helen smiled and gave her brother-in-law a kiss. She was a short, slender woman with a bob of curly brown hair. "The kids wanted to stay up to see Uncle Ike, but they couldn't keep their eyes open."

"I'd love to see them . . . maybe tomorrow?" And with that, Eisenhower dropped into one of the wood chairs at the kitchen table.

Helen placed a heaping plate of food in front of him—meat loaf and mashed potatoes with gravy and carrots. Eisenhower wolfed it down. He hadn't eaten since breakfast on the train.

"I suppose what you're working on is top secret," said Milt after his brother finished devouring his meal.

"Afraid so. What are you up to, Milt? You're a mover and shaker around DC."

"I just finished an assignment the President gave me to establish the Overseas Information Agency."

"Is that a propaganda operation?"

"The agency's responsibility is to inform the world of American attitudes and activities."

"In other words, propaganda like Goebbels produces!"

The lines around Milton's mouth hardened. "There's an important difference between us and the Nazis. The information we disseminate is truthful."

"I didn't mean to offend," replied Eisenhower. "I was only teasing you. I know it's important in this war for people to know what they're fighting for." Eisenhower gave a yawn. "I need to get some shut-eye."

Milton grabbed his brother's suitcase and led him up the stairs to the second-floor guest bedroom. After changing into his pajamas, Eisenhower fell into an exhausted sleep.

CHAPTER 3

At 4:30 a.m., Eisenhower was standing in his brother's living room when a pair of headlights turned into the driveway. He opened the front door and walked out into thirty-degree air and biting wind. When his driver opened a rear car door, he hastily slid in. As they drove through quiet Virginia suburbs, he reflected on the past two weeks in the War Department.

Shipping was in short supply, but Somervell had secured some coveted transports. Eisenhower had been able to dispatch ships from San Francisco and New York to Australia loaded with vital supplies, including ammunition and fighter planes. Leaving no stone unturned, he concocted a scheme to hire blockade runners in Australia to deliver supplies to the Philippines.

While Eisenhower was heartened by these small achievements, he knew they would matter little without the support of the navy. Roosevelt had directed the navy to do what it could to help the Philippines, but the only supplies being delivered arrived on submarines with scant cargo capacity.

Progress had been made in securing a supply line to Australia. The three critical islands—Fiji, New Zealand, and New Caledonia—were in Allied hands, but they remained targets for future Japanese aggression. Eisenhower determined New Zealand was strong enough to provide its own defense and had secured authorization to send American troops to Fiji, a British possession.

New Caledonia, a French possession, had repudiated the pro-Nazi Vichy government formed in the wake of the 1940 French-German armistice and joined Charles de Gaulle's Free French movement that vowed to carry on the fight against the Nazis. Eisenhower had approval to send American soldiers to New Caledonia, but de Gaulle had yet to agree to receive them.

At 5:00 a.m., Eisenhower was at his desk. He had the ability to acutely focus, and the hours flew by. His concentration was interrupted when Beetle Smith knocked on his open door, holding a document.

Smith's intense, piercing eyes were full of fire. "Churchill is staying in the White House and has taken full advantage of his unfettered access to the President. You won't fucking believe what's happened!"

As Eisenhower read the document Smith handed him, his blood pressure rose, and the veins on his neck throbbed. "What in the hell is going on? Churchill persuaded Roosevelt to give the British the reinforcements I'm sending to Australia? This is a disaster for our defense of the Pacific!"

"Hopefully it won't stick," replied Smith. "Marshall is at the White House, trying to convince FDR of the folly of such a deal."

"You mean the President made this deal without consulting Marshall?"

"Yes, Roosevelt can be a wheeler-dealer. Marshall is determined to change the President's mind."

After Smith left, Eisenhower tilted his head back in dismay. *How in the hell can the War Department manage a global war when the President makes military decisions without consulting its chief?*

Barely an hour later, Gerow poked his head into Eisenhower's office. "I've found just the man for your blockade-busting operation, Ike! Come to my office."

When Eisenhower entered Gerow's office with its large window overlooking the reflecting pool, he saw a familiar face, the former secretary of war, Patrick Hurley.

Eisenhower knew Hurley from his days working in the War Department in the 1930s. Born in a log cabin in the Oklahoma

Territory, Hurley was a rugged frontiersman who grew up hunting with the Choctaws.

Hurley embraced Eisenhower in a bear hug. "It's great to see you, Ike! I came to volunteer for service. Gee said you had a job for me?"

"Mr. Secretary, we're going to hire blockade runners in Australia to get supplies to MacArthur, and we need a man of boundless energy and bravery to run that operation. In other words, someone like you."

"That's the type of challenge I can get excited about," Hurley said with a broad grin. "What's the budget?"

"You'll have ten million dollars to induce men to run the Japanese blockade."

Hurley was lost in thought for a minute. "Okay, I'll do it. When do you want me to leave?"

Eisenhower smiled. "Midnight and be prepared to be overseas for quite a while."

"I'm leaving tonight?"

"Yes, speed in getting the operation up and running is essential," replied Eisenhower.

"At least I'll have time to see my lawyer and revise my will!" Hurley said as he turned to leave.

When Eisenhower returned to his office, there were two messages on his desk. De Gaulle had agreed to have US troops protect New Caledonia, and Marshall had changed the President's mind—the troops would not be diverted from Australia.

At 8:00 a.m. the next day, Eisenhower called Mamie from his office.

She answered sleepily. "I'm happy to be woken up by the sound of your voice, darling."

"I love hearing your voice, honey. I miss you so, so much. It looks like I'm going to be working in the War Department for a while. I want you here, but housing in Washington is insanely hard to secure. How do you feel about living with me at Milt and Helen's?"

"If that's how it must be," she said in a wavering voice. "They're lovely people, and I'm sure they'll make me feel welcome." There was a pause; then the words came rushing out. "But I know you. I bet you haven't even left your desk to look for a place for us to live!"

Eisenhower felt sheepish. "You're right; I haven't. I've been too busy. But what I said about the housing crush is true."

"I'll make a deal with you," replied Mamie, her voice strong and steady. "I'll live with you at Milt and Helen's *if* you promise to make a real effort to find us a place to live."

"That's a deal," replied Eisenhower with enthusiasm. "I'll make the travel arrangements. Honey, I can't wait to see you."

At 8:30 a.m., Eisenhower left his office and walked down Constitution Avenue to the Federal Reserve Building to attend a joint US-British meeting of staff officers. Upon entering the Federal Bank's boardroom, he eyed the leather chairs surrounding the large conference table. As a junior officer, he was attending as an observer. He sat in a hardwood chair against the wall with the junior officers of both nations.

The meeting was cochaired by Marshall and his British counterpart, Field Marshal Sir John Dill.

Marshall opened the meeting. "I propose that in each theater where our forces fight together, there should be one man vested with authority to command all the troops, air, ground, and ships of both nations. I've discussed this proposal with President Roosevelt, and it has his full endorsement."

"We don't have a theater commander with the authority you suggest over His Majesty's armed forces," Dill replied. "In each theater, we have army, navy, and air commanders on an equal level. No commander has authority to insist a sister service take any specific action. Theater commanders must cooperate to achieve coordinated action. We find this committee system works quite well."

"The United States has a similar history, where the army and navy are equals without power to direct the other service's actions," replied Marshall. "During World War One, I witnessed just how dysfunctional allied fighting can be when there is no unity of command. What I'm proposing may appear radical, but I believe it's quite necessary."

"We understand how important the unity-of-command concept is to the United States," Dill grudgingly acknowledged, "and we'll give your proposal the most serious and careful consideration."

"Sir John, if our forces are not integrated into a unified command, there'll be a lack of cohesion that will harm our chances of success." Marshall moved on to the proposal he had fleshed out with Eisenhower as a sweetener. "I suggest ABDA [Australian, British, Dutch, American] be the first Allied unified command led by General Sir Archibald Wavell."

Dill responded respectfully. "Your suggestion that an English general command all Allied forces in the Far East is interesting. We have a lot to digest. I suggest we take a break to caucus."

Before the resumption of the meeting, Marshall approached Eisenhower. The chief spoke softly so as not to be overheard by those milling about. "Dill says the Royal Navy is deeply opposed to unity of command, given its long history of independence. They don't want to take orders from an army officer. He told me I have to persuade Churchill to overrule the Royal Navy if we're to have unity of command in this war."

It was the last day of 1941, and Eisenhower was on his fourth cup of coffee when Gerow knocked on his door and then stuck his head in. "The boss wants to see us."

When the two friends entered the chief's office, Marshall was smiling. Eisenhower was surprised: he had never seen the man smile!

"I'm happy to report Churchill overruled the objections of the Royal Navy!" Marshall said almost giddily. "We're going to have unity of command!"

"How did you manage that?" asked Gerow.

"First, I had the President work on the Prime Minister. He told me Churchill was inclined to support the Royal Navy, but he would hear me out if I went to see him. The President arranged for me to meet the PM yesterday morning in the White House.

"When I got there, I was shown into Churchill's bedroom." Marshall laughed. "He was still in his pajamas, smoking a cigar with a glass of whisky by his bed! He gruffly told me to state my case.

"When I finished, he waved his cigar at me and asked, 'What in the name of God would an army officer like Wavell know about naval warfare?' He went on to cite the names of great English admirals and the magnificent battles they'd won without the interference of some ignorant army officer. I responded Wavell would control strategy, not naval tactics. All theater operations had to be under one man to avoid the mistakes of the last war."

Marshall chuckled. "At this point, Churchill interrupted our meeting to take his bath! Fifteen minutes later, he came out of the bathroom with that ample middle of his wrapped in a towel and still smoking his cigar. And that's when he said, 'Marshall, you have to take the worst of me with the best!'"

"Churchill sounds like a real character." Eisenhower grinned.

"He's an original; that's for sure," replied Marshall. "He and I continued to argue for some time. Finally, he said he admired the broad-mindedness of my concept and would discuss it with his military advisers. This morning, the President informed me Churchill has agreed to unified command in each theater where Allied countries are fighting together." Marshall looked down at the pile of papers on his desk. "We've spent enough time discussing this little victory in structuring our alliance with the British. It's time to get back to work."

That night, Eisenhower left his office well after dark and arrived at Milt and Helen's house before their children had gone to bed. He enjoyed the time he was able to spend playing with twelve-year-old Buddy and five-year-old Ruth.

After his niece and nephew were asleep, Eisenhower called Mamie. "Honey, happy New Year! I can't wait to hold you in my arms!"

"I can't either!" replied Mamie in her sweet voice. "You've been gone two and a half weeks, but it feels like two and a half years!"

"You'll be here next week, so our wait's almost over."

At midnight, Milt opened a bottle of champagne. As the brothers and Helen raised toasts for a better year and speedy victory in the war, Eisenhower thought about his aging parents in Abilene, Kansas.

David and Ida Eisenhower were deeply religious. They didn't drink and would not be toasting the New Year. Without much money, they had raised six rambunctious boys, all of whom turned out successful. Even though his parents were pacifists, they hadn't objected to his choice of West Point, because it offered him a free college education.

On this New Year's Eve, Eisenhower hoped David and Ida would be proud of him, defending the country that allowed them religious freedom in a world embroiled in war.

CHAPTER 4

On January 4, 1942, Eisenhower and Gerow were summoned to Marshall's office. They found the chief standing with his hands behind his back, staring out the window at heavily falling snow. At their entrance, Marshall turned and beckoned them to sit.

"Eisenhower, I've decided you need to join Gerow with having access to information we get from a most secret source. Army code breakers have been able to decipher certain Japanese radio messages, and the information culled from this source is called Magic. Given your role as our top strategist for the Pacific, I've determined you need access to Magic. The Japanese believe their codes are unbreakable, so you must never do anything to compromise this secret."

"Understood, sir."

Marshall handed Eisenhower a three-page document. "This is the latest Magic intelligence."

Eisenhower read the intercept that described Japanese plans for an invasion of the Dutch East Indies.

When he finished reading, Marshall said, "It's no surprise the Japanese intend to invade the Dutch islands, and right now we have precious few resources to aid the Dutch defense forces. I want you to do your best to provide them some help."

"Yes, sir."

"You can return to your duties."

When Gerow and Eisenhower reached the War Plans suite, Gerow asked Eisenhower to come to his office. "I'm relieved the chief has taken you into the Magic circle, Ike. It's been awkward trying to convey information to you without talking about Magic."

"It's nice being part of the club," Eisenhower agreed. Then he paused, thinking. "Gee, did Magic give any advance warning of the Pearl Harbor attack?"

Gerow squeezed his hands together nervously before responding. "Not exactly."

Eisenhower's quick temper fired up at the hedging response. "What the hell does that mean?"

"The Magic intercepts showed the intensity of Japan's anger over Roosevelt's economic sanctions and implied the possibility of war if negotiations to ease the sanctions were unsuccessful. On November 26, the President called Marshall to the White House and told him negotiations with Japan were at an impasse. At that meeting, Secretary of State Cordell Hull said he feared the Japanese were prepared to attack without warning. Marshall briefed me on the White House meeting, and I prepared a message to all our territories in the Pacific, including Hawaii, warning a Japanese attack was possible at any moment, and to take appropriate precautions."

"My God, we had knowledge of a potential attack and were still taken by surprise!" Eisenhower exclaimed, the unexpected news filling him with disgust.

Gerow shook his head as if trying to dispel a bad dream. "Magic produced a final warning, an intercept on December 6 telling the Japanese embassy in Washington to burn codes and destroy cipher machines."

"That kind of action could only mean war."

"Yes, but we didn't know *where*. Pearl Harbor wasn't mentioned. The intercept had to be translated into English, and it only reached Marshall on Sunday morning. With the time difference between Washington and Hawaii, this was before the attack started. Marshall sent a warning to all Pacific commands, but it wasn't received in Hawaii until the attack was underway."

"What about the navy?" queried Eisenhower. "They must have equal access to Magic?"

"They had the same intelligence information as General Marshall,"

Gerow confirmed. "Our Pacific naval forces were warned of a possible Jap attack."

Eisenhower stood. "I need to take a walk."

He moved toward the Munitions Building's front door, his mind racing. The Magic intercepts showed Roosevelt knew his inflexible negotiating position was likely to lead to war with Japan.

Flinging open the exit door, Eisenhower bolted out into the winter storm. He marched forward, flicking snow from his face and ignoring the harsh winds as his anger boiled. The army and navy commanders in Hawaii had *ten days' warning* of a possible attack, and yet had been caught napping! Roosevelt may have wanted war, but he sure as hell didn't want American forces unprepared for an attack. *Brave American sailors and soldiers are dead because of the military's incompetence!*

By the time Eisenhower turned back toward the Munitions Building, his fury had dissipated. He couldn't change the past; he had to focus on the present. The war continued to go poorly: the Americans had lost the islands of Wake and Guam, and the British had lost Hong Kong. While MacArthur was fighting bravely in the Philippines, the situation was hopeless with the navy refusing to ferry in supplies and reinforcements.

Eisenhower sat down at his desk, feeling low. He picked up the phone and called Mamie. She had a way of soothing his nerves and lifting his spirits during difficult times.

When she answered, he said, "Darling, I needed to hear your voice."

"Is something wrong, Ike? You sound down."

"It's been a tough day," he admitted with a sigh.

"Oh, Ike, I wish I were there to give you a big hug."

Thinking about having Mamie in his arms was exciting. "You'll be here soon, darling, and I'm really looking forward to that hug."

The Beaux-Arts Union Station was packed with humanity and pulsing with activity. There were hundreds of faces in the crowd, but one face stood out immediately, even though its owner was slight of stature.

Eisenhower waved as soon as he picked Mamie out in the crowd in the Great Hall. They moved toward one another to embrace and kiss.

"I've missed you, darling," she said, her eyes shining.

"I'm happy to have you in my arms!" He gave her a tight squeeze to prove it.

Eisenhower picked up his wife's suitcase and led her out of the cavernous train terminal. Outside, they found his driver, who chauffeured them to Milton's home in Falls Church.

After getting Mamie settled in the small guest room and spending an hour catching up on the doings at Fort Sam, Eisenhower ordered his driver to take him to the Munitions Building. He felt bad about not spending more time with Mamie, but his sense of duty compelled him to return to work. With problems mounting faster than solutions, he couldn't slack off from work to be with the love of his life.

He hoped his grueling work schedule wouldn't affect Mamie, whose health could be fragile.

CHAPTER 5

At 9:00 p.m., Eisenhower wearily walked out of the Munitions Building to end his workday. His efforts to get aid to the Philippines had amounted to little. Some of Hurley's blockade runners had gotten through, but the supplies they delivered fell far short of MacArthur's needs.

As his driver slowly navigated Virginia's icy roads, he thought about Mamie. Eisenhower felt terrible his heavy work schedule left so little time to spend with her.

In her five weeks of living in Falls Church, Mamie had left the house only to go on shopping trips with Helen and for doctor visits. Mamie's health suffered when she was under stress, and in the last week she had experienced a recurrence of dizzy spells where she had to lean on furniture, walls, whatever was available to avoid falling.

When Eisenhower reached Milt's house, Helen warmly greeted him. "I'll have dinner on the table in a few minutes. There'll only be three of us tonight. The kids are asleep, and FDR sent Milt to Tennessee."

"What's happening in Tennessee?"

"Something to do with the Tennessee Valley Authority."

Their discussion was interrupted when Eisenhower saw Mamie unsteadily coming down the stairs, holding on to the banister. He quickly moved to help her.

"How's my gal today?" he said cheerfully as he grabbed hold of her hand.

She smiled at his words, a hint of color gracing her complexion. "Better now that you're here, darling."

During dinner, Eisenhower casually asked Mamie, "How did your doctor's appointment go?"

"He thinks my balance issues may be due to an inner-ear problem, but none of the tests confirmed a diagnosis. It's frustrating not knowing what's causing this dizziness."

Eisenhower placed his hand on Mamie's. "Don't worry, darling. I'm sure they'll figure out the cause and a way to treat it."

After dinner, Eisenhower helped his wife climb the stairs to the guest bedroom. With the door closed behind them, she sat down on the bed.

"Ike," she said in an accusatory tone, "you haven't honored your promise to find us a place in DC. I feel cooped up living way out here in Virginia. I want to live in Washington, like we did in the thirties. Many of our friends from those days are still there. If we had a place in Washington, I could see some of them—socialize a bit, not feel so isolated."

"I've tried. I called the Wyoming Apartments where we used to live, and they have a waiting list a mile long, as does every other apartment building in Washington."

Eisenhower sat down on the bed beside Mamie and took her hand. "Your happiness is important to me; I'll redouble my effort to find us a place."

"Thank you, Ike. I know you can find us an apartment if you put your mind to it."

The next morning, Eisenhower approached Gerow for help. "I need to find an apartment in the city for Mamie; she needs to be around more people than just my brother's family. Any suggestions?"

Gerow thoughtfully stroked his chin. "That's a tough one. With federal employment growing by leaps and bounds, Washington is bursting at the seams."

"There must be someone who can pull a few strings and conjure up an apartment!" Eisenhower said in an urgent tone.

"Hmm . . . hey, you remember Harry Butcher?"

Eisenhower pictured the outgoing, gregarious Iowan who worked for CBS Radio. "Sure. Mamie and I used to have dinner with Butch and his wife, Ruth."

"He now runs CBS's Washington operation. He's very connected in the city. You should give him a call."

Eisenhower immediately called CBS. It took a while, but he finally got Butcher on the line.

"Butch, this is Ike Eisenhower."

"You're a blast from the past."

"I'm back in the War Department, and I have a favor to ask."

"Happy to help an old friend," Butcher said jovially.

"Mamie and I need to find an apartment in the city."

"You're asking for a miracle, not a favor."

"I've heard you can pull rabbits out of a hat!"

Butcher roared with laughter. "I didn't realize you had such a good sense of humor! Listen, Ike, I was serious when I said you were looking for a miracle." Butcher paused. "I have an idea or two, though. I'll look into them and get back to you."

Two days later, Eisenhower's phone rang at his desk in War Plans.

"Ike, it's Butch. I have a lead for you on a place."

Eisenhower was excited. "That's great."

"If you want this apartment, you need to jump on it today or it will be gone."

Eisenhower stared at the stack of documents in his inbox. "I can't get away today."

"You have to if you want this place."

Eisenhower was torn; he didn't have time to leave work to find an apartment, but he knew how happy Mamie would be if he found a spot in the city. "All right. Where's this apartment?"

"You know the Wardman Park Hotel?"

"Sure, it's just off Connecticut Avenue up near the zoo."

"There is a one-bedroom apartment available in the residential tower. Can you meet me there in an hour?"

Eisenhower hesitated. Then he thought of Mamie's unhappiness. "Yes, I'll be there."

Eisenhower arrived a few minutes early in the affluent, mostly residential Woodley Park neighborhood. The Wardman Park was an attractive redbrick building surrounded by elm and birch trees, their branches barren in the winter. Looking around, he knew Mamie would love the area. Not only did he see several restaurants and a grocery store close by, but they had friends who lived in Woodley Park.

When Butcher arrived, Eisenhower asked, "How did you find an apartment in this neighborhood?"

"Ruth and I live here in the CBS corporate apartment. The apartment you're going to see just came open. There's a waiting list, but I used my persuasive skills to get you first crack at it."

The property manager gave them a tour, which didn't last long. The apartment wasn't large—a single bedroom, one bath, a living room, and a kitchenette. Without calling Mamie to discuss it first, Eisenhower signed the lease. He knew she would be over the moon with the location.

But his sense of good fortune didn't last long. When he returned to the Munitions Building, he received sobering news. The British stronghold of Singapore, the Gibraltar of the East, had fallen, and more than eighty-five thousand British Commonwealth soldiers had been taken prisoner.

Late that afternoon, Eisenhower received a message to see Marshall. Once he was seated, the chief made a startling announcement.

"Eisenhower, we're reorganizing the War Department. War Plans is being abolished and replaced by the newly created Operations Division, the OPD. The War Plans staff will transition to OPD. Gerow is being transferred to a field command. You're going to run OPD."

Eisenhower was dumbstruck. He had no inkling such a change was being contemplated, and while the promotion to head OPD was flattering, it likely meant he would spend the rest of the war in Washington.

"Sir, I'm appreciative of your confidence in me. But I don't want to be chained to a desk for the rest of the war. I want a combat command."

Marshall's jaw muscles tightened, and his eyes narrowed. "Have you ever commanded troops in battle?"

Eisenhower knew he was being put in his place. The chief must know his service record—that he had spent World War I training tankers in Gettysburg, on the fields of Pickett's famous charge. "No, sir. I never deployed to France in the last war."

Marshall was silent for a few moments, then leaned forward. "It's my job to place officers in the best positions for their skills. You have an outstanding record as a staff officer and have performed well during your time in War Plans. In my opinion, you're more valuable to the army running OPD than commanding troops. Your position heading OPD is one of critical importance. Your shop will write my orders relating to strategies, tactics, and operations in all theaters of war. I want you to operate OPD as if it were my staff command post in the field."

Eisenhower sighed. He was a good soldier and would accept the assignment without further argument. "Sir, it's a big job you've given me. I'll perform it to the best of my ability."

Marshall sat back in his chair. "I know this sounds harsh after denying you a field command. In this war, generals will get additional stars on their shoulders for commanding troops in combat and not for sitting behind a desk in the War Department."

Eisenhower's temper had been on low boil, and now it exploded. "Goddamnit, I don't care about promotions; I just want to do my part to win the war! If that locks me to a desk, so be it!"

When Marshall didn't respond, Eisenhower knew the meeting was over. As he opened the door, he looked back toward the chief. There was a faint smile on his face.

Eisenhower headed straight to Gerow's office.

"Gee, I just came from meeting with Marshall."

"Ike, congratulations on your promotion! I'm sure you'll do a swell job."

"Honestly, I'm envious of you getting a field command. What outfit are you getting?"

"The Twenty-Ninth Infantry Division, a National Guard outfit. Marshall is promoting me to major general, so I'm getting a second star."

Eisenhower smiled. "That's great! I'm sure you'll do a bang-up job!"

Gerow looked down before confiding, "The reality is I'm being booted out of here. On my watch, we had Pearl Harbor, lost Wake and Guam, and the Philippines are sure to fall. I pray to God you do better!"

CHAPTER 6

The move to Wardman Park did wonders for Mamie's health. Her diz-ziness quickly disappeared, and she began having lunches with old friends. At the beginning of March, she asked her husband, "I want to do something for the war effort. Do you have any suggestions?"

Eisenhower was pleased with her desire to volunteer. "Some of the OPD wives do waitering in the canteens. Does that have any appeal?"

She smiled. "I like the idea of waiting on our soldier boys. Some of them are as young as Johnny. Yes, I'd like that."

"Great! I'll see it gets arranged."

A week later, Eisenhower was surprised when he came home to find Mamie wearing a military-style uniform, complete with a tie and a captain's hat with a white stripe. The green jacket had a patch iden-tifying her as a female volunteer. The tailored uniform fit her figure in a flattering way, and it was clear Mamie knew it did. When she saw Eisenhower looking at her outfit, she did a pirouette.

"What do you think?" she said with a wide grin.

Eisenhower whistled. "You look great, honey! I didn't know can-teen volunteers wore uniforms."

"I've learned the women's volunteer movement started with the Stage Door Canteen in New York. Those New York ladies wanted to look sharp for our servicemen and developed this uniform."

"So, you ordered and paid for the uniform?" asked Eisenhower.

A look of concern flashed in Mamie's eyes. "Are you angry with me for spending the money?"

"Absolutely not. I love the uniform! Especially the way you look in it!"

The plight of the Philippines was weighing on Eisenhower. The navy refused to run convoys from Australia, and the President wouldn't order them to take the risk. American and Filipino troops were bottled up on the Bataan Peninsula, while MacArthur was isolated on Corregidor Island in Manila Bay. Food, medical supplies, and ammunition were fast running out. *The only area in the world where the US Army is engaged in combat has been abandoned by the American government.*

But as the head of OPD, Eisenhower had the whole world to worry about. Marshall had tasked him with devising a plan for getting American troops into the war against Germany. At 2:00 p.m., he was in the chief's office to present his plan for Europe.

With his usual directness, Marshall asked, "What's the best way to take on the Germans?"

"Sir, I recommend building up a large Allied force in England and then invading occupied France across the English Channel. The shortest way to Germany is through France."

"When would we be ready for an invasion of France?"

"The earliest date is April 1943," replied Eisenhower. "Many preliminary steps need to be taken, including securing air supremacy, constructing specialized landing craft, and building up our forces in England. Even if all these steps are accomplished sooner, notoriously bad weather over the English Channel would preclude an invasion from October through March."

Marshall leaned forward. "That's more than a year away. I don't know if the President will wait that long for Americans to begin fighting Nazis. The Russians are barely hanging on and need some action from us to pressure the Germans. Do you have an alternative that allows for fighting in 1942?"

"Yes, but it involves high risks."

Marshall waved his hand, signaling, "Let's have what you got."

"We could do a limited assault this year somewhere on the French coast with the goal of establishing a bridgehead on the continent. The attack would have to be launched by September, before the fall storms start."

"What are the challenges with an invasion of France this year?"

"It will be impossible by September to gain control of the air, and the invasion would lack punch," Eisenhower explained. "A million more soldiers would be available for a 1943 attack than for one this year. Also, a shortage of specialized landing craft would limit the size of our invading force. Particularly worrying is a scarcity of a British invention—a large narrow draft boat they call a 'Landing Ship Tank,' LST for short—that can land tanks on beaches."

"The navy has control over ship construction. Have you met with Admiral King, the new chief naval officer?" asked Marshall.

"Yes, I met with King. He wasn't cooperative."

"Ernie King can be quite difficult," replied Marshall. "His daughter described him as the most even-tempered admiral in the navy—he's in a rage all the time!"

Eisenhower laughed at the first joke he heard Marshall tell. "You pegged King. He made it clear building landing craft for a European invasion is a low priority for the navy."

"I'll take the landing craft issue up with King."

"Thank you, sir."

"Are you recommending a 1942 invasion to relieve pressure on the Red Army despite the risks?" asked Marshall.

"Only if it appeared the Russians were about to drop out of the war. Then a 1942 attack could be justified as an emergency measure to keep them in the fight."

Marshall was silent, absorbed in thought. After a few minutes, he said, "I agree with your reasoning. I'll take your proposals up with the President."

When Eisenhower got back to his office, there was a telegram on his desk. It brought the sad news his father had passed away.

It wasn't a shock; his father had been ill for the last year. Eisenhower felt sadness at the news, but not overwhelming grief: his father had been a quiet, withdrawn man who had difficulty expressing his feelings for his children.

I should travel to Abilene for the funeral to support Mother. But my brothers will be there for her. Perhaps I'm being narcissistic, but managing OPD is too important to the war effort to be interrupted by long trips to and from Kansas. It's no time to engage in sacred customs. I'm going to stay here and keep working.

Eisenhower closed his office door, bowed his head, and prayed for his father's soul.

Milt and Helen traveled to Abilene for David Eisenhower's funeral. On their return, they came to the Wardman Park for dinner. While they were having dessert, Eisenhower said to Milt, who had been unusually quiet during dinner, "You seem to be taking Dad's loss hard."

"I am, but that's not the only reason for my dark mood. The President gave me a distasteful job."

"What job, Milt?" asked Mamie.

Milt looked at his sister-in-law. "Yesterday, FDR called me to the Oval Office. Normally he's relaxed and usually starts meetings with pleasantries or an amusing story. Not yesterday. He looked stressed and was quite blunt. He told me I had a new job—I was to immediately set up a new agency, the War Relocation Authority, the WRA. Its purpose is to remove Japanese Americans from the Pacific coast and put them in internment camps in interior states."

Eisenhower knew from Magic reports that Japan was trying to recruit Japanese Americans for espionage activities. "You mean, removing those Japanese Americans who have been identified as security threats?"

"No! The intent is to remove *all* Japanese Americans from the Pacific coast—men, women, and children! The President issued an executive order allowing the secretary of war to establish military zones wherein the military commander can exclude any person he wants."

"You're going to remove whole families, even if they're American citizens?" asked Mamie incredulously.

"That's the plan. The President said West Coast politicians and newspapers have created public hysteria over possible sabotage and spying by Japanese Americans. FDR told me the removal program must be implemented with the greatest possible speed."

"This seems like a drastic overreaction," said Eisenhower.

"I agree!" Milt said passionately. "Most Japanese are law-abiding, hardworking people who haven't done anything to warrant being uprooted from their homes."

"Have you talked to the military commanders on the Pacific coast?" asked Eisenhower. "What's the threat level?"

"I spoke with General Dewitt, commander of the Western Defense Command. He told me he couldn't tell the difference between loyal and disloyal Japanese Americans. They all look the same to him, and the FBI agreed with him."

"You seem pretty bothered by the assignment. Are you going to keep the job?" asked Eisenhower.

"I must balance my unease with the fact we're at war and the President has given me an assignment he believes is important for national security. I'm going to keep the job for the time being. Perhaps I can exert some influence to see this upheaval in the lives of Japanese Americans is carried out in a humane fashion."

CHAPTER 7

When the alarm clock rang at 4:00 a.m., Eisenhower sleepily reached out and turned it off. One advantage of living in Washington was a shorter commute. He could sleep longer and still be at his desk at 5:00 a.m.

In bed beside him, Mamie yawned. "Ike, I'll get up and make you breakfast."

"It's not necessary, darling. Go back to sleep."

Mamie sat up. "I hardly see you. You're worth losing a little sleep over!"

Eisenhower watched her with affection as she clambered out of bed before he got up to shower and dress. Then he went into the kitchenette, where Mamie had brewed a pot of coffee. Pouring himself a cup, he watched as his wife scrambled eggs and toasted bread.

Eisenhower was proud Mamie had mastered kitchen basics. When they were first married, she didn't know how to cook. She had grown up in an affluent home in Denver where her family's servants did all the cooking and cleaning.

Eisenhower had experienced quite the opposite upbringing: his parents had required him and his five brothers to rotate chores, including the cooking. He enjoyed cooking and prepared most of the meals in the early years of his marriage to Mamie.

Eisenhower looked at his watch; it was 4:40 a.m. As he got up from the table, Mamie reminded him, "Milt is having dinner with us tonight. Please try to be home by nine."

"I'll do my best."

He left the apartment, taking the elevator to the lobby and walking out into the fresh morning air. His new driver, Mickey McKeogh, was waiting for him on Woodley Road.

McKeogh, a former New York City bellhop, had been Eisenhower's orderly at Fort Sam. Eisenhower valued McKeogh's competence and strong sense of loyalty, and arranged for his transfer to Washington.

McKeogh, who had a round face and thick brown hair, opened the rear door as Eisenhower approached. "Good morning, boss."

"Good morning, Mickey."

McKeogh put the car in gear, and at the light turned onto the nearly deserted Connecticut Avenue. On the drive to the Munitions Building, Eisenhower thought about the ongoing Philippines tragedy.

The American and Filipino soldiers couldn't hold out much longer. The President had ordered MacArthur to leave Corregidor Island. MacArthur took his wife, four-year-old son, and a few close aides with him. When they made it through the Japanese blockade, MacArthur received a hero's welcome in Australia.

Eisenhower's feelings about MacArthur were mixed. He admired the man's brilliant intellect but deplored his megalomania. MacArthur was a pathological egotist whose visions of grandeur irritated the hell out of Eisenhower. He thanked God he worked for Marshall, a man he admired and respected.

He had been at work for three hours when the irrepressible Bill Somervell appeared at his doorway.

"I want to show you my baby! You can't say no today; you've turned me down five times already."

"Bill, I'm buried in work. I can't get away," Eisenhower protested, waving his hand at the stacks of paperwork on his desk.

"I won't take no for an answer this time. You'll only be gone an hour."

Somervell was as persistent as an avalanche—no wonder he got things accomplished! Eisenhower knew he would continue to be hounded until he gave in, so he might as well get it over with. "Okay, let's go."

As they walked out of the Munitions Building, Eisenhower thought about the power Somervell had gained in Marshall's War Department reorganization. The army had been divided into three huge commands, the Army Ground Forces, the Army Air Forces, and the Army Service Forces (ASF) under Somervell.

The two men went out into bright sunshine and pleasant sixty-five-degree April weather. Somervell's driver headed west on Constitution Avenue and turned past the majestic Lincoln Memorial to get on the Memorial Bridge.

Ahead, Eisenhower spied the former plantation of General Robert E. Lee's wife. During the Civil War, the federal government had confiscated the plantation for failure to pay an insurrectionist tax and created Arlington National Cemetery.

The driver turned onto the George Washington Memorial Parkway and quickly exited to an enormous construction site swarming with thirteen thousand workers. Somervell beamed and puffed out his chest like a rooster. "There she is, Ike! My baby—the new War Department building!"

"Why do you call this place 'your baby'?"

Somervell's eyes sparkled. "I never get tired of telling the story! In July 1941, I was asked to come up with plans for a new building for the War Department. That was a Thursday afternoon. I got hold of architect George Bergstrom and Major Hugh Casey, my chief engineer. I gave them until nine a.m. Monday to design the building. I told them I wanted a modern office building large enough for forty thousand workers and to examine a building site next to Arlington National Cemetery. Monday morning, they presented me with a design for a pentagonal building with five concentric office corridor rings. I was quite pleased with the distinctive design."

"Why shape it like a pentagon?"

"That fit the contour of the original construction site near the cemetery. Some congressmen ended up protesting the building would be too close to the cemetery, and Roosevelt forced me to move it here. I didn't want to waste time having the building redesigned, so I kept the original plans. This will be the largest office building in the world, and it's being built in record time!"

The men were standing with their backs to the Potomac. Eisenhower turned and looked across the river at Washington where the Jefferson Memorial was under construction in West Potomac Park. Its white marble gleamed in the sunlight. He turned back toward the Pentagon. "It looks like part of it is almost complete."

"I'm building the Pentagon in sections. When the first section is complete in April, we'll move personnel in, just eight months after construction started."

"That's an incredible achievement, Bill."

"No other man in America could have gotten the Pentagon built as fast as me!"

True to his word, Somervell kept it to a quick tour of the Pentagon site and had Eisenhower back at his desk in an hour. A message awaited him to see the chief.

Eisenhower was surprised by the news Marshall delivered.

"Eisenhower, I've told you not to expect a promotion working in the War Department. In your case, I've changed my mind. I view you almost as a field operations officer, sort of a subordinate commander. I've asked the President to promote you to major general."

Only eight months ago, Eisenhower was a colonel, and now he would be a two-star general. Mamie would be so proud!

During dinner that night with Mamie and Milt, Eisenhower casually said, "I'm getting a second star."

Mamie's cheeks flushed, and she clapped her hands in joy. "That's fabulous, honey! You've earned it! I'm so proud of you!"

She got up and went into the kitchen while Milt was shaking his hand.

"Congratulations, Ike!"

Mamie came back, holding a bottle of champagne. She held it up with a huge smile. "I've had this stashed away for a special occasion, and your promotion to major general counts!"

She popped the cork, and they toasted his promotion.

After dinner, Eisenhower asked Milt, "What's going on with the WRA?"

"It's been hectic. I've made several trips to San Francisco to assess the situation in person and meet with leading Japanese Americans there. Mike Masaoka heads an advisory council that represents those ordered to be interned. He told me people are worried about what's going to happen to their property. I met with officials of the Federal Reserve Bank in San Francisco. They've agreed to protect the physical assets of evacuees by renting their properties and depositing the income in the name of the property owner.

"I also convened a conference of western governors in Salt Lake City. I told them the hysteria occurring on the Pacific coast didn't have to prevail in their intermountain states; after all, none of the evacuees has been charged with disloyalty. I was completely shocked when many of the governors started yelling at me. They're outraged the WRA wants to move Japanese Americans into their states. One governor threatened the evacuees would be hanging from trees if we dared bring any into his state."

"Who made that threat?" asked Eisenhower, angered by the lynch-mob mentality.

"I don't want to name the many governors who were outrageously hostile; it's too politically sensitive. The only reasonable governor was Ralph Carr of Colorado. He's willing to accept evacuees in his state."

After Milt left, Eisenhower was ready for some sleep. But when he entered the bedroom, he stopped short. Mamie was wearing a skimpy nightgown and bright red lipstick. The scent of her favorite perfume floated in the air.

Eisenhower felt desire rise in his loins, and he forgot about sleep. He approached Mamie, and they embraced.

His wife purred in his ear, "Come to bed, darling."

CHAPTER 8

Eisenhower was used to impromptu orders to see Marshall. Usually, he found the chief with a stern, noncommittal expression on his face, but today he looked satisfied.

"The President has approved the War Department recommendations for engaging the Germans," said Marshall. "There will be three interrelated plans.

"Bolero will be a buildup of American forces in England leading to Roundup, a spring 1943 invasion of France. Sledgehammer will be an invasion of France this year, *if* the Russians are on the precipice of dropping out of the war. OPD should immediately begin formulating detailed plans."

"Congratulations, sir! It's good the President has accepted your counsel."

The chief gave a slight nod of acknowledgment. "While I've developed a solid working relationship with the President, I'm under no illusion he'll always accept my advice. He's extremely self-confident in his own judgment."

"Did you have the opportunity to resolve the landing craft issue with Admiral King?"

"When I met with King, he wouldn't budge. King and I took it to Roosevelt, who compromised. He ordered the navy to expedite a landing craft construction program to support the 1943 invasion of France, but not at the level I requested." Marshall shrugged. "The President said the army always requests double what it needs."

There was some truth to Roosevelt's point, but Eisenhower held his tongue.

"The President is sending me and Harry Hopkins to London to try to get the British on board with our plans," Marshall continued.

Eisenhower knew Hopkins was Roosevelt's closest adviser; indeed, the man lived in the White House. He was the President's diplomatic troubleshooter.

"When are you leaving?"

"Tomorrow. Since I'll be out of the country for God knows how long, you need to be aware of an audacious operation the President approved. We're going to bomb Tokyo."

"What?" Eisenhower asked, shocked. The closest US airfield was on Midway Island, twenty-five hundred miles from Japan. "How can we possibly bomb Tokyo?"

"By launching bombers off an aircraft carrier."

Eisenhower was slack jawed. "I didn't know a bomber could launch from a carrier!"

"A B-24 can take off from, but not land on a carrier," the chief clarified. "After bombing Japan, the pilots are going to land in the part of China controlled by Chiang Kai-shek. Jimmy Doolittle, the stunt pilot, is leading the operation. Two days ago, the carrier *Hornet* with sixteen B-24s on board left San Francisco. At this point, it's in the hands of the navy. I doubt we'll have a role to play, but I wanted you in the loop as my backup."

On April 9, Eisenhower was in a Bolero planning meeting when an aide handed him a note. He read it with sorrow. After four months of fighting on the Bataan Peninsula, twenty-five thousand US and fifty-five thousand Filipino troops had surrendered. Only Corregidor Island remained unconquered.

Eisenhower was friends with many of the soldiers, both American and Filipino, who were now captives of the Japanese. He had heard stories of Japanese brutality toward British, Australian, and Dutch prisoners of war. He sent up a silent prayer to God that the new captives wouldn't suffer similar mistreatment.

Marshall sent periodic reports from London on the status of his negotiations with the British. On April 14, he cabled agreement had been reached in principle, although "many if not most hold reservations over this or that."

On his return, Marshall briefed Eisenhower.

"Churchill and his advisers quickly agreed to Bolero. They liked the idea of filling up their island with American soldiers. But they dragged their heels at the thought of invading France. The British don't want to cross the English Channel until the Germans have been significantly weakened. Churchill kept suggesting periphery campaigns in the Mediterranean. He's particularly keen on invading French North Africa."

"Do you think the Brits' experience in getting pushed off the Continent at Dunkirk is inhibiting their strategic thinking?" asked Eisenhower.

"Undoubtedly so." Marshall paused. "Hopkins turned out to be a big help. Churchill knows he's a confidant of Roosevelt, and Hopkins made it clear the President wants to begin the liberation of occupied Europe with an invasion of France. After days of discussion, Churchill finally agreed to Roundup."

"What's Hopkins like?"

"He's candid and insightful. Churchill began calling him 'Lord Root of the Matter' for his insistence on focusing on the essence of a problem." Marshall poured himself a glass of water. "It was an even bigger challenge to secure their agreement on Sledgehammer. Particularly opposed was Sir Alan Brooke, who's replaced Dill as chief of the Imperial General Staff. He was very outspoken against a 1942 invasion of France, saying it was bound to fail and could turn into a disaster."

"Did he understand it wouldn't be undertaken unless the Soviets were in the direst circumstances?"

"That's exactly what I told Brooke. I got the impression he thought I was a poor strategist for even suggesting an assault on France in 1942. In a rather superior tone, he reminded me the English fought the Germans in France in 1940, and they were in a better position to evaluate the chances of a successful 1942 attack than the Americans."

Eisenhower didn't appreciate the English thinking their American cousins were naive in matters of war. This Brooke sounded arrogant and full of himself.

"It took time," the chief continued, "but eventually Churchill approved Sledgehammer, saying he fully supported Roosevelt's vision for prosecuting the war."

Marshall concluded the meeting with an order. "Eisenhower, I want you to live on Fort Myer. I need my most important subordinates close by. I reserved Quarters Seven for you."

Fort Myer! Mamie would be thrilled. The homes on the base were attractive and spacious. The base had been carved out of Lee's Arlington plantation and sat across the Potomac River from Washington. Eisenhower's good friend George Patton had been a post commander, and he and Mamie had attended parties at Patton's Fort Myer house. Eisenhower took his leave with a smile on his face.

That evening when Eisenhower got home, Mamie was reading a book. After they kissed, he said excitedly, "I have some news for you: We're moving to Fort Myer! Marshall wants me living close to him."

"Oh my, we'll be moving into a large house." She paused, then frowned. "Another move, so soon. Sometimes I feel like a football kicked from place to place."

Eisenhower was surprised by her lack of enthusiasm. *Will this move affect her health?* He reached out and took her hand. In a reassuring voice he said, "Honey, I think we'll love being at Fort Myer."

"It's just . . . jarring having to move so soon after getting settled in here." Then Mamie's eyes lit up. "I do enjoy home decorating. I'll get our stuff out of storage at Fort Sam."

Eisenhower was happy Mamie's spirits had perked up. "Honey, I'm sure you'll turn Quarters Seven into a swell home for us."

The next day, the Japanese acknowledged to the world Doolittle's raiders had succeeded in bombing Tokyo. The news had an electric effect on the morale of people across the nation. Against seemingly impossible odds, the Americans had bombed their enemy's capital!

Ominously, there had been no communication from the bombing crews. *Have any of them made it to China?*

CHAPTER 9

Spring arrived, transforming Washington from a dreary gray city into one full of color. Cherry blossom trees, a 1912 gift of friendship from Japan, were in full bloom in West Potomac Park. The change in seasons didn't brighten Eisenhower's mood. Five months into the war, America's only success was Doolittle's raid, and even that was bittersweet because nobody knew whether any of the raiders had survived the attack.

Midmorning Eisenhower's office phone rang: the chief wanted to see him. Once Eisenhower was seated in front of Marshall's desk, his boss studied him with a penetrating gaze for an uncomfortable length of time.

"Eisenhower, you look tired and ragged around the edges. I know you've been working herculean hours, and your effort is appreciated. But I want you to get more sleep and some exercise. Consider horseback riding for exercise. I ride as often as I can. Riding helps clear my mind—lets me focus on the big picture."

Marshall's criticism surprised Eisenhower: there was a war on, and men were supposed to push themselves to their limits and beyond. He fought to hold his anger in abeyance.

"I know I'm driven, sir. My parents instilled the value of hard work in me."

"A good work ethic is commendable, but ignoring the needs of your body is not. I'm ordering you to spend fewer hours in the office."

There was no use fighting his boss. "Sir, I'll take your advice—trim the hours I spend in the office and get some exercise."

"Good."

And with that, the chief dismissed Eisenhower.

He arrived at their new Fort Myer home at 7:00 p.m. Their furniture had arrived from storage in San Antonio, and Mamie had quickly transformed a sterile house into a comfortable home.

She welcomed her husband with a kiss. "You're home early. I don't have dinner ready."

"Marshall chewed me out today for working too hard! Can you believe that!"

"He's right," Mamie said, pushing back. "I'm worried you're going to drop dead from a heart attack."

"I don't need you piling on!" Eisenhower growled, her words offending his pride. "I'm a grown man. I know how to take care of myself!"

"You'll die from overwork before the war is over!" Mamie argued. "You've gained weight, and the bags under your eyes attest to your sleep deprivation. I'm happy Marshall's ordered you to pull back."

Eisenhower opened his mouth to argue, then closed it. *Calm down,* he told himself. He didn't want to fight with Mamie.

Taking a deep breath, he pulled out a pack of Lucky Strikes. He offered the pack to Mamie, who took a cigarette. He did the same. They spent a few minutes smoking in silence.

After crushing out his cigarette, Eisenhower said, "I apologize for losing my temper. I don't like to be told what to do." He smiled. "Of course, that's not news to you."

Mamie laughed. "You're as stubborn as an ornery mule."

Eisenhower straightened his back as if coming to attention. "I'm making a resolution to take Marshall's advice, and yours too. I'm going to approach work like a normal human being." He appraised his wife with an appreciative eye. "And we'll have more time to spend together."

Mamie blushed. "That would be lovely, Ike."

The next day, May 6, Eisenhower arrived at his desk at 7:00 a.m., having enjoyed a romantic evening and an extra two hours of sleep. He was greeted with the news the heroic American and Filipino defenders on Corregidor Island in Manila Bay, the last holdouts against the Japanese invaders, had finally succumbed. The battle for the Philippines was over.

Eisenhower put his face in his hands as he thought of those brave souls who were now Japanese captives. The stories of Japanese brutalities toward the American and Filipino soldiers who had surrendered on the Bataan Peninsula were shocking. The few men who escaped during the long march to the prison camps told chilling tales of Japanese atrocities, random shootings, and bayonet stabbings for no apparent reason. The prisoners received little food or water during the hot, dusty march, resulting in many dying from malnutrition, heatstroke, and disease. Despicably, the Japanese used sun torture as punishment for perceived misbehaviors. They forced accused prisoners to sit in the open under scorching tropical sunlight without any head covering. Anyone who had the audacity to ask for water in the torrid heat was shot. Thousands of prisoners had died during what was being called "the Bataan Death March."

Eisenhower said a silent prayer for the prisoners. He raised his face from his hands and picked up a memo from his inbox. Relying on his gift of concentration, he set his mind to focus on the urgent matter it detailed.

That evening, Milt and Helen came to Quarters Seven for dinner. Mamie enjoyed playing hostess. During Eisenhower's 1920s assignment with the American Battlefield Commission in Paris, Mamie's parties had been so popular, their apartment became known as "Club Eisenhower."

While they were enjoying cocktails in the living room, Eisenhower asked his brother, "What's happening at the WRA?"

"My latest challenge is finding homes for three thousand Japanese American college students being forced to evacuate the Pacific coast.

I'm just sickened with the bigotry of many of our American colleges and universities."

"No college will accept them?" asked Mamie incredulously.

"Initially, that was the case," Milt said with a look of disgust. "I tried to establish a committee of leading educators to help place these students, but all I received were flimsy excuses. Not a single person agreed to be on the committee!

"Then someone suggested I call Clarence Pickett, a prominent Quaker leader. Pickett accepted my request for help with alacrity, and he's been terrific. His sister was a Quaker missionary in Japan, and through her, he developed deep feelings of compassion for Japanese Americans. He's traveled to numerous colleges and universities and, through persuasion and perseverance, placed many of these deserving students in new schools. Pickett promised he won't stop until every single student has found a new home to continue their education."

After Milt and Helen left, Eisenhower walked out onto the porch and lit a cigarette. The army was still gathering facts about the horrors of the Bataan Death March and hadn't yet released the details to the public. As he watched the smoke from his cigarette drift off into the air, Eisenhower wondered whether Milt would feel such compassion for Japanese Americans if he knew their compatriots were brutally murdering and torturing American and Filipino prisoners of war.

Eisenhower finished his cigarette and lit another. *Yes,* he concluded, *Milt would act in the same fashion.* Their pious parents had taught their sons with religious fervor—until it was part of the boys' souls—to always do what was morally right.

The Japanese Americans were not culpable for war crimes being committed by the Jap army. They should be treated with the fairness all Americans deserved.

Eisenhower had again been summoned to Marshall's office. This time the chief was in a subdued mood.

"When I was in England," Marshall began, "I didn't feel a sense of urgency from our London office to support the Bolero buildup. I spent little time with General Chaney who runs that operation, so perhaps

I'm being unfair. I want you to go to England, make an independent assessment of Chaney, and bring back recommendations for the organization and development of our European forces. When can you leave?"

"I can leave in two days."

"Before you go, meet with Somervell and discuss how his shop will handle supplies in Europe."

Eisenhower found Somervell studying Pentagon blueprints. "Marshall said I should check with you on how ASF will work in Europe."

Somervell sat back. "We'll handle all supply and service functions, taking a huge burden off the theater commander."

"Have you considered the theater commander may be unhappy not having control over his supplies?"

Somervell's face darkened. "The ground and air force generals want to control everything, including supplies! Marshall put *me* in charge of logistics, and I'm going to exercise that control!"

Eisenhower raised his hands in a gesture meant to calm Somervell. "I didn't mean to get you riled up."

"I'm not going to concede an *ounce* of my authority! Whoever becomes theater commander will have to work within the structure Marshall created, meaning ASF controls supplies!"

Eisenhower was starting to feel sorry for whoever the theater commander would be. *That man is going to be knee-deep in army politics!*

When Eisenhower got to Quarters Seven that evening, Mamie was in a bubbly mood. She greeted him with a sparkling smile. "I'm enjoying living on Fort Myer! General Marshall's wife, Katherine, has been very friendly toward me. Really, everyone on the base has been great."

"It's great to hear you're happy here. I've got a bit of news for you. I'm going to England on a temporary assignment."

Mamie's face fell, and she looked down at the wooden floor. "How long are you going to be gone?" she asked in a soft voice.

"A week or two."

"It's awfully lonely when you're away," she admitted.

Eisenhower went to Mamie and rested his hands on her shoulders.

"Honey, there's a war going on. I must go where duty sends me. Remember, you're my Rock of Gibraltar."

She nodded. "I remember."

CHAPTER 10

Eisenhower left Washington in a B-17 Flying Fortress that was being ferried to England to serve in the US Eighth Air Force. He was accompanied by General Mark Wayne Clark, a close friend since their West Point days. They arrived in London on May 26 and were taken to 20 Grosvenor Square. The redbrick apartment building in the fashionable Mayfair district had been converted into offices for the American army.

General James Chaney, head of the Special Army Observers Group, greeted them in a conference room overlooking Grosvenor Square Park. After exchanging pleasantries, Eisenhower asked, "General Chaney, how'd you end up in England?"

"I was sent over here in 1940 to observe the Battle of Britain."

"That had to be a special experience," said Clark in an awed tone.

"Unforgettable!" Chaney agreed. "I spent my days at Royal Air Force bases and watched the dogfights in the skies. Those young Brit pilots punished the Luftwaffe—they saved this country from the Nazis! If the Germans had destroyed the Royal Air Force, they would've invaded England and this island would be under Hitler's jackboot. Churchill summed it up perfectly, 'Never was so much owed by so many to so few.'"

An aide entered the room with a pot of coffee, interrupting the conversation. The three generals eagerly filled their cups, and a sweet coffee aroma filled the room.

"After the Battle of Britain, I returned home," Chaney continued. "In May 1941, the army sent me back to England to head the Observers Group. Of course, that was before Pearl Harbor, and America was neutral. We were the army's eyes and ears in England, reporting on what was happening over here. Once America was in the war, our role changed. Currently our focus is working with the Brits to build bases for the Army Air Forces so we can start bombing Germany."

"What's your role in Bolero?" asked Eisenhower.

"I'm working with Bill Somervell and the Brits to build infrastructure to host American soldiers for the invasion of France."

"How's the construction going?" asked Eisenhower.

"We're still in the planning stages."

"What schedule does your staff work?" asked Clark.

"Eight to six, Monday through Friday."

Eisenhower thought, *What the hell? Doesn't Chaney know there's a war on?* But he held his tongue.

At the end of their meeting, Eisenhower asked, "Jim, how do we get to our hotel?"

"All visiting generals are provided with an English woman driver. One should be waiting for you in front of the building."

"Why not an American soldier?" asked Clark. "Not that I'm complaining!"

The men laughed.

"When the Brits thought Hitler was going to invade, they took down all the road and street signs. Americans trying to drive in London get hopelessly lost!" Chaney explained with a rueful shake of his head. "As for why a woman, the Brits are short on manpower, so they often use women for jobs like driving."

When Eisenhower and Clark walked out of 20 Grosvenor Square, there was an olive-painted American Packard curbside but no driver. Minutes passed, and Eisenhower's patience frayed. "Where in the hell is this woman who is supposed to be our driver?"

The tall and lanky Clark looked up and down the street. He lifted an arm and pointed to a woman in uniform hurrying toward them. "I bet that's her."

Eisenhower followed Clark's arm and saw a brunette in a military uniform hustling down the sidewalk. When she reached them, she was breathing hard.

Looking at the taller of the two men, she asked Clark in a lilting English accent, "Are you General Eisenhower?"

Clark laughed. "No." He pointed at Eisenhower. "He's the one you're looking for."

She turned to Eisenhower. "I'm Kay Summersby. Sorry, sir, for not being present when you came out of your headquarters. I've been waiting all day for you and was starving. I ran off to get a quick bite."

Eisenhower snapped, "Miss Summersby, I insist all my aides be punctual! I'll excuse you just this time, as I did not directly communicate with you when you should be available."

Summersby's eyes narrowed, and her face tightened. "It's Mrs. Summersby, sir!" she said, her voice clipped. "Now, where do you wish to go?"

"Claridge's Hotel."

The smile on Summersby's face was thin as she opened the rear door of the car for the Americans. Two minutes after pulling away from the curb, she stopped in front of the redbrick Claridge's. The elegant hotel was an integral part of the London social scene, and the exile home of the Kings of Norway, Greece, and Yugoslavia.

Eisenhower felt silly as she opened the rear door. "If I'd known it was so close, I would've walked. Mrs. Summersby, please be here at eight a.m. tomorrow."

A uniformed doorman wearing a black top hat welcomed them, opening the hotel's front door. As the generals walked across the black-and-white tiled lobby floor, Clark said conversationally, "She's attractive."

"Who's attractive?" Eisenhower wondered.

"Are you blind? The driver, Summersby."

Eisenhower thought back, but he couldn't recall what the driver looked like. "I was so annoyed by her lateness, I didn't pay attention to her appearance."

"It's a good thing you're a general and not a scout!" Clark joked. "You would've flunked the awareness course."

Eisenhower laughed. "See you at dinner, Wayne."

When he got to his room, Eisenhower went to the desk and found stationery embossed with Claridge's logo. He penned a quick letter to Mamie:

Just made it to London. It was a bumpy ride as we hit a lot of bad weather. The hotel on this stationery is too swanky for my humble tastes! I miss you already and love you dearly.

During dinner, served by a waiter wearing a red jacket and velvet breeches, Clark asked, "What do you think of our hotel?"

Eisenhower waved his arm at the high-ceilinged dining room with its multiple arches and chandeliers. "This place is too fancy for my taste," he said gruffly. "My room has red wallpaper, like a goddamn boudoir."

"It's a pretty luxurious place," Clark agreed.

"It's too plush and overdecorated for a simple Kansas boy like me."

Clark laughed. "I doubt living in luxury for a week is going to turn you into a dandy."

"Wayne, what's your opinion of Chaney?" asked Eisenhower, getting to the point of the trip.

"I liked him, but he's not the man to implement the Bolero buildup. I didn't sense the unrelenting drive of a Bill Somervell."

"I agree," Eisenhower said, spearing a bite of his steak. "Chaney and his staff seemed too comfortable in their Grosvenor Square offices, and they're working bankers' hours. Marshall's intuition was on the mark—Chaney's not the man for Europe."

The next morning, Summersby was waiting for the American generals outside of Claridge's. Eisenhower looked at her closely as he approached.

She was tall, with an athletic build. Her oval-shaped face was enhanced with makeup and lipstick, and she had penciled her eyebrows. Clark was right: Summersby was an attractive woman, and someone who took time to make the most of her looks.

Summersby opened the car's rear door for them, then returned to standing rigidly at attention. "Where to, sir?"

"The War Office," replied Eisenhower. Before he stepped into the car, he turned back to her. "I apologize for losing my temper yesterday. You had a legitimate reason for being late and didn't deserve a tongue-lashing."

Her stern demeanor dissolved into a smile. "Thank you, General Eisenhower."

Summersby dropped them off in Whitehall in front of an ornate Edwardian-era office building with circular towers at its corners.

"Mrs. Summersby, we'll be in meetings here all day. Please pick us up at six p.m.," Eisenhower said.

"Yes, sir."

Eisenhower and Clark approached the soldier standing at the front door. After introducing themselves, Eisenhower said, "We have a meeting with Lord Mountbatten."

The man looked at his clipboard. "You're expected. One of the guards inside will escort you to his office."

The American generals were escorted up a marble staircase and down a long corridor to Mountbatten's office. An admiral and a member of the royal family, the tall and thin Mountbatten warmly greeted his visitors. "We're happy to have you Yanks on our side."

Eisenhower shook Mountbatten's outstretched hand. "I'm Dwight Eisenhower, but please call me Ike. Just about everyone does."

When Clark shook hands, he said, "I'm Mark Clark. Please call me Mark. Everybody does, except Ike, who for some reason uses my middle name, Wayne!"

"I love American informality. Please call me Dickie."

After they were comfortably situated in Mountbatten's wood-paneled office, Eisenhower said, "Dickie, we're interested in your Combined Operations command. We have nothing like it in our armed forces."

"Ah, a subject close to my heart. After Dunkirk, Churchill created a special force comprising volunteers from the navy, army, and air force under a single commander. We call our soldiers 'commandos.' The men are subjected to a rigorous training course, and those who finish it emerge as elite warriors. Our mission is to raid the coastlines of Nazi-occupied countries."

"Was it hard integrating the three services into a single command?" asked Clark.

"It was challenging at first because each service thought they were superior to the other two. But the stress of combat missions broke down those barriers and has forged a real camaraderie among the men."

"I've heard you've studied the challenges of landing men and supplies on beaches," said Eisenhower.

"I've gathered a group of scientists to analyze every aspect of an amphibious invasion—the tides, winds, cloud cover, and whether the beach can support tanks—the list of subjects is quite expansive! We've developed specialized landing craft for getting men and supplies to the beaches, and we've shared the designs with the US."

"I'm aware of your generosity with the landing craft designs," replied Eisenhower. "Our navy is building landing craft for the invasion of France."

"We're going to use LSTs for the first time in combat conditions when we raid the French port of Dieppe," Mountbatten said. "We want to see if a fortified port can be taken by direct assault."

"Is Dieppe a precursor to a full-fledged invasion?" asked Clark.

"No, it's a test of our equipment and theories for a seaborne assault. I can't see invading France before 1943."

"Have you seen our plans for an invasion of France this year?" questioned Eisenhower.

"I have. But without air supremacy and with the limited forces available, I don't believe a permanent lodgment can be established in France this year."

"You realize such an invasion would only take place if the Russians were about to collapse?" asked Eisenhower.

"Ike, I understand it's a contingent plan. But a failed 1942 invasion will not help the Soviets. The Germans have ample forces in France to repulse an attack without weakening the Russian front."

After lunch, Mountbatten escorted Clark and Eisenhower to the office of Sir Alan Brooke, Churchill's top general.

Brooke was from a long line of Northern Ireland Ulster men who had served the English Crown for centuries. He was slightly stoop-shouldered, with dark hair, a beak-like nose, and horn-rimmed glasses. He greeted Eisenhower and Clark politely, but without the warmth exhibited by Mountbatten.

After the Americans expressed a preference for informality in names, Brooke looked faintly amused. "You can call me Alan. My close friends call me Brookie, but we're not close friends."

At first Eisenhower thought Brooke was joking, but the look on Brooke's face suggested otherwise. "Alan, we're here to see the Bolero buildup goes smoothly."

"You'll get complete cooperation from us. Whatever you need, let me know, and I'll do my best to honor the request."

"Thank you, Alan," replied Eisenhower. "I'm interested in your thoughts on Sledgehammer."

"Total bloody rubbish! A stupid plan that's bound to fail!" Brooke spoke in a clipped, staccato voice, the words flying out of his mouth like pistol shots. "And I told General Marshall as much. You Americans have a lot to learn. You've no appreciation for how good the Wehrmacht is. I fought in France, and I was on the beach at Dunkirk. We need to avoid reckless, futile attacks if we're going to win the war."

Brooke's condescending attitude angered Eisenhower, but he did his best not to show it. "Alan, if you're so opposed to a potential 1942 invasion, why did your government agree to it?"

"That was Churchill's call. He wants the alliance with America to work. But it's foolhardy to agree to a suicide mission simply to curry favor with Roosevelt," Brooke said dismissively.

Eisenhower was tired of being patronized. "If this alliance is going to work, you need to respect your ally, and frankly, I've felt a level of disrespect in your repudiation of Sledgehammer!"

"I'm a soldier, not a diplomat!" Brooke shot back. "I can be blunt when I express myself. You need to develop a tougher skin, Ike."

Eisenhower saw no point in continuing to argue with Brooke. "I appreciate your candor, Alan. Let's discuss the Bolero buildup."

The men spent the rest of the afternoon focused on creating the infrastructure to house and train American soldiers in England for a 1943 invasion of France.

As the American generals were leaving, Brooke said, "If you gentlemen have time, I suggest you attend the army maneuvers General Bernard Montgomery is conducting at the end of the week."

"Thank you, Alan, for the invite," replied Eisenhower. "We'll be sure to attend Montgomery's show."

CHAPTER 11

Summersby was driving the American generals to the county of Kent to observe Montgomery's maneuvers. As the car traveled past farmers' fields filled with strawberries and hazelnuts and through villages with stone houses, Clark asked, "Mrs. Summersby, remind me of your first name?"

"Kay, sir."

"Do you mind if I call you Kay?" Clark asked.

"Call me Kay if you'd like," she replied in a congenial tone.

Clark continued. "Can you tell us a little bit about yourself?"

"I grew up on a run-down estate on a lovely green island surrounded by a river in County Cork, Ireland."

Eisenhower was surprised. "You don't have an Irish accent."

"My mother's English. When she separated from my Irish father, she brought me to live in London, and I picked up an English accent."

"Is your husband in the army?" asked Clark.

"My ex-husband is in the army; we divorced before the war. But I'm engaged to one of yours, Colonel Dick Arnold."

"What outfit is he in?" asked Clark.

"Dick's a combat engineer in the Seventeenth Armored Engineer Battalion."

"Those combat engineers are brave fellows," Eisenhower noted. "They're often in front of the infantry, blowing up mines."

"I know," Summersby said, her voice dropping a level. "I'll be worried sick about Dick when he goes into battle."

"Kay, what did you do before the war?" asked Clark.

"I was a fashion model for Worth's of Paris at their shop in Mayfair. When the war came, I volunteered and was placed in the Mechanized Transport Corps. During the Blitz, I drove an ambulance."

Eisenhower was curious. "What was being in the Blitz like?"

"Pure hell—blood, death, body parts, and shattered buildings everywhere." Summersby's hands tightened on the steering wheel as she described the Nazi terror campaign. "For eight months, Hitler tried to break our will to fight with nightly bombing raids that killed thousands of civilians. I drove ambulances piled with bodies looking for a morgue that wasn't filled to capacity. It was . . . a horrific experience."

Eisenhower seethed with anger over the barbaric tactics. "Those goddamn Nazi bastards, killing innocent civilians!"

Conversation in the car lapsed, with the driver and the generals lost in their own thoughts.

When the car reached Montgomery's headquarters, the English general greeted them. He was a short, fit man who radiated energy.

"You're the first Americans I've met since you gents got into the war! I'm happy to see you're finally gearing up to get into the fight with us."

After Eisenhower asked to be called Ike, Montgomery chuckled. "I'm fine with informality; please call me Monty. I know you've met Brooke. Do you know his nickname?"

Clark replied, "Brookie?"

"That's only for his best friends. Most people call him 'Colonel Shrapnel' for his cutting remarks."

"He doesn't hold punches; that's for sure," replied Eisenhower.

After observing the English soldiers' field maneuvers in which the troops practiced attacking a ridgeline held by the enemy, Eisenhower and Clark attended a lecture by Montgomery on what could be learned from the exercise. The high school classroom was filled with British officers and the two Americans.

Ten minutes into the presentation, Eisenhower lit a cigarette. Montgomery stopped speaking and sniffed the air. "Is someone smoking?"

Eisenhower raised his hand.

In a curt tone Montgomery snapped, "I do not allow smoking in my presence."

Eisenhower was nonplussed: he had never been reprimanded for smoking. He dropped the cigarette on the floor and ground it out with his boot.

Montgomery smirked. "Thank you, Ike."

Once they were in the car on the way back to London, Clark said, "Monty was really obnoxious, scolding you for smoking."

Eisenhower couldn't have agreed more. "He's arrogant and full of himself, that's for sure!" When he saw Summersby's eyes in the rear-view mirror looking at him, he added, "Kay, you can never repeat what you hear in this car."

"Of course, sir," replied Summersby. "You can trust me to be discreet."

Eisenhower was packing for home when he noticed an envelope slipped under his hotel room door. He opened it and learned that his flight was delayed a day because of mechanical problems with the plane.

He called Clark. "Any ideas what we should do with our free day?"

"Why don't we go sightseeing?"

"Behave like tourists?" Eisenhower scoffed.

"Why the hell not?" was Clark's laughing rejoinder. "Let's have Kay show us London."

"Okay, okay, we'll be tourists."

The two men found Summersby outside the hotel at the appointed time to take them to the airfield.

"Kay, our flight is delayed a day," Eisenhower informed her. "Could you give us a tour of your beautiful city?"

"Of course!" she responded excitedly.

After a few minutes of driving, Summersby parked the car. She pointed across the street. "That's Westminster Abbey, where coronations of our kings and queens take place."

They got out of the car and walked toward the church. As he neared the abbey, Eisenhower studied the Gothic revival facade with its many large glass windows. He was impressed by the architecture, particularly the soaring twin towers.

Clark suddenly pointed up. "There're workers on the roof."

"During the Blitz, the roof caught fire," Summersby explained. "The wooden beams burned, and the roof crashed into the nave. London firemen had to work all night to save the abbey."

"Can we go inside?" asked Clark.

Summersby shook her head. "I'm sorry, the abbey's been closed during the week since the bombing. If you'd like, we could walk to Westminster Palace, home to Parliament. It's close by."

"Sure," Eisenhower responded.

In a few minutes, they were in front of a large Gothic revival building with the iconic Big Ben clock tower at the north end. The bomb damage here was extensive. The site was swaddled in scaffolding.

"The same bombing raid that damaged Westminster Abbey in May 1941 destroyed Parliament's Commons Chamber," said Summersby. "You can see it's being rebuilt."

"Kay, do you feel up to showing us where you drove ambulances during the Blitz?" asked Clark.

"I have no problem showing you. I was stationed in the East End near the docks."

In the East End, the damage was more severe. Whole blocks had been destroyed, buildings cut in half, and the skeletons of tenement buildings that remained seemed ready to crumble. The scarred landscape's sidewalks were crowded with people carrying on with everyday life.

"I drove through these streets with only fires from the bombing to light my way," Summersby said in a low voice. "The men in my crew pulled bodies out of buildings and piled them into the ambulance with only a tag on the toe—well, that is, if there was a foot. Many of the bodies were burned and disfigured and missing limbs. All that was left of some bodies were bits and pieces, which the men put in canvas bags."

Summersby stopped talking suddenly and, with one hand remaining on the wheel, opened her handbag and pulled out a handkerchief.

"Kay, are you okay?" asked Clark.

Summersby nodded as she used the handkerchief to dry her tears.

"I got emotional thinking about all the horrors Hitler has wreaked on us. I'm . . . I'm sorry. Not very professional of me."

"No need to apologize. It's understandable. Viewing all . . . this brings home what the war is about to us as well," Eisenhower said tersely. "The Nazis and their brutal ways will not prevail."

The next day, Summersby drove Clark and Eisenhower to the RAF Northolt base for their flight. As the generals got out of the car, Eisenhower reached into the bag he was carrying and pulled out a box of Hershey's chocolates. He handed it to Summersby.

"Kay, this is a little token of appreciation from the two of us for doing such a wonderful job driving us around."

Summersby squealed like a schoolgirl who had gotten a special wish granted. "Oh my gosh, I haven't had chocolate in ages!"

Impulsively she hugged Eisenhower and Clark. Both men were a little red in the face when Summersby released them.

"Kay, if we ever come back to London, would you drive for us again?" asked Eisenhower.

"With pleasure!" Summersby laughed, giving the two men a salute before she returned to the car and headed off to find out who would be her next assignment.

CHAPTER 12

On his return to Washington, Eisenhower went directly to the Munitions Building to brief Marshall. While the first section of the Pentagon had opened six weeks earlier, Marshall had yet to move. June's oppressive heat and humidity had arrived, and the window air-conditioning unit in the chief's office was humming.

"What should I do with Chaney?" asked Marshall.

"Sir, General Chaney is out of touch with the priorities of the War Department. I recommend he be replaced."

"Do you have a suggestion for a replacement?"

"General Joe McNarney would be an excellent choice," replied Eisenhower, recommending Marshall's deputy chief of staff. "He headed the War Department reorganization committee, is intimately familiar with your thinking, and well acquainted with the British."

The chief steepled his fingers in front of his face, lost in thought for several minutes. "Eisenhower, draft a memorandum outlining a European command structure. I want to know what the organization will look like before I decide who will run it."

Eisenhower spent the rest of the day working through the stacks of memorandums that had accumulated during his absence. When he got home to Quarters Seven at 8:00 p.m., Mamie welcomed him with a hug and a kiss.

"Ike, I'm so happy you're home. I miss you terribly when you're gone."

"I missed you too, honey."

"What was London like?"

"Beaten up from the Blitz, and very dark at night as there's a strict blackout in effect. But I saw determination in the eyes of the people there! The English stood alone against Hitler when everyone else had given up the fight, and I respect them greatly for that. I'm glad they're our allies."

Eisenhower spied a pair of candles on the dining room table, a sign Mamie was thinking of a romantic evening.

He smiled affectionately at her. "Let's enjoy our reunion."

Mamie's cheeks took on a rosy glow, and her blue eyes sparkled with mischief. "Yes, let's."

The next day, Eisenhower woke up tired but with happy thoughts of the romantic reunion with Mamie. He would have enjoyed lingering at home, but the memo Marshall wanted couldn't wait.

Once he reached his office, Eisenhower closed his office door to avoid interruptions. The closed door didn't deter Beetle Smith, who knocked on it and then opened it without waiting for a reply. "Ike, you got a minute?"

"I'm knee-deep in preparing a memorandum for the chief, and you know he wants his requests fulfilled ASAP!"

"I'll be quick," Smith promised. "I know you like getting the latest scoop. Well, Churchill is coming to Washington again."

"I bet he wants to back out of Sledgehammer," Eisenhower said thoughtfully, rubbing his chin with his fingers. "The British high command, especially Brooke, is opposed to that operation."

"All I know is he wants to confer on grand strategy with the President. The chief's nervous because Churchill is going straight to FDR's home in Hyde Park. He's worried Churchill will influence the President into supporting one of his schemes for nibbling around the edges of Hitler's Europe."

Smith took his leave, and Eisenhower returned to working on his memorandum. It called for a European Theater of Operations (ETO) where the ETO commander would exercise planning and operational control over all American forces in Europe, including the Army Air Forces and the navy. Eisenhower emphasized that the American commander needed to be at least a three-star lieutenant general to gain the respect of senior British military leaders like the caustic Brooke.

It took Eisenhower two days to flesh out the details of the European command. When he presented it to Marshall, he said, "Sir, here is the blueprint for organizing our European operations."

Marshall raised an eyebrow at Eisenhower's choice of words. "You seem pretty confident I'll accept your recommendations."

"I apologize if I sounded cocky, sir."

"I'll read your 'blueprint' very carefully. And Eisenhower, you may well be the man who executes it."

The very idea was startling; it seemed like a mere fantasy! *Can Marshall really be considering making me commanding officer in Europe? Surely Marshall would appoint a more senior general with combat experience for such an important post.* The stunned Eisenhower simply replied, "That would be a great honor, sir."

Three days later, Eisenhower was summoned to Marshall's office. As was his custom, the chief got straight to the point.

"I've studied your recommendations and agree with the approach you want to take. I recommended to the President you be the ETO commander, and he agreed."

Every nerve in Eisenhower's body pulsed. *My dream of getting a field command has come true! And what a grand command it is: the liberation of Europe from the iron grip of Nazi tyranny!*

"Thank you, sir, for your trust in me," replied Eisenhower in the calmest voice he could muster.

Marshall stood. "The President wants to see us now."

As they walked out of the Munitions Building, Eisenhower thought about Roosevelt, whom he had met several times before over the plight of the Philippines. FDR had impressed him with his intelligence and infectiously positive personality.

Eight minutes after getting into Marshall's car, the two men were at the White House. When Marshall and Eisenhower entered the Oval

Office, the President was sitting in an armless wheelchair behind the Resolute desk, an 1880 gift from Queen Victoria.

Roosevelt wore rimless glasses and was smoking a cigarette in a holder, his large head tilted slightly to the left like a lion in repose. He smiled at his visitors with the easy grace of a man used to being in charge.

"Ike, General Marshall says you're the man to command Europe." FDR spoke in a modulated voice and the clear diction of a master communicator. "It's a big job, but I'm confident you can handle it. Competence runs in your family. Your brother Milton always does a bang-up job when I give him a tough assignment."

"Thank you, Mr. President. It's an honor and privilege to be selected for such an important command."

Roosevelt rolled his wheelchair around the Resolute desk and pointed to a yellow couch on a blue-gray rug, beckoning the generals to sit. "I want to bring you up to date on my meetings with the Prime Minister. The British are completely opposed to Sledgehammer, believing it has no chance of success."

"I don't agree with that assessment," Marshall protested. "Admittedly, it would be a desperate step, but a necessary risk if the alternative were the Russians abandoning the war."

"I didn't agree it's impossible," replied Roosevelt. "I'm only relaying the British viewpoint. Churchill wants to invade French North Africa, which does have a certain appeal."

"Mr. President, the War Department is opposed to an African operation," replied Marshall. "We would disperse our forces, making it unlikely we could invade France in 1943."

"Well, I simply cannot allow American troops to remain idle during 1942; they must engage the Nazis somewhere." The President looked at Eisenhower. "The Prime Minister wants to meet you. Please see my secretary, and she'll have someone escort you to his bedroom." FDR laughed. "Churchill's bedroom also serves as his office."

Eisenhower left the Oval Office and was soon escorted to the second-floor living quarters. After a short wait, he was shown into the Prime Minister's bedroom.

Churchill was balding, short, and portly. His roundish face had a pink glow to it, accented by the large cigar he was smoking. "I understand you prefer being called Ike."

"Yes, Mr. Prime Minister. Everyone except General Marshall calls me Ike."

"Marshall is rather formal, isn't he?" Churchill reached for a decanter of whisky. "Will you share a drink with me?"

"A small one," Eisenhower replied, wanting to be polite.

Churchill filled two glasses and handed one to Eisenhower.

"I received favorable reports on you from your London trip. Dickie Mountbatten in particular sang your praises."

"It was a very informative visit. I was quite intrigued with Mountbatten's command."

"Combined Operations is my brainchild," Churchill said with evident pride. "The commandos have made successful raids in Norway and France, which have infuriated the Führer." Churchill paused, taking the measure of Eisenhower. "We are now opposed to Sledgehammer. Our military experts looked at it every which way and concluded it would be a suicide mission."

Eisenhower responded more loudly than he intended. "General Marshall and I do not agree with that conclusion!"

"You can't be wedded to an unsound operation," Churchill argued. "You need to have a flexible mind! Take me—I've been an outspoken anti-Communist my whole life, but when Hitler invaded Russia, I immediately made an alliance with Stalin." Churchill took a sip of whisky and smiled broadly. "After all, if Hitler invaded hell, I'd at least make a favorable reference to the devil in the House of Commons!"

Eisenhower laughed heartily.

"I like a man who has a sense of humor," Churchill said as he chuckled at his own joke. He then pointed his cigar at Eisenhower. "It's important our nations get along—that the great Anglo-American alliance functions smoothly. The President and I have established a strong relationship. I feel you and I will develop a good relationship as well."

"I'm confident we'll have an *excellent* relationship," replied Eisenhower, who liked that Churchill was open and direct.

An aide knocked on the door; Marshall was ready to leave.

Churchill walked Eisenhower to the door. "Ike, I look forward to working with you in England."

"I as well, sir."

On the short ride to Fort Myer that evening, Eisenhower thought about how his European assignment would affect Mamie. She would be happy he received such an important command, but also uneasy about being left alone in the States.

He found Mamie in the living room, writing a letter. Upon seeing him, she asked, "How was your day?"

"Consequential. Marshall is sending me to London to command our European operation."

Mamie's face grew pale as she stammered out, "You got . . . your field command?"

"I know this came out of the blue, but it will be okay. We've been separated before; it's simply part of army life."

His words had a desired effect. Mamie straightened her spine and replied in a firm voice, "I'm so proud of you. I want to give you a congratulatory hug."

When they embraced, Eisenhower could feel the tension in her body.

"Try and relax, Mamie. We've overcome every challenge God has thrown at us."

"You know me too well!" Mamie said with lips that shook slightly.

Eisenhower pulled out a pack of Lucky Strikes and offered one to Mamie, who accepted. He lit her cigarette, then his. They sat together on their green sofa.

She inhaled deeply and slowly expelled the smoke. "How long will you be gone?"

"It's impossible to predict. If I do a good job, it could be a while."

She fell silent, smoking her cigarette.

Eisenhower knew from experience something more was bothering her. "Mamie, what is it? You're brooding; what's your concern?"

"I know I shouldn't worry about something like this," she admitted, "but I hear stories from the other wives about their husbands having affairs with loose English women."

Eisenhower laughed. "I'm an old duffer." He ran a hand over his bald forehead. "And not that attractive. You don't have to worry about women throwing themselves at me."

"Don't knock your looks with me!" There was fire in Mamie's eyes. "You're a handsome man, and you'll be the commanding general! Some floozy is bound to cast her eye on you!"

He laughed. "I promise you won't hear any stories about me running around with some floozy." Eisenhower patted his stomach. "I'm starving; let's eat."

In the middle of dinner, Mamie suddenly put down her fork. "Oh my goodness, Ike! They're going to kick me off Fort Myer! I'll lose this house, and I already have it decorated. I can't believe I'll be moving again!" she said miserably. "I can't eat another bite."

"What on earth are you talking about?" Eisenhower questioned, baffled.

"All the wives talk about it—if their husband is stationed outside of Washington, they get thrown off the base. There're too many important generals in Washington, and not enough homes on Fort Myer for them."

He hadn't expected this turn of events. "It'll be fine, Mamie. I'll talk to Marshall and ask him to allow you to stay on at Fort Myer."

While Eisenhower didn't like to ask for favors, he'd make an exception to ensure his wife stayed secure and happy in their new home while he was overseas.

CHAPTER 13

Marshall, being a man of strong virtue, refused to bend the rules. Eisenhower added "find a place for Mamie to live" to his list of tasks to accomplish before leaving for England.

Eisenhower started putting together his staff. He began with the easiest selection: Mickey McKeogh would be his orderly. He was a known commodity, competent and loyal.

Then he considered the most important position: chief of staff, his right-hand man. His chief needed to be a smart, efficient hard-nosed driver of people, yet when circumstances required, diplomatic. Beetle Smith met the specifications, but he was a favorite of Marshall's, who might not let him go. Eisenhower thought hard about a second choice but came up empty. It had to be Smith.

He also wanted one of his aides to be a trusted friend, someone he could confide in during stressful times. Harry Butcher fit the bill, but he had been called up in the Naval Reserve, and the army had no control over him.

Eisenhower had an appointment with Ernie King to discuss the unity-of-command issue. He would ask the ornery admiral to assign a navy man to the army.

That afternoon, Eisenhower received a surprise visitor: the President of the Philippines, Manuel Quezon, who had fled his occupied country and established a government-in-exile in Washington. Eisenhower had come to know Quezon well during his time in the Philippines when they worked closely together in establishing a Filipino army.

Eisenhower shook Quezon's hand. "Mr. President, it's good to see you again. I feel great sadness for the plight of our brave soldiers and for your people under Japanese occupation."

"It's a dark time for my country," replied a haggard-looking Quezon. "I know I stopped by without any notice and it's clear you're busy, so I'll get to the point. As a token of appreciation for all you did for the Filipino people during your years in Manila, my government is providing you this stipend for services rendered."

Quezon stretched out his hand, holding a check. Eisenhower took it and was astounded when he saw the amount: $100,000. The sum was more than twenty times his annual salary!

Eisenhower handed the check back to Quezon. "Mr. President, thank you so much, but I can't accept this check. The American government paid me for the services I performed for your government."

Quezon's eyes widened in surprise. "Ike, the government of the Philippines wants you to have this money. I personally know how much time and effort you devoted to my people. It's only fair you be rewarded for such valuable service."

"Sir, I'm deeply honored by your acknowledgment of my efforts in behalf of the Filipino people, but I cannot accept payment from a foreign power."

Quezon persisted with his offer. "But . . . General MacArthur accepted his stipend."

The news was appalling. "Sir, I believe it's inappropriate for an American officer to accept money from a foreign government. I must refuse your offer."

Quezon's look of surprise was replaced with one of respect. "If you change your mind, please contact me."

The next day when Eisenhower met with King in his office, the admiral got straight to the point. "I've read your paper about unity of command in the ETO and spoken with Marshall. I'm wary of setting a precedent." King pulled a large cigar out of his pocket. "If that flamboyant son of a bitch MacArthur had written this memo and requested control over the navy, my answer would be, 'Hell, no!'"

"I'm well acquainted with General MacArthur, and given his ego-centric personality, I fully understand why you wouldn't want him commanding naval forces."

King roared with laughter, then lit the cigar. "You know how to play your cards, Ike. Nothing warms my heart faster than hearing crit-icism of MacArthur. That man has been a giant pain in the ass! The reality is our naval forces in Europe are going to be paltry compared with what we'll have in the Pacific. The big show for the navy is the war with Japan. In the Pacific, we are going to control the action, not the army. MacArthur stubbornly refuses to acknowledge that reality."

"Sir, I understand your position. The Pacific is a different theater with different considerations. In Europe, we need unity of command to seamlessly coordinate naval support for the army's invasion of France."

"You're proposing the first unified command of army and navy forces in American history, and you want a goddamn army officer to be top dog!" King bellowed. "I was ready to tell you to go to hell before you walked in, and I still might."

King swiveled his chair to look out on the reflecting pool, all the while puffing on his cigar. Time passed. The room filled with smoke and the smell of tobacco, and Eisenhower feared the age-old rivalry between the army and navy was going to scuttle unity of command in the ETO. Finally, the admiral swung his chair back toward his visitor.

"I'll agree to unity of command with two conditions. First, it only applies to Europe. The navy will never be under army command in the Pacific! Second, the army only controls strategy; the navy remains fully in control of tactics. Are the conditions acceptable?"

"I'll have to clear them with Marshall, but, yes, I'm confident we have a deal." Eisenhower paused. "Admiral King, could I ask you for a favor?"

"What in the hell do you want now? I just gave you the biggest fucking favor I've ever given anyone!"

"I would like a Naval Reserve officer assigned to my staff."

"Why?"

"He's extremely capable, and he's also a personal friend."

"What's his name?"

"Harry Butcher."

"I've never heard of him, so you can have him," King said dismissively. "Now, get the hell out of here; I've got work to do!"

The next day, Eisenhower met with Marshall and requested Beetle Smith for his chief of staff.

Marshall frowned. "I can't let Smith go. He's critical to our ongoing negotiations with Churchill and his advisers. Smith is so obviously competent; he's earned their respect."

"I understand General Smith's importance here in Washington," Eisenhower acknowledged. "He's the ablest staff officer in the army. But it's a huge job I have in England, and I need a man with Smith's talents to ensure the ETO is established on a firm foundation. What you just said about the British respect for Smith means he should be in England, where we'll be dealing with the Brits every day."

Marshall's frown deepened. "I understand why you want Smith, but for now he stays here."

Eisenhower wasn't happy and inwardly resolved to continue to push for Smith. But for now, he moved on. "Sir, have you decided on a commander for the US Second Corps, the first combat troops sent to England under the Bolero plan?"

"Do you have a recommendation?"

"General Mark Wayne Clark would be an excellent choice."

"You two are pretty close," Marshall observed.

"While we're friends, I suggested Clark because he's an able general," Eisenhower emphasized.

"Since you want Clark, who I agree is competent, I'll approve his appointment and send him to England with you."

Back in his office, Eisenhower called Butcher, who was still at CBS Radio tidying up his affairs before joining the navy.

"Butch, I want you to serve on my staff in London."

There was silence, then an earnest, "I'd love to, but have you forgotten I'm in the navy?"

"Not a problem," Eisenhower said casually. "Admiral King has approved it."

"Are you joking?"

"God's truth. You'll be my naval aide."

"London sounds good—really good."

"Why don't you and Ruth come over to Fort Myer for dinner tonight, and we'll talk more about it? Milt and Helen will be there too."

"Okay, we'll be there."

"One more thing—I need to find a place for Mamie to live while I'm gone. Got any ideas for me?"

"Let me think about it—again!" Butcher said with a laugh.

That evening during cocktail hour, Mamie asked, "Ike, have you found a place for me to live?"

Eisenhower turned to Butcher. "Butch, any luck finding a place for Mamie?"

"Ruth and I were talking about it on the way over. I've persuaded CBS to allow Ruth to stay in the CBS-owned apartment in the Wardman Park while I'm in the military. Mamie could have the spare bedroom and live with Ruth."

Ruth chimed in, "Mamie, I'd love sharing the apartment with you! I hate the idea of living alone, and you and I get along so well. What do you say?" she asked with a twinkle in her eye and a wave of her glass.

Mamie slowly began nodding her head as her smile grew wider. "I think it's a grand idea. Oh, Ruth, I don't want to live alone either!"

Eisenhower had reservations but chose not to voice them to the group.

The matter seemingly settled, Butcher asked, "Milt, is the rumor I heard true? You're no longer running the WRA?"

"Thank goodness I'm not!" Milt affirmed in a voice rich with gratitude. "That was the most disagreeable job I've ever had."

"What happened?" asked Mamie. "How did you get out of it?"

"Before I was given the WRA post, the President asked me to study how the government disseminates war news. I recommended forming a new agency to control the flow of news to ensure nothing is made public that could benefit our enemies. Well, last week the President finally acted on my recommendation and established the Office of War Information, OWI.

"FDR called me to the White House and informed me I will be the OWI's associate director—it's the number two position. He's given the OWI a second mission too, one of keeping morale and patriotism high on the home front. We're going to use all the media channels, radio broadcasts, motion pictures, newspapers, and even posters to keep support for our fighting men high."

As the dinner guests left, they congratulated Mamie for hosting such an enjoyable evening. She beamed with pride.

After everyone was gone, Eisenhower took Mamie's hand and led her to the green sofa. "Honey, I've concerns with your living with Ruth Butcher."

"What are you talking about, Ike?"

"Ruth drinks too much for my taste. I've noticed you tend to drink more when you're with her."

Mamie took her time in responding. "Ruth does love her martinis. But don't worry about me! I'll be careful not to have more than one drink a day."

Eisenhower smiled. "That's great, honey."

He still had reservations Ruth would be a bad influence on Mamie, but with the housing crunch, living with Ruth was Mamie's only option for staying in the city.

It had been a whirlwind two weeks. Marshall had the President promote Eisenhower to a three-star lieutenant general, and the chief gave him everything he asked for—except Beetle Smith.

It was time for Eisenhower to leave Fort Myer to assume his European command. He went into his living room, where he found Mamie reading a book. He was startled by her appearance: she had donned one of her favorite bright blue dresses and put on a pearl choker. It was more formal than her usual daytime attire; she had made an extra effort to look beautiful on their last day together. The realization warmed his heart.

"Darling, it's time for me to go."

She stood. "I packed pictures of Johnny and me for your desk."

"Thanks. I'll be sure to prominently display them. I'm going to have the pilot fly over Fort Myer. I'll call you right before we take off. Please stand by the flagpole on the parade ground so I can look down and see you one last time before I head overseas. I should be able to spot you in that bright blue color."

"That's such a sweet gesture, Ike."

They kissed, and Eisenhower gave her a bear hug. "Goodbye, honey."

"Goodbye, my love," Mamie said, tears running down her cheeks.

CHAPTER 14

When Eisenhower arrived in London on June 24 to assume command of the ETO, he was disappointed to discover Kay Summersby was not his assigned driver. He had brought some fresh fruit, nearly impossible to get in wartime England, as a gift for her.

He was taken to US Army headquarters at 20 Grosvenor Square. As he exited the vehicle, Eisenhower was surprised by several press photographers snapping pictures with popping flashbulbs.

Once inside, he was escorted to a small office facing the park in Grosvenor Square. The first thing he did was open his briefcase and pull out the pictures of Mamie and Johnny. As promised, he placed them on a corner of his desk.

After getting a cup of coffee, he convened a meeting of his staff officers in the basement cafeteria.

"I'm Ike Eisenhower, your new theater commander. I come from the War Department, where we've been working seven days a week since Pearl Harbor. Beginning immediately, this staff is going on a seven-day schedule too."

There were groans and mutterings under their breath from many in attendance. They were used to a leisurely five-day workweek.

Eisenhower's neck turned red as his anger rose. "If you're not prepared for hard work, I'll be happy to send you back to the States!"

The noise in the room stopped.

"I insist you approach your work with an enthusiastic, can-do, get-it-done attitude. I'm an optimist, and I know the Allies are going to win this war! I will not tolerate defeatism in any form. Anyone who cannot accept my rules should ask for reassignment."

Eisenhower pulled out his Lucky Strikes and took a cigarette. "All policy making involving the ETO will be done in *England*." He pointed the cigarette at his audience. "The days of 'passing the buck' to Washington for decisions are over. You need to take accountability and accomplish your assigned tasks. We need to plan and successfully execute the largest amphibious invasion in the history of warfare! Hitler's Fortress Europe must be breached, and France successfully invaded. You'll be given jobs where obstacles will appear insurmountable. You need to apply old-fashioned Yankee ingenuity and come up with solutions, not excuses. I don't want to hear why something can't be done. Any questions?"

No hands went up. A sea of tense faces stared at him.

"Any of you play football?" Eisenhower asked unexpectedly.

More than half of those present raised their arms.

"I played football at West Point and later coached at many army bases. My assignments were often determined by the base commander's desire for a winning team rather than my qualifications as an officer."

Laughter rippled through the room at the self-deprecating humor.

"A great football team involves teamwork," Eisenhower continued, "everyone pulling in the same direction toward a common goal. That's what we need to do here—work as a unified team to come up with a plan to liberate Europe from the Nazis."

Every eyeball in the room was on Eisenhower. He had accomplished his purpose. These officers knew their days of treating war as a casual affair were over.

"All right, men, I've spoken my piece. Let's get back to work."

Mamie had requested her husband write often. Two days after arriving in England, Eisenhower wrote her his first letter:

The army has me living in Claridge's, a stuffy old hotel

more fit for an exiled King than a small-town Kansas boy. Press photographers took some pictures, so you may see my mug showing up in a newspaper. I've been assigned a man too old to fight as a chauffeur. I wish you were here with me. Being separated only deepens my love for you.

When Butcher arrived in London at the beginning of July, there was a message to see Eisenhower in his hotel room. When Butcher knocked on the door, Eisenhower was swift to open it.

"Butch, I'm happy you're here." He rested a hand on Butcher's shoulder momentarily. It was great to see a real friend.

"Pretty nice digs, Ike," Butcher said, casting an appreciative eye at the luxurious Louis XV–style wood furniture.

"This place is too damn fancy for my taste," Eisenhower growled. He pointed to a wall. "Look at that red-and-gold patterned wallpaper. I can't decide if I'm sleeping in a brothel or a funeral parlor! First thing, you need to find me a new hotel!"

"Okay, Ike," Butcher laughed good-naturedly. "I'll see if I can find you a less pretentious place to live."

"That's not all," Eisenhower said, responding with a grin. "I've been bombarded with social invitations. I want you to screen out all the purely civilian get-togethers. I only want to attend military functions, and as few of those as possible."

"Will do. Have you accepted any invites?"

"A few. Dickie Mountbatten invited me to spend a night at his country home. I thought a house in the country would be a cozy small place, so I told Mickey to pack me light. It turned out to be a huge house complete with butler and servants!

"Dickie had a valet escort me to a large exquisitely decorated suite. I thought the valet was going to have a stroke when he opened my suitcase and found only a toothbrush, razor, and pajamas. I felt like Dorothy in *The Wizard of Oz*—another simple Kansan thrust into a strange, far-off world!"

"You're not used to rubbing shoulders with the aristocracy." Butcher smiled. "You'll figure out how to handle yourself quick enough."

"Not sure about that! I'll give you another example of how out of place I've felt in the London social scene. I attended a dinner party where the King was present. After dinner, our ambassador, John Winant, pulled me aside and told me I had violated an important custom."

"What custom?" asked Butcher.

"I smoked a cigarette before the traditional toast to the King. How in the hell was I supposed to know that was a no-no!"

As he concluded the tale, Eisenhower yawned. Butcher took note and got up to leave.

"One more thing," Eisenhower said hurriedly. "I want you to keep a diary of events I attend, places I go, people I see, and when significant events occur. Nothing too detailed, just a chronological catalog of my activities in the ETO."

"Okay, Ike, but best that I go now. You need to get some sleep."

Two days later, Butcher was in Eisenhower's Grosvenor Square office.

"Ike, I found you a new hotel, the Dorchester on Park Lane. It's the first hotel in the world built with reinforced concrete—it's one of the safest buildings in London!"

"Is it a stuffy place for rich people, like Claridge's?"

"It's definitely posh, and I'm sure plenty of rich people stay there. But it's got a more modern feel than Claridge's and is a notch less pretentious."

Eisenhower wasn't happy. "Can't you find me something more low-key?"

"Look, Ike. You're the commanding American general; you can't stay in a dump!"

Eisenhower sighed. "I appreciate your candor. Let's go look at this hotel."

The general frowned when they entered the Dorchester's elegant lobby. The glitzy marble shouted upscale exclusivity. Eisenhower's opinion of the hotel changed when he toured the two-bedroom suite Butcher had put on hold. The room's wallpaper was a neutral beige color. The brownstone fireplace, solid mahogany furniture, and cherrywood desk were masculine in appearance. Eisenhower found the spacious balcony overlooking leafy Hyde Park appealing.

He moved into the Dorchester—and invited Butcher to share the suite.

Eisenhower received an invitation from Churchill to spend a night at Chequers, the country home of British Prime Ministers. It was an invite he couldn't refuse.

It was a forty-mile drive from London into the Buckinghamshire countryside. After an hour and a quarter, Eisenhower's car turned off a country road onto a smaller road that twisted and turned between hedgerows and beech trees.

When they drove into open parkland, Eisenhower saw a small guardhouse, and beyond it, a stately Tudor country house. Its exterior was a yellowish-reddish brick color. The driver stopped at the guardhouse and was quickly waved through.

As soon as the car stopped in front of Chequers, Churchill bounded out of the house, holding an unlit cigar. He was wearing carpet slippers and a loose-fitting yellow smock with paint stains. "Welcome, Ike!"

Eisenhower appreciated Churchill's relaxed and casual attitude. *Perhaps with Churchill, I won't make any faux pas?*

"Mr. Prime Minister, it's a pleasure to see you again."

As they entered the stately manor, Eisenhower, who loved history, asked, "How did this house become the Prime Minister's country residence?"

"After World War One, the owner of Chequers, Arthur Lee, saw a need for Prime Ministers to have a country estate to entertain dignitaries and for a place for them to relax away from the pressures of London. He donated the house and land to the government."

Churchill stopped in a two-story room with wood paneling and an alabaster fireplace. Comfortable furniture in the middle of the room formed a conversation pit. A massive chandelier hung from the ceiling, and a large window filled the room with light.

"This is the Great Hall, my favorite room," Churchill said.

He motioned for Eisenhower to sit, then asked, "Will you agree Sledgehammer should be scrapped?"

"I don't agree it's inevitable Sledgehammer will fail. I'll admit it's a risky venture, but one worth taking if the alternative is the Russians stop fighting the Nazis."

"You can't stage Sledgehammer without our help and participation. The War Cabinet is united in its opposition."

Eisenhower fought to control his temper over the British backsliding. "You're breaking a commitment you made to General Marshall!"

"I agreed in good faith," Churchill retorted. "I've only changed my position when it became manifest it would fail."

A servant came in with a bottle of whisky and two glasses. Churchill poured them each a generous portion of the amber-colored liquor. After handing Eisenhower his glass, the Prime Minister said, "Let's address North Africa, which is a far more promising venture than an invasion of France this year. All true Frenchmen hate the Nazis. The French African Empire will come to our side if we arrive in force on its beaches."

Eisenhower was prepared to rebut the Africa strategy, which he deeply opposed. "That certainly didn't happen in 1940, when Charles de Gaulle, supported by an English fleet, showed up off the coast of Dakar. The French colonial army chose to fight and repulsed the invasion. The Dakar experience strongly suggests the French would resist an Allied invasion of North Africa."

"Dakar was a debacle," Churchill admitted. "De Gaulle believed the French colonial administrator, Pierre Boisson, would accept him and come over to the Free French cause. We discovered that French officers who stayed loyal to Vichy hate de Gaulle for his constant efforts to undermine the Vichy regime. In any future African endeavor, we'll exclude him from participation." Churchill sipped his whisky. "Have you met de Gaulle?"

"I haven't had the pleasure."

"I doubt you'll find meeting de Gaulle a pleasure. He's a prickly character who's anti-British, even though we're bankrolling his Free French operation."

"Why support him, then?"

"He was the only French officer to speak out forcibly against the despicable French-Nazi armistice and the pro-German government that was established at Vichy. De Gaulle approached me and asked for financial support to form a French army in exile and to spark a resistance movement in Metropolitan France. We let de Gaulle use the BBC to broadcast speeches into France, and to the French people he's become the symbol of French resistance to Hitler. Yet de Gaulle shows no gratitude for our support."

Eisenhower turned the focus of the conversation back to Africa. "The United States is opposed to a North Africa invasion for more reasons than the risk of French opposition. A more important objection is it would disperse our forces and preclude the invasion of France in 1943. Merely nibbling around the edges of Hitler's empire will surely prolong the war. The surest and quickest way to victory is to invade France, push the Nazi army back into Germany, and destroy it there."

"Invading France is not the only clear path to victory," argued Churchill. "There are alternative approaches that may be better! If we clear the Hun out of Africa, we'll secure the Middle East and open the Mediterranean to Allied shipping. From an African base, we could attack the soft underbelly of Europe through Italy or the Balkans."

"I don't know why you think Italy or the Balkans would be easy places to attack," replied Eisenhower. "They're mountainous areas well suited to defense."

"The Italians have no heart for this war!" proclaimed Churchill. "If we invaded Italy, I think the Italians would surrender. Most Italians hate the Nazis."

The two men continued to debate grand strategy for hours until Churchill announced, "It's time for my nap."

After his siesta, Churchill found Eisenhower in his quarters and brought him into a first-floor room filled with bookcases. "This is the Long Gallery. There are more than five thousand books here, most collected before Chequers was given to the government."

Churchill stopped in front of a bookcase and pushed it. To Eisenhower's amazement, it opened. *A secret door!*

Observing the look of surprise on his guest's face, Churchill glowed like a little boy who had pulled off a magic trick. "This secret door leads to the Cromwell Corridor," he explained. "Come, follow me."

They entered a corridor lined with paintings.

"Oliver Cromwell's descendants owned this home for two hundred years. There are oil paintings here of Cromwell and his family from the 1650s, when he was Lord Protector of England."

After a short tour, they returned to the Long Gallery. There, Churchill put a hand on Eisenhower's shoulder. "I enjoyed our discussion of military strategy. I invite you to lunch with me weekly so we can have frequent and frank discussions."

Eisenhower knew Churchill had an ulterior motive: to shape his thinking. But having the lunches could be a two-way street; perhaps Eisenhower could influence him as well. "I'm happy to accept."

"Good, this Tuesday will be our first lunch." Churchill looked at his watch. "Speaking of food, it's time to eat."

Dinner was a small affair with only Churchill's wife, Clementine, joining them. She was formally dressed in a long black dress, a three-strand pearl necklace, and black pumps. Her elegant appearance contrasted with her husband's blue zip-up siren suit of his own design that accentuated his egg-like shape.

"Good evening, General Eisenhower," Clementine said warmly. "Welcome to Chequers."

"Thank you; please call me Ike."

She smiled. "And please call me Clementine!"

Midway through dinner, Churchill unexpectedly said, "You can talk about the war if you want while we eat. I don't keep any secrets from Clemmie."

The revelation shocked Eisenhower. He would never share military secrets with Mamie, however close they were!

Clementine saw the look that crossed Eisenhower's face at the disclosure. "Don't worry, General Eisenhower," she said. "I'm most discreet with Winston's secrets."

Her reassurance was comforting. "Thank you, Clementine."

After dinner, the trio watched a movie in the Long Gallery, *That Hamilton Woman*, starring Vivien Leigh and Laurence Olivier. It told the story of Admiral Horatio Nelson's mistress.

When Nelson died in the film during the Battle of Trafalgar, Churchill began sobbing uncontrollably. Clementine leaned over to Eisenhower and whispered, "Winston's a very emotional man."

After the movie, Churchill took Eisenhower to the Great Room and expounded on numerous topics, always with a drink in hand. The verbose statesman recounted his experiences in the Boer War and opined on the quality of English tea. Then he asked, "Did you study the 1898 Battle of Omdurman in the Sudan War at West Point?"

"I did. That battle featured the last cavalry charge of the British army."

"I was in that charge," Churchill said, a gleam in his eye. "I was a lieutenant in the Twenty-First Lancers. We numbered four hundred and charged what appeared to be a small detachment of dervishes. It was a trap! Fifteen hundred dervishes were hidden behind a hill, and they quickly surrounded us. I put away my sword and pulled out my pistol. I killed three dervishes as we fought our way out—it's hard to miss when the enemy is only a foot away! The Lancers suffered twenty-five percent casualties, but God was looking over me, and I suffered nary a scratch."

Eisenhower was captivated by Churchill's vivid description. "What a memory for a soldier to cherish."

It wasn't until 2:00 a.m. that the sixty-seven-year-old Prime Minister released the exhausted general for sleep.

CHAPTER 15

The Tuesday after his Chequers visit, Eisenhower passed through security at the end of Downing Street and walked a short distance to a black door with the number 10 on it. A uniformed policeman greeted him.

"General Eisenhower, you're expected."

The policeman knocked on the door. An usher opened it, and Eisenhower entered the London home of the British Prime Minister. He was led through the entrance hall with its black-and-white checkerboard floor and down a narrow corridor to the Cabinet conference room. Churchill was inside, speaking with a silver-haired man with a receding hairline.

Upon Eisenhower's arrival, the Prime Minister turned, cigar in hand. "Ike, let me introduce you to Stewart Menzies, head of MI6, our foreign intelligence service. I invited Stewart so he could brief you on a most secret project."

The three men sat on comfortable leather chairs at the end of a long walnut conference table.

Menzies spoke with the cultured accent of the British upper class. "The Germans arrogantly believe the radio encryption codes created by their Enigma machine are unbreakable. The Nazis cannot fathom mortal men deciphering Enigma messages, because daily, the machine's electric rotors create more than a hundred million letter combinations. But the Enigma has a flaw."

Menzies paused a moment for dramatic effect. "General, this flaw was discovered by Polish intelligence, and it is that an encoded letter never appears in the plaintext message as itself. For example, an encoded *a* could never be a plaintext *a*; an encoded *b* could never be a plaintext *b*, and so on. Of course, even with that flaw, breaking a code that changes every day with millions of possible letter combinations would seem impossible."

Churchill interjected, "But we're cleverer than the Hun! We invented a machine to do the calculations!"

After a glance of annoyance at Churchill for interrupting his monologue, Menzies continued. "We have a code-breaking operation at Bletchley Park, a country estate outside of London. A Cambridge mathematician, Alan Turing, has built a machine that mimics the Enigma's three rotors. Each day, Turing's machine explores millions of possible code-letter combinations exploiting the Enigma's flaw— that a coded letter cannot appear as itself in the plaintext message. It looks for 'cribs,' or phrases that appear in German radio messages in the same format virtually every day, such as 'the weather forecast,' 'nothing to report,' or 'Heil Hitler.' Using the cribs, Turing's machine eliminates impossible letter combinations. What's left are a manageable number of possible letter associations that our code breakers use to decipher German radio messages."

"We can read German radio signals within hours of their being sent!" Churchill chortled. "It's the intelligence coup of the century! We call the decoded messages 'Ultra,' as in 'ultrasecret.'"

Menzies's voice was less exuberant than Churchill's. "While we've had remarkable success, the Germans haven't sat idle. They've improved the Enigma over time, sometimes throwing us in the blind while we catch up. In February, the German navy started using a four-rotor Enigma machine, and we haven't yet cracked its code. The blackout in naval intelligence has resulted in a significant increase in convoy losses."

"Stewart, you like to puncture my balloon," Churchill said, his face darkening. "Ike, the Battle of the Atlantic is my biggest concern. Without Ultra intelligence, the German U-boats are feasting on our merchant shipping, and we're suffering horrific losses in men and matériel. We must defeat the U-boat menace to keep Hitler from starving us into submission!"

"Winston," Menzies reassured, "Turing is working full-time on cracking the navy Enigma code. He's a brilliant man. I'm sure he'll accomplish it."

"God, I hope so, and soon!" Churchill looked at Eisenhower. "Very few people know about the existence of Ultra. I've approved you as the senior American general in England to receive Ultra intercepts."

While he was excited to be privy to the secret intelligence, Eisenhower knew such information wasn't a panacea. "Our experience with breaking the Japanese radio code was that the picture revealed was frequently incomplete."

"You're right," replied Menzies. "Ultra is often just a piece of a puzzle, and additional military intelligence is needed to understand German intentions."

Churchill patted his stomach. "Let's go to lunch."

Menzies excused himself. "Winston, I need to get back to MI6."

Churchill led Eisenhower downstairs to a room set up for their luncheon. "During the Blitz, it became too dangerous to continue working and living in this old house. The government built new offices and a flat for Clemmie and me above the Cabinet War Rooms in the NPO basements."

"NPO?" asked a bewildered Eisenhower.

"The New Public Offices Building," replied the Prime Minister. "To keep a connection with 10 Downing Street, I've christened our flat Number 10 Annexe. Clemmie's made the flat quite comfortable." Churchill tapped the ash off the end of his cigar as he sat down at the dining table. "The Blitz ended when Hitler invaded Russia, and now London only receives sporadic bombing raids. Some days I prefer to work and dine here. I had this bombproof dining room built in the space where typists used to work."

During lunch, Churchill asked, "Do you have time for a tour of the Cabinet War Rooms, Ike? It's only a five-minute walk from here."

Eisenhower was curious to see where Churchill conducted the war. "I'd love a tour."

When the men left Number 10, they were followed by the Prime

Minister's ever-present bodyguard, Inspector Walter Thompson. As the trio approached the NPO, Churchill pointed to a corner of the building facing Saint James's Park.

"Number 10 Annexe is on the ground floor. The Cabinet War Rooms are in the basements."

Churchill and Eisenhower entered the NPO and proceeded to a door that led to a spiral staircase. It took them down to the first basement. "This level has offices and meeting rooms," said Churchill. "The level below has beds for the secretaries and staff to sleep. The Cabinet War Rooms are manned twenty-four hours a day."

Churchill led his guest down a cramped corridor. Men and women they passed nodded and smiled at the Prime Minister.

Soon Churchill and Eisenhower entered a room with a rectangular table surrounded by hardwood chairs. "This is the Cabinet Room where we have our most important meetings, attended by my key ministers, advisers, and our chiefs of staff. That chair in the center of the table with the red box is mine. Those three chairs directly across from mine are for my military chiefs."

Eisenhower surveyed the room. It was quite intimate in size. "I bet you've had some intense meetings in here."

"We have. Brooke likes to challenge me, claiming I'm putting forth crackpot ideas." Churchill laughed. "Sometimes he's right."

The next room they entered had a table in the middle at which five men were working. The walls were covered with maps.

"This is the Map Room," Churchill said, pointing to a wall. "The pins on that map show the current location of convoys coming from the New World to England." He pointed to the opposite wall. "That map shows the current disposition of our forces fighting in the African desert. The green color line demarks the location of the English Eighth Army, and the black line Rommel's Afrika Korps."

"How often are these maps updated?" asked Eisenhower.

"Constantly—twenty-four hours a day."

"I gather you like maps!"

"I do love maps. You can't manage a worldwide war without a great knowledge of geography and topography."

They went out into the corridor, and Churchill showed Eisenhower a small utilitarian bedroom next to the Map Room. "This is my bedroom, which I rarely use. I'm much happier sleeping in Number 10 Annexe. Before we end the tour, I want to show you one more room."

Soon they entered a small room filled with broadcasting equipment.

"I've made a number of broadcasts from here to the nation." Churchill suddenly choked up. Tears began rolling down his cheeks. "Excuse me, Ike," he apologized. "I'm a sentimental man. This room invokes very intense memories of the darkest days of the war." Churchill pulled out a handkerchief and wiped the tears off his face. "Well, did you enjoy the tour?"

"It was fascinating," Eisenhower enthused. "I feel I'm in the nerve center of the war."

CHAPTER 16

Flying back from an inspection trip to Northern Ireland, Eisenhower put on his reading glasses and pulled out a memorandum from his briefcase. It was from his supply chief, Johnny Lee.

The War Department has prioritized sending combat soldiers to England at the expense of ASF soldiers. My operation is severely understaffed, and we have fallen behind inventorying supplies arriving from the States. The situation is made exponentially worse because many cargo boxes arrive with incomplete documentation of their contents. Despite the challenges, I promise you the supply operation will run smoothly when crunch time comes.

Eisenhower rubbed his temple as he set the memo aside. A poor logistics operation could cripple an army. He hoped Lee's self-confidence in being able to deliver when it mattered was warranted.

At the airfield, Eisenhower was expecting to be greeted by his West Point classmate and friend General Carl "Tooey" Spaatz, head of the US Eighth Air Force. They were going to lunch at Spaatz's headquarters in Bushy Park. As Eisenhower exited the plane, he spotted Kay Summersby standing beside Spaatz.

He walked to Spaatz and shook hands. "Thanks for meeting me. I'm looking forward to lunch."

"Me too, Ike."

Eisenhower turned toward Summersby. "Kay, how has Tooey been treating you?"

"Oh, General Spaatz is a great boss!"

"Would you like to drive for me again?"

Before Summersby could answer, Spaatz interjected, "You can't take Kay from me! She's the best driver I've had."

Eisenhower turned to Spaatz and in a jovial tone said, "Now, Tooey, be reasonable! Kay drove for me before being assigned to you."

"Ike, before Kay, my drivers were awful, frequently late, and often got me lost! Kay knows her way around London like a taxi driver."

Eisenhower changed the subject. "Kay, when you have a chance, stop by 20 Grosvenor Square. I brought some fruit from America for you."

Summersby beamed. "That's fabulous! I can come by tomorrow."

"Stop trying to bribe my driver!" growled Spaatz.

Eisenhower just smiled.

The next afternoon, Eisenhower was in his office contemplating the news that Marshall, King, and Hopkins were on their way to London to have it out with the British over Sledgehammer, when his intercom rang. Summersby was here.

When she entered his office, looking radiant and smiling brightly, Eisenhower handed her a box containing oranges, lemons, and grapefruits. "Here's your fruit, Kay. Enjoy."

She clapped her hands. "I haven't had fresh fruit in years!"

"Can I ask you who you like driving for better, me or Tooey?"

Without hesitation she responded, "You, General Eisenhower."

"Why?"

"General Spaatz always asks how long it should take to get to where he needs to go. If I say, 'Twenty minutes,' he'll respond, 'Do it in fifteen minutes!' I feel more like a fighter pilot than a driver careening through London to meet his demands."

"Do you want me to see whether I can have you drive for me again?"

"That would be lovely!" she enthused.

Eisenhower grinned broadly. "I'll see if I can make it happen."

A few days later, Summersby received an order assigning her as Eisenhower's driver.

On July 18, the American delegation arrived for a showdown with the British. Eisenhower joined his countrymen in the chief's hotel suite at Claridge's to discuss strategy.

Marshall's blue eyes glowed with intensity. "Eisenhower, the President insists American soldiers enter the fight against the Nazis in 1942. I've been ordered to make a deal with the British while I'm in London. Is there any way we can persuade Churchill to support Sledgehammer?"

"Sir, that's going to be difficult." Eisenhower's voice reflected the frustration he felt. "His advisers, led by Brooke, believe Sledgehammer is bound to fail. I've tried to convince Churchill otherwise, but he wouldn't budge."

"Why are the Brits so opposed to Sledgehammer?" asked King.

"The Germans drove them out of France in 1940," replied Eisenhower. "And they were lucky the Nazis didn't capture the entire English army at Dunkirk. A failed Sledgehammer would require the evacuation of the invading force. I believe Churchill and Brooke are fearful the Dunkirk miracle can't be replicated."

"Why does Brooke believe the invasion will fail?" asked Hopkins, whose pale face and frail body reflected his courageous battle with stomach cancer.

Eisenhower didn't hide from Hopkins the enormous risks a 1942 invasion posed. "There are three main reasons for Brooke's opposition. First, a lack of air supremacy would lead to unacceptable naval losses, including troop transports. Second, it would be a weak assault comprising only five divisions, whereas the Germans have twenty-five divisions in France that could be mustered in opposition. Third, there are too few LSTs to deliver the minimally required number of tanks to the beaches. Brooke believes that, without armored support, the invading force would be overwhelmed by a German counterattack."

Marshall pointed a finger at Eisenhower. "I want you to prepare rebuttals to every objection Brooke has to Sledgehammer! I anticipate Churchill will advocate for an invasion of French North Africa. Prepare a memorandum on why invading North Africa is a bad strategy!"

Eisenhower readily accepted that he and his staff would be working day and night preparing the reports Marshall demanded. He doubted his memorandum would change Brooke's or Churchill's minds. They were as stubborn as the British bulldog image.

On July 26, Marshall summoned Eisenhower to his room at Claridge's. The chief greeted the general's arrival with an air of resignation.

"We finished our meetings with the British. We couldn't get them to agree to Sledgehammer. It's going to be North Africa. Churchill suggested an American commander for the operation, as there is bad blood between the French and the English."

Eisenhower knew French hostility toward the English stemmed from a British attack on a portion of the French fleet at the Algerian port of Mers el-Kebir. Churchill wanted to prevent the French warships from falling into German hands, but the British attack resulted in the deaths of thirteen hundred French sailors.

The words Marshall said next shocked Eisenhower. "You're going to command the African campaign. It's been given the code name Torch."

Marshall is putting me in command of an operation I oppose!

Eisenhower quickly pushed aside his surprise and focused on the challenges of an African invasion. "I doubt we'll be welcomed by the colonial administrators with open arms just because we're Americans. I think we'll have to fight the French army."

"I think so too," replied Marshall. "I'm also concerned with the Spaniards. Franco owes Hitler for his support during the Spanish Civil War, and if he allows German planes to operate from air bases in Spain and Spanish Morocco, Hitler could close the Strait of Gibraltar." Marshall shook his head. "Our forces in the Mediterranean would be trapped."

"How quickly is Torch to be launched?"

"As soon as possible. Churchill and Roosevelt are impatient leaders. Prepare the invasion plans in concert with the British and the War Department."

"Yes, sir," Eisenhower responded crisply.

"And I want you to continue working on the 1943 invasion of France even though it's doubtful the resources will be available to pull it off. I'm putting a lot on your plate, but I have confidence you can handle it."

With this kind of workload, Eisenhower needed all the help he could get. "Sir, I hate to be a pest, but I'm renewing my request to have General Smith assigned as my chief of staff. Now that I'm running the ETO and planning the African invasion, I need Smith."

"You're very persistent in pursuing Smith," Marshall said with a deep frown.

"Only because we'd make a great team," Eisenhower said earnestly. "I understand he's valuable in Washington, but Smith would be invaluable here. You know he can crack heads and get things done! He is also adept at dealing with the Brits."

Marshall sighed. "Okay. You can have Smith. But it will be at least six weeks before I can release him."

CHAPTER 17

As ordered, Eisenhower turned his attention to Torch. The first thing he did was create Allied Force Headquarters (AFHQ) in Norfolk House, a modern office building on Saint James's Square. He was intent on building an integrated operation with Americans and British working together at every level of AFHQ.

He knew things wouldn't always be smooth going, given the multitude of accents, slang usage, and xenophobic biases of officers from both countries. But he zealously pushed his international teamwork approach. He was pleased when British officers began to join the Americans for morning coffee, and the Yanks reciprocated by joining the Brits for afternoon tea.

Eisenhower was hard at work when Butcher entered his office at AFHQ.

"There's a story spreading like wildfire about you," Butch said.

"What story?"

"That you sent an American officer back to the States for calling a British officer 'a Limey son of a bitch.'"

Eisenhower laced his fingers together as he regarded Butcher. "Do you believe it?"

Butcher stared hard at Eisenhower. "I could see you doing it. You're always talking about breaking down the walls of nationality."

"The answer is I didn't, but I'm happy people believe I did. Confirm the story to anyone who asks," Eisenhower ordered. "I want officers to understand the lengths I'll go to forge a harmonious alliance."

Once Butcher left, he returned to studying the reports he had requested on French North Africa. Morocco, Algeria, and Tunisia had a combined population of 17,000,000, mostly Muslim with a Jewish minority of 450,000. There were 175,000 French citizens, mostly settlers and government officials. French colonial administrators had proven adroit at managing underlying tensions between French colonials and the natives, and between the Muslims and Jews. Eisenhower needed the French to continue their day-to-day administration because he wouldn't have sufficient forces to administer and police the three large territories.

The vast geographic scope of Torch posed logistical challenges. The major cities were distant from each other. It was 640 miles from Casablanca to Algiers, and 600 miles from Algiers to Tunis. Only a dilapidated single-track railroad ran from Casablanca to Algiers and on to Tunis.

The geographic detail that most troubled Eisenhower was that Spain and its African colony, Spanish Morocco, controlled both sides of the eight-mile-wide Strait of Gibraltar. Marshall was right to be wary of Franco allowing Hitler to close access to the Mediterranean Sea.

AFHQ quickly produced a plan for Torch, one championed by Brooke and endorsed by Eisenhower. The invading forces would sail from ports in the British Isles and America directly to the beaches of Algeria. The initial goal was to wrest control of Algeria from the Nazi-collaborating Vichy government and bring the French North African Army to the side of the Allies—or at worst, neutralize it. French Morocco would be isolated, and if its colonial administrators didn't throw their hat in with the Allies, it could be attacked from Algeria. Once an African base was secure, Eisenhower would move eastward and try to capture Tunisia before the Nazis, who were sure to invade that French colony with troops garrisoned in nearby Sicily and Sardinia.

After Tunisia was in Allied control, Eisenhower would move into

Libya and attack Erwin Rommel's Afrika Korps and his Italian allies. The English Eighth Army under Montgomery would attack westward from its Egyptian base. The two-pronged Allied attack would be a deadly vise, ensnaring and crushing the Germans and their Italian allies.

It was a bold but risky plan. If Franco allowed Hitler to close the Strait of Gibraltar, it could end in disaster. Eisenhower believed putting all their forces in the Mediterranean was worth the risk because it heightened the chances of capturing Tunisia before the Germans. Without Tunisia as a base, Hitler would have no land force that could block the Torch armies from reaching Rommel's rear.

Once Washington reviewed the plan, Marshall insisted on an additional landing at Casablanca on the Atlantic Ocean. He wanted an escape hatch in case Franco allowed Hitler to close the Strait of Gibraltar.

There were too few Allied ships to support all the proposed landings, and the invasion plan became a struggle between Brooke and Marshall, the two dominant personalities on the Combined Chiefs of Staff. Both chiefs wanted their way, and cables with conflicting strategic approaches flew back and forth between London and Washington.

Weeks passed, and to Eisenhower's dismay, the great transatlantic essay contest continued, without agreement on an invasion plan.

Finally, Churchill contacted Roosevelt, and a compromise was reached. The US Navy reluctantly agreed to provide more ships, and the British dropped their demand for landings east of Algiers. The final plan called for two landings in Algeria at Oran and Algiers, and one in Morocco at Casablanca.

Eisenhower was in his office when an aide delivered a cable from Marshall:

```
Do you have a recommendation for a commander for the
Casablanca task force?
```

He replied with the name of his old friend George Patton, now a two-star general. They had formed a bond in 1919 at Fort Meade where they discovered a shared passion for tank warfare.

When Marshall agreed to his choice, Eisenhower was thrilled. Soon, Patton would be on his way to London to help with the planning.

Eisenhower ate most dinners in his Dorchester suite from room service. Since Butcher had started an affair with a nurse, the general ate alone most nights. Tonight was an exception: his naval aide was in the suite, sharing dinner with his boss.

Butcher took the opportunity to raise a matter there hadn't been time to fit in during Eisenhower's frenzied workday. "Ike, you need to resolve a censorship issue. We've had complaints from the press the army won't let them report on pub fights between white and Black soldiers."

"What's causing the fights?"

"Usually, they involve a Black soldier socializing with an English girl. The English don't segregate Blacks like we do in the States, and some English girls have been dating Blacks. Some of the white troops have taken exception, leading to the altercations. The censors want the army to appear to be one big happy family."

"I believe in a free press. Lift the censorship order. I don't think a few stories about interracial tension are going to undermine the war effort."

As they were cleaning up from dinner, Eisenhower said, "Butch, you need to find me a hideaway on the outskirts of London—someplace I can escape to. Living in a hotel in the center of the city is driving me crazy. I can't walk through the lobby without being accosted by people who want to shake my hand or give me advice on how to conduct the war."

"What do you have in mind?"

"Nothing fancy. Just a small, secluded house where I can have some privacy."

"I'm on it."

Eisenhower walked out of AFHQ to visit Churchill for his weekly lunch. Summersby was at the curb waiting for him.

Her green eyes sparkled in the bright sunshine. "Where to, sir?"

"Number 10 Annexe."

As she navigated London traffic, Eisenhower thought about his chauffeur. Her upbeat, bubbly personality was a pleasant respite during his jam-packed, stressful workdays. And she was damn attractive. Her uniform didn't hide her full figure, and while he knew he shouldn't covet a woman other than Mamie, he couldn't deny his attraction to Summersby. He told himself to suppress the thoughts; he had never cheated on Mamie and didn't plan to start now.

Summersby dropped him off in front of the NPO.

Churchill's flat was comfortably furnished with overstuffed chairs and a red leather sofa. The walls were adorned with landscape paintings the PM had painted at Chartwell, his country home.

Before lunch, Eisenhower and Churchill had a glass of brandy.

"Ike, all of our operations are preceded by deception plans; we want the element of surprise on our side. For Torch, we've floated two fake operations to fool the Germans. Regarding the Moroccan convoy, we've put out a story that there'll be another attempt to capture Dakar. That deception should work, as ships headed to Dakar would pass close to Casablanca. For the convoys passing through the Strait of Gibraltar, the story is it's another relief force headed for the besieged island of Malta."

"Why would German intelligence put much credence in the convoy ruses?"

"Because the information is coming from spies they trust."

The news baffled Eisenhower. He could only utter a lame, "What?"

"We've captured every German agent in England," Churchill said, his chest puffing up with pride. "Some have been executed, while others have agreed to be double agents. The double agents are run by the Double Cross Committee. We know from Ultra intercepts that the Germans highly value the information they receive from these double agents."

"How can you be sure you've captured *every* German spy?"

"We've seen no evidence from Ultra of any agent operating in England not under our control."

Eisenhower marveled at British ingenuity and duplicity. "Your intelligence operations are an unbelievable advantage for the Allies!"

Churchill smiled. "We're outwitting the bastards!"

At the end of the luncheon, Churchill asked, "Is it true you have an attractive English woman as your driver?"

Eisenhower was taken aback by the question, surprised a man as busy as Churchill would care about the looks of a general's driver. "She's half-Irish, but yes, she's darn attractive."

Churchill wore an impish grin. "I'll walk out with you so you can introduce me."

When they got outside, Eisenhower made the introductions. Churchill took Summersby's hand.

"Kay, take good care of Ike. He's a precious commodity in this war."

Summersby's face glowed. "Mr. Prime Minister, I'll take good care of the general!"

CHAPTER 18

After a long and wearying day, Eisenhower entered his Dorchester suite to a ringing phone. He feared it was Churchill asking for a spur-of-the-moment meeting, something he was prone to do. Reluctantly he answered the phone.

"Ike, is that you?"

Eisenhower recognized the high, squeaky voice. "Georgie! You're in London?"

"I've just arrived," Patton replied. "The army put me up at Claridge's."

"You're rich, so you're probably used to plush places that look like brothels," Eisenhower said jovially.

Patton, the wealthiest man in the American army, laughed.

"Georgie, why don't you come over to the Dorchester for dinner? My suitemate, Harry Butcher, is out."

"That sounds good. I'll grab a bottle of whisky so we can really enjoy the evening."

"Let me know what you want, and I'll put our order in. It can take a while for the food to come up."

"What do you recommend?"

"What's available varies. Even with the food rationing, they sometimes have steak. They usually have baked cod."

"Order the steak well done, if they have it; otherwise, I'll have the cod."

When Patton arrived, the two old friends embraced. "Ike, look at you, a three-star general! I remember when I used to rank *you!*"

"You were the first officer I thought of when Marshall asked for a recommendation."

"Thanks for your support," replied Patton earnestly. "I know I'm destined to do great things in this war." His voice rose an octave. "You know I've been a warrior through many generations! I fought with Alexander the Great, the Vikings, Napoleon, and many others. All those previous experiences have prepared me to defeat the Nazis!"

Eisenhower was well versed in Patton's belief in reincarnation. "You've put in the work, that's for sure, Georgie. What do you think of Torch?"

"Hmm, let's see. . . . I'm attacking the Moroccan coast in November when there are fifty-foot swells coming off the Atlantic and the fucking French are likely to outnumber my invading force! Worst of all, I don't have time to adequately train my men. Other than those little imperfections, the plan is just peachy."

Eisenhower shared his friend's frustration. "I was opposed to the Moroccan landing, but Marshall wants an escape hatch if the Germans close the Strait of Gibraltar."

There was a knock on the door. Their dinner had arrived.

As they sat down to eat, Patton asked, "Do you like living in a hotel?"

"I hate it!" Eisenhower said passionately. "It's like living in a fucking fishbowl! I have an aide looking for a house on the outskirts of London where I can have some privacy."

After dinner, Patton poured them each a shot of whisky, and they went out on the balcony. It was a moonless night, and with the blackout, Hyde Park was barely visible. The hum of traffic drifted up from Park Lane as the two men talked.

After a slow sip of his whisky, Patton said, "There is one thing I know about Torch—whatever obstacles the dumbass planners create, my troops will overcome them, because I can inspire my men to super-human effort!"

"I love your confidence, Georgie. I'm glad you're on the Allies' side!"

"Allies? The goddamn English have done nothing but lose battle after battle! We Americans can teach those smug sons of bitches how to fight!"

Eisenhower took a step back, aggrieved at his friend's attitude. "Goddamnit, you need to lose that kind of talk right now! Roosevelt and Churchill have forged a grand alliance, and we have our role to play. I don't want to hear any stories about you bad-mouthing the British!"

"Whose side are you on?" Patton shot back. "Have you forgotten you're an *American*?"

Eisenhower's eyes blazed fire in the darkness. "I haven't forgotten I'm a simple Kansas boy who has been tasked with creating the first unified Allied command in world history! I've been working hard to forge a command where British and Americans work together in an atmosphere of mutual respect. Too many officers of both nationalities think they're made of superior material to their counterpart across the pond!" Eisenhower pointed an accusing finger at Patton. "You're a perfect example of that problematic officer. I don't want you to make my job harder than it already is by throwing verbal grenades at our British cousins!"

"Okay, okay, I get your point." Patton held up his hands in mock surrender. "I'll control my tongue."

"Thanks, Georgie. I don't want the alliance to fall apart because we're fighting each other more than the Germans!"

Once Patton left, Eisenhower was too keyed up to sleep. He looked around his room before pulling out a battered Zane Grey Western. Losing himself in stories of heroes, desperadoes, gun-toting sheriffs, violent shoot-outs, and romance among frontier pioneers relaxed him.

After an hour of reading, Eisenhower drifted off to sleep, the novel open on his chest.

The next morning, a *Life* magazine reporter interviewed Eisenhower for a human-interest story. After the interview, *Life*'s photographer, Margaret Bourke-White, a tall, slim woman with curly brown hair, began taking photographs for the article.

Eisenhower insisted one of her shots be with his closest aides—his army family. That's when he noticed Summersby was present, waiting at the back of the room to take him to his upcoming meeting. When she made no move forward to be in the picture, Eisenhower held up his hand for Bourke-White to wait.

"Kay, I want you in the picture too."

She smiled. "Am I part of your army family, General?"

"You certainly are! You spend enough time with me to qualify for family membership. Get in the picture."

That night, Eisenhower read his weekly letter from Mamie:

I'm enjoying waitressing in the canteen. Some of the soldiers flirt with me. Their harmless advances make me feel young!

Please include as much detail as you can about your living environment and who you're working with. I feel detached and lonely being across the ocean from you. I love you so, so much!

As he sealed the letter he had written in response, he thought about the fact he described every aide so that his wife could imagine his daily life in England with a single exception—Kay.

Mamie still believed he had a male driver, which was true at the time he first wrote her. Because she suffered such insecurity and jealousy over other women sharing his life when the two of them were apart, it was a decision he felt compelled to make. Back in 1935, Mamie had refused to accompany him to the Philippines because she had hated their time in the Panama Canal Zone and didn't want to live in another tropical climate. It went on that way for a year, but she hurried over when she heard he was playing golf with Marian Huff, the pretty wife of a naval officer. It didn't make sense to upset Mamie and cause her to worry because he had a woman driver. *Some things are better left unwritten.*

That night as Eisenhower was drifting off to sleep, a thought hit him: *Will I regret the impulsive decision to include Kay in a picture that could appear in a magazine read by millions of Americans?*

The next day, Eisenhower and Butcher were eating breakfast in their Dorchester suite when Mickey delivered the morning paper. The banner headline read:

COMMANDOS RAID DIEPPE: HEAVY FIGHTING

Eisenhower knew the raid had been scheduled to take place the previous day, August 19, and that fifty US Army Rangers were participating in the attack—the first American soldiers to engage the Germans. Eisenhower read through the article quickly; it ended with a report of a Nazi radio broadcast claiming the Dieppe raid had been a "disaster" for the Allies.

He set breakfast aside, troubled. He wouldn't have to wait long to find out if the Nazi report was true. He was scheduled to meet Mountbatten in an hour in his British War Department office to hear the results of the attack.

Eisenhower found Mountbatten in a somber mood.

"The raid went bloody poorly, Ike. We lost the element of surprise when the first landing craft ran into a German convoy three miles from the beach. The German shore defenders were alerted, and they gave our boys a hot reception. Most of the men didn't get off the beach."

Eisenhower asked with a tinge of nervousness, "Did the LSTs work well?"

"The LSTs were able to land our tanks on the beach. The problems came ashore: Dieppe's pebble beach proved less than ideal for tank maneuvers. Its seawall was an obstacle only a few of our tanks overcame. Most of the tanks became sitting ducks and were taken out by German artillery fire."

"How did the Americans perform?"

"Superbly. First-class soldiers."

"How bad were the casualties?"

Mountbatten's face darkened. "Horrific. More than fifty percent. A third of the raiding force are German prisoners."

Eisenhower shook his head, sad for those who gave their life in the fight for freedom and for the soldiers who would spend the rest of the war in a Nazi prison camp. "There were more troops in the attack than just commandos, weren't there?"

"Yes, the bulk of the attacking force were Canadian soldiers. They covered themselves with glory. I've heard numerous stories of their gallantry and bravery." Mountbatten became pensive. "Despite the heroics of their soldiers, I fear Dieppe will be remembered as a dark day in Canada."

Eisenhower realized Dieppe had been a disaster but diplomatically said, "I'm sure there are important lessons to be learned from the attack."

"I've had those same thoughts. We'll study Dieppe and learn from our mistakes. The next time we attack France, we'll be better prepared."

CHAPTER 19

The latest letter from Mamie made Eisenhower sad:

I don't know if you realize it, but you're famous in America. Newspapers and magazines are filled with stories about the humble man from Abilene who is leading our forces in Europe. I'm so proud of you, Ike! But there's a downside for me. I'm being stalked by reporters. They wait for me in the lobby of the Wardman Park and approach me at restaurants with questions about you. I don't want to say anything stupid, so I generally say "no comment," which seems to irritate some reporters.

I don't like being in the limelight. I had a dizzy spell and fell at the canteen. I've given up volunteer work and stay in the apartment as much as possible.

His life's story had become grist for the newspaper and magazine mills. To feed the public's thirst for information, Eisenhower's mother and brothers had been interviewed, and as far as he knew had suffered no ill effects. But Mamie was in a wartime capital teeming with reporters and had difficulty coping with stress.

He was thinking of what to write in response when Butcher knocked on his open door. He looked up, grateful for the interruption.

"I found your hideaway."

"Where is it?"

"A place called Kingston upon Thames. It's a suburban area south-west of London, about a half-hour drive."

"What's the place like?"

"It's a two-story Tudor home named Telegraph Cottage. It has five bedrooms, but only one bathroom. It's set on ten acres; it's very private, very secluded."

"That house sounds promising."

"The place backs up on a golf course. If you ever get time, you could play a few holes to relax."

"That would be great. I enjoy golf."

"One more bonus! Telegraph Cottage is close to Richmond Park, where you could get some exercise horseback riding."

"Butch, that house sounds perfect."

"That's good, because I already rented it," Butcher said with a wry smile.

"That's presumptuous!" Eisenhower said with a grin.

"You're always preaching your subordinates should take responsibility and get things done."

Eisenhower laughed. "True."

After Butcher left, Eisenhower worked on his letter to Mamie:

Honey, I'm so sorry your health is suffering and the press is hounding you. You can give interviews if you want to; there is nothing you could say that would bother me. The hullabaloo over me will likely fade soon.

Getting out of Washington may relieve the pressure you're feeling. You could go to San Antonio and visit your sister or to Denver to see your parents. Remember you're my gal, and I'll love you forever and ever!

He walked out of the office and handed the letter to an aide. "Get this mailed ASAP."

Eisenhower went back to working on Torch. Planning the largest amphibious invasion in history when Allied shipping capacity was constantly shrinking because of Nazi U-boat attacks was nerve-racking. By 7:00 p.m., Eisenhower was worn down.

He found Butcher. "Tell Kay to get the car. I want to see Telegraph Cottage."

When they exited Norfolk House, Summersby was standing by the car.

"Where to, General?"

"Butch will tell you. He's found a hideaway for me outside of London."

Once she learned the location of Telegraph Cottage, Summersby said exuberantly, "That's a lovely area close to Richmond Park, which is quite beautiful too!"

"Kay, is it true you can go horseback riding in Richmond Park?" asked Eisenhower as he and Butcher settled into the back seat of the car.

"Oh yes! There are several stables that rent horses, and there are bridle paths in the park. Do you ride, General?"

"I learned to ride at West Point."

"I grew up riding horses in Ireland. I'm quite a horse lady!" She laughed.

"Kay, would you like to go riding with me sometime?" asked Eisenhower, who thought Summersby, with her bubbly personality, would prove good company.

"Love to!"

At Kingston upon Thames, Butcher directed Summersby to turn off Warren Road onto a driveway that wound through a pine forest. At the end of the driveway lay a Tudor home that looked like it had fallen out of a fairy tale.

Telegraph Cottage had a steep slate roof, yellow brick walls, and a red chimney. Well-trimmed bushes and trees surrounded the property.

Butcher unlocked the cottage's front door and gave Eisenhower and Summersby a tour. There was a furnished living room with a stone fireplace, game table, and French doors that opened onto a terrace. The dining room had a round oak table with six chairs. On the upper floor were five small bedrooms. Eisenhower opened a dresser in one and laughed. It contained a French-style commode.

"Well, that's an upgrade over the outhouse I used as a child!"

By the time the tour finished, Eisenhower was enthralled. "Butch,

I love Telegraph Cottage. Now tell me the bad news—how much is this place costing me?"

"Thirty-two dollars a week, and that includes the gardener."

Eisenhower was relieved. It was less expensive than he had feared.

Eisenhower tasked Mickey McKeogh with setting up Telegraph Cottage as a home and managing its operation. He told McKeogh to keep the fridge and pantry well stocked, and to always have a stack of Western novels available in his bedroom. He had a telephone installed in his bedroom for top-secret calls.

McKeogh moved some of Eisenhower's clothes there from the Dorchester, purchased bed linens and towels, and secured bathroom supplies. Two Black soldiers, John Moaney and John Hunt, were assigned to do the cleaning and cooking.

When McKeogh asked if he could live at Telegraph Cottage, Eisenhower readily agreed.

Very quickly, Telegraph Cottage felt like a home. Eisenhower sought refuge there whenever his schedule permitted. Butcher found him some golf clubs, and he enjoyed playing a hole or two when he had time at the course that abutted the property.

One evening on the drive out of London, Summersby said, "General, I've heard you've been playing a few holes of golf. I'm a pretty good golfer. If you ever want company when you play, I'm happy to volunteer!"

He considered her offer. He had been playing alone, and having a partner could be fun. "Okay, Kay, we'll play two holes when we get to Telegraph Cottage."

On their first outing, Eisenhower saw she was a good golfer. He was quite taken with how graceful she looked swinging a golf club. The short golf outings became a weekly routine, with Summersby staying afterward for dinner.

Eisenhower didn't think it fair for her to have to drive back to London for the night, only to come back to pick him up early the next morning. He had Tooey Spaatz find her housing at nearby Bushy Park, headquarters of the US Eighth Air Force.

Eisenhower loved bridge, and whenever possible played a few rubbers after dinner at Telegraph Cottage. On a night when the fourth for the bridge game canceled, Eisenhower asked Summersby on the way out of London, "Are you a bridge player?"

"I grew up playing the game with my family, but I haven't played in probably ten years. I used to be pretty good."

Eisenhower hesitated before asking her to join his bridge game; he didn't enjoy playing with someone who didn't match his skill. But he decided to give her a chance.

Kay surprised him with her bidding sophistication and ability to fulfill contracts, and soon the two were regular bridge partners.

One morning as she drove Eisenhower back to London, Summersby asked, "General, do you know what Londoners are calling Grosvenor Square?"

"I've no idea."

"Eisenhower Platz."

He laughed. "It's good to know people still have a sense of humor."

"I have another question for you. What's missing from Telegraph Cottage?"

"Kay, you're stumping me today. What's missing?"

"A dog!"

"You want a dog?"

"I think Telegraph Cottage needs a dog! I'm not saying it has to be *my* dog," she clarified.

Eisenhower had grown up with dogs in Abilene. Dogs were great stress-reducers, and God knew he needed to reduce his stress.

"Kay, I'd like to get *you* a dog, but I'm concerned some people may find a general giving a dog to his chauffeur a bit odd. I'm going to ask Butch to get a dog for me, and over time it will become your dog. We'll keep the pup at Telegraph Cottage."

Summersby squealed as she pumped her hands against the wheel, "That's smashing!"

Eisenhower smiled at her excitement. "Kay, what kind of dog would you like?"

"I had a Scottish terrier growing up."

"Okay then, it will be a Scottie!"

When he got to the office, he found Butcher. "I have an assignment for you—I want a dog."

Butcher sighed; another odd job to do! "Do you have a preference for breed?"

"A Scottie."

"Like Fala, FDR's dog."

"Exactly!" Eisenhower laughed, thinking about the little dog the President had made an honorary private in the army.

That night before dinner, Eisenhower noticed McKeogh was tense; his shoulders were tight, and his usual smile was missing. "Mickey, is something wrong?"

"Boss, I got a letter from Mrs. Eisenhower saying you don't write her often enough. She's asked me to write her once a week, giving her details about your activities. She wants to feel more of a connection with what's going on over here."

Eisenhower wasn't thrilled Mamie wanted someone in his army family spying on him, but he understood her desire to stay connected. "It's okay, Mickey. Mamie's been feeling lonely and detached lately. I'm fine with you writing her. I want her to be happy and content while I'm over here." Eisenhower paused. "Just don't disclose any military secrets, and definitely don't mention Kay! Mamie's worried that a less-than-virtuous English woman will seduce me! Of course, Kay's not that type of woman, and I don't want any unfounded worries to affect my wife's health."

"Don't worry, boss," Mickey replied, the tension draining from his body. "I won't write Mrs. Eisenhower a word about Kay or any other woman for that matter."

CHAPTER 20

Beetle Smith finally arrived in England on September 6, 1942. He was sitting with Eisenhower at Telegraph Cottage before a crackling fire. "Beetle, I'm glad you're finally on board! Marshall sure as hell didn't want to let you go."

"Thanks a million for getting me out of Washington. Working for Marshall was a privilege, but I belong in the field!"

"What's the War Department's perspective on Torch?"

"That it's political bullshit!" Smith said with acid in his voice. "FDR wants Americans fighting Germans before the November midterm elections, and Churchill convinced him the only fucking way that could happen was an invasion of North Africa!"

"Politics controlling strategy!" Eisenhower seethed with anger. "What really bothers me is that Torch makes an invasion of France impossible in 1943. Dispersing our forces in fringe theaters like North Africa is going to prolong the war!"

"Are you sure we can't still invade France in 1943?" asked Smith.

"There isn't a snowball's chance in hell there'll be an invasion of France in 1943! The Bolero buildup won't happen with all our shipping diverted to Africa. Speaking of shipping, what's going on with the navy? Churchill and Brooke have been bitching the navy's shortchanging Torch."

"Ernie King has a lot on his plate," Smith explained. "We won the Battle of Guadalcanal but at a terrific cost to the navy. King lost twenty-nine ships defending the Marines. The Pacific campaign is King's focus. He only gives Europe what the President forces him to."

"That's been painfully obvious."

"How are Torch preparations going?"

"I'm concerned with our logistics operation." Eisenhower grabbed a poker and stoked the fire. "Troops arrive on converted cruise ships like the *Queen Mary*, while their supplies follow on slower cargo ships often with incomplete documentation. A substantial amount of matériel has been misplaced. Johnny Lee is short on manpower to locate and inventory supplies." Eisenhower grunted. "It's been hellishly difficult trying to train men who haven't received their equipment. Can you look into the logistics quagmire?"

"I'll get on it," Beetle promised.

Two days later, Smith flew through Eisenhower's office door like a bull that had seen a red flag.

Startled, Eisenhower asked, "Have you a handle on our logistics problems, Beetle?"

Smith took a seat before unloading his frustration. "The supply situation is a fucking, chaotic mess! Virtually all our supplies are shipped from the Port of New York, and speed over organization has been their motto! The ships arrive jammed to the gills with spotty documentation. The amount of lost matériel is astronomical!"

Eisenhower felt a rising sense of unease. "That's been the problem since I got to England. Johnny Lee has repeatedly promised he would get on top of it."

"To be fair, Lee has been dealt a bad hand," replied Smith, calming down a little. "Still, I'm not impressed with his operation. I don't get the feeling they're working with a sense of urgency. And this *is* a true emergency; the lack of identifiable supplies could derail Torch! You don't have enough guns to give our soldiers. You may have to cut back the size of the landings."

Eisenhower had known the situation was bad, but it was far worse than he had envisioned. He got Lee on the phone.

"Johnny, I hear your supply operation is fucking out of control!" Eisenhower roared by way of greeting.

"I'll admit there's been some confusion and misplaced supplies, but we're diligently working on sorting it out," Lee said confidently.

"Don't blow smoke up my ass! I want you to personally get on top of this! Have your men work twenty-four hours a day, and have Washington send additional supplies to make up for the shortages. Time is of the essence! Do you understand me?"

"You've made yourself very clear, Ike," Lee replied in a flat, dispassionate voice.

"Good!" Eisenhower yelled before he slammed down the phone.

"You sure gave Lee a good ass-chewing."

"I'm not proud I lost my temper, but hell's bells! Sometimes you really need to come down hard on people."

"Ike, you may be interested to know an acronym I learned from one of Lee's soldiers. SNAFU sums up our supply problems."

"What the hell does 'SNAFU' mean?"

Smith smiled. "Situation normal, all fucked up!"

"SNAFU! I'll have to remember that. It perfectly describes Lee's operation."

Within a week of Eisenhower's lambasting Lee, the supply situation began to improve. Critical items thought lost were located. Equipment was stripped from units training in the US and sent to England to make up for the shortfalls in essential Torch matériel. It would be close, but it appeared the fifty-five thousand American soldiers in the British Isles earmarked for Torch would be adequately equipped for the invasion.

Eisenhower read the cable from Marshall:

Robert Murphy, the State Department expert on French North Africa, is on his way to London to brief you on his recent trip there as the President's special envoy.

He looked up at a knock on his open door; it was Smith.

"Got a minute, Ike?"

"Sure, if you have good news."

"Then I should come back later," Smith said with a rueful shake of the head.

Eisenhower waved him in. "What's the problem?"

"Nazi U-boats have sunk four more cargo ships that were to take part in Torch. Even worse, the Brits lost an aircraft carrier that was going to provide air support for the landings."

Eisenhower gave a heavy sigh, weary of seeing his limited shipping capacity shrink. "I have a meeting with Clark this afternoon. We're triaging our equipment and supplies and leaving behind thousands of tons of material not essential to the success of the initial landings." He rubbed his bald forehead; his veins were throbbing. "We're launching the largest amphibious invasion in history on a shoestring because of those goddamn U-boats!"

Murphy arrived in England a week after Smith. Eisenhower had him brought to Telegraph Cottage. He invited Clark and Smith to join him in welcoming the diplomat.

Everyone settled before the fireplace that radiated warmth into the chilly room. A side table had a pot of coffee.

"Bob, we're eager to learn about North Africa," Eisenhower prompted.

Murphy, a career diplomat, had blue eyes, broad shoulders, and a squarish face. "First, you need a little background on the Vichy government in order to understand North Africa. The French-German armistice in 1940 left the Nazis in control of northern France, including Paris. A new French government established in the spa town of Vichy controls southern France and the French Overseas Empire. Marshal Pétain runs Vichy with dictatorial powers. He and his closest advisers believe Hitler will win the war and are working hand in glove with the Nazis."

Murphy poured himself a cup of coffee. "At the time of the armistice, Charles de Gaulle fled France and, with Churchill's backing, established the Free French movement to continue the fight against the

Nazis. De Gaulle tried to recruit French North Africa to his cause but was rebuffed. The colonial administrators accepted Vichy as France's legitimate government, and pledged allegiance to Pétain."

"Don't the Frenchmen controlling North Africa understand Vichy is collaborating with the Nazis?" asked Smith.

"I met with all the high-ranking colonial officials when I was in North Africa. They understand the Nazi influence, but under the French code of honor feel obligated to support Vichy."

"Do you believe Pétain will order his North African forces to oppose an Allied invasion?" asked Clark.

"Yes," replied Murphy, "because he'll incur Hitler's wrath if he doesn't."

The room fell silent.

After a minute, Eisenhower asked, "Do you have any good news to share?"

"There is an underground movement composed of junior officers and civilians opposed to Vichy rule," Murphy explained. "I've spoken with the underground's leader, General Charles Mast. He told me he would welcome an Allied invasion. I'm returning to North Africa next week, and I can seek his cooperation if you want me to."

"Go ahead and meet with Mast, but don't divulge invasion details without my direct approval," said Eisenhower. "Did you discuss with Mast how he could help us?"

"I did. Mast believes General Henri Giraud could inspire French soldiers to support an Allied invasion. Ever since Giraud daringly escaped from a Nazi prison, he's been something of a national hero in France. The Nazis demanded Vichy return Giraud to Germany, but even Pétain wouldn't go that far. He has Giraud under house arrest in Lyon. There is one complication with Giraud—he wants to command all Allied forces on French soil."

"That's impossible!" replied Eisenhower to the preposterous proposition of a defeated Frenchman taking control of an Allied army. "Giraud will not command American and British troops! If he chooses to help us, you can tell him he can command those French forces who come over to the Allied cause. But he'll always be subordinate to my overall command."

"I understand," replied Murphy.

"Can we get Giraud out of France and into North Africa?" asked Smith.

"Giraud is confident the French Resistance can smuggle him out of Lyon and transport him to the Mediterranean coast. We'll have to figure out a way to get Giraud across the sea to Algeria."

"Do you know the size and quality of the French forces?" asked Eisenhower.

Murphy opened his briefcase and pulled out a folder. He handed it to Eisenhower.

"This is all the information Mast gave me. There are one hundred twenty-five thousand soldiers in the aggregate, with sixty thousand in Morocco, fifty thousand in Algeria, and fifteen thousand in Tunisia. It's a professionally trained army led by experienced French commanders. Most of the troops are natives. Mast told me their biggest weakness is a lack of modern weapons, particularly tanks."

"How do you think the general public will react to the invasion?" asked Clark.

"Most people will probably be indifferent. The Jews are the only group likely to welcome the invasion because they're worried the Nazis will force the French to send them to German concentration camps. Jews make up half of the Algiers underground."

When the meeting was over and everyone had departed Telegraph Cottage, Eisenhower lit a cigarette and paced the grounds. The knowledge that the French would fight and his green, undertrained troops would wade ashore in Africa under enemy fire heightened his pulse rate. *Goddamnit, Torch could turn into a disaster.*

CHAPTER 21

October 14, 1942, was Eisenhower's fifty-second birthday. When his chauffeured car reached Telegraph Cottage at 8:00 p.m., Summersby said, "General, I need to get gas. I'll be back for dinner."

"Okay, Kay."

While Eisenhower wasn't sentimental about his birthday, he was a bit disappointed nobody had wished him a happy birthday. He opened the front door and walked into a totally dark house. *What the hell is going on? Is there a power outage?*

He turned on the light in the foyer; it worked! With a sigh of relief, he made his way to the living room. When he flipped the light switch, he was met with a chorus of "Happy birthday, Ike!" from Harry Butcher, Tooey Spaatz, Beetle Smith, Mickey McKeogh, John Moaney, and John Hunt. They were joined by Summersby, who had snuck in behind the general to join the festivities.

Eisenhower flashed a wide grin, the one that millions around the world had seen on newspaper and magazine covers. "Thank you, all!"

Mickey went into the kitchen and emerged with a birthday cake with three stars representing Eisenhower's status as a three-star general. Butcher uncorked a bottle of champagne for all to enjoy.

Being at a celebration reminded Eisenhower of Mamie and her enjoyment in playing hostess. He dearly missed his wife and wished she were here to celebrate with him.

Summersby disappeared, only to return a minute later. She presented him with a small black Scottie puppy.

It was love at first sight! Eisenhower held the little dog, who wagged his tail vigorously while licking and kissing the general's face.

Summersby clapped her hands. "General, I'm so happy you like the dog!"

"Thank you, Kay," responded Eisenhower. "I've always loved dogs, and I can tell this little character is going to be a good buddy."

"Ike, what are you going to call him?" asked Spaatz.

Eisenhower stared at the puppy's face for a moment. "Telek."

"That's a funny name for a dog," Butcher responded. "What the heck does Telek mean?"

Eisenhower laughed. "It's top secret, just like my presence at Telegraph Cottage!"

After dinner Eisenhower and Summersby took Telek out in the backyard. They sat on a stone bench while the puppy frolicked in the yard. Summersby threw a stick toward Telek, who picked it up and began chewing it with gusto.

Eisenhower laughed at Telek's antics as the little dog darted here and there, sometimes tripping over his own feet. He turned toward Summersby, "Thank you, Kay, for being such an upbeat, positive person. When I'm with you, I can relax, unwind from the pressures of my job. I need a bit of downtime when I don't think about the war to keep my sanity."

"General, it's a privilege for me to be of service."

"Kay, I'd really like it if you would call me 'Ike' when we're alone. We've become friends now, not just driver and officer."

Summersby eyed him steadily before a smile spread across her features. "Okay, I'll call you Ike. But just when it's the two of us."

Eisenhower returned his attention to the puppy, who was now chasing his tail. "Are you at all curious as to why I called the dog Telek?"

"I am, actually. It's an unusual name. I've never heard it before."

"It's a combination of Telegraph Cottage and Kay. I wanted to name the puppy after things that make me happy. I'm happy when I'm here, and I'm happy when I'm with you."

"That's sweet, Ike," Summersby said, reaching over to briefly squeeze his hand.

At her touch, an electric shock surged through Eisenhower's body; it was as if he had touched a live wire! His mouth dropped open, and he couldn't say a word.

Goddamnit, I'm married and Summersby is engaged! How can I feel so attracted to a woman who isn't my Mamie?

Eisenhower sat frozen in place, unable to move. Summersby didn't notice. She moved off to play with Telek, picking up the stick and giving it a toss.

After a few minutes of watching the game of chase, Eisenhower regained his bearings. *Better to spend the rest of the evening with a group of people than alone with Summersby.* He moved forward and picked up the dog. "Kay, we should go inside and join the party."

That night, Eisenhower slept poorly. He felt torn over his attraction to Summersby and his devotion to Mamie. This attraction to another woman—one of Mamie's biggest fears—was happening.

He rolled over in bed with a heavy sigh. Kay certainly was striking in her well-fitting uniforms, and her makeup enhanced her naturally good looks. But the attraction was deeper than her physical beauty. He liked the sunniness of her personality and her self-confidence.

Kay's temperament stood in stark contrast to Mamie's, Eisenhower realized uneasily. Mamie was prone to nerves and worrying, and had an insecurity that came out in full force when she felt alone and isolated. Eisenhower loved Mamie for trying her best to be his rock, but she had an underlying frailness. While Mamie's love and affection comforted him in stressful situations, he was always on guard, watching out for her and her health.

With Summersby, there was no need for him to be a protector. He could truly relax around Kay.

And that, indeed, is attractive.

The next morning, Summersby was her usual buoyant self when she picked Eisenhower up. "Good morning, General! Do you want to take Telek to the office with you today?"

"Do you think that's a good idea?" replied a skeptical Eisenhower. "He's not been trained."

"You should enjoy Telek as much as possible! One of your aides can take him out to Grosvenor Square to do his business."

"Okay, I'll get the little imp."

Telek rode in the front with Summersby while Eisenhower got to work in the back seat, reading a memorandum he pulled out of his briefcase.

After a few minutes, he put down the memo. "Kay, I don't feel like working yet. My workday is going to stretch long enough as it is. Why don't you tell me a little bit about your family? I know where you were raised, but not much else about your childhood."

She responded with an eagerness in her voice. "I'm the oldest of four children; I have two sisters and a brother. My father was a soldier like you. He retired as a lieutenant colonel in the Royal Munster Fusiliers. He's the one who taught me to shoot guns, ride horses, and sail boats."

"You were a tomboy!"

She laughed in agreement "Yes, indeed. My father raised me as he would a son. But my mother worked hard to ensure I learned some feminine skills, like the proper application of makeup." Summersby paused. "Can I ask about your childhood?"

"Sure, that's fair," Eisenhower agreed. "I grew up in Abilene, Kansas, one of six boys. My father worked for a local dairy and didn't make a lot of money. When my uncle Abe decided to give up his veterinary practice and move west to Oklahoma to preach the Gospel, he gave my father his house, which included three acres of land and a barn. From that point on, we raised farm animals, like chickens and cows. All of us boys were required to do chores. There was never much money, though. We learned to make our own toys out of pieces of wood and metal."

"Oh, that's sad."

"Kay, I was never sad, and neither were my brothers! Our childhood was quite happy. We hunted, fished, and played sports. All of us became very self-reliant."

The sharing of childhood recollections ensued until they arrived at Grosvenor Square. Eisenhower carried Telek into his office. He emptied a box filled with cigarette cartons and placed the puppy in the box. Telek curled up and went to sleep.

A letter from Mamie awaited him on his desk. Just seeing the letter made Eisenhower feel guilty for being attracted to Summersby. He shook his head as he read through the letter. Mamie was continuing to have a rough time without him in the States:

Your concerns over Ruth's drinking in excess unfortunately have come true. She's heard stories Butch is having an affair with a nurse. Is he? Ruth can be an unpleasant drunk, and the living arrangement has become uncomfortable. I'm looking for my own apartment now. Thank goodness I know you're true to me. I love you with all my heart!

Eisenhower wrote a reply to Mamie, but he found he couldn't bring himself to tattle on his friend:

I'm sorry to hear about Ruth. You're smart to try to find your own place. I don't keep track of what Butch is doing when he's not working, and I'm not going to comment on rumors.

The staff got me a dog for my birthday, a little black Scottie. I like him a lot. You can't talk war to a dog!

I wish I were there to give you a big hug. I miss you and love you hugely!

Eisenhower had given Tooey Spaatz the job of forming a new air force to support the African invasion and the subsequent campaign against Axis forces. Spaatz created the Twelfth Air Force for Torch.

Spaatz was at AFHQ for a meeting with Eisenhower. He had brought Jimmy Doolittle with him.

After Spaatz made the introductions, Eisenhower said, "Jimmy, before we start the meeting, I'd love to hear about your attack on Japan."

Doolittle, a short, stocky man, obliged. "After Pearl Harbor, FDR demanded the military figure out a way to attack the Japanese mainland, and the navy came up with the idea of launching B-24s from an aircraft carrier. Knowledge of the actual operation was on a strictly need-to-know basis. Our crew members volunteered for a dangerous mission without any idea what they'd be doing. I didn't tell them we'd be attacking Japan until we were already at sea.

"When we were in the Pacific and went to launch, the seas were heavy, and the deck of the carrier was pitching up and down pretty dramatically. As I rolled my bomber down the Hornet, I was praying I wouldn't end up in the ocean. Fortunately, every crew got airborne."

"Is it true you had to launch early?" asked Eisenhower.

"We were spotted by a Japanese picket boat. I decided to launch immediately, even though we were two hundred miles farther from Japan than we planned. But despite the sighting, the Japanese were surprised when we started dropping bombs on Tokyo factories. They didn't shoot down any of our planes."

"You had tight security," Spaatz noted. "I'm pretty high up the food chain in the Army Air Forces, and I had no inkling there'd be a raid on Tokyo."

"Sorry about that, Tooey," replied Doolittle, who continued. "The early launch meant nobody had enough fuel to get to the designated landing sites. One bomber flew to Russia to land. All the other planes crash-landed along the Chinese coast in areas controlled by the Japanese."

"How many crew members made it back to the States?" asked Eisenhower.

"Sixty-eight out of eighty. Three were killed in the crash landings, and we believe the others were captured by the Japanese."

"How did you make it out of China?" asked Spaatz.

"We ended up scattered about in a rural farming area. Most of us were lucky to be found by Chinese farmers rather than Japanese soldiers.

"The farmers passed us on to resistance fighters, who took us in small groups to Chiang Kai-shek's headquarters in Chungking. From there, we flew out of China. Sadly, I've heard the Japanese exacted a terrible revenge on the Chinese who helped us." Doolittle shook his head in disgust.

"Stories of the Japanese brutality sicken me," Eisenhower said before he turned toward Spaatz. "What role is Jimmy going to play in Africa?"

"If you approve, Doolittle will command the Twelfth Air Force."

Eisenhower reached out and shook Doolittle's hand. "Congratulations on your new command, Jimmy!"

When the meeting with his air chiefs ended, Eisenhower departed for his weekly lunch with Churchill.

At Number 10 Annexe, the Prime Minister appeared tired but happy. "I'm just back from Moscow, where I met Stalin for the first time and told him there wouldn't be a second front in France in 1942. He was most unhappy to hear that news!"

"You're a brave man going into the bear's den with such bad news," Eisenhower commiserated.

"I went because such news needed to be delivered in person. It was awkward and uncomfortable at times. Stalin kept pressing for an attack somewhere on the French coast. I repeatedly explained the difficulties and extreme risk of a cross-channel attack. Finally, I asked if he ever wondered why Hitler hadn't invaded England in 1940."

"Did that logic work on Stalin?"

"No, he just looked glum and said he couldn't force us to invade France."

"Did you tell him about Torch?"

"Yes, he sees the value of kicking the Germans and Italians out of Africa and opening up the Mediterranean to Allied shipping."

"What did you think of Stalin?"

"I was surprised how knowledgeable he was on military strategy and tactics." Churchill chuckled. "Stalin threw a state dinner for me on my last night in Moscow. To show him I'm a proletarian at heart, I wore one of my painting smocks."

Eisenhower burst out laughing. Churchill had a unique style, and he wasn't afraid to show it!

An aide entered the room and handed Churchill a cable. He frowned as he read it.

"Ike, you remember the letter concerning Torch you wrote to the governor-general of Gibraltar?"

Eisenhower thought back to the letter he had written discussing the support he would need for his Torch headquarters in Gibraltar. "Yes, but that the letter was lost at sea when the courier's plane was shot down off the coast of Spain."

"You better read this." Eisenhower took the cable from Churchill's outstretched hand.

```
The body of the courier, carrying General Eisenhower's
letter to the governor-general of Gibraltar concerning
Torch preparations, washed ashore. The Spanish delivered
the corpse to the British embassy in Madrid. A search by
embassy security found the sensitive letter still sealed
inside the dead man's jacket.
```

"Do you think the Spaniards opened the letter and, after reading it, resealed it?" Eisenhower asked with rising anxiety. "If they did, Torch security has been blown!"

"In all probability they did," replied Churchill as he pulled a large cigar out of his pocket. "Franco's in bed with Hitler. There are Nazi spies all over Spain."

The veins in Eisenhower's temple began throbbing as his blood pressure rose. "But I don't know how we can do anything but proceed with our plans."

"I quite agree," replied Churchill as he lit his cigar. "We must go forward with the invasion."

On October 18, Eisenhower sat down at his desk to review the final Torch plans. The invasion was to appear to be an American-only enterprise, on the premise the French were less likely to fight Americans than the detested British.

Patton would lead the Casablanca attack. A task force of 34,500 men in a convoy of a hundred ships would sail directly from America.

Casablanca harbor had been deemed too hazardous for a direct assault, so the landings would be made north and south of Casablanca. The soldiers would advance in a pincer attack on the city.

General Lloyd Fredendall would command the Oran, Algeria, assault with thirty-nine thousand American troops. They would sail from Scotland and Northern Ireland. There would be beach landings east and west of Oran, and a direct assault on the Oran harbor. The soldiers from the beaches would move on the city and block reinforcements from reaching Oran.

The Algiers invasion plan was identical to Oran's. The initial assault would be led by American general Charles Ryder with a force of sixteen thousand. Once Algiers was secured, British general Kenneth Anderson would land his twenty-three thousand soldiers and rush to Tunisia in an effort to beat the Germans.

Over objections it was too hazardous an operation, Eisenhower authorized a twelve-hundred-mile flight from England to Algeria of American paratroopers, whose mission was to capture two airfields near Oran.

Eisenhower lit a cigarette and began pacing. The whole Torch operation felt like rolling dice at a craps table.

Did the Spaniards pass the dead courier's letter to the Germans?

Will the British deception plans work?

Will Nazi U-boats wreak havoc with the convoys?

Can Giraud be smuggled out of France? If Giraud gets to Algeria, will the French colonial army honor his orders?

If the French choose to fight, how will inexperienced American soldiers perform?

Eisenhower crushed out the cigarette and lit another; his heart was racing. *My first command will be my last if Torch is another Dieppe disaster.*

CHAPTER 22

November 8, D-Day for Torch, was three weeks away, and Eisenhower was worried about the preparedness of American soldiers. Training in the British Isles had been less than ideal, with some men having to train without their equipment. In two days, Eisenhower was traveling to Scotland to observe invasion exercises and get an accurate picture of the situation.

Smith entered Eisenhower's office, holding a document. "This is exciting!"

Intrigued, Eisenhower put on his reading glasses.

Bob Murphy wants an American delegation to meet with
General Mast in Algeria for a conference on how the French
underground can assist the Torch invasion. Mast thinks
the underground might be able to seize power during the
invasion. Murphy's scheduled the meeting for October 24
at an isolated house sixty miles west of Algiers. The
Americans should be delivered by submarine.

Eisenhower sat back in his chair to think through the startling request. It was only four days to the scheduled meeting.

"Beetle, call Clark and tell him I want to see him ASAP. Then contact Churchill and see if Clark and I can see him today."

Two hours later, Clark and Eisenhower were in the underground

Cabinet War Rooms sitting directly opposite the PM in the chairs normally reserved for the British chiefs of staff. Sitting beside the PM was
Brooke. Smoke from Churchill's cigar created a blue haze in the low-
ceilinged room.

After hearing details of Murphy's message, Churchill exclaimed,
"This is a tremendous opportunity! With Mast's help, we may be able
to take North Africa without spilling French blood! Your delegation
can fly to Gibraltar and then take a British submarine to Algeria."

"Who is going to lead the American delegation?" asked Brooke.

"Wayne is going," replied Eisenhower.

"Ah! The American Eagle," chirped Churchill. He had given the
nickname to Clark because of his prominent nose.

"What invasion details can I divulge to Mast?" asked Clark.

"None," replied Brooke haughtily. "The French can't be trusted to
keep secrets."

That evening, Clark, accompanied by three American officers, left
for Gibraltar.

On the drive into London the next morning, Eisenhower said, "Kay,
I'm leaving England soon. I may be gone for a long time, perhaps the
rest of the war."

It took Summersby a moment to respond. "I've heard rumors about
an impending invasion, so I'm not shocked. I'll miss you, Ike. It's been
a wonderful experience being part of your army family."

"Kay, the thing is, I'll need a driver. But I want you to know it will
be dangerous duty. I'll be in a war zone."

She didn't hesitate. "I don't mind danger! And I'm sure Dick will be
in the invasion, so I might be able to see him occasionally. I'd love to
go if you'll take me."

"Are you sure? You'll be treated like a regular soldier. And don't
underestimate the risk you'll be taking if you go."

"I'm not afraid. I want to go with you!" she said with firmness in
her voice.

Eisenhower was pleased Kay accepted his invitation. He planned to reassemble his army family in Algiers once it was in Allied hands, and Kay had become an integral part of that family.

"Okay, I'll make it happen."

Summersby shrieked, "That's smashing! I'm so excited!"

The next day, Eisenhower was pouring himself a cup of coffee in the AFHQ break room when Butcher approached him.

"Do you have a few minutes to talk, Ike?"

"Sure. What's on your mind?"

"Umm, well . . ." Butcher looked down at his feet before he shot a glance at Eisenhower's face. "This needs to be a private conversation."

Eisenhower was used to the need for confidentiality. "Of course. Let's go into my office."

When they were in Eisenhower's office with the door closed, Butcher said, "I don't think it's a good idea for you to take Kay to Africa."

Eisenhower was taken aback. "Why?"

"There's gossip the two of you are having an affair."

"Nothing like that is happening between me and Kay," protested Eisenhower. "You know I adore Mamie!"

"The mere fact you're taking an attractive woman to Africa to drive for you is bound to generate rumors."

"I find this funny coming from you, Butch, since you're the one having an affair."

"I'm a nobody. The press has absolutely no interest in my affair. You, on the other hand, have become the face of the American army. A story about Ike Eisenhower, the all-American boy from Abilene, having an affair with a thirty-four-year-old Englishwoman would be front-page news."

Eisenhower swiveled his chair and looked out at Saint James's Square. Butcher's advice made logical sense. Mamie would be devastated if she heard rumors he was having an affair. It was quite a few minutes before he turned his chair back to face Butcher.

"As sage as your advice is, Butch, I can't take it. Kay is just too important to me. She's always upbeat and optimistic. At the end of a stressful day, I can relax around her and take my mind off the war. I'm not changing my mind. Kay's coming to Africa with us."

Eisenhower was on his way to Scotland in a luxurious private train car, *Bayonet,* to watch the US First Division practice amphibious landings. Churchill had provided him with the railcar, but just like he had with Claridge's, Eisenhower was finding it too damn fancy for his taste.

Paneled in teak, the car offered a sitting room, an office, and sleeping quarters for four. *This must be how the King of England travels,* Eisenhower thought wryly, casting his eyes at the ceiling.

He shifted awkwardly in his seat, concerned about traveling alone with Kay in the palatial railcar. Butcher, Clark, and Summersby had been scheduled to travel with him, but Butcher was bedridden with a high fever, and Clark was on his way to Algeria. Eisenhower hadn't planned on it being just the two of them on this trip, and the situation made him uneasy after the conversation with Butcher.

Eisenhower spent the first two hours reading reports on the last-minute revisions to cargo-shipping schedules due to U-boat attacks. When he finished, he glanced over at Kay, who was reading a book—a romance novel. *How ironic!*

Eisenhower thought about the many men he knew who were having affairs. Beetle Smith had started sleeping with the pretty nurse treating his ulcer, and Butcher was openly talking about divorcing Ruth after the war. *So, what is holding me back from seeing if Kay is open to an affair? Is it my devotion to Mamie, Kay's engagement, or the need to live a moral life instilled in me by my parents?*

He had growing feelings for Kay . . . but should he tell her? If he wanted to take a chance on the romance, this would be a good time—a perfect time—to do so. But he was devoted to Mamie, and he knew he would always love her. The thought of committing adultery made him queasy.

The trip to Inverness, Scotland, took sixteen hours. He had plenty of time to ponder.

Before dinner, served by a porter in the train dining car, Summersby changed into a green dress that accented her figure. With her makeup and red lipstick, she looked glamorous.

After dinner they moved to his sitting room and sat facing each other in brown leather chairs. Eisenhower decided to put a toe in the water.

"Kay, I, I, uh . . ."

He lapsed into silence as he looked at Summersby. *Goddamnit, I can't express my feelings!*

Summersby looked at him with concern in her green eyes. "What is it, Ike? Are you okay?"

"Yes," he managed, "I just wanted to say . . . our relationship is important to me. I enjoy being around you. And I'm starting to have . . . to have feelings for you."

She stared at him without speaking. Her silence stood in stark contrast to her usual loquaciousness.

Eisenhower felt like a schoolboy who had overstepped the bounds, crushing on a pretty girl. His heart dropped in his chest; his stomach began a slow churn.

Finally, Summersby spoke in a quiet voice. "I've growing feelings for you as well, but I'm engaged to Dick. I love him, and we're going to have a family together."

"I've never been unfaithful to Mamie in all our years. I'm conflicted as hell when it comes to you." Eisenhower broke into a sweat. "Honor and loyalty are of immense importance to me."

She smiled. "You're a good man, Ike Eisenhower."

He smiled back. "Well, this has been awkward." He stood. "I need to get some work done. Best if I get to it."

The train was scheduled to arrive at Inverness at 1:00 a.m. At 9:00 p.m., Eisenhower put the memo he had been reading back in his briefcase.

He stood. "Kay, I'm going to bed. I want to get a few hours of sleep before our arrival."

She looked up from her book. "I've been thinking about what you said about your feelings for me. I can't get it out of my mind. I love Dick, but I'm attracted to you too. I want to give you a good-night kiss."

She stood and approached him; their lips lightly touched. Instantly Eisenhower was aroused. He found her red lips sweet, her perfume intoxicating. The kiss deepened. He wrapped her in his arms. She pressed her body firmly against his.

After a few minutes, he released her from the embrace. "I can't bring myself to go any farther. My emotions . . . they're all mixed up."

"Mine too," she said, carefully smoothing down her dress.

Eisenhower smiled at her and then entered his sleeping compartment.

When the alarm clock rang at 12:30 a.m., Eisenhower awoke, exhausted. It had been a long time before he had been able to fall asleep. He felt equal amounts of lust for Kay and guilt for being on the precipice of betraying Mamie.

Eisenhower got out of bed quickly, grateful that getting dressed for the bitter Scottish weather would provide a distraction from his thoughts.

The train reached Inverness on schedule, with Scotland greeting *Bayonet* with high winds and sheets of freezing rain. Eisenhower and Summersby had prepared for the weather by donning heavy jackets, rain slickers, and rubber boots.

After descending the train steps, they were greeted by a soldier with a waiting car. First, the man opened the rear door for Eisenhower. Then he handed the keys to Summersby and opened the driver's door for her.

Summersby slid behind the wheel. She reached into her jacket and pulled out maps of the roads leading to the landing sites. She had memorized the routes in London before boarding the train.

"Kay, is this typical Scottish weather?"

"Appalling weather is the norm from my experience!" Summersby laughed as she put the car in gear and set out for the closest landing beach.

When they reached the designated area, Eisenhower slogged through driving rain and mud to the shoreline. There, he carefully observed the maneuvers. He was not happy with what he saw.

In the darkness, the landing craft came ashore at the wrong locations. Once on land, there was confusion among the soldiers about what to do next.

During the long, bleak night, Eisenhower visited four different landing sites and encountered similar problems everywhere. Most of the officers looked befuddled, and the soldiers under their commands milled around, unsure of where to go.

The lack of preparedness and demonstrated skill was unsettling. Eisenhower hoped his green troops learned valuable lessons from the dismal practice exercises and would perform better when they hit the Algerian beaches.

At daybreak, Eisenhower and Summersby were back on the *Bayonet*, heading south to London. Their only desire after the miserable all-nighter was for sleep. After a quick breakfast, they retired to their separate sleeping compartments.

That evening before dinner, Summersby came out of her compartment, wearing the same dress she had the night before. She looked stunning, and Eisenhower's pulse quickened, his attraction to her undeniable. He told himself to get a grip.

"Kay, about last night. I'm not sorry I expressed my feelings for you, but our relationship can't be more than an affectionate friendship. I can't be unfaithful to Mamie."

She smiled. "I feel the same way. I'm going to marry Dick, and I want to remain faithful to him."

On Clark's return from Algeria, Eisenhower brought him to Telegraph Cottage for a debriefing. The friends sat close to a blazing fire.

"I'm eager to hear about your trip, Wayne."

"When we got to Gibraltar, a young British submarine commander named Bill Jewel met us. We immediately boarded his sub and departed. When I was on board, Bill introduced me to three British commandos whose job was to transport us from sea to shore and back to the sub."

A grin cracked Eisenhower's face as he teased. "With your height, I bet you bumped your head a few times in that sub."

Clark laughed. "I had to bend myself like a pretzel to fit through small openings. When I went to the head, I literally had to crawl on all fours to get there!"

"Did you have any trouble getting ashore?"

"No, we got a signal light from the house at midnight. The commandos put three wood-framed canoes in the water two miles from shore and paddled us in.

"We landed on a wide beach with nobody about. There was a steep bluff covered with vegetation, and we rushed across the beach to hide the canoes. Just as we got to the bluff, Murphy and some Frenchmen were coming down a path. They led our little party up the hill to a stone house overlooking the Mediterranean. That's where we met Mast and a few of his aides."

"Can Mast help us?"

"He thinks so. His underground will act to immobilize key military installations and officers when the invasion occurs. He's hopeful French soldiers will obey General Giraud's orders if he can be gotten to North Africa. Mast will try to seize power if Giraud doesn't make it."

"Did Mast provide us with any information on the current disposition of French forces?"

Clark reached for his briefcase on the floor. He pulled out four files that smelled like the sea and handed them to Eisenhower. "In these files are the locations and strengths of their army and naval units, the locations of gasoline and ammunition supply dumps, and details about their harbors and airports."

Eisenhower wrinkled his nose before he asked, "Why do these files smell like they've spent time in salt water?"

"It's a hell of a story! During the meeting with Mast, the owner of the house got a call the French police were on their way to search the place. We hastily hid in a small wine cellar."

"How did the police know to raid the house?" Eisenhower interrupted Clark's recounting, leaning forward in his armchair with interest.

"The owner had sent away his Arab servants, and they went to the police and suggested the house was being used for a smuggling operation. It was a ticklish situation, but Murphy showed his diplomatic credentials to the police and said they were having a discreet party—that there were gentlemen and ladies occupying themselves in the bedrooms. He told the police that if they didn't want to cause an international incident, they needed to leave."

"That bluff worked?"

"It did. After that scare, the homeowner told us to leave—he was afraid the police would come back. So we went down to the beach but had to wait for darkness to rendezvous with the sub.

"When nightfall came, a strong wind was blowing large waves off the Mediterranean. The lead commando thought we should wait for the wind to lessen. I overruled him. Knowing I would get soaked, I took off my pants and shirt and put them in a watertight bag. It proved impossible to make headway in the heavy waves. The canoe capsized, and my clothes got washed away."

Eisenhower roared with laughter. "That sounds like a Keystone Cops caper!"

Clark smiled ruefully. "It sounds funny now. We waited for hours for the wind to subside. By four a.m., I felt we couldn't wait any longer to try to escape, and we launched the canoes. We were able to get past the first breaker, but the next wave capsized all the canoes. Our musette bags were filled with the documents Mast had given me. We had tied the bags to our arms so we didn't lose any documents when we capsized. We doggy-paddled for a long time before spotting the sub in the darkness."

Eisenhower sat back in his armchair, impressed. "Quite a story, Wayne."

Clark laughed as he gave an eye roll. "There were some close calls, but the trip was worth it."

CHAPTER 23

Momentous events were unfolding. Patton's Torch task force was at sea, and American and British soldiers were boarding transports in Scotland and Northern Ireland. In Egypt, the British Eighth Army, under Montgomery's command, had attacked Hitler's favorite general, Erwin Rommel, and his famed Afrika Korps at El Alamein. Early reports indicated the battle was going favorably for the British.

Eisenhower was at his desk, pen in hand, when a bark disturbed his concentration. He looked down. Telek wanted some attention. He picked the puppy up and rubbed his ears. Then Eisenhower put Telek in his box. The puppy curled up and shut his eyes. Eisenhower returned his attention to finishing the letter he was writing Mamie.

You're my gal, my everything. I'm a lucky man to have you as my wife. I can't wait to come home to you. Being away from you only deepens my love for you!

Eisenhower set down his pen: his flirtation with Kay was just that. After the war, Kay would go off with her fiancé, Colonel Dick Arnold, while he would return to Mamie in the States and be as happy as he had always been in the marriage.

His letter to Mamie finished, Eisenhower opened a desk drawer and took out three coins—an American silver dollar, an English five-guinea gold piece, and a French franc. One coin for each of the victorious Allies of World War I.

He rubbed the coins before putting them in a round leather coin purse with a fold-over flap he had purchased just for these special coins. He knew some people had more luck than others. From now on, these would be his lucky coins!

He looked at his watch—time to go. He strode into his office's waiting area to find Kay. She looked up from a magazine.

"Ready, General?"

"Yes, let's go."

Summersby, with Telek riding in the front seat beside her, drove Eisenhower out of London. Their destination was a remote railway spur, where *Bayonet* was waiting to take him to Bournemouth, a resort town on the south coast of England. From there, Eisenhower would fly to Gibraltar and establish his Torch headquarters.

When they got to the rail spur, Summersby opened his door while holding Telek in one arm. Eisenhower climbed out and scratched the dog's chin.

"Now, be a good boy for Kay," he instructed.

"Safe travels, Ike."

He looked fondly at Kay before he smiled. "I'll be seeing you soon, Kay. Promise."

When *Bayonet* reached Bournemouth, it was raining heavily, and a thirty-mile-an-hour wind was blowing. Eisenhower went to the airfield and found Major Paul Tibbets, the pilot who would be flying him to Gibraltar. Tooey Spaatz had picked Tibbets for the assignment, telling Eisenhower Tibbets was the best pilot in the Army Air Forces.

"Major, it's nasty out here!" Eisenhower hollered through the wind. "Can we leave tonight?"

"It would be highly risky in this abominable weather!" Tibbets shouted back. "And this weather is expected to last for two more days."

"I'll wait one night. Tomorrow, though, we're going, hell or high water, so be prepared!"

The next night, the weather hadn't broken. Eisenhower went to the airfield and found Tibbets. "Are we going tonight?"

"General, I don't recommend flying in this weather. But if you insist, I'll take you."

Eisenhower reached into his pocket and rubbed his lucky coins before he commanded, "Let's go."

The crew and their passenger climbed into the plane and got ready to take off. The B-17 rumbled down the runway, buffeted by wind and rain. When the wheels left the ground, the plane shook violently.

As the plane ascended, the shaking intensified. The aircraft bounced up, down, and sideways, all the while making unsettling creaking noises. Eisenhower felt a stab of fear. *Is the B-17 going to break apart in the fury of the storm?*

The plane's shaking persisted for a nerve-shattering two hours until encountering calm air.

Before the landing in Gibraltar, Tibbets advised Eisenhower, "The landing strip is very short. I'll have to slam the brakes as soon as the wheels touch. It's going to be a jarring landing."

"Thanks for the warning."

When Tibbets hit the brakes, the force was so great, Eisenhower thought the harness holding his arms would break loose and he would be hurled into the bulkhead. Mercifully, the harness held, and the plane came to a halt before careening into the Mediterranean. Eisenhower's legs were so wobbly, he could barely stand. Tibbets helped him off the plane.

"Thank you, Major, for being such a skilled pilot," said a grateful Eisenhower. "I feel like you saved my life."

Tibbets smiled. "I saved my life too!"

After Tibbets took his leave, Eisenhower studied the profile of the mountain that was the Rock of Gibraltar, one of the two Pillars of Hercules that marked the end of the known world to the ancients. Its white-and-green peak towered over the Mediterranean.

Being here and seeing the famed mountain made Eisenhower think of Mamie's pledge to be the family's "Rock of Gibraltar." He was proud of her for trying to be strong, but he worried about her health from the triple stressors of his long absence, the unwanted press attention, and Ruth's drinking.

His thoughts were interrupted by the governor-general of Gibraltar, Sir Frank Mason-MacFarlane, a tall man with a gaunt face. After welcoming Eisenhower, the governor-general drove him to a tunnel complex carved out of the Rock of Gibraltar.

As they entered the tunnel, Eisenhower asked, "How big is this place?"

"It's quite elaborate! There are twenty-five miles of tunnels in this rock. There's a power-generating station, a telephone exchange, a hospital, a water distillation plant, and even a bakery."

Eisenhower was initially impressed with the massive complex. His opinion began to change as he followed Mason-MacFarlane down a side tunnel, lit by faint lights. The air was stagnant, and it stank. Water dripped down from porous limestone rock as the men moved through the cold passageway.

Mason-MacFarlane stopped and used a key to open the door of a small office. Two feeble light bulbs hung over two desks. One wall had a map of French North Africa. "This is your office." Mason-MacFarlane chuckled as he handed the key to Eisenhower. "Not exactly Claridge's."

Eisenhower sighed. *What a depressing location for a command post.* Clark was arriving the next day and would share the cramped space with him. It was fortunate he was a good friend.

Once his new headquarters was up and running, Eisenhower decided it would be a good idea to add to his quotient of luck. Legend had it that touching a Gibraltar monkey brought good fortune. At Eisenhower's request, the British provided him with a driver to take him up the Rock of Gibraltar on a narrow switchback road to find a monkey.

When his driver located a group of monkeys, Eisenhower warily approached. He was happy to be able to pat one on the head without being bitten.

Upon returning to his cold and clammy tunnel office, Eisenhower found British admiral Andrew Browne Cunningham—ABC to his friends—awaiting him.

Eisenhower had worked closely with Cunningham in planning Torch and had come away impressed with his ability to orchestrate the navy's support of a complicated invasion involving hundreds of ships.

"Giraud has escaped from France and is on a sub headed to Gibraltar!" said Cunningham, his broad, flat face breaking into a smile.

"That's great news!"

"Do you want to see the first Allied ships pass through the Strait of Gibraltar?"

"Hell, yes!" Eisenhower responded. He was excited; months of planning would soon be turned into action!

They exited the tunnel to a waiting car and driver. They headed toward Europa Point, the southernmost tip of Gibraltar. Before reaching it, the driver turned off the paved road and headed up the side of the mountain on a twisting, potholed trail. After a few minutes, the car stopped.

Cunningham pointed up. "For the best view, we need to climb up to the headland above the strait."

Cunningham led the way, walking up the rocky path with the quick and steady gait of a seasoned seaman. Eisenhower had trouble keeping up with the older man, the knee he hurt playing football at West Point hindering his movement on the uneven ground.

When the two men reached the perfect vantage spot, Eisenhower was out of breath. When he saw the silhouette of blacked-out Allied ships passing Gibraltar, he thanked the Lord that thus far the convoys had avoided the deadly U-boats. He reached into his pocket and vigorously rubbed his lucky coins, his pulse racing.

In less than forty-eight hours, the troops will hit the beaches!

The next afternoon, Eisenhower was anxiously awaiting the arrival of French general Henri Giraud, when Clark returned from the teletype room with a sober expression.

"Something wrong, Wayne?"

"A submarine near Casablanca is reporting high winds and large waves crashing against the shoreline. If the winds don't subside, Patton will have to postpone his landings."

"Goddamnit, we'll lose the element of surprise!" Eisenhower rubbed his forehead. He felt his veins throbbing.

At 2:30 p.m., Giraud appeared in the Americans' tunnel office. Sporting a large mustache and wearing rumpled civilian clothes, the six-foot-three Frenchman towered over the five-foot-ten Eisenhower.

Through an interpreter, he dramatically announced, with a raised arm, "Giraud has arrived!" Then he kissed the Americans on each cheek.

Eisenhower thought it strange the French general referred to himself in the third person, but he shrugged it aside. "Welcome, General Giraud, to the Allied team! I'm prepared to make you the civilian governor of French North Africa and the commander of all French forces who join the Allied cause."

Giraud looked puzzled as he listened to the interpreter translate.

"General," Eisenhower continued, "we have prepared a speech for you to give on a radio broadcast tonight that can be heard in Algeria and Morocco."

Eisenhower handed Giraud a document written in French that called for the French army not to resist the Allied invasion.

Giraud studied the statement. "Giraud cannot give this speech."

Eisenhower was surprised. "Why not?"

"This paper says *you'll* be in command of Allied forces in North Africa. That can't be. A Frenchman *must be* in command of all forces fighting on French soil, including American and British soldiers! General Mast promised Giraud he would be in command. You must be subordinate to Giraud!"

A shocked Eisenhower replied, "General, there's been a misunderstanding. I must retain ultimate command. President Roosevelt and Prime Minister Churchill have vested me with command. I cannot relinquish such a sacred obligation to anyone."

"It would be a family disgrace for Giraud not to command all forces fighting on French soil! What would the French people think?"

Eisenhower and Clark took turns trying to get Giraud to be reasonable. Hours passed, and the Frenchman refused to budge. Finally, he imperiously announced, "Giraud will return to France if he can't be in command."

"No, you won't," snapped Clark. "You came on a one-way submarine!"

Eisenhower interceded. He knew Giraud had made a daring escape from a German prison, and perhaps telling his story would put the Frenchman in a more agreeable mood.

"General Giraud, can you tell us how you escaped from Germany?" Giraud's eyes lit up at the request.

"The Nazis put Giraud and other captured French generals in Königstein Castle, a medieval fortress built on the edge of a cliff with a one-hundred-foot drop. The Germans thought Königstein was escape-proof and permitted Giraud to take unescorted walks. Giraud discovered a blind spot, a corner where, at night, a man would have a few undetected minutes to attach a rope to the wall and lower himself to the ground."

"How did you secure that rope?" asked Clark.

"Giraud ingeniously made a rope," the French general crowed. "He had been a prisoner in World War One, and he knew the same could happen again in this war. Giraud worked out a cipher code with his wife so they could communicate in secret. In a letter, Giraud asked her to send him food packages tied up with plenty of good, strong cord. Giraud received frequent food parcels from his wife and used the cords to braid a rope."

"That was clever," Eisenhower complimented, "although I'm surprised a cord rope could hold your weight."

"Giraud knew the rope needed strengthening," Giraud said haughtily. "To make it stronger, Giraud had his wife send him telephone wire hidden in jars of strawberry jam. It took two years to make a one-hundred-foot rope out of the cords and telephone wire. When it was ready, Giraud's wife contacted the French Resistance. They sent a man who spoke perfect German to meet Giraud on the designated escape date.

"Giraud's plan worked perfectly! When he lowered himself from the fortress, the man was waiting for him on the ground. He gave him civilian clothes and fake identity papers. Giraud had perfected his German while in captivity just so he could pose as a civilian one day!

"Giraud and the Resistance man rode on German trains close to the Swiss border. When Giraud learned the Nazis had launched a manhunt for him, they left the train and hiked over the mountains into Switzerland."

While Giraud's story was fascinating, the telling of it didn't make the tall Frenchman more malleable, and another fruitless hour passed.

Finally, Eisenhower couldn't take it anymore. He ended the marathon meeting that was going nowhere, and at 9:00 p.m. he fled to his room in the Convent, the residence of the British governor of Gibraltar.

In the bedroom, Eisenhower tossed and turned. He couldn't fall asleep. How in the hell could Giraud be so misinformed as to his role?

The invasion will proceed without help from the imperious Frenchman.

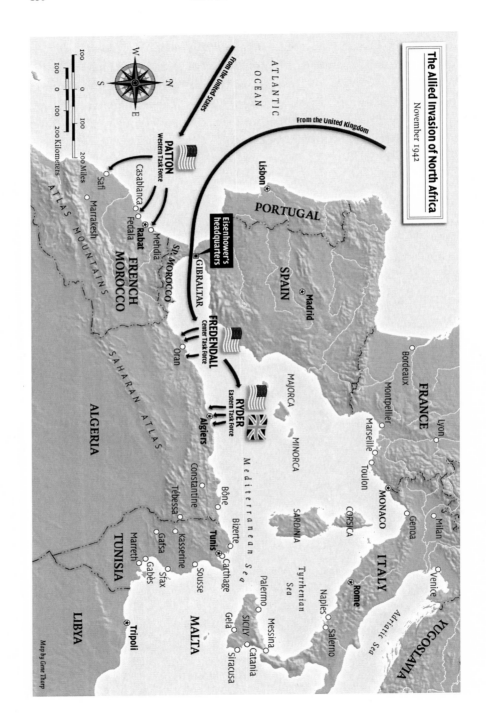

The Allied Invasion of North Africa
November 1942

From the United States

From the United Kingdom

ATLANTIC OCEAN

PATTON
Western Task Force

Lisbon

PORTUGAL

SPAIN

Madrid

Safi

Marrakesh

Casablanca

Fedala
Rabat
Mehdia
Sp. MOROCCO

FRENCH MOROCCO

Eisenhower's headquarters

GIBRALTAR

ATLAS MOUNTAINS

SAHARAN ATLAS

ALGERIA

Oran

FREDENDALL
Center Task Force

RYDER
Eastern Task Force

Algiers

MAJORCA

MINORCA

Bordeaux

Montpellier

Marseille

Toulon

FRANCE

Lyon

MONACO

Genoa

Milan

ITALY

Venice

Rome

YUGOSLAVIA

Adriatic Sea

Mediterranean Sea

Constantine

Tébessa

Bône

Bizerte

Tunis

Carthage

SARDINIA

CORSICA

Tyrrhenian Sea

Palermo

Naples

Salerno

TUNISIA

Marreth

Gafsa

Kasserine

Gabès

Sfax

Sousse

Messina

Gela

SICILY

Catania

Siracusa

MALTA

LIBYA

Tripoli

Map by Gene Thorp

N
W E
S

100 0 100 200 Kilometers
100 0 100 200 Miles

CHAPTER 24

The Torch assaults were set for 1:00 a.m., and Eisenhower was back in his dismal tunnel office at midnight. There was an encouraging cable on his desk from Patton:

```
The good Lord has answered my prayers and moderated the
wind! I'm proceeding on schedule with the Casablanca
landings.
```

Clark tried to make small talk, but Eisenhower wasn't in the mood. As hours passed without information on the assaults, his body became as taut as a piano wire, and his blood-pressure level surged.

Finally, at 5:30 a.m., a cable came from General Charles Ryder in Algiers:

```
Beach landings were unopposed, but French army putting up
stiff resistance as we approach Algiers. The French navy
repulsed the assault on Algiers harbor.
```

"No surprise the French are fighting," said Clark.

Eisenhower took a deep breath and exhaled. "Looks like Mast's effort to seize control failed."

At 6:00 a.m., General Lloyd Fredendall reported from Oran:

```
Beach assaults successful with no opposition. Fierce
fighting on approach to Oran. Assault on Oran harbor
failed.
```

Eisenhower began pacing in the cramped office. "I hate being in this tunnel so far from the action. It's taking forever for reports to come through."

Clark stood and stretched his back. "I'm going to the teletype room to see if anything has come in from Patton."

"Wayne, while you're there, check on whether there's any information on the paratrooper assaults."

Clark returned in fifteen minutes.

"Any news, Wayne?"

"Nothing. Not a word from Patton, and the thirty-nine planes carrying the paratroopers seem to have vanished in thin air."

"How in the hell can we lose thirty-nine planes?" Eisenhower asked rhetorically, his heart racing.

"There is one bit of good news."

"What's that?" asked Eisenhower, desperate to hear something positive.

"There've been no reports of Nazi planes using Spanish airfields."

"Thank goodness."

Time passed slowly. *Too slowly.* The constant drip-drip of water from the limestone walls got on Eisenhower's nerves as he paced in his cell-like office.

At 8:30 a.m., Ryder reported:

```
Have learned Vichy's senior military commander, Admiral
François Darlan, is in Algiers. Darlan has taken control of
the French forces defending Algiers. Making slow progress
in advancement on the city.
```

"Goddamnit, what bad luck Darlan's in Algiers!" exclaimed Eisenhower. "He's sure to stiffen French resistance."

Finally, at 10:00 a.m. Patton reported:

```
The goddamn French are fighting! Landings made under
```

hostile fire. American blood being shed in Morocco.

Eisenhower seethed with anger. Brave American soldiers were dying at the hands of French troops who should have been on the Allied side fighting the Nazis.

An 11:00 a.m. message from Ryder brought some good news:

Have captured Algiers's Maison Blanche airfield.

As the day dragged on, Eisenhower learned the fate of the paratroopers. Strong winds and heavy rain had broken up the plane formations. Allied aircraft landed in Spain, Spanish Morocco, French Morocco, and Algeria. Only three planes found one of the targeted Oran air bases, and they were unceremoniously driven off by antiaircraft fire. The ambitious paratrooper assault had been a debacle.

In the late afternoon, a subdued Giraud appeared in Eisenhower's office. His overweening arrogance was absent. Through an interpreter he said, "Giraud has reconsidered his position. Giraud accepts General Eisenhower's authority and accepts the roles of governor-general and commander of French military forces."

"General Giraud, welcome to the Allied team!" said a relieved Eisenhower. "Tomorrow you and General Clark will fly to Algiers and bring an end to the fighting. You must persuade the French army to join the Allies in the fight against the Nazis!"

"Giraud will not fail!" He saluted and left.

At 6:00 p.m., Clark and Eisenhower were discussing their frustration with the French when a message was received from Ryder:

Darlan has ordered a cease-fire in Algiers but refuses to end hostilities in Oran and Casablanca.

"Why in the hell didn't Darlan end the fighting everywhere?" sputtered Eisenhower, throwing both hands up in the air. "God, I hope Giraud can deliver tomorrow and bring the French army to the side of the Allies."

"Am I empowered to deal with Darlan in the event Giraud doesn't get control of the French military?" asked Clark.

Eisenhower hesitated before responding. Darlan was an infamous Nazi collaborator who openly courted Hitler. "Try and avoid meeting with Darlan because of his association with the Nazis. But if he's the only one who can end the fighting, then deal with him. We need to be moving on Tunisia as quickly as possible."

The next day, Clark and Giraud flew to Algiers. Eisenhower impatiently awaited news. Finally, a late-afternoon cable arrived from Clark:

```
Giraud totally ineffective. His orders for the French to
cease fighting in Oran and Casablanca have been ignored.
Darlan has control of the military. Murphy is arranging for
me to meet with the admiral.
```

Eisenhower was enraged. So much effort and time had been invested in Giraud, and all for naught!

An 8:00 p.m. cable from Clark brought good news:

```
I met with Darlan and persuaded him to order a temporary
cease-fire in Oran and Casablanca. I'm attempting to get
Darlan to switch sides and join the Allies.
```

Eisenhower wanted to fly to Algiers to take control of the negotiations, but the weather was proving inhospitable yet again. Rain and fog had closed the Gibraltar airfield.

Events were moving at a fast pace. Hitler abrogated the armistice with France, and the German army occupied Vichy territory. Pétain fired Darlan for ordering the cease-fire and facilitated German troop movement into Tunisia.

Two days later, Eisenhower read a message from Clark with mixed feelings:

Have negotiated an agreement with Darlan subject to your
ratification. Darlan will become High Commissioner of
French North Africa in charge of civilian affairs, and
Giraud will control the military forces. The French will
join the Allies, and the North African Army will join the
fight against the Germans.

Eisenhower was happy the French would join the Allies but disturbed that Darlan, a man who had collaborated with Hitler, would control the government.

Impatiently he waited for Gibraltar's airfield to open. He needed to get to Algiers and determine whether to ratify the Darlan deal.

When the weather cleared on November 13, Eisenhower flew to Algiers. Murphy met him at the Maison Blanche airfield.

As they drove toward Algiers, Eisenhower asked the diplomat, "What happened the night of the invasion, Bob?"

"At one a.m., I went to the house of General Alphonse Juin, the senior French commander. I told him the invasion was happening and that General Giraud would take charge."

"I gather Giraud's name didn't carry much weight with him?"

"Juin said Giraud was a retired officer with no authority, and that because Darlan was in Algiers visiting his polio-stricken son, he was powerless to help. I had Juin call Darlan and tell him I had an urgent message for him."

"You spoke with Darlan the night of the invasion?" asked a surprised Eisenhower.

"Yes. Darlan appeared at Juin's residence within twenty minutes. When I told him Giraud would take charge, he laughed. Darlan said Giraud had the political sophistication of a child, and that he was, at best, a good commander of troops."

Eisenhower wished he had known Darlan's appraisal of Giraud before America put its political and military weight behind the Frenchman.

"Darlan claimed he needed to cable Pétain for instructions," Murphy continued. "But when he tried to leave, he was stopped by members of Mast's underground who had surrounded the house. Darlan came back inside and dramatically announced he was a prisoner of the Americans."

"Bob, you get caught up in the strangest affairs!" Eisenhower said, chuckling.

"It got even more strange! The underground fighters surrounding Juin's house were overpowered by the French army, and I was arrested at gunpoint. I was left under guard at Juin's house while Darlan and Juin left to supervise the defense of Algiers.

"In the afternoon, Darlan returned and released me from custody. He told me to find the senior American general and take him to Fort l'Empereur. Darlan provided me a chauffeur-driven limousine flying a white truce flag. It was a harrowing trip. We drove past French and American troops engaged in combat, with several bullets hitting our limousine.

"I found General Ryder on a beach outside of Algiers. I took Ryder to Fort l'Empereur, where he and Darlan signed a cease-fire stopping the fighting in Algiers."

By the time Murphy finished his tale, the car had stopped in front of the elegant Hotel Saint George. They were greeted by Clark, who escorted them to a conference room with the placard SALLE DE CONFÉRENCE PARIS. The high-ceilinged room had white crown molding, a glittering crystal chandelier, and paintings of Paris on the walls.

The three men sat in leather chairs around a walnut conference table.

"Wayne, what happened when you got to Algiers?" asked Eisenhower.

"Mast was under arrest, and Giraud's orders were ignored. Giraud told me he was powerless and that I should deal with Darlan.

"Murphy arranged a meeting for me with the admiral. Initially, Darlan claimed he couldn't stop the fighting in Oran and Morocco without Pétain's approval. I angrily pounded on the table and told him he had to end the bloodshed! He and I went back and forth for a while. Finally, Darlan ordered a cease-fire. A few hours later, Pétain fired him."

"Tell me more about this deal you reached with Darlan," Eisenhower asked as he lit a cigarette.

"It will greatly aid our advance into Tunisia!" Clark said fervently. "We'll control the airfields, seaports, and the railroad. The French will unload American cargo ships and store our supplies. And the French army will fight beside us in Tunisia."

"What's in it for Darlan?" asked Eisenhower.

"The French get to continue to administer their possessions without us interfering in their internal affairs."

"I see," said Eisenhower. "And how did Giraud get back in the picture?"

"I thought we should have a man in power who owed his position to the United States. I insisted Darlan cut a deal with Giraud to share power." Clark pulled a document out of his briefcase. "Ike, here's the draft agreement."

After reading it, Eisenhower asked, "What's the status of the French fleet?"

"Darlan ordered the fleet to leave the naval base at Toulon for North Africa, but nobody here believes the Germans will allow those ships to leave France."

Eisenhower turned his attention to Murphy. "Bob, do you have concerns about entering into an agreement with Darlan?"

"I do. Darlan has actively cooperated with the Germans, and that makes him a Fascist in the eyes of many. But he's the most powerful French official in North Africa. I don't think you have a choice but to deal with Darlan if you want French cooperation while you advance into Tunisia."

Eisenhower was quiet for a time, weighing the pros and cons. Clark's deal achieved all his immediate military needs. Having the French administer Algeria and Morocco was imperative because there were not enough Allied troops to impose a military occupation. Active French support would aid the invasion of Tunisia in innumerable ways, and securing the North African French as allies to fight the Nazis was a key Torch objective. But there was one big negative—and that was dealing with a Nazi collaborator.

Eisenhower thought about Churchill making an alliance with Joseph Stalin, a Communist dictator. *War indeed makes strange bedfellows.* There could be political fallout from dealing with Darlan, and the safe course would be to seek approval from Churchill and Roosevelt. But the problem with doing that was his advance into Tunisia would assuredly be delayed by another transatlantic essay contest. He was the man on the spot, and he needed to take responsibility and act. *Today.*

Eisenhower took a deep breath. "I'll ratify the Darlan deal. Bob, set up a meeting with Darlan as soon as possible."

An hour later, Darlan and Giraud were brought into the Paris conference room at the Hotel Saint George. Eyeballing them as they entered, Eisenhower suppressed a laugh. With Giraud towering over the diminutive Darlan, they resembled the cartoon characters Mutt and Jeff.

Giraud approached Eisenhower and insisted on kissing him on both cheeks. It was a custom he was beginning to loathe.

With Murphy interpreting, Eisenhower said, "I accept the Clark-Darlan Agreement. I welcome the French North African Empire to the grand Alliance to liberate the world from the tyranny of Hitler and Mussolini."

Eisenhower looked over at the round-faced Darlan in his French admiral's uniform; he was contentedly smoking a pipe. "Admiral, are you firmly with us in the crusade to defeat the Nazis?"

Darlan pointed his pipe at Eisenhower. "I hate the Nazis! France made an armistice with Hitler, which I was honor-bound to abide by. But Hitler has broken his promise not to occupy Vichy territory. His breach frees me of complying with the armistice."

Eisenhower recalled seeing pictures of Darlan befriending Hitler in Berchtesgaden. His disavowal of the Nazi dictator seemed disingenuous. *Darlan is indeed a slippery character—but he could still be useful.*

"Admiral, can you get French West Africa to drop its ties to Vichy and support the Allies? The naval and air bases in Dakar would be of great value."

"I'm on good terms with Pierre Boisson, the governor-general," Darlan boasted. "I'll talk to Boisson. Now that the Germans have broken the armistice, I think I can persuade him to join the Allies."

Eisenhower's nerves tingled with excitement. Dakar would be the closest African base to American air bases in Brazil. An invaluable air bridge could be established there to ferry supplies for his African operations. *If Darlan can deliver Dakar without firing a shot, I'll be ecstatic!*

Eisenhower left the Hotel Saint George, feeling he made the right decision to deal with Darlan. *Will my political bosses agree?*

CHAPTER 25

Newspaper columnists and radio broadcasters across America and England were outraged: *How can the great democracies do business with a man known to be a Nazi collaborator?* Edward R. Murrow, whose CBS Radio broadcasts were heard by millions, asked, "Are Americans waging war against the Nazis, or sleeping with them?" The *Christian Science Monitor* charged Eisenhower with immoral behavior for dealing with a Nazi collaborator. Roosevelt and Churchill were savaged in the press, and they demanded Eisenhower explain his reasoning for cutting the deal.

The American general spent days in his depressing Gibraltar tunnel office, writing memos in defense of the decision. The President and Prime Minister supported him on the narrow grounds of temporary military necessity.

While he knew the Darlan agreement would rankle some, Eisenhower found the vehemence of the personal attacks against him shocking. Despite the blowback, he firmly believed he made the correct decision. Before Darlan ended the fighting, more than eleven hundred American and British soldiers and sailors had been killed and thousands more wounded—and the North African French went from being an enemy to an ally.

Eisenhower's battered spirits fell further when intelligence reports showed the Nazis were winning the race for Tunisia. Hitler had moved swiftly, and aided by Vichy cooperation, quickly built up a formidable force.

General Anderson rushed his British troops into Tunisia. They got within eleven miles of Tunis before hitting stiff German resistance. Anderson's advance was hindered by frequent air attacks. The Germans dominated the skies, having the advantage of hard-surface airfields in Tunisia close to the front lines.

Doolittle's Twelfth Air Force was plagued by a score of problems. Planes that broke down proved difficult to repair because of a paucity of spare parts. Quickly constructed forward bases lacked antiaircraft batteries, and many planes on the ground were destroyed during German air raids. Heavy rain added to Doolittle's woes, turning dirt runways into mudholes, hampering operations.

Eisenhower ordered American and French soldiers forward as quickly as possible to reinforce Anderson. Combat units were broken up because of transport limitations, with Eisenhower putting a premium on speed over an orderly and well-supplied advance.

Feeling blue in his dismal tunnel office, he penned a letter to Mamie:

Please don't take offense if I sound irritable in this letter. I must deal with one headache after another. War, international politics, the press. I'm under pressure from all sides; there is only so much a man can put up with! . . . Remember, honey, I love you with all my heart.

He longed to leave Gibraltar and the depressing tunnel. But he couldn't until a secure communications system was in place in Algiers. Finally, on November 21, Eisenhower left Gibraltar for his new headquarters in the Hotel Saint George.

The grand hotel, built in the Moorish style by the French in 1889, stood atop a hill high above Algiers harbor. The building bustled with activity as staff, led by Smith, transferred from London.

When Eisenhower arrived in Algiers, there was a letter from Mamie waiting for him. He smiled; she was ready to defend his honor:

Reporters have tried to get me to comment on the

Darlan affair. I refuse. Those ignorant commentators attacking you don't know you're a man of the highest character. I'm sure you made the best decision in the circumstances. I'm as angry as a hornet at Roosevelt for failing to more vigorously support you. You'll always have my love and support.

In Algiers, Eisenhower moved into a Spanish-style villa that had sweeping views of the city, its crescent bay, and sparkling blue Mediterranean waters. It had two master bedrooms—which Eisenhower and Butcher occupied—and four smaller bedrooms. Admiral Cunningham occupied an adjacent villa in the two-villa compound.

It soon felt like home. Mickey flew in with Telek. Moaney and Hunt came to do the cooking and cleaning. And Kay would soon arrive on the British troop ship *Strathallan* with a group of nurses.

Eisenhower's army family was quickly reassembling.

Darlan arranged for a meeting in the Hotel Saint George's Paris conference room with Pierre Boisson, governor-general of French West Africa. They sat around the walnut conference table with Murphy translating the French for Eisenhower.

"Pierre, you no longer owe loyalty to Vichy," the little admiral said to start the meeting. "Ever since Hitler occupied southern France, Pétain has lacked the free will to act. Sadly, he's nothing more than Hitler's puppet. We must throw our lot in with the Americans and British and fight beside them to liberate our beloved France from the Nazis!"

Boisson pressed his lips tightly together before declaring, "I despise the Nazis, and I want a free France! Yet if I stop supporting Vichy, won't I be a traitor like de Gaulle?"

"Of course not!" Darlan smoothly responded. "The Nazi occupation of Vichy territory changes everything. We were loyal to Vichy because it was the lawful government of France, with freedom to govern southern France and our glorious overseas empire. Our faithfulness to Vichy was entirely proper. Now that Vichy is under the Nazi heel, there is no legitimate French authority to be loyal to!"

Boisson directed his eyes upward at the glittering crystal chandelier, lost in thought.

Darlan persisted with his argument. "You must confront reality! If the Germans win in Tunisia, they'll inevitably invade all of French Africa, including your cherished Dakar. For France to retain its African Empire after the war, the Germans must be defeated. You must see that?"

"What you're saying makes sense," replied Boisson, who then pointed a finger at Eisenhower. "But I'll not join the Allies until you force de Gaulle to stop attacking me on the radio station he controls in Brazzaville!"

"General Boisson, I don't understand," replied a puzzled Eisenhower. "What problem is de Gaulle causing you?"

"Brazzaville is the capital of French Equatorial Africa, which has joined de Gaulle's movement," Boisson explained, "and de Gaulle's propaganda broadcasts can be heard in Dakar. De Gaulle vilifies me personally and accuses my government of criminal misdeeds! His lies are causing problems with the natives. He must be ordered to stop these libelous broadcasts! You must stop that . . . that madman if you want me to join forces with you!"

"The British have influence over de Gaulle because they're funding his Free French movement," replied Eisenhower calmly. "I have no power over de Gaulle."

Boisson let Eisenhower's words sink in before replying. "I know the British want their sailors captured during the Battle of Dakar released from my prisons. That won't happen until de Gaulle stops attacking me and my government!"

"General Boisson, I believe you speak English?" Eisenhower asked unexpectedly.

Boisson's face registered surprise at the question. He responded in English. "Yes."

"Will you step away with me so we can have a one-on-one conversation?" Eisenhower wanted to talk soldier to soldier to plead his case.

Boisson assented, and they moved to a corner of the room out of earshot of the others.

Eisenhower spoke slowly, with a heartfelt earnestness. "It's imperative you bring West Africa into the Allied camp. Getting you on our side is incredibly important."

"What about the silencing of de Gaulle?"

"When I explain the circumstances, I think Churchill will do everything in his power to force de Gaulle to stop libeling you. However, I need to be honest. I don't know if Churchill can control de Gaulle."

Boisson grunted. "I appreciate your candor."

"General Boisson, we need the air and naval bases in Dakar to support our campaign against the Germans. Time is of the essence. Use of your territory will greatly facilitate bringing supplies from America to Africa. If you sign an agreement to join the Allies, I promise on my honor as a soldier I'll do everything humanely possible to see the British silence de Gaulle."

Boisson stared into Eisenhower's eyes. He must have appreciated what he saw there because, without another word, he walked back to the conference table and signed an agreement bringing French West Africa into the alliance to defeat the Nazis.

Eisenhower was elated. "General Boisson, when can American planes and ships begin using bases in Dakar?"

"My bases can be used immediately!"

On December 12, Eisenhower received a welcome visitor in his office at the Hotel Saint George: his brother Milton.

After the two men embraced, Milt appraised his brother. "How are you holding up?"

Eisenhower gave a heavy sigh. "I'm going through a rough patch. The rancor over the Darlan deal has been wearing on me."

"That's why I'm here. Roosevelt has been under siege from both the press and Congress over the Darlan agreement. He wants me to change the news narrative. The Darlan deal must be reported as a military necessity that ended the fighting, saving American lives."

"While that's true, Milt, the Darlan deal did a lot more than save lives. The French have become our allies! French troops are fighting beside American and British soldiers in Tunisia. Darlan was instrumental in securing strategic Dakar naval and air bases for our operations. And while he couldn't get the French fleet to come to North Africa, the French navy did the next best thing—scuttling its ships at Toulon when Hitler tried to seize them!"

"Thanks, Ike," Milt said appreciatively. "Knowing those additional facts will help me put the Darlan agreement in the proper light. Is there any potential negative news I should be prepared for when I meet the press?"

"You may be asked about the Jewish problem."

"What problem?" asked Milton with a puzzled expression.

"The head rabbi of Algiers has educated me on the vile discrimination perpetrated against the Jewish population," replied Eisenhower. "Vichy set quotas severely limiting the number of Jews who can be doctors and lawyers, and many Jewish professionals have been forced to give up their practices. Jews have been barred from all public service as well, including teaching. Just like Nazi Germany, Vichy tried to eliminate Jews from the economy by confiscating their businesses and giving them to French settlers."

"Can you get the anti-Semitic laws rescinded?"

"I met with Darlan and told him the laws against the Jews are repugnant and should be repealed. Darlan claimed rescinding the anti-Jewish laws would rile the Arabs and cause riots. I continued to insist these discriminatory laws needed to be lifted, and Darlan has finally agreed to do so."

"Has Darlan kept his word?"

"No, not yet. I have a meeting with Murphy this afternoon, and I'm going to seek his advice on how to make Darlan act."

"Good luck with getting the Jewish issue resolved." Milton stood to leave. "I should go now. I have to set up meetings with the press correspondents."

"Before you go, please tell me—how's Mamie holding up?"

Milt sat back down. "I'll be honest, Ike; she's had a few rough patches. That Ruth Butcher has Mamie drinking too much. When

Mamie fell in a canteen, a rumor spread around town that she was drunk."

"I don't believe that for a second!" exclaimed Eisenhower. "I'm sure it resulted from one of her dizzy spells."

"I have no idea if there's any truth to the rumor. But I did see Mamie tipsy at a party. I asked her if she'd like to live with us again, and she said no, she wanted to stay in the city."

"Milt, can you help Mamie find another apartment in Washington?" Eisenhower asked in a pleading voice.

"Of course, Ike. As soon as I get back to DC, I'll see what I can do."

That afternoon, Murphy visited Eisenhower in his office.

"Bob, I'm infuriated with Darlan for keeping the anti-Jewish laws in place. What can I do to force his hand?"

Murphy learned forward. "You should go slow with ending the restrictions on Jews."

"Why?" Eisenhower asked, perplexed. He had thought Murphy would agree with him.

"The Nazis have been using their propaganda machine to get the Arabs all worked up. They're saying you're Jewish, and that you're going to install a Jewish government that will persecute the Arabs."

Eisenhower couldn't believe his ears. "That's ridiculous!"

"We know the Germans are lying, but the average Arab on the street doesn't."

"You're telling me Darlan is right—the Arabs would riot?"

"That's a real risk. The Nazis are exploiting centuries-old resentments the Arabs have toward the Jews. Rescinding the Vichy laws could be the spark that sets the countryside ablaze!"

Eisenhower sat back heavily in his chair. "Rioting would disrupt our campaign to seize Tunisia. It's a risk I can't afford."

"Then lay off Darlan. Go slow with the Jews is my advice."

Eisenhower sighed. The needs of the military campaign to capture Tunisia had to take precedence over rescinding the unjust laws.

"Okay," he capitulated. "For now, I won't push Darlan. But please make sure we publicize to the Arabs I'm not Jewish!"

An hour later, Butcher came into Eisenhower's office, holding a *Life* magazine. "The article came out great! Nine pages with lots of pictures."

Eisenhower took the magazine from Butcher's outstretched hand. He enjoyed reading it until he saw the caption of the picture of his army family. It identified Kay as his "pretty Irish driver."

Mamie would be furious to learn of Summersby's existence in his inner circle from a national magazine. He had some explaining to do.

CHAPTER 26

As the sun rose over Algiers on December 22, Eisenhower was already at his office. He glanced over at Telek sleeping in the inbox and scratched the Scottie's ears while he thought about his troubles. The fast buildup of German forces in Tunisia had thwarted Allied efforts to quickly capture that French colony.

Eisenhower ruminated on his missteps. His rushing forward reinforcements helter-skelter had resulted in intermingled, confusing commands that hindered rather than helped Anderson's operations. His decision to leave half his trucks in England because of reduced shipping capacity had crippled the supply chain. While there were many reasons for the current stalemate—including the delay in advancing on Tunisia caused by French resistance to the Torch invasion; six hundred miles of harsh terrain between Algiers and Tunis; and a single-track railroad lacking sufficient locomotives and rolling stock—in Eisenhower's mind his rookie mistakes as an army commander were the foremost reason for the failure to take Tunisia.

He looked at his watch—time for his meeting with Beetle. Eisenhower got up quietly and left Telek sleeping peacefully. He found Smith in his office, looking somber. "Something wrong, Beetle?"

"The *Strathallan* was torpedoed."

Hmm . . . The name of that ship sounds familiar. Then it struck him like lightning: *Kay is on the Strathallan!*

Eisenhower became cold all over. *Is Kay gone? Has she drowned an agonizing death in the Mediterranean?*

He felt himself start to shake. A sadness gripped him, pulling him hard into darkness.

"Any word on survivors?" he managed to gasp out.

"Not yet. . . . Ike, are you okay?"

Eisenhower didn't respond. His normally organized, sharply focused mind had gone off the rails. He stood in front of Smith, completely mute.

Beetle stared hard at Eisenhower. "Look, Ike; we'll all miss Kay if she drowned, but you need to snap out of your funk," he said bluntly. "You're the Allied commander. You can't let the death of a single person rattle you."

Eisenhower took a deep breath. Smith was right: he had to be strong. The war was taking millions of victims, and he couldn't allow his feelings of despair to distract him from his duty. He was the commander, and he needed to show strength.

He gave a crisp nod. "Of course. I just needed some time to process that Kay may be gone."

Eisenhower called on his well of discipline to get through the meeting with Smith dealing with mounting logistical challenges.

That night before going to bed, Eisenhower bowed his head in prayer to Almighty God that Kay had survived the U-boat attack.

The next day, Eisenhower left as planned for the Tunisian battlefront. He was meeting Anderson to discuss launching a winter offensive. He traveled by car because incessant winter rains made air travel impossible.

The twenty-hour trip provided an unexpected benefit: it allowed Eisenhower time to mourn Kay in solitude, without needing to show a face of resilience and strength.

Eisenhower arrived at Anderson's headquarters on December 24, exhausted from the grueling trip. When he got out of the car, his feet sank into mud two feet deep. His rubber boots, overalls, heavy jacket, rain slicker, and knit hat protected him from the worst of the weather.

General Kenneth Anderson, a short, thickly built man, greeted Eisenhower in the farmhouse that served as his headquarters. They left together to survey the countryside in Anderson's staff car.

As they drove behind a slow-moving tank, Eisenhower observed four soldiers trying to pull a motorcycle out of the thick mud. The feat proved impossible despite their all-out efforts.

When they were back in Anderson's headquarters, a tired and discouraged Eisenhower asked, "Ken, can I get a cup of coffee?"

"Coffee?" asked Anderson with a marked Scottish brogue. "Sorry, old chap, we only have tea here."

Eisenhower groaned. He didn't like tea, but at least it had caffeine. "Okay, Ken, I'll have tea."

Once they were seated in the kitchen, each with a boiling cup of tea, Anderson said, "My meteorologist advises these Tunisian rains will last till spring. I don't see how we can conduct a winter offensive with the roads being virtually impassable because of the mud."

Grim-faced, Eisenhower nodded in agreement. "If I were in Algiers speaking with you by phone, I'd argue the point. But after what I saw today, I know you're right. There'll be no winter offensive."

Eisenhower was in the mess tent admiring an evergreen tree the troops had decorated for Christmas with a wild assortment of ornaments, including painted hand grenades, when he received a message. Smith had called, and it was urgent that Eisenhower call him.

He frowned. *So much is going wrong these days. . . . What's happened now?*

Eisenhower walked through the rain and mud back to Anderson's headquarters and got Smith on the phone. "What's up, Beetle?" he asked, bracing himself.

"Kay is safe. She was picked up by a British destroyer and is in Oran."

Relief swept over him. *Kay is alive!* His heart began to pound.

"Beetle, that news is the best Christmas present I've had in a long time! Send the Flying Fortress to Oran to pick her up and bring her to Algiers."

"Will do. I've one other piece of news. The little admiral has been assassinated."

"What? Darlan's dead?" Eisenhower asked, shocked. "What happened?"

"A twenty-year-old student who hates the Vichy government and wants to restore the French monarchy shot Darlan at point-blank range in the Hotel Palais d'Été."

While Eisenhower felt a rush of sympathy for Darlan's family—he had met his wife and polio-stricken son—it was a relief to have the controversial collaborator out of the picture.

"Beetle, I'm returning immediately to Algiers."

After an exhausting drive, Eisenhower reached Algiers Christmas night. Early the next morning, he was back at work in his office in the Hotel Saint George. There was a lot to get done, but the first thing he wanted to do, the first person he wanted to see, was Summersby.

When she entered his office wearing a rumpled skirt, a GI shirt, and bright red lipstick, the general flashed a huge grin and leapt to his feet. "Kay, I'm so happy to see you! What a nightmare to think you died in that U-boat attack."

The hug he gave her was crushing, and Summersby returned it with the same fierceness.

"Where did you get that shirt?" asked Eisenhower when he let go and took a step back.

"From Dick! He's stationed in Oran, and we were able to spend some time together! He scrounged up some clothes for me since my suitcase went down with the ship. I can't wait till his divorce comes through and we can be married."

Dick Arnold was a lucky man, thought Eisenhower. He pulled out a pack of cigarettes and offered Summersby one, which she readily accepted. He lit her cigarette, then his own.

"Do you feel comfortable talking about the U-boat attack?"

"Sure. It was the middle of the night right before we were to land at Oran. I was awakened by a terrific explosion. There were four of us in the cabin, and everyone stayed calm, although we all moved quickly. I put on a pair of shoes, then grabbed a coat and flashlight. The four of us made our way together to the lifeboat station. The ship was listing to the right when we reached the deck.

"The crew put the women in the first lifeboat. We were lowered into the water as destroyers were dropping depth charges, trying to sink the U-boat. Our little lifeboat rocked and rolled so much from the waves, I thought we'd capsize!

"The boat filled with freezing water. The crew furiously bailed out the water to keep us from sinking. My legs and feet literally turned blue from the cold. It was a miserable night before we were picked up the next morning."

"Were you scared?"

"Only when I thought the turbulence from the depth charges would overturn the lifeboat." Summersby took a drag on her cigarette and slowly exhaled the smoke. "Our spirits lifted when the sun came up and we started warming up. Margaret Bourke-White, the *Life* photographer, was in the lifeboat with us, and she started making jokes and taking pictures."

"Do you need some time off to recover?"

"Absolutely not! I'm ready to get to work."

Eisenhower smiled. Summersby was being her usual positive, upbeat self. Despite her near miss with death, her spirits were high.

"Good! Well then, you can drive me home tonight to the Villa Dar el-Ouard."

"What does that mean in English?"

"'Villa of the Family.' I find the name fitting. My army family means a lot to me," he said softly.

That night, when they got to the villa, Summersby stayed for dinner. Afterward, she was Eisenhower's partner for that evening's bridge game.

Over the next few days, Eisenhower worked hard to see that Giraud replaced the slain Darlan. He was concerned that Giraud lacked enough political acumen to succeed, but at least this man was untainted by any Vichy association. The action he took pleased Roosevelt and Churchill.

Wearing a bemused look on his face, Smith entered Eisenhower's office. "Roosevelt and Churchill are coming to Morocco for a conference."

"Are you pulling my leg, Beetle? They can't seriously be thinking of having a meeting in a war zone."

Smith handed Eisenhower the cable. "Here, read it for yourself." He put on his glasses.

President Roosevelt and Prime Minister Churchill have chosen Morocco as a location for a strategic conference with the Combined Chiefs in January 1943. Find a suitable location that can be safeguarded from enemy attack.

"Where do you think our government kingpins can have their confab without being murdered by the Nazis?" asked Eisenhower.

"Casablanca probably would be safest."

"Maybe, but the Germans periodically bomb Casablanca, and the Nazis must have spies there." Eisenhower walked to his large window overlooking Algiers. "Pay a visit to Patton in Casablanca and find a secure spot for the conference. I don't want Roosevelt's and Churchill's blood on my hands."

That night during a bridge game at Villa Dar el-Ouard, Algiers's air raid sirens went off. German night bombers were attacking the harbor. Everyone in the villa grabbed a helmet and went out on the terrace to watch the attack.

Antiaircraft fire lit up the night sky. Explosions from the bombs vibrated the ground, sending shock waves up the hillside that could be felt by those on the terrace. An oil tank on the harbor front exploded into a fiery ball of flame. The cacophony was deafening.

When shrapnel from the antiaircraft fire began falling on the terrace, Eisenhower ordered everyone inside. That's when he noticed Telek hiding under a sofa and quietly whimpering.

Poor dog. Maybe I shouldn't have brought him to a war zone.

Eisenhower picked Telek up and cuddled him to his chest. As he petted the dog's head, he said, "Don't be frightened, little fellow. Everything's going to be okay."

CHAPTER 27

Most days Eisenhower worked on the drive to his office. As it was the first day of 1943, he gave himself a few minutes to take in the allure of Algiers.

The city's white buildings rose like waves from the seashore up hills steeper than those in San Francisco. The history of many civilizations was jumbled together, with mosques, cathedrals, and synagogues blending into an eclectic mixture of Roman, Moorish, Arab, Ottoman, and French architecture. Algiers simply felt . . . exotic, and it showed in the contrast of well-dressed French colonials next to robed Arabs leading camels loaded with goods for the markets.

After Summersby dropped him off in the Hotel Saint George portico, Eisenhower took a moment to admire the purple bougainvillea and pink oleander vines that climbed the hotel walls. Before entering the bustling interior of AFHQ, he inhaled the refreshing smell of blooming flowers from the hotel's botanical garden.

The Saint George's interior contrasted sharply with its pleasant exterior. Inside, the hotel looked like a government office building. The lounge had been converted into a teletype center, with operators working at makeshift desks among the ottomans and brass tables. A long corridor led to Eisenhower's suite of three offices. Smith and Butcher shared the suite, together with the stenographers who took Eisenhower's frequent dictations.

Eisenhower's first visitor of the new year was Harold Macmillan, a tall Englishman with a dark mustache. His family-owned Macmillan Publishing was one of the world's largest publishing houses.

After the introductions were made and both men were comfortably seated, Eisenhower asked, "What's the purpose of your visit to Algiers?"

Macmillan responded in the cultured tone of a well-read Englishman, "I thought the Prime Minister advised you?"

"I got a cable from Churchill asking me to receive you, but it gave no inkling of why you're in Algiers."

"I'm a Cabinet-level minister to your headquarters."

Eisenhower looked at him thoughtfully. "What kind of minister?"

"I'm a politician. My job is to advise you on the British political perspective as matters come up."

Eisenhower sat back in his chair. "Ah, so you're here because of the Darlan affair?"

"I'm afraid so. The Darlan agreement caused quite a dustup in London. The PM wants to avoid any more political bombshells."

"So do I." Eisenhower pulled out a pack of Lucky Strikes and offered a cigarette to Macmillan, who waved it off as he pulled a cigar out of his pocket. There was silence as both men lit up.

"Harold, I can't understand why I'm so viciously attacked in the press. Christ on a Mountain! I'm no Fascist; I'm idealistic as hell!"

"The past is water under the bridge. You're a public figure now. You need to develop a tough skin, and not let the press attacks bother you."

"That's easy for you to say. The continuing press assaults on my ethics and morality sting like a snakebite."

Macmillan suddenly changed the subject. "You know, you can trust me because I'm a Hoosier."

Eisenhower arched an eyebrow in surprise. "You don't sound like you're from Indiana."

"My mother was born there."

"Then you're as American as Churchill!"

Both men enjoyed a laugh before Macmillan said, "I need to speak to you about de Gaulle."

"What about him?"

"The PM desires Giraud and de Gaulle join forces politically and militarily. De Gaulle's London committee should be merged with Giraud's North African administration. The Free French forces fighting with Montgomery should be combined with Giraud's North African Army."

Eisenhower's mood darkened. "Please don't drag me back into French politics!"

"I'm afraid I have to. We need you to persuade Giraud to enter into a power-sharing agreement with de Gaulle."

"Why do I have to be involved? Why can't *you* meet with Giraud?"

"I'll meet with Giraud and request his cooperation," Macmillan assured Eisenhower. "But your request will carry a lot more clout with him because America's rearming his army."

Eisenhower couldn't refuse a request from the British government. "Okay, I'll talk to Giraud."

After Macmillan left, Smith came into the office, back from his trip to Casablanca.

"Do you have time to discuss plans for the Casablanca conference, Ike?"

"What do you and Georgie have in mind?"

"He and I agree the best location for the conference is Anfa, a suburb four miles south of Casablanca. There's a modern hotel surrounded by upscale villas close to the Atlantic. We'll take over the hotel and the villas. Security will be tight—a three-deep barrier of barbwire fences guarded by Georgie's soldiers. Antiaircraft batteries will defend against a possible German bombing raid."

"Who's living in the surrounding villas?"

"Mostly wealthy French businessmen. They can find hotel rooms in Casablanca until the conference is over."

"Beetle, that sounds like as good a location and security arrangement as we can come up with. I approve the plan."

That afternoon, Eisenhower paid a call on Giraud at his large office in the Palais d'Été. Once again he suffered through being kissed on each cheek. The two men then sat around a marble-topped table in two leather oval-back armchairs.

"General Giraud, it's important to the war effort that French exile leaders form a unification committee."

"You want Giraud to work with de Gaulle?" Giraud asked haughtily.

"Yes, you and de Gaulle need to meet and work out an arrangement."

Giraud frowned. "De Gaulle is a self-promoter; he's become an ambitious politician. So he surely will agree. But Giraud has no interest in politics."

Eisenhower narrowed his eyes and held Giraud's gaze without blinking. "America is spending millions of dollars to rearm your army with the expectation there will a unified French army. You *must* work out an arrangement with de Gaulle."

Giraud's posture stiffened. "Are you threatening to cut off military aid?"

Eisenhower's words conveyed one thing, but his steely eyes with their direct gaze conveyed something else entirely. "I can't predict what Washington will do if you fail to cooperate."

Giraud pressed his lips together and paused a beat. "De Gaulle is only a one-star general while Giraud is a five-star general. He must be subordinate to Giraud."

"Does that mean you'll meet with de Gaulle?"

"If de Gaulle comes to Algiers, Giraud will meet with him."

CHAPTER 28

On January 15, 1943, Eisenhower boarded his B-17 to fly to Casablanca, accompanied by his diplomats, Murphy and Macmillan. A few hours into the flight, there was a deafening boom that sounded like exploding dynamite. Eisenhower looked out a window; one of the engines was blown apart! The plane rocked and pitched for two minutes before the pilot controlled the huge machine—it still had three working engines—and the flight became steady again.

Eisenhower knew the bomber could fly just fine with three engines, and soon dozed off.

A loud noise, like a crack of thunder, awakened the general. Eisenhower looked out a window—an engine was on fire!

The plane began flying erratically like an out-of-control roller coaster, inducing nausea in its passengers. Within ten minutes, the flight smoothed out, but the plane was gradually losing altitude.

The copilot came back and shouted, "Everybody needs to put on a parachute and stand near an open exit! We're unlikely to make it to Casablanca!" The copilot swiftly opened the exit doors and returned to the cockpit.

Eisenhower wriggled into his parachute. He gripped the fuselage and stared out at the craggy, snowcapped Atlas Mountains.

He didn't relish the opportunity to jump into the rugged landscape. Would his bad knee buckle when he hit the ground? Eisenhower reached in his pocket and rubbed his lucky coins.

Murphy was standing at the opposite door. "Ike, I've been saying my Hail Marys. If your religion has any special invocation to God, I suggest you use it."

"Good idea, Bob."

Eisenhower thought of his upbringing in the River Brethren Church, an offshoot of the Mennonites. While it was a pacifist religion, he felt certain God was on the side of the Allies. He lowered his head and closed his eyes. *Please, God, allow me to survive this flight so I can help the Allies rid the world of evil dictators.*

Eisenhower didn't fear dying; he was a soldier, and facing deadly risks was part of the job description. *But how will my death affect my wife and son whom I love with all my heart?*

Mamie was close to her parents and remaining sister; they would assuredly give her love and support as would Johnny.

He trusted Johnny was maturing into a self-sufficient man at West Point. He should be mentally tough enough to handle the death of his father.

His thoughts moved to Kay. He couldn't deny that she aroused in him immoral feelings of desire for a woman other than his wife. Thank God he hadn't broken his marital vows.

For the next hour, the stricken flight continued to jangle the nerves of all on board, but no command to jump came. Finally, the B-17 cleared the mountains and approached Casablanca.

The copilot came back and shouted, "Take your seats. Make sure your shoulders are in the restraining harnesses. We're coming in hot and fast!"

As the bomber approached the runway, it pitched up and down erratically. Panic overtook Murphy, who yelled, "We're going to crash!"

A minute later, the B-17 violently hit the ground, the force so hard it crushed the plane's landing gear. The plane slid on its belly, screeching sideways down the runway.

When the machine miraculously stopped in one piece, Eisenhower inwardly thanked God for answering everyone's prayers.

The passengers departed the plane on shaky legs. As soon as they exited, Eisenhower and his diplomats were put in the back seat of an army staff car, its windows smeared with mud. As with all VIPs attending the conference, their presence in Casablanca was a secret.

After passing through a series of security checkpoints Patton had set up, they arrived at the Anfa Hotel, a white four-story building shaped like a cruise ship. Eisenhower ate a quick meal before being escorted to a door with a printed placard: BUSINESS: COMBINED CHIEFS OF STAFF CONFERENCE.

He entered a conference room filled with sunlight and vases with fresh-cut flowers. Around a rectangular table sat the top brass of England and America. Marshall and Brooke cochaired the meeting.

Marshall asked, "General Eisenhower, would you provide the chiefs an update on the battle for Tunisia?"

After summarizing the campaign and the current stalemate, Eisenhower addressed combat strength. "The opposing forces in Tunisia are approximately equal in number. But we're building up our forces faster than the Germans and Italians. I expect we'll have a significant manpower advantage when we launch the spring offensive."

Eisenhower moved to stand by a wall map of North Africa. Pointing to the location in Libya where Montgomery's army was facing Rommel's Afrika Korps, he said, "The plan is to catch Rommel in a vise between Monty's men coming from the east and Torch forces coming from the west." Eisenhower used his hand to trace the Tunisian battlefront. "We now hold a line in Tunisia running two hundred miles from the north on the Mediterranean coast to the south touching the Sahara Desert. In March when the weather improves in Northern Tunisia, General Anderson will resume his offensive to capture Tunis."

Eisenhower paused. "I don't want to wait till March to strike a blow against the Germans. In Central Tunisia, it's possible to stage a winter assault. In two weeks, the US Second Corps will attack the city of Sfax on the Tunisian coast. Sfax is about midway between German general von Arnim's army facing Anderson and Rommel's army in Libya. The goal is twofold: cut off Rommel's supplies coming from Tunis and weaken the forces in front of Anderson by forcing von Arnim to react to the Sfax attack."

After Eisenhower outlined the details of his planned offensive, he asked for questions.

Brooke pounced, his sharp eyes boring into Eisenhower. "Do you see the dangers in your plan?"

"The biggest risk is we'll be too far from Anderson for him to provide support for the Second Corps if von Arnim attacks."

"Don't you think that's an extraordinary risk, exposing untried American troops to crack, battle-tested German soldiers without a force close by to provide support if things go poorly?" asked Brooke. "You're violating the cardinal rule of concentration of force!"

Eisenhower was angered by Brooke's lack of confidence in American soldiers. "While it's true the Second Corps hasn't been tested in battle, I have great confidence in the fighting abilities of US soldiers! I know I'm splitting my forces, but the risk is worth it to keep pressure on the Germans!"

Brooke persisted with his interrogation. "Have you considered your men, not Rommel's, could be the ones caught in a vise?"

"I have. Rommel is a long way from Sfax. It's highly unlikely we'd be attacked by both von Arnim and Rommel."

Brooke held up a piece of paper. "In your travels, you may not have seen the latest Ultra intercept. Rommel's Twenty-First Panzer Division has started moving into Tunisia."

The information blindsided Eisenhower. "I hadn't seen that intelligence."

"Does Rommel's movement change your thinking?"

Eisenhower's shoulders sagged. "It does."

Brooke spent the next half hour asking questions in a fashion suggesting Eisenhower had no strategic vision and had concocted a dangerously inept battle plan.

When Eisenhower left the conference room, he felt limp. Brooke had excoriated him.

He walked out of the hotel into bright sunlight and gently swaying palm trees. In the far distance, sunlight reflected off the white buildings of Casablanca. He looked east to the majestic Atlas Mountains and thanked God he hadn't had to use his parachute.

Eisenhower wasn't outside for more than a minute before a Secret Service agent approached. "General Eisenhower, the President wishes to see you."

Eisenhower nodded and followed the agent to the nearby Villa Dar es Saada, the House of Happiness. As he walked, Eisenhower looked out at the Atlantic, its large waves crashing against the shoreline. He told himself to buck up. He didn't want the President to see him looking downcast after the battering he had taken in the Combined Chiefs of Staff meeting.

Roosevelt's villa was art deco in design with porthole windows. Eisenhower was escorted to the living room, where the President sat in an armless wheelchair beneath a twenty-eight-foot-high ceiling.

FDR was in a jovial mood. "Ike, it's good to see you!" He pointed to a zebra-skin couch. "Come sit down."

"Does it feel good to be out of Washington, Mr. President?" Eisenhower said in a relaxed tone as he dropped onto the couch.

"It does! I feel like a schoolboy on holiday. I hadn't flown on an airplane in ten years. I made history—I'm the first President to have flown while in office!"

"What route did you take to get to Casablanca?"

Roosevelt smiled mischievously. "The trip had to be kept secret. I left Washington by train heading north, like I was going to my home in Hyde Park. In Baltimore the train turned south to Miami, where I took a Pan Am Clipper seaplane first to Trinidad and Tobago, and then to Brazil. From Brazil I flew across the Atlantic to Gambia, and then to Casablanca."

"How many days were you traveling?"

"Five days. It's been quite an adventure!"

Eisenhower admired Roosevelt's stamina and enthusiasm. For a sixty-year-old man afflicted with polio, such a trip must have been strenuous and tiring. Yet the President was full of energy.

Roosevelt continued. "I had the pilot fly over the Port of Dakar, and I saw the French battleship *Richelieu* with its fifteen-inch guns. It's a wonderful feeling knowing we now control such a powerful ship. It was validation I made the right decision to authorize Torch."

Eisenhower debated whether to bring up a subject that still weighed heavily on his mind. He decided to take the plunge. "Sir, I know the Darlan agreement was controversial, but without it, we would not have secured Dakar."

"I understood Darlan's value, and you did yeoman's work getting Boisson to join the Allies. But in the future, you need to leave the political decisions to me and Churchill."

Eisenhower wanted to protest there hadn't been time for a trans-atlantic essay contest, but the stern expression on the President's face signaled it was best he keep the thought to himself.

"What do you think of Giraud?" asked Roosevelt.

"He's an old soldier who hates the Germans and wants to fight. Giraud despises politics and lacks political sense," Eisenhower said bluntly. "He wants to focus all his attention on the army."

"Giraud's lack of interest in politics is concerning. But for better or worse, he's our man in North Africa. Churchill and I are going to force a shotgun wedding between our Frenchmen. Giraud will be the groom and de Gaulle the bride." The President paused while an aide served coffee. Once the aide left, he continued. "I don't trust de Gaulle. It's clear to me he's angling to seize power after we liberate France. I'm afraid de Gaulle wants a one-man government. I'm going to ensure the French people have the right of self-determination—we aren't going to foist de Gaulle on them. It's important to me de Gaulle ends up being subordinate to Giraud."

"Isn't it an internal French matter how they share power?"

"It certainly is not!" snapped Roosevelt. "We've conquered North Africa—we can dictate which Frenchmen are empowered here."

"I don't view us as conquerors," replied Eisenhower. "The French are now our allies. We need their logistical support for the Tunisian campaign. We also need them to administer Morocco and Algeria."

"Ike, remember we're rearming the French army. You need to en-sure Giraud, not de Gaulle, controls that army. Consider that an order from your commander in chief."

"Understood, sir."

Roosevelt sipped his coffee. "The British have advocated for an-other Mediterranean operation after you finish your work in Tunisia. Because we're building up large armies in Africa, I've agreed to Sicily being the next target."

"That's a logical step," Eisenhower said thoughtfully. "Taking Sicily could knock Italy out of the war."

"That's what Churchill thinks."

"What about France? Is Roundup dead?" asked Eisenhower.

"Absolutely not! The quickest way to win this war is to in-vade France. I'm a firm believer in that strategy. We're not leaving

Casablanca without a firm commitment from Churchill for a cross-channel attack."

The President changed direction. "Why weren't you able to capture Tunisia before the Germans built up their forces?"

Eisenhower explained the problems, including the ones caused by his decisions. He concluded with, "Mr. President, I take responsibility for the failure to achieve the mission's goal in 1942."

FDR nodded. "I like a man who is candid with me and calls it as it is."

Their meeting was interrupted by the arrival of Churchill. He went to Eisenhower and vigorously shook his hand. "Congratulations on pulling off Torch! It gives me intense pleasure to be having this conference in territory we liberated!"

The Prime Minister turned toward Roosevelt. "Franklin, it's cocktail hour, and I'm thirsty."

"Winston, you're always thirsty." Roosevelt smiled as he wheeled himself to a small bar. He started making highballs for the three of them. As he worked, the President asked, "Ike, when are you going to finish the job in Tunisia?"

While Eisenhower didn't like to guess, he needed to answer the question. "I think we'll have the Germans and Italians in the bag by the middle of May."

Handing Eisenhower his drink, the President said in his usual jocular tone, "I'm going to hold you to that deadline."

As he tasted the cocktail, Eisenhower thought perhaps the President wasn't joking. The Darlan affair had been a huge political headache for Roosevelt, and the current military stalemate had to be annoying. FDR would surely hear about his dismal performance at the Combined Chiefs meeting. He could be out of a job if he didn't capture Tunisia by his guesstimated date!

That night, Eisenhower stayed in Patton's villa inside the armed compound. He had managed to hold it together when he met with the President and later Churchill. By the time he got to his friend's villa at 7:30 p.m., he was drained of energy. His eyes lacked their normal luster, and his face was pallid.

"Ike, you look like you've been run over by a Mack truck!" exclaimed Patton.

"It's been a hell of a day." Eisenhower sighed. "The Fortress lost two engines, and I was lucky to get to Casablanca in one piece. Then Brooke skewered me at the chiefs conference. He made me look like a fool. It was humiliating."

"That sanctimonious bastard! I'd like to rip him a new asshole!" Patton said before pouring them each a whisky. He handed Eisenhower a glass. "You need to take the edge off."

"Thanks, Georgie. My neck's on the line too. If I don't deliver Tunisia by May, I think Roosevelt will replace me."

CHAPTER 29

The next morning, Eisenhower returned to Algiers on a replacement B-17 while his diplomats stayed behind to try to consummate the marriage of French generals.

Summersby was waiting for him at the Maison Blanche airfield. Her face registered shock at his drawn face and drooping posture.

"Ike, are you sick?" she asked with concern.

"I'm not physically ill, just worn down."

"I suggest you take the day off," she said, her voice regaining its usual lightness. "You need to recharge your batteries."

"You know I never take a day off," replied Eisenhower with a bit of a scowl, although inwardly he was pleased Summersby was worried about his welfare.

"You need to take at least *half* a day off, then," Summersby said with firmness. "The Allied cause will not be helped if you end up in the hospital suffering from exhaustion."

The general contemplated her suggestion. *A few hours' rest would do me good.*

"Kay, please drive me to the villa; I'm taking the morning off."

A week after his return from Casablanca, Eisenhower had regained his energy, self-confidence, and optimism for the future. He welcomed

Macmillan to his Hotel Saint George office to get the inside scoop on the French.

"Harold, was the marriage of French generals consummated?"

"I'm sorry, Ike; the answer is no."

Eisenhower was perplexed. "But . . . I saw a picture in the paper of Giraud and de Gaulle shaking hands! I thought it symbolized an agreement had been reached."

"That picture was a brilliant piece of propaganda orchestrated by Roosevelt. The conference was coming to an end, and Roosevelt asked de Gaulle to shake hands with Giraud in front of the photographers. Given how difficult de Gaulle had been, I was surprised he agreed."

Eisenhower frowned, profoundly disappointed. "What happened?"

"De Gaulle initially refused to come to Casablanca. Churchill was furious—in all my dealings with him, I've never seen him so angry! And he had a right to be. He's spent millions of pounds building up de Gaulle. The man has become a French hero, the leader of Free French forces, and with his BBC broadcasts into France, an inspiration to the Resistance. To use an analogy, de Gaulle was like a racehorse Churchill bred and trained, and when race time came, he refused to run."

"How did Churchill persuade de Gaulle to come to Casablanca?"

"He threatened to cut off his funding. Churchill and de Gaulle operate like an old married couple," Macmillan assessed. "Sometimes they have volcanic fights where threats are made. Afterward they realize they need each other, and the relationship continues.

"Once de Gaulle arrived in Casablanca, he was arrogantly aloof. Murphy and I prepared draft after draft of a merger arrangement. Showing his lack of interest in politics, Giraud accepted every suggested alliance without protest, whereas de Gaulle rejected each proposal with disdain."

"Where's Murphy?" asked Eisenhower.

"He's still with Roosevelt, undoubtedly discussing ways to limit de Gaulle's influence."

"Going forward, will you and Murphy handle French politics so I can focus on the battle for Tunisia? It needs my full attention."

Macmillan hedged. "Churchill still wants the French to form a unified front, and I'm to facilitate that process. There likely will be times I'll need your support."

Eisenhower rolled his eyes. He had heard enough about the quarrelsome French and changed subjects. "Were you involved in the President's statement that the Axis powers must unconditionally surrender?"

"No, that was Roosevelt's brainchild. I think it's a response to the Darlan agreement. No more deals with Fascists. The Germans, Italians, and Japanese must abjectly surrender."

The next day, Generals Marshall and Somervell arrived in Algiers along with Admiral King. As Eisenhower entered the Paris conference room to meet his visitors, he wondered if his stock had gone down in their eyes, given his less-than-stellar performance in Casablanca.

Marshall began the meeting. "Eisenhower, as you know, General Harold Alexander commands the British Middle East forces, including Montgomery's army. When Montgomery gets to the Tunisian border, Alexander will come under your command."

The news startled Eisenhower. Alexander had substantial command experience and held a higher rank in the English army than he did in the American army. *What the hell is going on?*

Marshall continued. "Alexander will become your deputy commander in charge of ground operations. Alexander's top airman, Arthur Tedder, will become commander of Mediterranean Air Forces, reporting to you. Admiral Cunningham will remain in charge of your naval force."

"Sir, I'm surprised Brooke would allow Alexander to serve under me, especially given the grilling he gave me in Casablanca."

Marshall's jaw muscles tightened. "Brooke did handle you roughly. If it's any consolation, Brooke is just as aggressive and cutting in his remarks toward me. That's his style."

"Ike, Brooke is a tough bird," King commented. "But in one area, he was complimentary of you. He thinks you've done a remarkable job in getting American and British officers to work together with little friction at AFHQ."

Eisenhower grunted. At least Brooke didn't think he was a total waste of a human being.

During a bathroom break, Eisenhower contemplated the changes in the command structure. He didn't like the chiefs picking his subordinates without any input from him, and he now had three experienced and well-regarded British officers as direct reports. Had Brooke maneuvered the chiefs to reduce his power by giving him only British subordinate commanders? Had he been kicked upstairs to a chairman-of-the-board position while the Brits took control of day-to-day field operations?

If that was Brooke's stratagem, Eisenhower thought angrily, he wouldn't go along with it. He was determined to exercise his authority as the top Allied commander.

When the meeting resumed, Marshall said, "After North Africa is secured, the next target is Sicily, operation Husky. The Allies will invade with two armies—one British, one American. Eisenhower, do you have a recommendation for who should command the American army?"

Without hesitation Eisenhower responded, "I recommend General Patton. He's smart, aggressive, and a good leader. The army is wasting Patton's talents keeping him in Morocco."

"I've been considering Patton," replied Marshall. He paused, lost in thought. "Okay, Patton's the man for Sicily."

At the end of the day, Summersby drove Eisenhower and Marshall to Villa Dar el-Ouard. As they were driving up the compound's palm-tree-lined driveway, Eisenhower said, "Sir, I'm giving you my bedroom for your stay in Algiers."

"That's not necessary. I don't want to inconvenience you."

"You're my guest. I insist."

Marshall nodded his acceptance.

When they entered the villa, Telek came running, barking and wagging his tail. Eisenhower leaned down and affectionately scratched the Scottie's chin. As Eisenhower led Marshall up the stairs to the second floor, Telek scampered after them.

When they got to the bedroom, Eisenhower said, "Sir, this is a very comfortable bed."

Just then a black ball of fur leapt onto the bed. Telek lifted his leg and relieved himself on the luxurious-looking maroon silk cover. The little dog then hopped on the pillow and repeated his transgression.

Eisenhower fumed as Marshall laughed.

"After spending ten days locked in meetings with Brooke, I needed some comic relief, and that dog of yours has provided it!"

The next day before the meetings began with his War Department visitors, Marshall approached Eisenhower. "You need to disengage yourself from French politics."

"I'd like nothing better, sir. But it may not be easy. Macmillan thinks Churchill wants me involved in forging a Giraud–de Gaulle détente."

"If Roosevelt or Churchill orders your involvement, you have no choice. Otherwise, spend all your time focused on Tunisia."

"Yes, sir."

"One more point. I think you could use a roving deputy—someone who can travel to forward commands, ask questions, dig around, and report back information essential for controlling the battlefront."

"I'd welcome that. Do you have someone in mind?"

Marshall reached into his jacket pocket and pulled out a list of names. "How's Major General Omar Bradley?"

"Go no farther. Brad and I were classmates at the Point. I trust his judgment. He'd make an excellent roving deputy."

"That was easy. I'll issue an order for Bradley to come to Africa."

In the afternoon, Eisenhower met with Somervell to discuss his supply needs.

"For the spring offensive, I need more trucks, tank transporters, locomotives, and railcars. I desperately need transportation to break supply bottlenecks."

"How many trucks do you need?" asked Somervell.

"At least five thousand."

They took a short break. When they reconvened, Somervell handed Eisenhower a list. "How does this look?"

Eisenhower scanned the document. There were fifty-four hundred trucks, seventy-two tank transporters, one hundred locomotives, and two hundred railcars.

"Bill, this would be a gift from heaven!"

"I can have a convoy ready to sail in three weeks, but it can't leave America without navy escorts. You need to persuade Ernie King to provide us some of his precious ships to make this happen."

King had already left Algiers, so Eisenhower sent him a cable noting the supply crisis and requesting the escort vessels. Then he waited.

When King cabled, Tell Somervell the escorts will be provided, Eisenhower pumped his fist in celebration. The navy had come through in the pinch!

CHAPTER 30

When Eisenhower came downstairs to the dining room the day after the Pentagon brass left Algiers, he found Butcher chatting with Summersby.

"Ike, General Marshall instructed me to take care of you," said Butcher.

"What are you talking about?"

"He gave me orders to keep you out of the office as much as possible, and in general have you do things that relax your mind and body—for example, he suggested you go horseback riding. He's concerned you're going to burn out from overwork."

"Butch, you're welcome to try. But I'm an old warhorse. I don't know how to slow down."

Summersby jumped in. "General Marshall is right! You need to pace yourself. If Butch can find some horses and a place to ride, I'd be happy to join you."

Suddenly the idea sounded pleasant. Eisenhower turned to Butcher. "Find some horses and a place for me and Kay to ride."

On the drive to the Hotel Saint George, Eisenhower pondered what to do with the French army in Tunisia. The Germans had repeatedly attacked the French, viewing them as a weak link in the Allied line. The French had been pushed back and suffered heavy casualties. The problem wasn't the fighting qualities of the French soldiers, but their lack of modern weapons, particularly tanks. The German tanks were so superior to the inferior armor of Giraud's troops, it wasn't a fair fight.

By the time Eisenhower reached his desk, he had determined to withdraw the French troops from the front line and hold them in reserve until they could be rearmed with American tanks. Withdrawing the French meant the Americans and the British would be stretched thin along the battlefront.

Eisenhower was knee-deep in memos when Smith entered his office.

"Churchill is paying us a visit."

"I can't be diverted from the fight for Tunisia. Why in the hell is he coming?" Eisenhower asked irritably.

"Murphy told me it's about French politics."

"Tell him not to come here. After the Darlan assassination, it's too dangerous for him to be in Algiers!"

"I'll try. But Churchill is fearless and stubborn. Telling him it's too dangerous in Algiers is like waving a red flag at a bull!"

Late in the afternoon, Smith gave Eisenhower the bad news. "Churchill insists on coming. He'll be here tomorrow."

"No surprise. Churchill charts his own course. See if Cunningham can host him."

The next day, February 5, Summersby drove Eisenhower to meet Churchill's plane. She looked in the rearview mirror at the general's tightly drawn face. "Is something wrong, Ike?"

"The PM is going to drag me back into the cesspool of French politics!" Eisenhower snapped. "I'm a soldier, not a fucking diplomat!"

Summersby chose to remain quiet the rest of the drive.

At the airfield, after disembarking from the plane and exchanging greetings with Eisenhower, the Prime Minister turned to Summersby.

"Kay, I thought I'd find you in Algiers. How do you like driving on the wrong side of the road?"

She laughed. "I've adapted, sir."

On the ride into Algiers, Churchill said, "I know I'm a distraction, and you don't want me here. But I couldn't leave Africa without persuading Giraud to invite de Gaulle to Algiers so they can iron out their differences. Could you host a luncheon for Giraud tomorrow at your headquarters?"

"Of course."

"Please support me in emphasizing to him how important it is to the war effort that he and de Gaulle come to an accommodation that unifies the French factions."

"I'll meet with Giraud after the luncheon to reinforce the points you make," replied Eisenhower.

"Thanks, Ike. We make a good team!"

That night, Eisenhower joined Churchill for dinner at Cunningham's villa. After a dinner of chicken fricassee cooked by Cunningham's French chef, Churchill asked, "Ike, have you been to Marrakesh?"

"No, I haven't."

"You must go before you leave Africa. The sunsets over the Atlas Mountains are some of the most beautiful you'll ever see."

"I'll put it on my to-do list," Eisenhower promised.

Churchill looked at the admiral. "ABC, have you been to Marrakesh?"

"Afraid not. There's no navy business there."

"I took the President to Marrakesh after the Casablanca conference," Churchill said. "We stayed at the Villa Taylor. It has a tower with magnificent views of the Atlas Mountains. Before sunset, two Secret Service agents formed a sling seat with their arms and carried Roosevelt up to the roof. FDR and I enjoyed highballs as the fading sunlight shone brilliant shades of purple on the snowcapped peaks."

"Sounds spectacular," said Eisenhower.

"I was so moved by the beauty that the next day, I painted my first picture of the war on that rooftop. I'm going to give that painting to Franklin as a gift. Would you like to see it? I can have an aide bring it down from my bedroom."

Eisenhower and Cunningham both asked to see the painting.

A few minutes later, an aide propped up Churchill's painting on an easel in the dining room. Eisenhower and Cunningham got up and closely examined the painting.

Purple snowcapped mountains under a wavy blue sky formed the background. In the foreground was the walled city of Marrakesh, with cypress and palm trees dotting the surrounding hillsides. The colors were bright and vibrant.

Eisenhower was impressed. "Sir, this is a striking painting."

Cunningham added, "You could make a living as a painter, sir!"

Churchill smiled. "I'm a man of many talents."

The energetic Prime Minister proceeded to keep Eisenhower and Cunningham up till 2:00 a.m. telling story after story.

The next day, a tired Eisenhower hosted Giraud for lunch. Churchill spoke broken French, which Murphy translated for Eisenhower. The gist of Churchill's comments was that French unity was of paramount importance, and Giraud must invite de Gaulle to Algiers to work out a power-sharing arrangement.

When the luncheon ended, Eisenhower asked Giraud and Murphy to come back to his office. Eisenhower asked Giraud, "Will you invite de Gaulle to North Africa?"

"Giraud doesn't trust de Gaulle. He's all about gaining power for himself. He treats Giraud with condescension! At Casablanca Giraud made every effort to accommodate the man's huge ego. But de Gaulle rejected every power-sharing proposal. Must Giraud deal with such an obnoxious man?"

"I've found in this world you sometimes have to work with disagreeable people," replied Eisenhower. "The French must be unified in the fight against the Nazis. I'll ensure you'll control the French army."

Giraud stood, his lips tightly pressed. "All Giraud desires is a liberated France. Giraud will think hard whether he can work with de Gaulle and will give Mr. Churchill an answer tomorrow."

The next day, Eisenhower was happy when he learned Giraud agreed to invite de Gaulle to Algiers. That night after dinner at Cunningham's villa, Eisenhower bid farewell to the Prime Minister, who left for the airfield and a flight back to England.

When he awakened the next morning, Eisenhower was unhappy to learn the Prime Minister's plane had developed mechanical problems and Churchill was still in Algiers. Eisenhower braced himself for another long night with the irrepressible Prime Minister.

That afternoon, Eisenhower reviewed an Ultra intercept; the Germans were planning an attack in Tunisia. The intelligence was maddeningly vague as to the location of the assault. Because Rommel's entire Afrika Korps had moved into southern Tunisia in front of the inexperienced US Second Corps, Eisenhower suspected the Americans were the target.

He got a stenographer and dictated a cable to US Second Corps Commander Lloyd Fredendall, with a copy to Anderson:

```
Intelligence suggests imminent German attack. Immediately
prepare defensive positions to receive assault that will
likely come through one of the mountain passes in front of
your troops.
```

Eisenhower wanted to travel to the front and inspect the Second Corps. First, though, he had one more evening to spend with Churchill.

That evening, the PM arrived for dinner at Eisenhower's villa, wearing a red zip-up one-piece garment with two breast pockets, roomy side pockets, and fold-over cuffs. Admiral Cunningham accompanied him, making quite a sartorial contrast in his crisply pressed, all-white naval uniform. Butcher joined the small dinner party.

While they were having cocktails on the terrace overlooking

Algiers, Butcher asked, "Mr. Prime Minister, why is the outfit you're wearing called a 'siren suit'?"

"Some reporter coined that phrase because you can don it quickly after hearing an air-raid siren. That can be important at night if you're sleeping quite naked in bed!" Churchill guffawed. "But in reality, this garment has nothing to do with the war. I designed this for practicality and comfort when I was laying bricks at Chartwell. I had my tailor make several of them in different colors. That was back in the 1930s, when I was in the political wilderness and had plenty of time for bricklaying!"

"Excuse my ignorance, but why were you in the 'political wilderness'?" asked Eisenhower.

"I was labeled a 'warmonger' for raising the alarm about Hitler and the Nazis!" Churchill's cheeks took on a pinkish hue. "No Prime Minister would have me in his cabinet. My colleagues heaped scorn on me when I protested Britain's unpreparedness for war. I had long periods of the black dog."

"'Black dog'?" asked a puzzled Butcher.

Churchill looked meditative and took a sip of his whisky before answering. "'Black dog' refers to being in a dark mood, feeling down with the world."

Cunningham broke the somber mood. "Sir, your predecessor in office, Neville Chamberlain, was a goddamn fool! His policy of appeasement virtually gave Europe to Hitler. The Allies are lucky to have a man with your foresight and strength as our wartime leader!"

"I'll toast to that!" said Eisenhower, raising his glass. "To the Prime Minister and victory over the forces of evil!"

They all clinked glasses.

Churchill began weeping. Pulling a handkerchief out of his pocket to wipe away the tears, he said, "Thank you all for your support. Sorry, I'm a crier."

It was another long night for Eisenhower. While he had grown fond of the PM and his unique character, he was a happy man when Churchill finally left Algiers.

CHAPTER 31

Summersby was driving Eisenhower in his armored Cadillac on the road to his forward headquarters in the ancient city of Constantine, Algeria. They were accompanied by two jeeps with mounted guns, a spare sedan, and a weapons carrier.

Before leaving Algiers, Eisenhower learned the President had sent his name to the Senate for promotion to four-star general. His reading of the tea leaves in Casablanca—that the President was losing faith in him—had been wrong. The realization was invigorating.

During the trip, he intently studied a map of Tunisia. The mountains ran north to south down the spine of the country. There were only a few passes that could be crossed easily. The German attack was certain to come through one of the passes. *Which one will it be?*

At the command post, Eisenhower sought out Anderson. He found him in his Map Room.

"Ken, do you agree with my assessment the Germans will attack the Second Corps?"

"You're wrong, Ike," Anderson replied bluntly. "They'll strike Fondouk Pass, where I had to replace the French troops. That pass is thinly held and vulnerable. I want to send my limited reserves to Fondouk."

Eisenhower pointed at the map. "I question whether the Germans would strike that far north. My gut tells me Rommel will attack farther south where the weather is better."

Anderson sighed in exasperation. "You're not analyzing the situation correctly. Rommel has been beaten up by Montgomery. He needs to recoup, lick his wounds. No, Rommel will not attack. Von Arnim with his fresher troops will attack Fondouk."

The dour Scotsman's condescending attitude irritated Eisenhower, but he reined in his annoyance. "Montgomery has stopped at Tripoli; his army is not pressing Rommel. And the Desert Fox is famous for being aggressive."

An aide entered the room. "Urgent message for you, sir."

The man handed a cable to Eisenhower. It was from AFHQ's intelligence chief, British officer Eric Mockler-Ferryman.

```
I've analyzed the Ultra intercepts and concluded the
Germans will attack Fondouk Pass.
```

Eisenhower passed the cable to Anderson. "I guess you're right. Go ahead and reinforce Fondouk."

From Constantine, Summersby drove Eisenhower south to Second Corps headquarters near Tébessa, Algeria. The route was littered with ruins of buildings built during Rome's six-hundred-year rule of North Africa. Doric, Corinthian, and Ionic columns stood as silent witnesses to the glories of ancient Rome. Eisenhower, a lover of history, imagined Roman Legions marching on the route they were traveling.

After they passed through the town of Tébessa, Summersby turned left and started the Cadillac up a narrow, twisting canyon road that ran between tall mountains. The road, constructed by the Corps of Engineers, led to Fredendall's headquarters.

When his car reached the end of the road, Eisenhower was amazed to see hundreds of engineers at work blasting an underground headquarters for Fredendall. *Why in the hell is Fredendall building an impregnable HQ? Is the man a damn coward?*

Eisenhower got out of the car and quickly approached Fredendall, a narrow-faced man with close-set eyes. "Lloyd, when did you decide to become a miner?"

Fredendall earnestly replied, "I'm building a secure headquarters."

"I can see that," Eisenhower replied, his words laced with sarcasm. "Have these engineers already built fortifications for the front-line troops?"

"No. The combat divisions have their own engineers for that work."

"How often do you go to the front and see for yourself what the situation is?"

"Not often, Ike. I need to be at the headquarters to control my commanders, who are spread out over a wide area."

"Well, I'm going to inspect the front now," Eisenhower said curtly. "Find me a guide and a driver. My driver needs some rest."

Soon Eisenhower was in a jeep headed toward the front lines in nearby Tunisia. His inspection trip lasted all night, and what he observed was disturbing.

The Second Corps was defending mountain passes but had constructed only partial defensive positions. The contrast between the feverish work at Fredendall's HQ and the lackadaisical approach exhibited by his subordinate front-line officers was shocking!

When he discovered a position where no minefield had been laid, Eisenhower sought out the responsible officer. "Lieutenant, why in the hell hasn't a minefield been sown here?"

The man fidgeted uncomfortably. "We've only been here two days, sir."

"When the Germans get to a new location, they get their mines laid in two hours! Now, get cracking and sow those fucking mines!"

"Yes, sir!" The wide-eyed soldier snapped a sloppy salute and ran off.

During the long night, Eisenhower visited a sixty-mile front between the Maknassy and Faïd Passes. Nowhere had strong defensive positions been constructed. He instructed the officers he met to urgently complete their work—the Germans could attack at any moment!

He was outraged to discover the strategic reserve, the US First Armored Division, was scattered about in penny packets. The isolated detachments were liable to be defeated in detail if they had to respond to a German attack that broke through the front lines.

The sun was rising as Eisenhower's jeep approached Fredendall's bunker. When the jeep stopped, Eisenhower leapt out, intent on reprimanding Fredendall for the sorry state of the Second Corps. But the words the first officer he encountered spoke stopped him dead in his tracks.

"General Eisenhower! Have you heard the Germans are attacking?"

"Where?"

"Faïd Pass."

Eisenhower's mind churned with visions of a looming disaster, one for which he felt responsible. Rather than entertaining Churchill and being entangled in French politics, he should have been up here inspecting the Second Corps, ensuring the troops were well positioned to receive a German attack. *It is pure negligence on my part that the Second Corps is so ill-prepared for their first battle!*

Eisenhower found Fredendall coming out of a meeting with his staff. He resisted the urge to rip into him; such a tongue-lashing would only undermine the man's self-confidence. Fredendall had commanded the Oran fight and performed well. Hopefully, he would rise to the occasion now.

Eisenhower fought to keep his tone even. "Lloyd, I found your men have not constructed strong defensive positions. Direct them to take advantage of the rugged terrain, control the high ground, and make extensive use of mines to impede the advancement of German armor."

"My men have been trained to take those steps! Some asses are going to be chewed out!" Fredendall yelled.

"The men need your leadership," Eisenhower said, balling his fist for emphasis. "Get them to fight like tigers and give the Germans hell!"

"I will, Ike!" Fredendall said with a bravado that was missing from his eyes.

Eisenhower gave him a reassuring pat on the shoulder before leaving to send a cable to Mockler-Ferryman asking for the latest intelligence:

```
Is the attack against the Second Corps a diversion to
draw reserve forces from Fondouk, where the main attack
will occur? Or are the Second Corps positions the true
objectives of the Germans?
```

As he waited for a reply, Eisenhower managed to get a few hours of sleep.

An officer woke him and handed him Mockler-Ferryman's reply. Eisenhower sat up, rubbing his eyes.

I'm convinced the Faïd Pass attack is a mere feint and the major assault will be at Fondouk.

Eisenhower decided to return to his command post in Constantine. It was the best place to communicate with Anderson, who, as Tunisian ground force commander, had the responsibility for repelling the German assault.

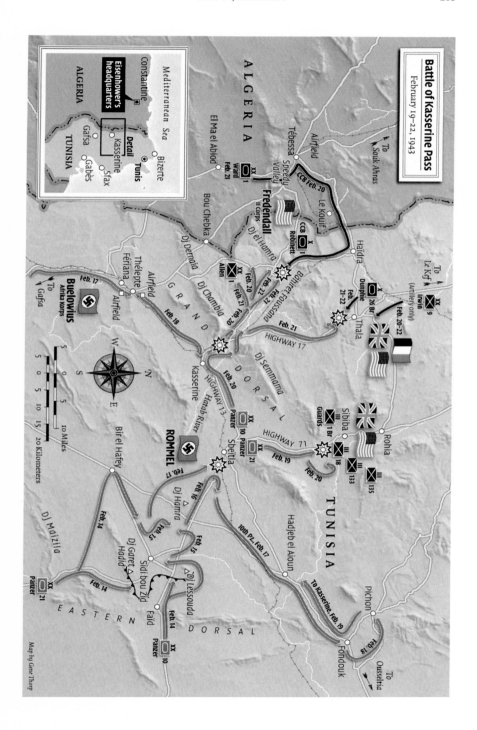

Battle of Kasserine Pass
February 19–22, 1943

Map by Gene Thorp

CHAPTER 32

When Eisenhower reached Constantine, he found Anderson in his office with a melancholy look in his eyes. "Ken, has Fondouk been attacked?"

"No, Ike." Anderson exhaled a deep breath. "Your gut instinct was right—Rommel is attacking the Second Corps."

Eisenhower took a step back, stunned by the news. How could Mockler-Ferryman's Ultra analysis have so missed the mark? He gathered himself to focus on the crisis at hand. "Is the Second Corps holding up?"

"Early reports are discouraging."

"Have you sent reinforcements to Fredendall?"

"Not yet. I think von Arnim may still attack in the north."

Eisenhower's temper erupted like a volcano. "Goddamnit! Send Fredendall all the men you can, including the French reserves!"

In the early days of the battle, the surprised and poorly prepared Americans recoiled from the force of the Afrika Korps assault. As Eisenhower feared, the US First Armored Division's scattered tank units were fed into the battle in piecemeal and defeated in detail by the advancing Germans.

Eisenhower ordered the US Ninth Division, with its artillery, to immediately start a 735-mile march from western Algeria to the battlefield. He stripped units training for the invasion of Sicily of their tanks, trucks, and ammunition, and shipped them to Fredendall. He ordered Doolittle's air force to focus its attention on supporting the Second Corps.

Two days into the battle, Eisenhower met with Anderson in the Constantine Map Room.

"Ike, I think we should order the Second Corps to fall back to the Kasserine Pass." Anderson pointed to a map of Tunisia. "That pass is only a half mile wide at its narrowest and flanked by four-thousand-foot-high mountains. It should be an exceptionally strong defensive position."

The recommendation made sense. Fredendall's men were being bludgeoned by Rommel. They needed to find a defensive position they could hold on to.

"Okay, Ken, order the retreat."

Forty-eight hours later, an ashen-faced Anderson found Eisenhower outside the Constantine headquarters, where he was pacing and smoking a cigarette.

"You look like you've seen a ghost, Ken."

"Our Kasserine position has collapsed."

"What the hell happened?"

"Rommel's men captured the mountainous high ground. The Americans are fleeing in a disorganized retreat."

Eisenhower put aside his shock and thought hard about what action to take. "Order the men to fight for every ridgeline. They need to buy time for reinforcements to arrive. We need to amass enough artillery to stop Rommel's tanks."

Over the next three days, the actions of the US Twenty-Sixth Armored Brigade, supported by remnants of the US Twenty-Sixth Infantry Division, averted a complete catastrophe. Taking a gallant stand, the soldiers fought desperately as they fell back from ridge to ridge. The Americans slowed down Rommel's progress in front of Thala, Tunisia. Time, bought with the Twenty-Sixth's blood, allowed British and French reinforcements to arrive and strengthen the precarious defensive line. The fortunes of the battle shifted when the US Ninth Infantry's artillery appeared. The combined Allied artillery punished Rommel's tanks, bringing his advance to a halt.

Eisenhower was in his Constantine command post when a cable came from Mockler-Ferryman:

```
An Ultra intercept revealed Rommel is planning to retreat.
He's running out of supplies and believes Montgomery will
soon threaten his rear.
```

Eisenhower lit a cigarette and paced his office. Rommel was vulnerable, with his supplies dwindling. It was the time to be aggressive. He went to Anderson's office.

"Rommel's preparing to retreat! Tomorrow, have our troops attack him aggressively!"

"That's a foolish move, Ike," Anderson protested. "Our forces are weak. If we attack, Rommel will surely counterattack and shatter our thin line. I say let Rommel go. We need to regroup and resupply."

Eisenhower faced a dilemma: *Should I follow my gut feeling that a bold counterattack would turn a losing hand into a winning one? Or should I heed Anderson's warning that it's a risky move that could spectacularly backfire?*

Eisenhower fretted. Maybe being cautious was the right play. . . . He wanted to act boldly like his hero Robert E. Lee, but if his gamble failed and Rommel broke through, the battered Second Corps could be annihilated.

Not trusting his own judgment, Eisenhower decided not to counterattack.

Rommel retreated, hindered only by air attacks from Doolittle's planes.

Eisenhower reflected on the battle during his long trip back to Algiers. His premonition of a disaster befalling the Second Corps had proven true. In a week, Rommel had pushed the US troops back eighty-five miles. In their first engagement with the Germans, the Americans had been humiliated in what the press was calling "the Battle of Kasserine Pass."

Kasserine has been a debacle. Who is to blame?

It was clear to Eisenhower the ultimate responsibility was his. Too much of his time and energy had been sucked into the vortex of French politics and entertaining Churchill. He hadn't spent enough time at the front to discover Fredendall's inadequacies.

Going forward, Alexander, who had taken a month to wrap up his affairs in Cairo, would be on board to command the ground forces. Alexander had experience fighting Rommel, and, after Kasserine, Eisenhower was happy to have him assume management of the front-line battle.

Changes had to be made. First on the chopping block was Mockler-Ferryman: Eisenhower had no tolerance for an intelligence chief who so misread the enemy's intentions.

Fredendall would have to be relieved. Who should replace him?

A smile came to Eisenhower's face: *George Patton, my old friend, is just the man to take over the Second Corps!* He would provide leadership, discipline, and fighting spirit. Yes, Patton was the perfect choice. He would pull Patton out of preparations for the invasion of Sicily and put him in charge of the badly beaten-up Second Corps for six weeks. His friend was sure to turn the Second Corps into a first-class fighting outfit in those six weeks.

For a few hours, Eisenhower dozed off in the back seat of the Cadillac. He awoke in a sweat, having dreamed of dead American soldiers, men who died because of his failure to effectively manage the battlefield. Eisenhower looked at his watch: 1:00 a.m.

He glanced out the window and observed in the moonlight that they were in the suburbs of Algiers. He needed to decompress. He decided to invite Kay in for a nightcap when they reached his villa. Being with her soothed his nerves.

He couldn't deny his desire for Kay; that kiss and embrace on the train had been scintillating. But he willed himself to suppress it; he would not cheat on Mamie!

Then a thought struck like a thunderbolt: *Can I justify a romance with Kay as a means to cope with the grueling burdens of command that are grinding on me like a millstone crushing grain? Would a wartime romance be an antidote to the pressures that assault me from every direction?*

When they reached his villa, Eisenhower asked, "Kay, will you come in and have a drink with me? I'm too keyed up to go to sleep."

"That would be lovely," Summersby said in a tired voice as she climbed slowly out of the car.

He led her into the library, closing the door after them. He poured them each a Johnnie Walker whisky, and they sat down on the green couch. For a time, they sat in companionable silence, taking sips of their whisky.

Eisenhower took a deep breath. He wanted to lay his cards—his emotional cards—on the table. "Kay, I've never expressed just how devastated I was when I heard your ship had been torpedoed. The thought of losing you was depressing as hell."

She cocked her head and smiled. "I'm happy you want me around. I have to confess; I want me around too!"

Eisenhower continued slowly. "When I contemplated my death on the flight to Casablanca, I thought about how deeply I cared for you."

She reached out and squeezed his hand. Tears filled her eyes. "You're important to me too."

He stared into her green eyes, and she held his gaze. *I desire this woman, but . . . but making love to her would be a betrayal of Mamie.*

She put her glass of whisky on a side table. "Ike, I should go. You need to get some sleep."

"Don't go, Kay." His mind had conjured up a rationale for a wartime romance, and he was ready to act. He put his whisky glass down and embraced Summersby. The two shared a long and passionate kiss. When their lips parted, he asked, "Kay, do you want to come upstairs to my bedroom?"

She stared at him for a long time. "I don't know what to do. I love Dick, and yet I have strong feelings for you."

"We're in the same boat," Eisenhower admitted. "I love Mamie, but I'm drawn to you. I've fought the urge to make a pass at you, but my ability to suppress my desire for you has, well, collapsed."

Summersby looked intently into Eisenhower's blue eyes. Then she took his hand and stood. "Let's go upstairs."

Their lovemaking was intense. Kay didn't leave the villa until 4:00 a.m.

Eisenhower fell into an exhausted sleep, only to awake to conflicting emotions. *Making love to Kay was exhilarating, everything I dreamed it would be, yet I've broken the sanctity of my marital vows, cheated on Mamie. I'll have to live with this sin the rest of my life.*

Eisenhower was waiting at the Maison Blanche airfield to meet Patton, who was making a brief stop on his way to the battlefront. He smiled as his flamboyant friend deplaned, wearing ivory-handled pistols. The two old friends embraced with hearty backslaps.

"It's good to see you, Georgie."

"I thanked the Almighty when I got your message. I dreaded having to wait till Sicily to get after the Nazis!"

Patton continued. "Is it true Fredendall was a goddamn coward during the battle, hiding his ass in his subterranean headquarters?"

The smile fell from Eisenhower's face. "We don't speak ill of our fellow officers."

"Ike, that's fucking headquarters talk! We've known each other too long for such namby-pamby niceties!"

Eisenhower stiffened. "I love your energy and your enthusiasm, but you need to watch your big mouth! I won't tolerate hearsay character assassination." He reached into his coat pocket, pulled out a letter, and handed it to Patton. "This letter authorizes you to assume control of the Second Corps as soon as you arrive. Fredendall has been told he's being relieved. Please don't embarrass him when you relieve him."

"No, of course I'll be classy," Patton replied with a wave of his hand. "You don't kick a man when he's down."

"Fredendall's men lack discipline and were poorly trained. I know those are deficiencies you'll correct. Be ruthless weeding out weak officers!" Eisenhower ordered. "GIs should be led by the best officers America can produce."

Patton gripped his pistols and puffed out his chest. "I'll turn the Second Corps into the best fighting outfit in the US Army! I can't wait to battle Rommel and give those Nazi sons of bitches the opportunity to die for their fucking Fatherland!"

Eisenhower reached out and shook Patton's hand. "Good luck and Godspeed!"

When Eisenhower got back to his office, there was a letter from Mamie on his desk. Eisenhower eyed it for a few moments before opening it.

How could you deceive me! Finding out you have an attractive woman driver from Life magazine was humiliating. One of my girlfriends made a catty remark about unfaithful husbands that brought me to tears.

I'm happy all the gossiping will stop now that you're in Africa and away from that woman. And, of course, I don't believe the nasty insinuations you're having an affair. My love for you has never wavered.

Eisenhower set the letter down. He felt terrible that Kay's existence was causing Mamie grief. What could he do in terms of the current situation? To correct her assumption and tell her Summersby was in Algiers—and worse, that he had slept with her—would do no good. He didn't like lying but saw no recourse.

Darling, I apologize for not mentioning Kay Summersby as my driver. I didn't want you worrying about me being seduced simply because my driver was a woman. And you needn't worry about Summersby having romantic intentions for me. She's deeply in love—engaged to an American officer, and soon to be married. My love for you is as strong as ever!

CHAPTER 33

Bright sunshine reflected off white Algerian roofs as Mickey served breakfast. Eisenhower and Sir Arthur Tedder, his new air chief, were dining alfresco on Villa Dar el-Ouard's terrace. The topic of conversation was whether ground force commanders or air chiefs would control the fighter planes and medium bombers that composed New Zealander Arthur "Mary" Coningham's tactical air forces.

Tedder was slender and spoke in a calm, erudite manner. "Ike, I've spent years fighting the Germans and Italians in the desert and have learned valuable lessons. One of the most important is that ground force commanders cannot be allowed to control air power."

It came as no surprise to Eisenhower that Tedder held a different perspective than he did. Being an infantry man, Eisenhower believed ground force commanders should control air power, just as they did a tank battalion.

"The War Department's Field Manual provides air forces should support the ground forces, and that's the policy I've implemented," replied Eisenhower. "Ground force commanders should have the authority to order air support for the grunts on the ground."

"The approach you've adopted has proved a bloody failure."

"How so?"

"Not concentrating air power is just as big a sin as not concentrating ground power," replied Tedder. "Think about the losses the American First Armored Division suffered in the Kasserine battle because it was broken up into penny packets. Letting ground commanders control air assets results in similar ineffective penny packets."

Eisenhower's eyes opened wide, and he put down his fork. What Tedder just said was a eureka moment! "Ted, your argument for concentration of air power makes sense. But my ground force commanders are going to be mad as hell if I take away their authority to call in air support!"

"We're not going to abandon support of the ground troops. I'm a firm believer in the closest possible cooperation between the air and ground forces, and the way to achieve that is to assign air advisers to each of the Allied armies fighting in Tunisia. The embedded airmen will liaise with Coningham's officers, who can see the big picture and order air strikes where they will be most effective. Your ground commanders can still request air support, and circumstances will dictate whether the request can be honored. We perfected this type of cooperation with Montgomery, and the system has worked well."

"Okay, you've convinced me," Eisenhower said. "Go ahead and implement your air-control plan."

On February 20, Alexander arrived in Tunisia and assumed his responsibilities as Eisenhower's ground force commander. After completing a tour of Allied forces, he met with Eisenhower at the Constantine command post.

Lean, fit, and deeply tanned from his time in the desert, Alexander started the conversation with his assessment of matters. "Ike, I'm sure you're painfully aware the Americans were roughly handled by the Germans. Your Fredendall chap was not up to the job. This Patton fellow seems cut from finer cloth."

"I'll be the first to admit the Americans performed poorly in their first encounter with the Germans. But I'm confident the Second Corps will show vast improvement under Patton's leadership."

"I hope that's true," replied Alexander with a note of skepticism.

"What about Anderson?" asked Eisenhower. "Do you think he's up to the job?"

"That dour Scot is not my cup of tea. He's unimaginative, lacks charisma, and doesn't inspire the men. But Anderson is competent. He can execute a battle plan."

"What's your take on the French?" asked Eisenhower.

"They're mostly native troops. Some of the units have good fighting qualities, but their lack of modern weapons puts them at a severe disadvantage against the Germans. Until they're reequipped, they're best suited for a reserve role."

"Alex, put together a plan for a spring offensive. I told the President we'd prevail in Tunisia by the middle of May, and that's a promise I plan to keep."

Butcher greeted Eisenhower on his return to Villa Dar el-Ouard. "How was the trip to Constantine?"

"Worthwhile. I think Alex will be a good ground force commander," Eisenhower said succinctly as he lit a cigarette. "Have you found a place for Kay and me to ride?"

"I have."

"Wonderful! Where?"

"I rented an abandoned farm about ten miles out of town."

"Did you find us some horses?"

"Of course—some Arabian stallions. They're magnificent."

"Good work, Butch."

"Thanks, Ike." Butcher laughed. "You won't believe it, but Kay has shown up in *Life* again."

"What?" Eisenhower gasped.

Butcher turned and picked up a magazine from a nearby table. He opened it to page forty-nine and handed it to Eisenhower. "Women in Lifeboats" by *Life* photographer Margaret Bourke-White told the story of the torpedoing of the *Strathallan*. An accompanying picture of a lifeboat filled with women had a caption identifying one of them as "Eisenhower's Irish driver, pretty Kay Summersby."

Eisenhower felt like a two-by-four had smacked him in the head. He was in a daze and having trouble focusing.

"Ike, are you okay?" Butcher asked with concern.

"Water. I need a glass of water," he said faintly.

After Butcher rushed off to the kitchen, Eisenhower tried to sort out his emotions. Foremost was his shame for causing Mamie so much sorrow by not telling her Summersby was still part of his life. *Mamie's health will undoubtedly suffer when she sees the article and photo—and I can only imagine her catty friend making more snide remarks about unfaithful husbands.*

When Butcher returned, Eisenhower gulped down the water, then asked, "Butch, how can I explain to Mamie why Kay is in Africa?"

"I'd tell her a plausible truth—you brought her to Africa to be close to her fiancé, Dick Arnold, whose unit is fighting in Tunisia. That's what I tell people who've asked me why Kay is here."

The next morning, Summersby drove Eisenhower and Butcher out of Algiers. After twenty minutes, Butcher instructed Summersby to turn off the road onto a dirt path. It led to a run-down white stucco farmhouse.

As they got out of the car, Eisenhower asked, "Butch, does this place have a name?"

"Sailor's Delight."

"That's a funny name for a farm. Did my naval aide make it up?"

Butcher just smiled.

They went straight to the stables, where Eisenhower and Summersby admired the Arabian horses. They were chestnut-colored with long, flowing manes, finely chiseled bone features, and arched necks. A few American soldiers were tending to the horses.

"Butch, get some Algerians to take care of the horses! These GIs should be fighting in Tunisia."

"I don't think that's wise," Butcher cautioned. "Your security is paramount, and after the Darlan assassination, we can't be too careful. These men grew up on horse farms, so they know what they're doing."

Eisenhower gave a heavy sigh. "As much as I hate to admit it, you're right."

At the sound of engine noises, Eisenhower turned around. A convoy of four jeeps filled with soldiers was pulling up in front of the stables.

"Butch, who in the hell are those men?"

"They're here to guard the farm while you and Kay ride."

"Christ on a mountain! I didn't want this to be a big production!" Eisenhower bellowed.

"You can yell at me all you want, but I take your security seriously," Butcher said without flinching. "The plan is for stable hands to live in the farmhouse. The security detail will only come out when you're here riding. They'll set up a picket line around the perimeter of the farm, and there'll be a roving patrol on the farm."

Eisenhower took a deep breath and exhaled. "Butch, you've done well. I apologize for losing my temper."

Butcher smiled. "No problem, boss."

Eisenhower changed his focus to riding. He had wanted to ride with Kay when they were at Telegraph Cottage, but there had never been time.

Once Eisenhower and Kay got on the horses, they started off at a trot. Soon the stallions were galloping across the undulating landscape, with Summersby controlling her spirited horse with ease. Eisenhower felt the stress and tension draining from his body. He hadn't felt this at ease in a long time.

He looked over at Summersby. *My God, the two women in my life are so different!*

Mamie didn't like physical exercise of any sort and had never flown out of fear. Kay rode a horse as naturally as a cowboy and was comfortable driving in a combat zone. Mamie was a worrier with an undiagnosed dizziness issue, while Kay was high-spirited and in great physical health. These two women, so different in makeup and personality, were part of the fabric of his life.

After an hour of vigorous riding, Summersby and Eisenhower dismounted on a headland overlooking blue Mediterranean waters. They tied their horses to a tree and walked up to the edge to enjoy the view.

"This shoreline reminds me of the French Riviera!" Summersby enthused.

He took her hand. "Kay, I love the time we spend together."

She looked at him with adoration. "I cherish my time with you, Ike."

He smiled and put his arm around her waist. She did the same.

The sound of an approaching jeep interrupted Eisenhower's

reverie. Without saying a word, he and Summersby quickly disengaged and stepped apart, united in their desire not to show signs of their affection for one another in front of others.

Soon the jeep came into view, with a driver and a soldier holding a submachine gun. The driver yelled out, "Good morning, General!"

Summersby and Eisenhower waved simultaneously as the jeep passed by on its patrol.

On the ride back to the stables, Eisenhower thought about Kay. *I'm a lucky man to have a beautiful and supportive woman to help me cope with the ungodly pressures of command. But when the war ends, I'm going to return home to my Mamie. And I will be loyal to her for the rest of my life!*

CHAPTER 34

Eisenhower picked up his glasses and read the letter from Mamie:

I'm shocked beyond belief that you brought Kay Summersby to Africa! The look I get from my girlfriends is one of pity. I don't believe you're having an affair. Please end the squalid rumors by sending that woman back to England! I love you dearly.

He understood why Mamie wanted him to get rid of Summersby, but he wasn't prepared to do it. She was an integral part of his wartime life.

He picked up his pen.

Darling, I understand your anger. I'm deeply sad that the Life articles have caused you pain. I brought Summersby to Africa so she could be close to her fiancé who is fighting here. She has a bubbly, upbeat personality that raises the spirits of all who meet her. She's done nothing to deserve being sent home. I'm sorry, but I can't honor your request. I love you with all my heart and can't wait for the day we're reunited!

Smith entered Eisenhower's office with a broad smile as he handed him a cable from the War Department. "Somervell's come through!"

A twenty-six-ship convoy loaded with trucks, locomotives, and other invaluable war materials was on its way to North Africa. Eisenhower laughed when he read the cable's last line: "If you should happen to want the Pentagon shipped over there, please try to give us about a week's notice."

On March 6, the emergency convoy arrived in Algiers. The precious trucks were immediately put to work hauling supplies and men. Eisenhower sent seven hundred trucks to Patton to mobilize the Second Corps.

Ever since Patton's successful invasion of Morocco, Eisenhower had lobbied Marshall to get his friend a third star. When the promotion came through, he decided to visit Patton at his headquarters in Gafsa, Tunisia, to celebrate the event and discuss plans for Patton's upcoming attack against Rommel.

Upon reaching Gafsa, the first man Eisenhower saw was Omar Bradley. The tall, bespectacled Missourian's first North African assignment as Eisenhower's roving eyes and ears had been to Fredendall's headquarters during the Second Corps's initiation to war. Bradley's assessment of Fredendall's poor performance had affirmed Eisenhower's own dismal view of the man and hastened his removal. Eisenhower had made Bradley the Second Corps's number two in command, with the thought he would take over command when Patton returned to Husky preparations.

"Brad, it's good to see you. Is Georgie whipping the Second Corps into shape?"

"Whipping is the right word," Bradley said with a tone of disapproval. "Patton's as coarse as a Brillo pad. He's hard on the men, and just about every sentence he utters contains a curse word. But he's getting results."

Eisenhower wasn't bothered by his friend's methods. He found Patton crossing the town square, wearing a leather, fur-lined pilot's jacket.

"Where'd you get that jacket, Georgie?"

"Doolittle gave it to me. I'm freezing my ass off out here!" Patton groused. "I had no idea Tunisia would be so fucking cold."

"I've learned to wear two pairs of wool underwear when I'm out here in the winter!" Eisenhower laughed as he reached out to shake Patton's hand. "Congratulations on getting your third star!"

"Thanks, Ike. I know you put in a good word for me, and it's truly appreciated." Patton pulled a paper out of his jacket pocket and handed it to Eisenhower. "Here's a letter I'm going to give the men the night before we attack."

Patton's letter was written the same way he talked, and one paragraph stood out:

We must be eager to kill, to inflict on the enemy, the hated enemy, wounds, death, and destruction. If we die killing, well and good, but if we fight hard enough, viciously enough, we will kill and live. Live to return to our family and our girls as conquering heroes—men of Mars.

He handed the letter back to Patton. "You sure know how to turn a phrase," he commented with a wry grin. "I've arranged for Alex to come down here so we can review the planned offensive together."

An hour later, Alexander arrived at Patton's office. The three men moved to stand close to a wall with a map of Tunisia nailed to it. Alexander put a finger on Tunisia's border with Libya.

"In the 1930s, the French built fortifications, called the Mareth Line, close to the border with Libya. They feared the Italians, who controlled Libya, would attack Tunisia. Now those fortifications are manned by German and Italian troops. Monty is preparing to attack the Mareth Line, but it will be a tough nut to crack."

Alexander turned to Patton. "I want you to attack the Germans holding the mountain passes in front of your troops." Alexander pointed again at the map. "Your attacks on the El Guettar and Maknassy Passes will be coordinated with Monty's assault on the Mareth Line. If you get control of the passes, that would be jolly good! But I don't want you going down to the coastal plain."

"If we break through, why in the hell shouldn't we drive to the coast?" Patton growled.

"I fear your men would get mauled by a German counterattack where Rommel can take full advantage of his panzer tanks," Alexander explained.

"Alex, that's fucking bullshit!" Patton raged. "You're tying my hands because Fredendall got his ass kicked by Rommel! I know what I'm doing on a battlefield! I can beat Rommel!"

"The Americans performed rather poorly in their first battle with the Germans," Alexander replied calmly, not reacting to Patton's anger. "Until your men prove themselves, I'm inclined to give them modest goals."

Eisenhower interceded. "Alex, why don't we take it one step at a time? If Georgie captures those mountain passes, we can reevaluate whether the Second Corps should be ordered forward."

"Fair enough, Ike," Alexander agreed.

After Alexander left, Patton turned his fury on Eisenhower. "You sure as hell didn't stand up for the American soldier!"

"Alex's criticism of how our men fought under Fredendall was fair. I know they're going to fight a hell of a lot better under you, but first we need to show our British cousins on the battlefield the American fighting man is equal to the German. Once we do that, we'll earn the Brits' respect."

Patton wasn't ready yet to take no for an answer. "You're Alex's boss. Can't you overrule him, and unshackle me from his restrictions?"

"I could, but I prefer you earn his respect on the battlefield. I'm confident you'll redeem American honor in the upcoming fight."

Splitting his forces, Patton simultaneously attacked the two passes, which were fifty miles apart. At El Guettar, Patton found few Germans in front of him and was able to secure the high ground on the west side of the pass. Then he dug in and prepared for a German counterattack, which Ultra intelligence revealed would come quickly.

When the Germans attacked El Guettar, Patton's artillery and tanks beat off the assault of the elite Tenth German Panzer Division, inflicting heavy losses. It was the first American victory against the Germans.

Eisenhower sent a cable to Patton:

```
Congratulations on your victory at El Guettar! The Hun will
soon learn to respect you.
```

Patton's effort to seize the Maknassy Pass faltered in the face of fierce German resistance.

After Montgomery failed to break the Mareth Line, Alexander ordered Patton to drive over the mountain passes and down to the coastal plain.

As Patton advanced through the El Guettar pass, he found the Germans holding the high ground on the eastern end. Repeated attacks by the Americans were bloodily turned away. At Maknassy, Patton also failed to break through. Montgomery finally managed to break the Mareth Line while Patton was still stuck in the mountain passes.

The frustration Patton experienced over being bottled up was intense, and it boiled over when a young aide was killed during a German air attack. Patton wrote in a situation report that a lack of air cover allowed the German air force to operate "almost at will."

Eisenhower was in his Algiers headquarters when he received Patton's report on April 1. Before he could respond to it, Tedder called.

"Ike, have you seen Patton's report?"

"I just read it."

"Well, Mary Coningham fired off a shot at Patton."

"What?" Eisenhower exclaimed in disbelief.

"Coningham sent a signal to all his air commands that he thought Patton's report was an April Fools' joke, and that the real problem was Second Corps's not being battleworthy."

"Goddamnit to hell, I've preached Allied unity until I'm blue in the face!" Eisenhower shouted. "Now these two prima donnas are doing their best to tear down the alliance! I can understand Patton's unhappiness with the lack of air cover, but he shouldn't have put it in a widely circulated situation report. And Coningham's response to it is outrageous. We can't have a British officer being so condescending and obnoxious toward Americans!"

"Ike, I've read Coningham the riot act," replied Tedder. "He knows he's stepped in it. I've told him to cancel the signal and to personally apologize to Patton."

"Ted, we need to placate Patton before he escalates the verbal battle. Go to Patton's headquarters with Tooey Spaatz and personally apologize."

Three days later, Tedder entered Eisenhower's Algiers office, covered in Tunisian dust.

"How'd your meeting with Georgie go?" asked Eisenhower.

"Tooey and I found Patton at his headquarters building in Gasfa. We apologized for Coningham's slur against the Second Corps. Just then, I heard the engine noises of German fighter bombers making a strafing run. Tooey and I hit the floor, but Patton didn't react at all. He just stayed in his chair! I reached up and pulled him down just as machine-gun bullets burst through the wall of his office and a bomb exploded, knocking the plaster off the ceiling. When the strafing was over, I asked Patton how he managed to stage a German air attack while we were visiting."

"What did Georgie say?"

"'I'll be damned if I know, but if I could find the sons of bitches who flew those planes, I'd mail each of them a medal!'"

Eisenhower roared with laughter. "That's a war story I'll remember."

CHAPTER 35

Eisenhower, his feet propped up on the railing, sat on his office balcony, enjoying the sunny April weather as he studied a map of Sicily. The island was the size of Vermont and had a triangular shape, like a three-corner hat. Volcanic Mount Etna dominated the rugged landscape. Sicily lay only ninety miles north of Tunisia, and the city of Messina in the island's northeast corner was a mere two miles from mainland Italy.

The door to his office opened and heavy footsteps heralded the approach of his chief of staff. Smith came out onto the balcony, holding a cable and looking sheepish.

"What's wrong, Beetle?"

"I really fucked up."

"What are you talking about?"

"Remember when I went to Tripoli in February to meet with Monty?"

"Yes."

"We were bantering, and Monty asked me what you'd give him if he broke the Mareth Line and captured Sfax in six weeks. Well, it's more than four hundred miles from Tripoli to Sfax, so I thought he couldn't possibly achieve both objectives in six weeks' time."

Montgomery has done the seemingly impossible. Smith must have wagered something big.

"Okay, Beetle, out with it. What did you bet?"

Beetle kept his eyes on the ground, unable to meet Eisenhower's eyes. "I told him you'd give him anything he wanted. He, umm, asked for a Flying Fortress complete with an American flight crew."

Eisenhower bolted up. "Monty doesn't expect me to honor such a stupid bet?"

"I'm afraid he does."

He handed Eisenhower a cable.

```
MOST IMMEDIATE: Personal from Montgomery to Eisenhower.
Have arrived Sfax 10 April. Recall our bet. Dispatch Flying
Fortress with American crew to Eighth Army, airfield to be
designated.
```

"That arrogant son of a bitch!" Eisenhower thundered.

"I'm sorry, Ike. I put you in a bad spot."

"Goddamnit, Beetle, if I don't honor the bet, Monty will tell everyone I'm not a man of honor!"

"You could tell the little bastard to go to hell and that I didn't have the authority to bind you to an insanely stupid bet."

Eisenhower sighed. "Everybody knows you're my right-hand man. You make agreements in my name all the time. If I repudiated your bet, I'd undermine your authority and hinder your effectiveness in dealing with the Brits. I don't welsh on my obligations, Beetle. I'll give Monty a Fortress."

Smith started to leave, then stopped and pulled a letter out of his jacket and handed it to Eisenhower. "I almost forgot; you got a letter from Mamie."

Eisenhower took a deep breath and opened it.

I'm not going to harp on the Summersby woman. You know how I feel. I trust you and know you're true to me. I love you, so, so much!

Two hours later, Smith returned to Eisenhower's office with another cable from Montgomery:

I object to the Husky plan because the English and American armies will be too far apart to be mutually supporting. The armies must land close to each other so the Allied forces can be concentrated.

Eisenhower knew Montgomery had a legitimate point—he was violating the rule of concentration of force. He was doing so for supply reasons: none of the Sicilian ports were large enough to support both armies. Two ports were considered essential, one for the British and one for the Americans. If a second port was not taken, one of the armies would have to receive all its supplies over beaches, for which there was no historical precedent. Eisenhower's planners had convinced him the need for a second port was worth the risk of not concentrating the armies.

"Beetle, set up a meeting for me to fly to Monty's headquarters to discuss Husky."

Three days later, Montgomery, wearing a black beret, brown sweater, and khaki pants, greeted Eisenhower with a crisp "Good to see you, old chap!" as he exited his plane. The English general gestured with a swagger stick toward a nearby B-17. "Thanks for the Fortress! It's a grand plane."

Eisenhower responded with a forced smile.

When they reached Montgomery's headquarters in a Tunisian school building, the two men got down to business.

"Ike, the Husky plan is a real dog's breakfast."

Eisenhower arched an eyebrow. "Is that some type of joke based on the Husky code name?"

"You Yanks don't know what 'a dog's breakfast' means?"

"I'm afraid not."

"It means a real mess, like you cook a meal that's so inedible, you give it to your dog for breakfast."

"Guess I have another English slang term to add to my vocabulary," Eisenhower said dryly.

"The Husky plan breaks every rule of common-sense battle

fighting!" Montgomery proclaimed passionately. "It has no chance of success! It's like a flock of birds fluttering down all over the Sicilian coast, nowhere in strength. The widely dispersed landings violate the rule of concentration of force."

"You have a valid point," Eisenhower agreed, "but our logistic experts claim the invasion will fail for lack of supplies if we don't immediately secure two ports."

"I'll come up with a better plan once I finish my work in Tunisia," Montgomery said smugly.

"We don't have the luxury of time. If we're going to modify plans, it must happen quickly."

"It's difficult to fight one campaign and plan another one at the same time!" Monty argued.

"I'll give you two weeks to propose a plan. Otherwise, we'll proceed with the plan we have."

Montgomery's eyes narrowed. "You Americans still have a lot to learn about making war. Your Patton chap likes to bluster about air cover, but he still hasn't broken through the mountain passes."

Eisenhower exploded and pointed a finger at the Englishman. "We have enough tension in our alliance without you throwing oil on the fire! Our Anglo-American coalition will break apart if senior officers make disparaging comments about their ally!"

"I only spoke the truth, Ike. You shouldn't be so sensitive."

"Goddamnit, Monty, don't you see we are in this war together? We need to be fighting the Germans and Italians, not each other."

"Look; I'll do my best to keep my opinions to myself. But I must warn you, I'm blunt by nature, and people tell me I'm often tactless."

Eisenhower sighed. *Montgomery is annoying, but there is no choice but to deal with him; the man is England's best field general.* "Very well, then. I need to leave now, but I look forward to receiving your Husky plan."

"Before you go, can you watch the movie *Desert Victory*, produced by the British army?"

"How long is it?"

"Just over an hour."

"Okay. Let's watch it."

The film depicted scenes of the Battle of El Alamein. The combat footage incorporated captured German film showing Rommel directing portions of the battle he lost to Montgomery. It ended with the capture of Tripoli and Montgomery's triumphant victory parade.

"Monty, that film was excellent! Is it being released to the public?"

"It's already showing in movie theaters in the UK and the States. I'm receiving fan mail, even marriage proposals!" Monty laughed. "This movie is making me famous."

On his flight back to Algiers, Eisenhower thought about his key subordinates, Patton and Montgomery. He tolerated his friend's eccentric behaviors and explosive temper because Patton was America's best field commander and, despite his rough edges, a likable person. He found Montgomery irritating as hell—a bad combination of egotism and rudeness. He sighed deeply. *One or both of these goddamn prima donnas is sure to cause me trouble.*

CHAPTER 36

When Eisenhower returned from his visit to Montgomery, there was a cable on his desk from Marshall. He read it with dismay:

The prestige of US soldiers has dropped in the minds of the media and the public after the Kasserine battle. The success of the *Desert Victory* movie has made Montgomery more popular in the US than any American officer. Publicity favorable to the American soldier is practically nonexistent with unfortunate results to national prestige. You need to take steps to improve the image of the American army.

That afternoon, Eisenhower held a press conference where he emphasized American contributions to the Tunisia campaign. He lauded Patton for his victory at El Guettar, and had Alexander issue a press release praising the fighting abilities of Patton and the Second Corps.

Eisenhower was studying Alexander's proposed plan for the final push to win the Battle of Tunisia. The Second Corps wasn't assigned a prominent role, and that bothered him. *How can I improve the public's perception of the American army without it having an important role*

in Tunisia?

The next day, he flew to the front to meet with Alexander. After exchanging pleasantries, he got straight to the point. "The Second Corps must play a significant role in the final battle for Tunisia."

"Bradley's taken over for Patton, and he has no track record," replied Alexander. "I don't know whether he'll be another Fredendall. That's why I have the Second Corps in a supporting role."

"I have every confidence in Brad." Eisenhower lit a cigarette. "But there is a bigger picture to consider. The American public is disappointed their soldiers haven't had success. That's a big problem, because there's considerable pressure on Roosevelt to abandon the 'Germany first' strategy. Without a significant victory by US troops in Tunisia, that pressure may become overwhelming. Most American soldiers could be sent to the Pacific to fight Japan, and England would be left to handle the Nazis without much help from us. Is that what you want?"

The blood drained from Alexander's face. He looked as white as a ghost. "Ike, you can't let that happen! We need American help to defeat the Germans."

"Then you need to revise your battle plan," Eisenhower said firmly.

By the end of the day, Alexander had drawn up a new plan. The Second Corps would use the trucks Somervell provided and move north toward the Tunisian coast. They were given the job of capturing Bizerte, the second-largest Tunisian port.

On his return to Algiers, Eisenhower summoned Tedder to get an update on the air campaign. The airman entered Eisenhower's office, smoking a long-stemmed briarwood pipe.

After he was comfortably seated, Tedder declared, "We've achieved air supremacy! Not only that, we've put a stranglehold on Axis supplies reaching Africa! Thanks to Ultra, we know the shipping invoices and sailing schedule of every Axis supply ship trying to reach Tunisia. My airmen could sink every ship, but that would raise suspicions that we've broken the German radio code. We're selective in our attacks, focusing most heavily on sinking ships carrying gasoline and ammunition."

"Great work, Ted!" Eisenhower was excited. "Your airmen have given us a decisive edge. I told Roosevelt we would capture Tunisia by the middle of May, and by golly, we're going to do it!"

On the eve of the spring offensive, Eisenhower traveled to the Tunisian battlefront to meet with Omar Bradley at his headquarters on a date farm. The Second Corps commander looked and talked like a midwestern schoolteacher, and the quiet confidence he exuded was comforting.

The two men studied a map laid flat on a table in Bradley's headquarters tent showing the disposition of Axis and Allied forces. The German and Italian armies formed a 120-mile arc protecting Tunis and Bizerte. The mountainous and hilly terrain was well suited for defense.

On the Allied left flank close to the Mediterranean were three battalions of the Corps Franc d'Afrique, an independent group of volunteers. Its ranks included Spaniards, Jews expelled from the French army by anti-Semitic laws, French supporters of de Gaulle, and Muslims who had failed to meet the standards for acceptance in native troop regiments. Giraud viewed the Corps Franc d'Afrique as a bunch of misfits and refused to allow them to fight with the regular French army.

Next to and south of the Corps Franc d'Afrique was Bradley's Second Corps. South of Bradley was Anderson's army, which connected to Giraud's French army that curved east toward the Mediterranean and linked up with Montgomery's army.

Bradley pointed toward the sector he planned to attack. "The valleys through these hills are like mousetraps. They're places our men would be bottled up and torn apart by German artillery on the surrounding hills. My plan is to hop from hilltop to hilltop, attacking along the sides of the hills and not in the valleys."

"Brad, you must be successful!" Eisenhower pumped his fist for emphasis. "We must have a clear American victory to rally support on the home front!"

"I'm confident we'll achieve victory," Bradley said pensively. "But the cost in blood will be high to drive the Krauts off those hills."

On April 22, a vast artillery barrage lit the night sky along the entire battlefront. Two hours later, Allied soldiers advanced. The Germans and Italians fought tenaciously from their entrenched positions on the high ground.

The Axis forces stopped the cocksure Montgomery in his tracks. Alexander transferred a portion of Montgomery's stalled army to Anderson, who had easier terrain to cross.

The Corps Franc d'Afrique and the French army fought bravely, but without great success due to a lack of modern armaments.

Bradley's attack made slow progress. The hillsides were filled with anti-personnel mines known as castrators because they sprang to the height of a man's belt before exploding. Day after day, fierce battles raged on hills known only by the number of meters they stood above sea level. The most difficult obstacle for the Americans was Hill 609: its elevation at almost two thousand feet gave the Germans a bird's-eye view of American troop movements.

During Bradley's fight for Hill 609, Anderson asked him to lend an infantry regiment to support the British army. Needing all the man-power available to take Hill 609, Bradley refused. Anderson protested to Eisenhower, who had returned to Algiers.

Eisenhower got Bradley on the phone. "Anderson's raising hell, claiming you're not being cooperative."

"We're in a vicious fight up here! Hill 609 is the linchpin of the German defense. The Krauts are fighting desperately, and we're suffering significant casualties. I can't afford to give Anderson a single man."

Eisenhower hesitated. As the Allied commander, he should allocate resources fairly. But he was also the American theater commander and bore ultimate responsibility for the performance of the American army.

Bradley continued. "Remember how important this campaign is for the reputation of the American army. We must whip the Germans—prove our boys are their equal on the battlefield."

"You're right, Brad. I'll tell Anderson you can't give him any reinforcements."

Once Eisenhower got off the phone, Smith entered his office. "Churchill is sending you a visitor."

"God Almighty, I need another visitor like I need a root canal! Who the hell is it?"

"Captain Ewen Montagu."

"Never heard of him. Do you know the purpose of his visit?"

Smith smiled. "He'll be presenting you with an interesting proposition."

"That sounds mysterious."

CHAPTER 37

On May 2, Montgomery boarded his Fortress and flew to Algiers to present his Husky plan. The fighting in Tunisia was in full cry, but Montgomery could afford to get away as his army wasn't playing a prominent role.

An hour before the scheduled meeting, Tedder visited Eisenhower's office. "Alex can't make the meeting today. Bad weather grounded his plane in Tunisia."

"That's too bad."

"ABC and I don't believe we should meet with Monty to discuss Husky without Alex being present," Tedder said earnestly.

"Why?"

"Alex serves as a counterweight to Monty's monstrous ego. Monty's become . . . delusional after his victories over Rommel. He thinks he's another Napoleon, which he's assuredly not! His success has more to do with Ultra intercepts telling him Rommel's every move and my airmen's destruction of Rommel's supply lines than any brilliant generalship on his part."

Stunned by his countrymen's disdain for Montgomery, Eisenhower leaned back in his chair and threaded his fingers together on his desktop. "Ted, assuming that's all true, I don't see why I shouldn't meet with him."

"ABC and I absolutely believe Alex must be at any Husky meeting where Monty is present." Tedder's thin face tightened. "We'll boycott the meeting today if you go forward."

Eisenhower had great respect for Tedder and Cunningham, and he wasn't going to alienate them if they felt this strongly about rescheduling a meeting. "Okay, I'll postpone the meeting until tomorrow."

The matter seemed settled until Smith came into Eisenhower's office an hour later. "Monty just saw me in the lavatory. He says he must return to Tunisia today. He wants to meet with you to discuss his plan."

"Tell him I won't meet with him without Alex being present. He can stay in Algiers tonight; the Eighth Army will survive another day without him."

A half hour later, Smith was back in Eisenhower's office.

"Monty insists he must return to Tunisia today. He wants me to chair a meeting with the planning staff where he can present his plan."

"Okay, you go ahead and meet with Monty and the planners. Tomorrow when Alex gets here, we'll have a meeting where you can present his plan."

That evening, Eisenhower was throwing a ball to Telek outside his villa when Cunningham came out to walk his Airedale. The dogs had become fast friends, and Telek raced up to the terrier to play.

Eisenhower followed Telek, and as the dogs frolicked, asked Cunningham, "Why do you dislike Monty?"

"When he captured Tripoli, that little bugger complained the navy didn't uncork the harbor fast enough." Cunningham's face darkened like a storm cloud. "Hell, we got that harbor open as quickly as humanly possible! What really angered me is Monty didn't complain to me or even Alex! No, he went straight to Brooke, who took his bullshit complaint to Churchill.

"Another thing that rankles me is he won't attack until his preparations are perfect," Cunningham sneered. "Nobody in this war but him has the luxury of perfect conditions before battle. Monty's method of operation is too velvet-arsed and Rolls-Royce for my taste!"

The next day in the Paris conference room, Eisenhower, Tedder, Cunningham, Alexander, and Smith gathered to discuss Husky.

Eisenhower convened the meeting. "Beetle, tell us about Monty's plan."

"First off, Monty admitted he's a tiresome person who always wants to get his way," Smith said with a straight face.

The room burst into laughter!

Smith continued. "Monty claims the British and American armies need to land close together to avoid a disaster in Sicily. He proposes his Eighth Army land on the southeast corner of Sicily, on the Pachino Peninsula, to capture Syracuse. He wants Patton's Seventh Army to land on the Gulf of Gela and capture the Italian airfields on the coastal plain. The two armies will be close enough to quickly link up."

"Under Monty's plan, Patton's men would have to receive supplies over beaches," said Cunningham. "Did Monty have an answer to the supply problem?"

"He said he would share the port of Syracuse with Patton, but we all know it's not large enough to support both armies," replied Smith.

"Monty is selfishly thinking only about his army," Tedder interjected. "Patton would be starved for supplies."

"I don't agree with that assessment," Smith said while opening his briefcase. He pulled out a picture of an unusual vehicle that looked like a boat with wheels, passing it around the room. "This is a DUKW, a two-and-a-half-ton swimming truck. It has a watertight hull and a propeller. It can ferry supplies from sea to shore. Once on land, the DUKW can drive to a supply dump with its cargo. I've seen a DUKW demonstration, and I was amazed at how well it worked."

Smith had already briefed his boss on the DUKW, but Eisenhower still had concerns. "Beetle, do you think the DUKWs can effectively supply Patton's army over the beaches?"

"The DUKWs should be able to deliver the bulk of his supplies. I believe Patton's army will be sufficiently provisioned if some supplies come through Syracuse and the others by air, once the airfields are captured."

Hours of discussion followed. At the end of the day, Montgomery's plan for the invasion of Sicily was approved.

The next morning, the mysterious Captain Ewen Montagu was shown into Eisenhower's office. His uniform revealed he was a captain in the Royal Navy.

"Captain, what proposition have you brought me?" Eisenhower asked after the two men shook hands and were seated.

"It's a deception operation to fool the Germans into believing Sicily will not be invaded."

"We engage in deception plans all the time. Why would Mr. Churchill send you to Algiers to personally brief me on this one?"

"The Prime Minister is enamored of the plan but realizes it's a high-risk operation and will only approve it if you give your blessing."

"Tell me about the plan."

"Operation Mincemeat involves taking a dead body from an English morgue, dressing it as an English officer, and transporting it by submarine to a location off the Spanish coast. The corpse's lungs will be filled with seawater to simulate a drowning victim and then launched on a tide that will carry it onto a Spanish beach. Attached to a wrist will be an attaché case containing letters suggesting the Allies will launch two invasions in the Mediterranean, one in Sardinia and the other in Greece or possibly Crete, but not Sicily. The hope is the Spanish will believe the body comes from an airplane crash off the coast and will turn the documents over to the Germans."

"Interesting. Your plan reminds me of a real situation we had before the Torch operation, where a letter I wrote ended up in the hands of the Spaniards."

"Yes, I'm aware of that. We believe your letter was copied and passed on to the Germans before the corpse was returned."

"But the Germans didn't act on the information."

"Your letter to the governor-general of Gibraltar merely advised him Gibraltar would be your headquarters for Torch. The letter didn't disclose North Africa would be invaded. The Double Cross Committee used its agents to feed the Germans information the Allies had no interest in North Africa."

Eisenhower smiled. "It's impressive how British intelligence constantly outwits the Germans!" Then, an ominous thought entered his mind. "If the Nazis believe Mincemeat is a deception scheme, they'd conclude Sicily is the target and heavily reinforce it."

"That's the risk the Prime Minister saw," Montagu confirmed. "If an autopsy is conducted, it would reveal the death wasn't caused by drowning. German suspicions would be aroused, and they would likely conclude that Sicily is the target. We're counting on Spain being a Catholic country with an aversion to autopsies for the plan to work. Because Mincemeat could spectacularly backfire, Churchill wants you to personally approve it or kill it."

"Can you give me details concerning the deception documents?"

"We created a fictitious character and placed him on Lord Mountbatten's staff. We chose the name 'William Martin' of the Royal Marines, as there are several officers by that name. The Germans, who will undoubtedly check, shouldn't suspect a fraud is being perpetrated on them.

"We also prepared personal correspondence to high-ranking Allied officials to provide clues as to where the Allies could strike in the Mediterranean." Montagu reached into his briefcase and brought out a packet of papers. He handed it to Eisenhower. "Here are the letters."

Eisenhower read the first letter from a senior officer in the British War Department addressed to General Alexander:

The Germans are reinforcing their forces on Greece and Crete, and the Allies need to increase the size of the invasion force. . . . Sicily is a deception target. . . . The amphibious landing exercises occurring in Algeria and Tunisia and the bombing of Sicilian airfields support the deception.

Eisenhower nodded his head in appreciation as he said, "I like how you are planting clues focusing the Germans on the Eastern Mediterranean and away from Sicily." He picked up the second letter, from Mountbatten to Admiral Cunningham:

I think you'll find Martin of great assistance. He was involved in the Dieppe raid and is an expert on landing craft. . . . As soon as the assault is over, Martin must immediately return to London. . . . Hopefully he'll have time to pick up some sardines to bring home.

Eisenhower laughed as he looked up from the letter. "The reference to sardines is a clever way to point the Nazis at Sardinia."

The third letter was from Mountbatten and addressed to him! Eisenhower gave a surprised smile before he read on.

Ike, would you write an introductory message for the American readership of a pamphlet describing my Combined Operations Command? Bill Martin, a member of my staff, will provide you proofs of the pamphlet.

Eisenhower set down the letter, puzzled. "This letter doesn't have any invasion clues."

"We needed Martin to be carrying enough documents to justify having an attaché case, and the proof pages will provide the bulk we need." Montagu pulled a few more things out of his briefcase, which he was holding in his lap. "This is what we call 'pocket litter.'" He handed one item after another to Eisenhower. "Ticket stubs from a West End theater, a receipt for a new shirt, a book of stamps, keys, cigarettes, matches, and a photo."

Eisenhower studied the photo. It showed a pretty girl standing on a beach with her hair flying in the breeze. "Who is she?"

"A clerk in MI5 where I work. She's posing as Martin's fiancée."

"Captain, are you a poker player?"

"Not my game, sir."

"The very clever scheme you've concocted is like a big-stakes poker game. Mincemeat will either be a huge win, making the invasion easier, or a horrible loss, leading Hitler to fortify Sicily to such an extent the invasion will be a bloody failure."

Eisenhower lit a cigarette, stood, and began pacing. Minutes passed. Then he stopped and took a deep breath. "I like the boldness of the plan. Let's do it and pray to God the Spaniards don't do an autopsy!"

CHAPTER 38

On May 5, Eisenhower traveled to the front. He found Bradley inside a camouflaged tent beside an olive grove.

"Welcome to the final show!" Bradley enthused. "I've coordinated with Anderson to attack along our forty-mile line simultaneously with his assault. The Germans are on the ropes. At three a.m., there'll be an intense artillery barrage; then we'll surge forward with overwhelming force and crack the Kraut line!"

"Brad, you've done a great job turning the Second Corps into battle-hardened soldiers. America can be justifiably proud of its men. If it's not a distraction, can I tour Hill 609 now that you've captured it?"

"Sure. I'll have an aide run you up there in my jeep."

A half hour later, Eisenhower was atop Hill 609. It was a hellish scene. Severed body parts littered the ground. The bloated corpses yet to be buried reminded him of pictures from the battles of Gettysburg and Antietam.

He used binoculars to scan the countryside. He spotted German troops dug in across the valley, and American soldiers assembling for the nighttime assault. Eisenhower felt a nervous energy anticipating the ultimate battle.

When he returned to Bradley's headquarters, he noticed a fierce-looking Moroccan Goumier clad in a brown-gray hooded cloak and sandals. A menacing curved sword hung from his belt.

"Brad, what's that French Goum doing here?"

"I accepted Giraud's offer of a regiment of Goums. They're from Berber tribes in the Moroccan mountains, and they know how to stealthily navigate these hills. I've used them for reconnaissance missions, and they've performed exceedingly well. The Goums strike fear in the Germans for their reputation for cutting off ears. The Krauts believe the French pay the Goums ten francs per ear."

"Is that true?"

Bradley smirked. "The Goums have undoubtedly cut off a few ears, but the French are too cheap to pay for them."

Anderson's and Bradley's attacks shattered German and Italian lines. Tedder's planes dominated the sky, flying more than two thousand sorties, and the Royal Navy effectively blockaded the coastline. Cunningham's order of the day summed up the Allied mentality: "Sink, burn, and destroy. Let nothing pass."

Within forty-eight hours, the British had captured Tunis, and the Americans, Bizerte.

When Eisenhower visited Anderson's headquarters, he heard stories of the British entering Tunis so quickly that German officers, not realizing the city had fallen, were captured in barbershops, bars, and brothels. The only person he encountered who wasn't jubilant was Anderson.

"Ken, what's wrong?" Eisenhower asked, perplexed.

"I just read a news dispatch filed by a British journalist saying it was *Montgomery's* army that captured Tunis! That's a total falsehood. My army was given no credit! Monty has the press in his pocket, and it's not fair. My men deserve recognition for what they've accomplished."

"I agree. I'll issue a press release giving your soldiers the praise and acknowledgment they so richly deserve."

"Thank you, Ike; you're a fair-minded man."

By May 12, it was over, his promise to the President fulfilled: Eisenhower had won the Battle of Tunisia, and more than 250,000 German and Italian prisoners were taken into captivity.

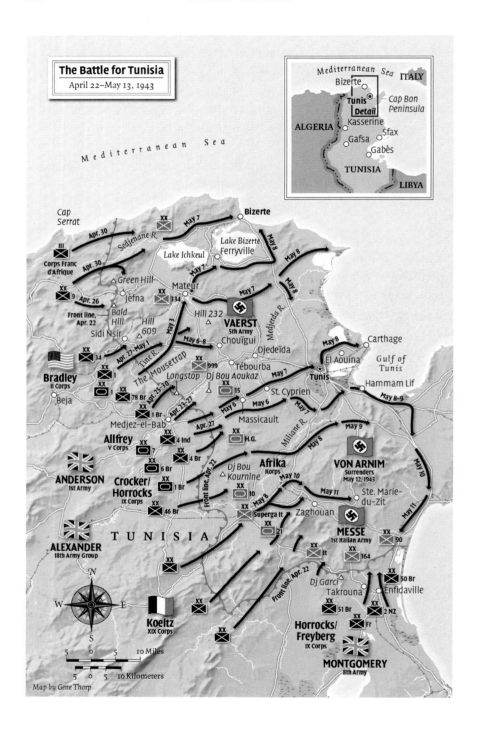

The Battle for Tunisia
April 22–May 13, 1943

Map by Gene Thorp

Eisenhower was anxious to focus on Husky and didn't want a victory parade to celebrate the Allied success in North Africa. But when Giraud insisted French pride warranted a parade, he acquiesced.

May 20 was a sunny, ninety-degree day in Tunis as Giraud and Eisenhower took their places of honor in the reviewing stand along Avenue Gallieni. Alexander, Tedder, Cunningham, Anderson, and his two diplomats, Murphy and Macmillan, joined them. Montgomery was absent, his army having its victory parade in Tripoli.

A large crowd jammed the palm-tree-lined parade route. People in homes along the route hung out their windows in anticipation of the spectacle. Every rooftop was filled with people.

At noon, booming cannon fire announced the beginning of the parade. Heading the procession was the French Foreign Legion Band wearing white hats, followed by Giraud's assortment of colorful native troops.

A cavalry regiment of Algerian Spahis wearing red cloaks and holding their sabers in the air in salute rode by on white horses. Then, the Chasseurs d'Afrique, wearing blue tunics and red pants, cantered by on their horses. The French infantry marched past, Muslim Moroccan and Algerian regiments wearing turbans; Black Senegalese Tirailleurs wearing dark blue forage hats and khaki uniforms; Algerian Zouave units wearing red kepis, blue coats, and white pantaloons; the Goums waving their menacing swords; and the French Foreign Legion, its ranks including blond-haired Poles. Tedder's air armada flew overhead, adding to the pageantry.

Sweating in the sweltering heat, Eisenhower stood the entire time, returning the salutes of the passing troops. He hoped he wouldn't pass out before the parade ended.

After the colorful French came the Americans in their olive-green uniforms, led by a band playing "The Stars and Stripes Forever." Enthusiastic spectators screamed, *"Vive l'Amérique!"*

Tears welled in Eisenhower's eyes as the Americans marched by. His countrymen had come so far from their disastrous encounter with Rommel in the Kasserine battle. They had fought with valor and learned invaluable battlefield lessons. Strong leaders like Patton and Bradley had emerged, while weak ones like Fredendall had been weeded out. The Allies had overcome adversity and emerged winners.

Eisenhower was proud he had turned the French from adversaries to allies and cleared the African continent of Axis forces. Even though he hadn't been a fan of having this parade, the victory the Allies achieved was something to be celebrated and honored.

After the Americans came the British Fifty-First Highland Division band, led by a drum major and bagpiper wearing kilts and playing the traditional Scottish folk song "Flowers of the Forest." The band put on a show in front of the reviewing stand. The drum major twirled his large baton and then threw it high in the sky; continuing to march, he caught it effortlessly on its descent. The band slow-marched past the reviewing stand, then countermarched back in front of the Allied brass before turning around and fast-marching off.

British soldiers followed, wearing khaki short-sleeve shirts, shorts, and knee socks. Units from the United Kingdom, Australia, New Zealand, and India filed past.

By now, Eisenhower's arm was sore from saluting, and he was wilting in the intense heat. The parade was to have been two hours long, but it was now close to three hours, and men kept coming! *Goddamnit, the French and British must have included more than their allocated number of units!*

Last were de Gaulle's Free French soldiers, led by General Philippe Leclerc, who had fought with Montgomery. The Free French refused to march with Giraud's men.

The parade finally ended, and Eisenhower wearily left the reviewing stand to fly back to Algiers on his Fortress. The two diplomats, Murphy and Macmillan, hitched a ride with him.

Eisenhower was close to dropping off to sleep when Macmillan approached his seat.

"Ike, you have to see this!" Macmillan said excitedly, pointing out the window at a large convoy passing below. "That is the first convoy since 1941 that has ventured this far west in the Mediterranean! There sail the fruits of your great victory!"

Eisenhower opened his eyes and peered out the window. So tired just a moment ago, he felt a surge of energy flow through his body at the sight.

"Harold, it's not my victory," he corrected. "It was an *Allied* victory! Our grand alliance is working!"

CHAPTER 39

Eisenhower had gathered his subordinates in the Hotel Saint George's high-ceilinged Paris conference room. The fate of Operation Corkscrew—the invasion of the Italian island of Pantelleria—was up for debate.

Pantelleria had an airfield, and the planes there posed a threat to the Husky invasion fleet. The island was heavily fortified and boasted sheer cliffs with no beaches for an invasion landing. Only an assault on Pantelleria's fortified harbor was possible.

Eisenhower started the meeting by stating his position. "I believe Pantelleria must be taken before we launch Husky. If the island is captured, we eliminate the Italian planes and gain an airfield Allied planes can use to support the invasion."

"It will be a bloodbath if we attack that fortress island," Alexander objected vehemently. "Pantelleria is the Italian Gibraltar, and it's unassailable! An attack would be another Dieppe disaster. I can't see losing good men for no gain."

Eisenhower was unbowed by Alexander's fears. "There're only Italians on Pantelleria, and I think they've had their fill of fighting."

"Ike, you're being pigheaded," Alexander shot back. "If Corkscrew fails, the adverse effect on morale would be significant."

"Ted, can your planes bombard the hell out of that island day and night?" interjected Cunningham.

"If Ike orders it, yes, but I don't think that's the best use of our air forces," warned Tedder.

"That's a great idea, ABC!" Eisenhower said before looking at Tedder. "Let's make this an experiment—whether round-the-clock bombing, aimed at not only destroying enemy defenses, but also denying garrison troops any chance for sleep, can reduce their will to fight."

"Ike, you have my support," said Cunningham. "The navy will blockade Pantelleria to prevent it from being reinforced and resupplied."

Eisenhower sat back and contemplated his decision. His gut told him to take the risk. "I like having consensus for major decisions, but sometimes that's impossible. I'm sorry, Alex, but we're going to attack Pantelleria."

Alexander's prediction of a Pantelleria bloodbath was weighing heavily on Eisenhower's mind as Summersby drove him back to his villa. He knew deaths were inevitable in war, but he wasn't a dispassionate person who could order a suicide attack. His body felt tight, the stress seeping into his bones.

Summersby eyed him in the rearview mirror. "Ike, you seem unusually tense. We haven't been to Sailor's Delight in a while. I think it will do you good to get some exercise."

"Good idea, Kay. Tomorrow morning we'll go out to the farm and do a long ride."

As Summersby navigated a steep Algerian hill, Eisenhower thought about their relationship. Kay was a pillar of strength in his life, perpetually optimistic and upbeat. Yet his infidelity to Mamie was always floating at the back of his mind, and at times his immoral conduct attacked his conscience with a vengeance.

He tried to damp down the guilt by reminding himself he was resolved to atone for his sins by doing the right thing when the war ended. He would return to Mamie and resume his old life.

The next morning, Eisenhower and Summersby were galloping across Sailor's Delight under blue skies. When their horses slowed to a canter, Summersby said, "I came out here last week when you were at the front. I did some exploring and found a quiet spot where we could have a picnic lunch. What do you think?"

Eisenhower noticed saddlebags on her horse. "A picnic lunch sounds great."

After two hours of vigorous riding, Summersby led Eisenhower off one of their favorite trails and through a small patch of woods to an oval-shaped swale. They tied their horses to a tree, and Summersby grabbed the saddlebags.

Eisenhower followed her into a depression in the undulating landscape. The swale was six feet deep and very secluded. He helped her spread a blanket on the bottom of the swale, which was relatively flat.

Summersby reached into a saddlebag and pulled out two Algerian oranges, a half loaf of French bread, a piece of French Cantal cheese, and a bottle of Algerian red wine. From the other saddlebag, she took out plates, knives, wineglasses, and a corkscrew.

"Kay, this is quite a spread."

"I thought a picnic would be fun. I could tell you needed a break."

He uncorked the wine and poured them each a glass. "When I'm with you, I don't think about the war."

She smiled. "That makes me happy. I'm following Churchill's order to take good care of you."

They enjoyed their lunch in peace—no roving patrol disturbed them. When they finished eating, Eisenhower refilled the wineglasses, and they spoke of their families, swapping stories of sibling rivalries.

As they rode back to the stables, Eisenhower felt reenergized. *I made the right decision bringing Kay to Africa. Nothing de-stresses me more than being with Kay.*

Macmillan was waiting for Eisenhower when he returned to his office from Sailor's Delight.

"De Gaulle is due in Algiers on May 30. Churchill wants your support in getting Giraud to make a deal with de Gaulle."

He took a seat behind his desk before he responded, lamenting his political bosses' insistence he meddle in French politics. "That puts me in an awkward spot. The President has made it clear he doesn't trust de Gaulle. The best I can do is tell Giraud America favors him forming a political union with the Free French."

"If we want a strong France after the war, then de Gaulle should be supported!" the diplomat argued. "While he's arrogant and often disagreeable, he's the only Frenchman strong enough to keep postwar France from spiraling into chaos. De Gaulle has proven to be an adept political leader, whereas Giraud is a simple old soldier—someone totally naive in political matters."

Eisenhower gave a heavy sigh. "Harold, I think it's best to let the French work it out for themselves."

Macmillan stared hard at the American. "His Majesty's government requests your assistance in brokering a deal between Giraud and de Gaulle."

God, how I wish I could stay out of French politics! But I can't refuse a request from Churchill.

"I'll do my best, given the limitations Roosevelt has imposed upon me."

After Macmillan left, Eisenhower went to Smith's office. He knew Churchill was in Washington and plans were being formulated for Allied objectives after Sicily.

"Any news from Washington, Beetle?"

Smith handed Eisenhower a cable. "This just came in from Marshall."

No agreement was reached at the Washington conference for a Mediterranean objective after Husky. I'm coming to Algiers with Churchill and Brooke where a final decision will be made.

He handed the cable back to Smith. "Should be interesting. Make sure Churchill stays with Cunningham. I love the PM, but he's exhausting."

Smith laughed. "I'll see to it."

On May 28, Churchill, Marshall, and Brooke arrived in Algiers. Eisenhower and Cunningham met the VIPs at the airport.

Churchill enthusiastically shook Eisenhower's hand. "Congratulations on your great victory!"

"Sir, it wasn't my victory. It was an Allied victory."

"Of course," Churchill agreed heartily. "You've done a magnificent job creating a unified headquarters!"

As they walked toward the parked cars, Eisenhower asked Churchill, "What's the status of Mincemeat?"

"I'm happy you approved that brilliant deception. Ultra reports show the Spaniards recovered the body and passed the letters to the Hun—they've concluded they're legitimate! The deception played beautifully on Hitler's fear we'd strike through the Balkans, the source of many of his natural resources. A panzer division in France has already been ordered to Greece."

"Any movement of German troops out of Sicily?"

"Not yet, no. But they haven't sent in any reinforcements either."

"Has the autopsy threat passed?"

"Thank goodness, yes. The Spanish returned the body to us intact."

By this point, the group of men had reached the vehicles. Churchill and Brooke got into Cunningham's car, and Marshall got into Eisenhower's car.

When they reached Eisenhower's office, Marshall briefed him on the Washington conference.

"It was a difficult meeting. Churchill was reluctant to agree to a fixed date for the invasion of France. He's totally focused on invading Italy."

"Did he finally agree to an invasion date?"

"Yes, May 1, 1944. By the way, Roundup has become Overlord."

"Why the change?"

"That was Churchill's idea. He takes . . . a childish pleasure playing around with code names."

Eisenhower laughed. "Churchill has never lost his childhood energy; that's for sure."

"While I admire Churchill, he can be extremely difficult to deal with," replied Marshall. "I persuaded Roosevelt not to give in to his demand for an Italian invasion. Eisenhower, the decision of where to go after Sicily has been left for you to decide."

"It's my decision?" said a surprised Eisenhower.

"Yes, that's why Churchill is in Algiers—to lobby you to invade Italy."

"An invasion of Italy could knock it out of the war."

"But at what cost?" asked Marshall. "We cannot allow the British to deplete our resources through endless battles in the Mediterranean. We must build up Allied forces in England for Overlord."

"I agree, sir. Overlord is of paramount importance. If Italy is invaded, the objectives should be limited."

"What objectives would you set?"

Eisenhower considered the question. "Eliminate Italy as Hitler's ally and force the Germans to defend the Italian Peninsula, which would weaken Nazi forces in Russia and France. A second objective would be securing the Foggia airfield complex so that we could bomb Germany from the south."

Marshall was silent for a few minutes as he thought about Eisenhower's ideas. Finally, he said, "I can support those goals. For your information, Churchill reluctantly agreed to a weakening of Mediterranean operations. In November, seven divisions will be shipped to England to train for Overlord. The British have proven slippery when it comes to honoring their commitments, and I expect Churchill will try to wiggle out of this one. But I will not let the British, under any circumstances, break this commitment," he said emphatically.

"I understand, sir."

"And I will not agree to having a single American soldier fight anywhere east of Italy! I think England's interest in the Mediterranean has as much to do with preserving its empire as it does with winning the war. If Churchill wants to attack the Balkans or a Greek island, he can do it with British troops. Other than Italy, the only Mediterranean targets I would approve are Sardinia and Corsica."

The next day on Villa Dar el-Ouard's terrace, Churchill, Brooke, Marshall, and Eisenhower sat down to discuss grand strategy. As they talked, each man periodically eyed an Allied convoy approaching Algiers off in the distance on the Mediterranean.

Churchill pointed his Cuban cigar at Eisenhower. "Ike, you must see Italy is a great prize! If the Italians surrender, Hitler would be left alone. The morale boost for the Allies and the corresponding body blow to the Nazis would be of stupendous value! With Italy out of the war, Hitler would need German troops to replace the Italian soldiers who had been defending the Balkans and Italy. His southern flank would be vulnerable to Allied attack."

A pensive Eisenhower replied, "Italy, with its many mountains, would be a tough nut to crack if defended by the Germans."

"And there would be no guarantee of victory, with the limited resources that will be devoted to the Mediterranean," added Marshall.

Churchill's pinkish face darkened. "You're being pessimists. America is a country of optimists!"

"We have more than a million soldiers in the Mediterranean," said Brooke. "We can't let those troops sit idle after Sicily until Overlord next May. We must mount another Mediterranean operation."

"What about targeting Sardinia?" asked Eisenhower. "Control of that island would provide a base to attack southern France or northern Italy."

Churchill scoffed. "Attacking Sardinia is playing for small fish!" He laughed heartily at his double entendre. "Compelling Italy to quit the war is the only endeavor worthy of our great Allied enterprise. The alternative between Italy and Sardinia is the difference between a glorious campaign, where we could capture the eternal city of Rome, and a mere convenience!"

That night after dinner, Churchill cornered Eisenhower. "De Gaulle arrives in Algiers tomorrow. I need your help in seeing Giraud and de Gaulle join forces."

"Mr. Prime Minister," Eisenhower said carefully, "you must be aware of the President's bitter animus toward de Gaulle?"

"I am. Franklin's made no secret of his dislike of de Gaulle. The President has a blind spot when it comes to France. He thinks its days as a great country are finished. I don't. Postwar Europe will need a strong, robust France, and de Gaulle is the only man who can make that happen."

"The President has made it clear that my role is to restrain de Gaulle and promote Giraud."

"We have formulated a plan where de Gaulle and Giraud would be copresidents of a French Committee of National Liberation [FCNL] that would be headquartered in Algiers. Could you use your influence with Giraud to have him agree to this new committee?"

"I'll have to check with Washington. If they approve, I'll work with you to see the de Gaulle–Giraud marriage is consummated."

"Thanks, Ike."

As the night wore on, the Prime Minister seemed to gain energy while Eisenhower began to droop. He longed for sleep. He urged himself to stay awake as Churchill spoke about many subjects, including diaries.

"It's an unwise man who keeps a dairy."

"Why is that?" asked Eisenhower.

"Over the course of a long war, one's opinion on various subjects is bound to change from time to time. You may record an observation that turns out to be ludicrously wrong. A historian can use a day-to-day diary to make his subject look foolish."

Eisenhower remained silent. He didn't volunteer Butcher was maintaining a diary so there would be a historical record of his command.

Churchill continued. "After the war, I'll write a history of this great conflict. You can be sure I'll look astute, a man with great foresight who managed the war with brilliance! I'll never look foolish."

CHAPTER 40

Churchill stayed in Algiers for eight days and at every opportunity lobbied Eisenhower to make Italy the next invasion target. But Eisenhower wouldn't give Churchill the answer he wanted. He followed Marshall's advice to wait to see how the Sicilian invasion unfolded before deciding on Italy. He set up two planning staffs, one for Italy and the other for Sardinia. When the persistent Prime Minister's plane finally left for London, Eisenhower was both exhausted and relieved.

Roosevelt signed off on a French copresidency, and Macmillan and Murphy took the lead in consummating the de Gaulle–Giraud marriage. True to his word to Churchill, Eisenhower urged Giraud to reach an agreement with de Gaulle. He was pleased when the French generals agreed to serve as copresidents of the FCNL.

At midnight on June 9, Eisenhower climbed into his Fortress and flew to Bône, Algeria. He was going to observe a naval attack on Pantelleria. Mussolini had spent twenty years fortifying the island, and he was eager to get a close-up look before the invasion.

Once he landed, a jeep took him to the harbor. As he boarded the HMS *Aurora*, a light cruiser, Admiral Cunningham greeted him.

"Welcome aboard, Ike! We'll be an hour delayed while we clear the channel of Italian mines."

"Will there be floating mines in the water when we sail?" asked Eisenhower.

"Yes, but at the speed we'll be going, the bow wave will keep them away from the ship. It would be the worst luck if the ship hits a mine!"

After hearing this, Eisenhower slept fitfully on the eve of his first naval battle.

At 6:00 a.m. the next day, the general was on the bridge with Cunningham, watching as a steady stream of B-17s flew overhead. They were carrying out his order to bomb Pantelleria around the clock.

By 10:00 a.m., the *Aurora* was located off Pantelleria, joining a flotilla of six British cruisers and ten destroyers. Eisenhower watched the B-17s drop massive bomb loads on the small island.

Cunningham yelled over the sounds of the explosions, "Do you still want to participate in the attack?"

"Absolutely!"

"It will be dangerous," Cunningham cautioned, "because we'll be within range of the shore batteries."

Eisenhower felt like a teenager who was skipping school to go on an adventure. "You can't fight a war without exposing yourself to danger."

By 11:00 a.m., the *Aurora* and the other British ships were a mile and half off the harbor. Eisenhower stood on the bridge and studied the shoreline with binoculars. He could see shore guns embedded in rock lobbing shells at them. One shell exploded two hundred feet from the ship. Cunningham approached, holding out some white cotton balls.

"Put these in your ears, Ike. It's going to get loud."

Eisenhower nodded his assent and stuffed the cotton balls in his ears. Barely a minute later, nine six-inch guns exploded in unison with the guns on the other fifteen warships. The *Aurora* rocked, rolled, and vibrated with a suddenness that threw Eisenhower off-balance. Only a quick grab of the rail kept him from crashing onto the deck. A crescendo of noise rolled over him, and the pungent odor of cordite stung his nostrils. Eisenhower steadied himself and focused his binoculars on the island. With all the dust and smoke, it was hard to tell where the shells were exploding. The only thing clear was that the little island was taking a hellish pounding.

In an hour, the *Aurora* fired 150 shells into Pantelleria. The other warships fired a similar number.

On the way back to Algeria, Eisenhower sought out Cunningham.

"Thank you for allowing this old infantry man to see the Royal Navy in action. It's a day I'll never forget!"

Cunningham beamed. "It was a jolly good show, wasn't it?"

"Yes, indeed!" replied Eisenhower. "The shore batteries weren't as active as I would have expected. Do you think they're running out of ammunition?"

"Our naval blockade has been quite effective. The Italians are running out of everything, including food."

CHAPTER 41

When Eisenhower returned to his office in Algiers, there was a message to call Murphy. He placed the call with trepidation: the diplomat rarely delivered good news.

Murphy was true to form. "De Gaulle has resigned from the FCNL! French unity has been shattered!"

"Why did he resign?" asked an exasperated Eisenhower.

"De Gaulle wants all the senior Vichy administrators fired. He claims they're traitors to France, supporting a Nazi-collaborating government. He particularly wants the head of Pierre Boisson, who humiliated him in the Battle of Dakar. When Giraud refused to agree to the firings, de Gaulle quit."

"Goddamnit, the French act like bickering schoolchildren! Can you get de Gaulle to rejoin the FCNL?"

"Harold and I are trying. But de Gaulle is stubborn as hell."

"Bob, please keep me out of French politics! I don't have time to deal with their bullshit!" Eisenhower slammed the phone so hard that the receiver cracked.

That afternoon, Eisenhower was focused on Husky preparations when his new intelligence chief, Kenneth Strong, a tall Englishman, entered his office to deliver disturbing news.

"I'm fearful de Gaulle will use force to wrest political control from Giraud!"

Eisenhower set down his reading glasses. "What in the hell are you talking about?"

"More than three thousand Free French soldiers are in Algiers. They've gone AWOL from their camp in Tunisia. Their purpose appears to be to recruit away Giraud's troops to serve with the Free French, and they're having success. Soon de Gaulle will have more soldiers loyal to him in the city than Giraud!"

"What a goddamn mess! The French are causing me more problems than the Nazis!" Eisenhower rose to his feet, lit a cigarette, and began pacing. "I can't believe de Gaulle would lead an armed insurrection to seize power. He'd surely lose Churchill's support. I'll send Murphy and Macmillan to de Gaulle to discover his intentions."

Shortly after Strong left, a somber-looking Smith entered Eisenhower's office.

"What is it, Beetle?"

"Dick Arnold, Kay's fiancé, has been killed."

No death in a war zone surprised Eisenhower, yet the news still jolted him. His voice was soft when he asked, "How?"

"He was supervising clearing a minefield in Tunisia, and one of his men tripped a mine. Do you want me to tell Kay?"

"No. I'll tell her."

That evening before dinner at Villa Dar el-Ouard, Eisenhower said with a heavy voice, "Kay, I need to speak with you. Please come into the library."

When they were alone in the library with the door shut, Eisenhower said, "There is no easy way to tell you what's happened, so I'll give it to you straight."

Mute for once, Summersby began trembling as she stood before him.

"Dick's been killed."

Tears welled in her eyes; then she burst into sobs, and her body began convulsing.

Eisenhower put a comforting arm around her shoulders. He led her to a green leather couch where they sat down. He held her tight as she continued to cry and shake.

It was clear Summersby loved Arnold deeply. Eisenhower understood how a person could have more than one love interest, because he was still deeply in love with Mamie.

"Go ahead and cry," he encouraged. "You're grieving the loss of a loved one, and the pain needs to come out."

After a time, she pulled back and asked, "How did Dick die?"

"He was supervising clearing a minefield near Bizerte. Dick was standing beside one of his soldiers who tripped a mine."

She nodded, her eyes unfocused.

"Kay, you need to take some time off to grieve. I suggest you go to Sailor's Delight and stay as long as you want. I've found activity helps me get through sorrowful times. If you're up to it, I suggest you go riding. The only people there are the soldiers looking after the horses, and they'll respect your privacy. Or, if you want to return to England, I'll arrange it."

Kay was silent for a long time, then in a low, mournful voice said, "Thank you for being so considerate. I'll take your advice and go to Sailor's Delight."

June 11 was D-Day for the Pantelleria assault. Eisenhower's stomach was in a knot, just as it was before the Torch invasion. He rubbed his lucky coins and prayed Alexander was wrong—that Corkscrew wouldn't be a bloodbath.

At 12:30 p.m., Smith burst into Eisenhower's office, a huge smile on his face. "Cunningham reports Pantelleria has surrendered! They ran up a white flag as the landing craft were approaching the harbor. There were no casualties!"

Eisenhower jumped out of his chair and embraced Smith. "We took the Italian Gibraltar without losing a single man!"

The two generals hopped up and down in celebration of the bloodless victory as if their team had won the World Series.

Eisenhower was still feeling elated when a cable came from Roosevelt:

I promised Pierre Boisson at Casablanca there would be
no retaliation against him for his service to the Vichy
government. You cannot allow the FCNL to fire Boisson from
his position as governor-general of French West Africa.

Goddamnit to hell, why can't I be allowed to do my job as a soldier?
I should be focusing on Husky, not infernal French politics!

Eisenhower slammed the cable on his desk with such force his
hand hurt.

To calm down, he left his office for a walk in the hotel's botanical
garden. The tranquil garden with its swaying palm trees and lush vegetation calmed his angst until his mind turned to the safety of the VIP
visitor due tomorrow, the King of England.

Eisenhower prayed George VI's visit wouldn't be marred by violence between supporters of the feuding French generals.

Eisenhower, with Mickey McKeogh as his driver, met King George VI
at the Maison Blanche airfield. When the King descended from the
plane, a swarm of senior British officers greeted him. After exchanging
pleasantries with them, the trim and fit-looking King headed straight
for Eisenhower's car.

"Ike, this is my first trip outside of England since the war started,"
the King said as he got into the back seat next to Eisenhower. "I feel like
a man on hol-holiday. I'm excited to see the troops and visit Malta."

When he first met the King, Eisenhower had been shocked that
the ruler stuttered. But the King had been a pillar of strength for his
embattled nation during the Battle of Britain, refusing to flee with the
royal family to the safety of Canada when many advocated for him to
do so. Instead, he and his family stayed in Buckingham Palace, sharing the danger of the Blitz with their countrymen. The English people
adored the man, stutter and all.

"Your Majesty, I'm concerned about your visit to Malta. Axis aircraft flying from Sicily and Italy have been active in attacking Malta.
Whether you go by plane or ship, it's a dangerous trip. I recommend
you stay in North Africa."

The King's demeanor transformed into one of fierce determination. "The Maltese people have suffered horri-horribly. Despite constant bombings and with little food throughout 1942, they refused to give in. The exceptional hero-heroism of the people has been an inspiration to me. Last year I awarded the entire population the George Cross—it's the highest civilian honor I can bestow. Nothing will stop me from going to Malta!"

The King's passion and desire to reward the Maltese people for their courage with a royal visit was moving. "Sir, I'm withdrawing my objection to your Malta visit."

"Thank you, Ike."

After dropping the King off at a British officer's villa, Eisenhower went to his office in the Hotel Saint George. Murphy and Macmillan were waiting to brief him on their meeting with de Gaulle.

Murphy took the lead. "De Gaulle said any fears his supporters would use violence to gain control are baseless. He spent most of our meeting being indignant over American and English intrusions into what he asserts are purely internal French affairs, particularly the President's insistence that Boisson be retained. He spoke scathingly about Roosevelt's refusal to recognize him as the leader of the French government in exile."

"De Gaulle appeared pleased Roosevelt is upset with him, because it means he has the President's attention," Macmillan added. "De Gaulle's fixated on the French deciding Boisson's fate, claiming it's a matter of French sovereignty and he cannot yield to Roosevelt. I calmed de Gaulle by telling him the King was arriving today and would host a dinner for him and Giraud."

"Do you think that's a wise move?" asked Eisenhower.

"I think the dinner will help soothe troubled waters," replied Macmillan. "It plays to de Gaulle's massive ego to be hosted by a head of state. The King speaks passable French and is used to hosting foreign dignitaries."

"Harold, how do you think this is going to play out?" asked Eisenhower, who had found Macmillan had better insight into the French mentality than Murphy.

"The FCNL is not going to fire Boisson. They're fearful if they do, Roosevelt will stop rearming the French army." Macmillan paused.

"Ike, I think the time has come for you to hold a meeting with de Gaulle and Giraud. Explain to both how important it is to the Allied war effort that Giraud command the army."

Try as he might, Eisenhower just couldn't avoid getting in the middle of French politics. "Okay," he acquiesced. "Arrange the meeting."

Eisenhower decided Murphy and Macmillan would not attend the meeting; he wanted it to be an intimate gathering of the three generals. A staff officer fluent in French would translate.

As the time for the meeting approached, Eisenhower was hopeful he could get the two egocentric Frenchmen to mend their fences. De Gaulle's dinner with the King had been a success—a good sign.

At the appointed time, Giraud arrived at Villa Dar el-Ouard and joined Eisenhower on the terrace. The two men kept the conversation to inconsequential matters until de Gaulle's arrival. He came late, striding out to the terrace, his six-foot-four frame ramrod-straight and his prominent Roman nose held high in the air.

Eisenhower stood to greet his guest, but before he could utter a welcome, de Gaulle began to speak.

"I attend this meeting as the President of the French government. It's appropriate I'm here, as it is customary in times of war for heads of state to visit commanding generals. General Eisenhower, I respect you as a fellow soldier and acknowledge your success in ridding Africa of Nazis, for which action you deserve the profound gratitude of the French people. If you wish to make a request of me concerning use of French forces, be assured I am disposed to give you satisfaction if such a request is compatible with the interests of France."

Recovering from his surprise over de Gaulle's audacity of anointing himself President of France, Eisenhower replied, "General de Gaulle, I think you're aware I'm preparing for a major operation. It's important the current command structure of the French army remain unchanged."

"You mean Giraud must remain in control of the army?" questioned de Gaulle as he remained standing.

"Precisely. It's the position of the American government that I only deal with Giraud on military matters."

"And if I refuse this demand that intrudes on French sovereignty?" asked de Gaulle with pressed lips.

Eisenhower was blunt. "If Giraud doesn't remain in charge of the army, America will stop rearming it."

"You're asking for a commitment I cannot give." De Gaulle pointed a finger at Eisenhower. "Who commands the French army is for the French government to decide, not you!"

"I understand your position, but I have no flexibility. I'm solely focused on immediate military necessities."

"You have leverage, threatening to stop rearming the French army." A very thin smile appeared on de Gaulle's face. "Do you remember, my dear general, in World War One, the Americans arrived in France without any tanks or airplanes, and the French gave those military arms to the Americans?"

"You're correct," replied Eisenhower. "France did help arm the American army during the First World War."

"Did France demand the right to designate the commanding general of the American army?" de Gaulle asked, his face as hard as stone.

Eisenhower ruefully admitted, "France made no such demands. The historical analogy, while interesting, doesn't alter the current situation. Giraud must remain in control of the army."

At last Giraud interjected his opinion. "Giraud's only concerns are getting modern arms for the army and liberating France. We must be partners with General Eisenhower, not troublemakers engaging in acts that hurt the alliance just to show our independence." He paused and continued with words laced with acid. "And please stop playing make-believe games like you're President of France."

De Gaulle glared first at Giraud, then Eisenhower. Without uttering another word, he turned his back to them and walked off the terrace, through the villa, and out the front door.

CHAPTER 42

Eisenhower had no more time to deal with the French; Husky demanded his attention. The invasion was three weeks away, and a huge armada of more than three thousand ships of every description was assembling across the southern rim of the Mediterranean Sea. Every port in Algeria, Tunisia, Libya, Egypt, and Palestine was crammed full of Allied vessels. Allied convoys would also embark from Malta and Scotland. Husky would be the largest amphibious invasion in world history.

Finding the right weather conditions for the invasion had been challenging. A certain amount of moonlight was needed for pilots to find paratrooper drop zones. The moonlight requirement upset the navy, which wanted to approach the beaches in total darkness to avoid air attacks and shelling from shore batteries. Finally, a consensus was reached: a second-quarter waxing moon would provide enough light for the paratroopers to drop at midnight and sufficient darkness for the navy to approach Sicilian beaches at 2:45 a.m.

On July 10, 1943, American paratroopers would jump into Sicily while British airborne soldiers landed by glider before seven infantry divisions hit the island's beaches on a hundred-mile front. All told, 160,000 Allied troops would assault an island defended by 350,000 Axis soldiers, three-quarters of them Italians.

Eisenhower opened the final Husky planning meeting in the Paris conference room with a question for his intelligence chief.

"Ken, what's the latest on Mincemeat?"

"Hitler's taken the bait, more than doubling the number of troops in Greece and strengthening the garrison in Sardinia." Strong looked at his notes. "But it's not all good news. The Germans have sent the Hermann Göring Division into Sicily, with some troops deployed close to the beaches Patton will attack."

"The Hermann Göring Division is sure to counterattack Patton," said Eisenhower worriedly. "His men are going to be sorely tested in the early days of the invasion."

"The navy will help Patton," assured Cunningham. "We're sending in naval gun spotters with Patton's men. The warships will be Patton's floating artillery."

"Thanks, ABC. I think Georgie is going to need your guns." Eisenhower turned his attention to logistics. "What's the latest feedback on training exercises with the DUKWs?"

"They've performed perfectly during practice maneuvers. A most ingenious invention!" enthused Cunningham.

"Are there any landing craft issues?" asked Eisenhower.

"They've done well in training exercises," said Cunningham, "but I've some concerns with how they're being used in Husky."

Eisenhower felt a jolt of anxiety. "What concerns?"

"The landing craft will be loaded with soldiers, tanks, and vehicles in North Africa. Then they'll cross the Mediterranean and discharge their precious cargo on Sicilian beaches. I'm worried about the craft's seaworthiness if caught in a storm with maximum loads on board."

"Can anything be done at this point?"

"No. There's a shortage of shipping, so we can't lighten the loads. Using the landing craft for a shore-to-shore attack is a necessity. We'll just have to live with the risk."

Eisenhower nodded. Calculated risks were unavoidable in war. "ABC, can you provide an update on the convoys?"

Cunningham walked to a wall map of the Mediterranean. He put a finger on Gozo Island near Malta. "This is the marshaling area for all convoys. We want any snooping Axis plane that spots a convoy to believe the attack will come east of Sicily, against either Sardinia or

Corsica. From Gozo, minesweepers will lead the way to Sicily, clearing a path for the convoys."

Eisenhower turned his head toward Alexander. "Alex, could you provide the latest on the beach assaults?"

Holding a pointer, Alexander walked to a wall map of Sicily. He tapped the Gulf of Noto. "Monty will land along a thirty-mile stretch of the coast near Syracuse. The Canadian First Division sailing from Scotland will land on the southern side of the Peninsula. British Airborne troops will land by glider and capture a key bridge at Ponte Grande. Monty's objective is to capture Syracuse. The Canadians will move west and link up with Patton's men near Ragusa."

Alexander tapped his pointer on the Gulf of Gela. "Patton will land here and in the first three days, capture five airfields on the coastal plain. The Eighty-Second Airborne will parachute in three hours before the invasion and capture the high ground above the beaches to block foreseeable counterattacks from nearby Italian and German forces."

Eisenhower asked, "Ted, are we winning the air battle?"

"We sure as hell are!" Tedder replied, a note of pride in his voice. "We've achieved a two-to-one edge in combat air strength. Every day we continue to whittle away Axis air strength."

By the time the meeting concluded, Eisenhower was confident everything hard work and careful preparation could accomplish was being done to make Husky a success.

When he got back to his office, there was a letter from Mamie on his desk. He smiled as he read it:

I finally found an apartment of my own. A one-bedroom directly across the hall from Ruth's apartment in the Wardman Park came open. The manager gave it to me even though there were people ahead of me on the waiting list. I think he likes having your wife living in his building! I can't wait till you come home to me. I love you!

Eisenhower put the letter down with a sigh. The arrival of every one of his wife's letters made him question his dual life.

He thought about Kay. *Should I step back from our intimacy to give her ample time to grieve Arnold's death? A break might allow me to mentally prepare to end the affair.*

The next day, Eisenhower was in the kitchenette area of his office suite when Summersby walked in. While her face had a healthy tan, her eyes were missing their normal sparkle.

"Kay, you're back! How are you feeling?"

"Not great," she responded in a flat, emotionless voice.

After filling his coffee mug, Eisenhower asked Summersby to come to his office.

Once she was seated, he said softly, "I can see from your face you took my advice and did some riding."

"I did, and it was good therapy." She paused, looked down, then back at Eisenhower's face. "I'm saddened by Dick's death. He was a great guy, gregarious and fun-loving. We were so happy together." She sighed. "But so many of my girlfriends have lost husbands and boyfriends in this war that I can't take a pity-me attitude. I'm ready to get back to work."

"Have you thought about going back to England to be around your friends and family?"

"I want to stay here and work for you; it's important to me. I feel I'm doing my part to beat the Nazis!" she said, a bit of her natural spunk resurfacing.

"That's great, Kay." Eisenhower flashed her a grin. "I was thinking that we should, ah, take a step back in the, ah, intimate part of our relationship. Dick's death was a traumatic event, and you need more time to mourn him."

Tears welled up in Summersby's eyes, and Eisenhower handed her a handkerchief. She dabbed at her cheeks.

"I was thinking the same thing, Ike. Thanks for being so understanding."

That night, Eisenhower dined at Cunningham's villa, where he savored the delicious Mediterranean seafood stew the French chef had prepared. During dinner, the admiral recounted the King's journey to Malta.

"I picked His Majesty up in Tripoli, where he met with some of Monty's troops."

"Did you encounter any Axis attacks on the way to Malta?"

"Thank God, no. There were reports of Italian submarines around Malta, but no torpedoes were shot at us. During the day, we had a fighter escort that kept the Axis planes away."

"How was his reception in Malta?"

"Obviously, his visit had to be kept secret. It wasn't until five a.m. that we informed the governor-general the King would arrive in Valletta at eight a.m. We constructed a special platform in front of the bridge so all on land could see the King as we sailed in."

Tears began to fill up in the admiral's eyes as he continued to reminisce. "It was the most magnificent scene I've witnessed in my long career! The King stood alone on the platform in a white naval uniform. As we sailed into the Grand Harbour, all the cliffs and forts on both sides of the harbor were jam-packed with humanity. Soldiers, sailors, and Maltese civilians filled every square inch the eye could see.

"The King received a roaring, thunderous reception. Choirs were singing, bands playing, and people waving flags. It was an incredibly joyous occasion. The King toured the island in a motorcade, and everywhere he went, there were mobs of people screaming and cheering for him." The admiral wiped away the tears now dripping down from his cheeks. "It was a memorable day."

Cunningham's show of emotion moved Eisenhower. Malta held special meaning for British military leaders like Cunningham. They had made herculean efforts to break the Axis siege and save the strategic island.

Eisenhower thought the Maltese and their British saviors represented the best in the human spirit, their sacrifices allowing the Allies to hold out in the Mediterranean during the darkest days of the war.

The next morning, Eisenhower received a call from Murphy. The dip-lomat sounded excited. "Boisson has resigned! This clears the way for de Gaulle to rejoin the FCNL as copresident with Giraud."

"Bob, make it happen!" Eisenhower ordered. "I want to be forever gone from French politics!"

That evening, the King of England hosted a dinner in the Hotel Saint George's Paris conference room; Tedder, Cunningham, and Eisenhower attended. At the conclusion of the meal, the King stood and walked to the front of the room.

"I wish to honor this hum-humble American who has united our two great nations' fighting men. General Eisenhower has created a truly integrated international headquarters for the first time in world history! He has led us to a great vic-victory in Africa and soon will lead us to victory in Sicily! For all he has accomplished, it is my great honor to present General Eisenhower with the Grand Cross of the Most Honorable Order of the Bath. It is the highest honor that I as King can give to a non-British subject."

He beckoned for Eisenhower to come forward. Eisenhower stood up and approached George VI. The King carefully placed a broad ma-roon sash with a medal across Eisenhower's chest.

After Eisenhower returned to his seat, Tedder and Cunningham offered their congratulations.

"Ike, it's a privilege to serve under you," said Tedder.

Cunningham added, "I didn't know what to expect when I was told our commanding general would be a midlevel American general who had never seen combat. But the King hit the mark! You've cre-ated an integrated Anglo-American command structure and earned the respect of your subordinates. It's an honor for me to be your naval commander."

Eisenhower swelled with pride. Having the support of the King and senior British military leaders was validation he had grown into his role as Allied commander.

CHAPTER 43

De Gaulle agreed to rejoin the FCNL as a coequal with Giraud, quieting French political issues for the time being. The bothersome French would have only a small representation in Husky: Patton had requested the Fourth Moroccan Goums to fight with the American army.

Eisenhower turned his attention to his army's media coverage. He was disturbed by a spate of articles and broadcasts speculating which target the Allies would attack next. He got headaches from reading media pundits predicting Sicily would be invaded. Eisenhower scheduled a press conference to address the issue.

When Eisenhower entered the Hotel Saint George's ballroom, he was happy to see every member of the Algiers media in attendance.

"Gentlemen," he began, "it's natural once a campaign ends to wonder where the next one will begin. I'm concerned the speculation many of you are engaging in as to our next move is giving aid to the enemy, who surely reads your stories and listens to your broadcasts. I've decided to take you into my confidence. The target is Sicily."

There was a stunned silence in the room. Reporters gaped and stared in disbelief that they had been told a military secret of immense importance.

Eisenhower continued. "You must absolutely keep this information secret! You now have the same level of heavy responsibility to keep this secret as my staff and I do. I expect your articles and broadcasts will contain no more speculation as to where the next invasion will fall."

And with that, Eisenhower briskly strode out of the room. His press conference was over.

With D-Day for Husky fast approaching, Eisenhower wanted to visit as many units as possible. He started with a trip to Patton's headquarters, where the two generals greeted each other like the two old friends they were.

"Georgie, you look like you've lost some weight!"

"I have. I've been running and swimming. I've even cut back on alcohol and smoking."

"Getting back in Olympic shape?" Eisenhower quipped.

Patton, who had competed in the 1912 Stockholm Olympics in the modern pentathlon and finished fifth, laughed. "Those days are long gone. I'm just getting in campaign shape."

Eisenhower turned serious. "Georgie, do you have any concerns with the invasion plan?"

"Those goddamn swimming trucks better perform as advertised, or my men will be throwing rocks rather than shooting bullets!"

"Everybody's assured me the DUKWs will perform well," Eisenhower said, keeping his tone casual as he lit a cigarette. "How's training gone?"

"I've worked the troops hard. Some of them hate me, but I don't care. I know they'll fight like tiger cats once they're unleashed on the Krauts and Dagos." Patton smiled. "I love leading men into battle— it's the most magnificent competition a human can engage in! When I speak to the men, I tell them there is no better death than to die in battle for a noble and glorious cause!"

"Do you think you come across as too much of a hard-ass?"

"I *am* a hard-ass! I'm proud they call me 'Old Blood and Guts.' But the soldiers know I'm not a humorless hard-ass. One of my favorite lines when I speak to them about your impossible-to-enforce anti-fraternization policy with local women is an army that can't fuck can't fight!"

Eisenhower laughed so hard that tears sprang to his eyes. He enjoyed being with Patton.

"I know you'll get the most out of your men. I have every confidence in you."

"You should, Ike. The American army is going to conquer Sicily!"

Eisenhower's next stop was the Tunisian airfield of the Ninety-Ninth Fighter Squadron, an all-Black outfit. The army was officially segregated under America's separate-but-equal doctrine sanctioned by the Supreme Court, with most colored troops serving in noncombat roles in the supply services. Under congressional pressure, the army did create some all-Black combat units. The Ninety-Ninth had trained in Tuskegee, Alabama, and seen its first combat protecting the bombers attacking Pantelleria. Eisenhower had overruled a staff officer who argued the Black troops didn't merit a visit. All American soldiers under his command deserved to be seen by their commanding general.

Lieutenant Colonel Benjamin O. Davis Jr., the fourth Black in history to have graduated from West Point, was there to greet him on the dusty, desolate airfield. The thirty-year-old Davis saluted smartly. "Welcome to the Ninety-Ninth, General Eisenhower!"

As he shook Davis's hand, Eisenhower said, "Please call me Ike. Just about everybody does."

Davis smiled broadly. "Ike, I have the men assembled for your inspection."

They got into a jeep and headed toward the center of the base. As they drove past parked Curtiss P-40 Warhawk fighters, Eisenhower said, "I've received good reports from Jimmy Doolittle on your squadron's performance protecting the B-17s attacking Pantelleria."

"Thank you, sir. We got our first kill of an enemy plane yesterday in the Strait of Sicily."

"Please identify that airman for me. I want to personally congratulate him."

In a few minutes, they reached the center of the base. An American flag flapped in the breeze from a tall flagpole.

Every man in the Ninety-Ninth stood at attention, prepared to be inspected by Eisenhower. In a booming voice the general said, "At ease, men."

There was a shuffling of feet as men assumed a more natural posture.

He continued. "You men have a difficult and dangerous job, taking on the Axis fighters. You're an integral part of the Allied team, protecting our bombers. I respect your bravery and thank you for your service to your country." Eisenhower then asked, "Who's played on a baseball or football team?"

Most arms shot into the air.

Eisenhower grinned. "An army is like a sports team. Everybody has a designated role to play. The best teams, the ones that win championships, have a selfless character to them; winning is more important than individual glory. The Allied army is now a winning army. We vanquished the Germans and Italians here in North Africa, and we're not going to stop beating those bastards until we grind their armies into dust!" He balled his fist and thrust his arm into the air for emphasis. "Are you men with me in the crusade to crush the Nazis and Fascists?"

A chorus of "yes" and "hell yes" erupted from the men of the Ninety-Ninth.

After lunch in the mess tent, Davis introduced Eisenhower to Charles Hall of Brazil, Indiana, the first Black pilot to shoot down an enemy plane.

Eisenhower asked, "Lieutenant Hall, can you tell me about your encounter with the enemy?"

Hall smiled with evident pride. "I saw a German Focke-Wulf attacking a B-17. I managed to come in behind the Jerry and fired a long burst into the fuselage. The plane fell like a stone toward the sea. I followed it down and saw it crash into the water."

"Congratulations, Lieutenant, on your first kill!" said Eisenhower, vigorously shaking Hall's hand. "It's because of brave fellows like you that we're going to win this war."

Eisenhower left Tunisia, impressed with the Ninety-Ninth. Davis's airmen had an esprit de corps and desire to take the fight to the Germans and Italians. He was proud these Black Americans were acquitting themselves well in combat. He didn't subscribe to the thinking of some that Black soldiers were inferior to white troops.

Eisenhower wondered about the contradiction between America's fight against the evil practices of the Nazis and the army's segregation of Black soldiers. He knew many of his fellow officers endorsed the army's policy of segregation. If the army was going to become integrated, the President would have to order it.

CHAPTER 44

On July 8, Eisenhower took off for Malta. He was happy his stratagem of making the press guardians of a military secret was working. Media speculation surrounding the next Allied target had ended, and there had been no leaks.

The plane's landing approach took him over Valletta, the capital city. Eisenhower pressed his face against the window and looked down at heaps of rubble seemingly everywhere. The city had been battered by incessant Axis bombing.

Upon landing, Eisenhower stepped out into blistering hundred-degree heat and into a waiting car. It took him to Valletta, where Admiral Cunningham awaited him atop the Lascaris Bastion, a military strongpoint the British built in the 1850s to bolster the already formidable defenses of Valletta that the Knights of Malta had begun erecting in the 1500s.

"Welcome to Malta, Ike!" Cunningham said with enthusiasm. The admiral pointed to the harbor that formed an amphitheater, with forts and heights on both sides. "This would have been a grand vantage point to witness the King's entrance to Valletta."

Eisenhower envisioned the V-shaped harbor filled with thousands of screaming, cheering people welcoming the English King. *What a spectacular scene it must have been!*

Cunningham led him down a long flight of stairs that ended in a courtyard under a large arch. At the end of the courtyard was a door guarded by two British soldiers. As Cunningham and Eisenhower approached, the soldiers saluted and opened the door. They entered a tunnel complex built by the Knights in the sixteenth century and enlarged and modernized by the British.

Cunningham and Eisenhower descended a poorly lit stone corridor, passing doors leading to side tunnels. Eisenhower eyed the condensation on the limestone walls and greenish mold on the ceiling. As dampness penetrated his bones, he inhaled an unhealthy concoction of smells. *Goddamnit, this place reminds me of that wretched tunnel in Gibraltar!*

Cunningham sensed Eisenhower's reaction.

"Ike, these tunnels may be gloomy and a bit smelly, but they're totally bombproof. We're deep under the Saints Peter and Paul Bastion. There's forty feet of rock above our heads. We're very safe in here."

The farther underground they went, the colder it got. Eisenhower began shivering. "It's freezing in here!"

"Yes, it's a bit chilly in this part of the tunnel complex. I'll have an aide get you an overcoat. Ah, here's the office we've set aside for your use."

Eisenhower entered the room and found a small desk with a light bulb dangling over it, three wicker chairs, an oil-burning stove, a small rug, and a blanket to ward off the chill.

"Let me show you the War Room," Cunningham offered. "I think you'll find it a bit more impressive than your office!"

Eisenhower followed the admiral down a corridor that opened into a room with a thirty-foot ceiling and a viewing gallery. Huge maps covered the surfaces of every wall.

Eisenhower's ill thoughts about the tunnel complex began to dissipate as he surveyed the War Room. One wall held a twenty-foot-high, thirteen-foot-wide collage of reconnaissance photographs of Sicily. It looked amazingly complete.

"ABC, how much of Sicily is captured in these pictures?"

"All ten thousand square miles."

Eisenhower moved in front of another wall. This one had a map of Sicily with the landing beaches identified by different colors. A third wall had colored lines showing the convoys approaching Sicily. A table in the center of the room was covered with a map of the

Mediterranean. Eisenhower noted, not for the first time, how close Malta was to Sicily—a mere fifty-five miles.

"Have there been any U-boat attacks?" asked Eisenhower.

"Three Canadian ships sailing from Scotland have been torpedoed. Fortunately, no troop transports were hit. Early reports are sixty men were lost, along with five hundred trucks and most of their communication gear."

Eisenhower sighed; the U-boat menace was a constant thorn in his side.

Wearing an overcoat, he spent the day going over the latest developments. Ultra intercepts showed the Germans didn't expect an attack on Sicily. The element of surprise favored the Allies.

The only disconcerting news was the meteorology forecast. A polar air mass was heading south across Europe and would collide with a small cold front in the Mediterranean. The result would be strong easterly winds off the Sicilian coast, which could imperil Patton's landing. Montgomery would be less impacted—the contour of the coastline would block the winds from hitting his beaches.

Eisenhower reached into his pocket and rubbed his lucky coins. *God, please make the weather forecast wrong.*

That night, Eisenhower was driven to Verdala Palace, a castle built by the Knights in 1586 and now the home of Malta's governor-general. Under a moonlit sky, he saw windmills turning furiously in forty-mile-an-hour wind. His anxiety level matched the intensity of the wind.

At the square-shaped castle, a valet escorted Eisenhower to an enormous second-floor bedroom and unpacked his valise. He took no interest in the furnishings. He couldn't take his mind off the wind menace.

The governor-general hosted him for dinner. Eisenhower's stomach was in a knot. He hardly touched his food. The wind had taken away his appetite.

The next day, Eisenhower was back in his dimly lit tunnel office. Tedder and Alexander had arrived. Cunningham joined them for a high-level meeting in the cramped space.

"Ted, have we achieved air dominance?" asked Eisenhower.

"We're close. I don't believe Axis planes can materially affect the invasion."

"ABC, can Patton make his assault in these conditions?" asked Alexander.

"If the current gale-force winds persist, they'll batter Patton's landing craft broadside as they approach the beaches. The lightweight landing craft will likely be swamped in the turbulent waves."

Eisenhower imagined thousands of GIs drowning in the Mediterranean Sea. "ABC, how late can I make a decision to postpone the invasion?"

"We'd need at least four hours' notice to inform the ships if you decide to postpone."

An hour later, Eisenhower was working in his dank office when Cunningham appeared.

"Ike, I met with the Royal Navy's meteorologist. He predicted the wind would slacken to twenty-five miles an hour by eleven p.m."

"Can Patton's men land safely in those conditions?"

Cunningham was pensive. "The landing craft have never been tested with full loads in those winds. Frankly, it's a close call."

"What percentage of the time is your meteorologist accurate?"

Cunningham took his time answering. "About eighty percent of the time."

A 20-percent error rate wasn't reassuring. Eisenhower felt the anxiety of a person who must make a monumental decision.

If the forecast was wrong and the winds didn't moderate, Patton's men would drown, and paratrooper and glider planes would be blown far off course. If he postponed, Axis planes in the morning were sure to spot the huge armada prepared to assault Sicily, and the element of surprise would be lost. If he chose to proceed with the invasion despite the strong winds, the Germans and Italians would be caught off guard, not thinking the Allies would attack into the teeth of gale-force winds.

Eisenhower took a deep breath and rubbed his lucky coins. "It's a go. Let the convoys proceed."

It was 7:00 p.m. when Eisenhower left the tunnel for dinner, his stomach clenched as tightly as a fist. *The winds haven't subsided. Surely the soldiers in the landing craft are going through hell.*

Eisenhower proved a poor dinner companion, barely speaking to the governor-general of Malta. He picked at his food. The unrelenting wind consumed his thoughts.

As soon as dinner was over, he went to Delimara Lighthouse, hoping to catch a glimpse of the paratrooper and glider planes on their way to Sicily. At first, he was excited to see British glider planes being towed by American C-47s, but his heart caught in his chest when he saw the violent effect of the wind on the gliders. They were being tossed about like leaves in a windstorm. *Have I made a horrible mistake in going forward?*

He went back to his tunnel office, resolved to take full responsibility if his decision to proceed ended in disaster. An 11:00 p.m. weather briefing brought news the winds had moderated to the predicted twenty-five miles an hour. The speed was still too high for Eisenhower's liking, and his right hand was sore from rubbing his lucky coins.

He ordered a cot be placed in his office. At midnight he went to sleep. He woke at 3:00 a.m. and went to Cunningham's office, where he found the admiral speaking with Tedder.

"Any news?" asked an anxious Eisenhower.

"Yes, and it's good!" replied Cunningham. "Patton's men made it through the rough seas and landed on the Gela beaches, while Montgomery's troops have landed on the Pachino Peninsula!"

Eisenhower let out a sigh of relief. "Ted, any reports from the paratrooper and glider-borne troops?"

"Not yet, Ike. I'll let you know as soon I hear something."

An hour later, Tedder wore a somber face as he entered Eisenhower's office.

"What's happened, Ted?"

"Quite a few of the British gliders have fallen into the sea. I fear catastrophic casualties."

Eisenhower rubbed his forehead; he felt sick. "I bet the goddamn wind pushed those gliders into the sea."

Tedder replied tersely, "Maybe."

"Any communication from paratroopers?" asked a worried Eisenhower.

Tedder ominously shook his head. "Not a word."

CHAPTER 45

Eisenhower was aboard the HMS *Petard* sailing to Sicily. The past two days had brought a combination of elation due to scattered reports the American and British armies were firmly ashore and frustration over a lack of status reports from Patton. Marshall frequently asked him for updates, and he could only feebly reply, "Things appear to be going well."

At daybreak the *Petard* arrived off Licata, Sicily. Eisenhower gazed at the Sicilian hills, golden in the morning sun. As the ship moved east, parallel to the coast, he stood at the railing and surveyed the shoreline through binoculars.

The beaches were crowded with soldiers and supplies. The newfangled DUKWs were hauling supplies to the shore, and LSTs were discharging tanks on the beaches. Beyond the shoreline, black columns of smoke identified areas of intense fighting.

The *Petard* dropped anchor two miles from Gela's shore. The American warship *Monrovia*, Patton's headquarters ship, was anchored nearby.

Eisenhower clambered into a launch that skimmed across the water to the *Monrovia*. Patton and Admiral Ken Hewitt, the American fleet commander, greeted him.

Admiral Hewitt saluted. "Welcome aboard, General Eisenhower."

Eisenhower returned the salute. "Thank you, Admiral, and please call me Ike. The navy's done a magnificent job in difficult conditions!"

Hewitt beamed. "Thank you, Ike."

Eisenhower turned to Patton, who in a joyous voice announced, "The American army has successfully invaded Europe!"

"Georgie, I want to hear all the details!"

"Come to my cabin where we can be comfortable."

Once they were alone, Eisenhower pointed a finger at Patton. "I have a bone to pick!"

"What in the hell are you talking about?"

Eisenhower's temper rushed out like water through a broken dam. "I haven't gotten a single goddamn report from you! You've kept me in the dark, and that's unacceptable!"

Patton's face darkened. He looked ready to punch Eisenhower in the face.

"That's fucking unfair, Ike! I've written you several reports, but they must not have been transmitted. There's been overwhelming cable traffic on this goddamn boat because it's *Hewitt's* flagship. He's managing more than a thousand ships, and the fucking navy gives *Hewitt's* cables priority over mine!"

Eisenhower took a deep breath and exhaled. "I shouldn't have come down on you so hard. It's frustrating as hell to have Marshall pressing me for details and being able to report only generalities."

"Apology accepted. Now, do you want a battle report, or do you want to chew me out some more?"

Eisenhower waved his hand. "Please, give me as much detail as possible."

"We had rough seas getting to Sicily. Those poor bastards on the landing craft must have been puking their guts out! It got so bad Hewitt talked to me about breaking radio silence and asking you for permission to postpone the invasion. We huddled with his weather forecaster, who predicted the winds would moderate." Patton took a drag on his cigarette and exhaled the smoke. "Thank goodness you had the balls not to call off the invasion."

Eisenhower nodded an acknowledgment, and Patton continued.

"The winds died down some, and we were able to get ashore without too many mishaps. We lost a few dozen men to landing craft accidents caused by the big waves." Patton stubbed out his cigarette. "We got off the beaches fairly easily. The Italians were not expecting an attack during a ferocious storm."

"What happened to our paratroopers?" asked Eisenhower.

"The high winds broke up their plane formations, and they ended up scattered all over Sicily. But those paratroopers are resourceful bastards! They started cutting telephone wires and ambushing enemy patrols. We've learned from captured soldiers they created a great deal of confusion.

"A few hundred did grab the high ground above the Gela beaches and bravely beat off the initial German and Italian counterattacks," Patton said with evident pride in the airborne troops. "But they couldn't hold off the Hermann Göring Panzers. Those goddamn German tanks came close to cutting my army in half."

"What happened?"

"I was ashore yesterday in Gela when the Germans and Italians counterattacked. We had no trouble beating off the Eyeties, but the Hermann Göring Division was another story. The paratroopers up on Biazza Ridge did a hell of a job slowing those sons of bitches down, but eventually the German tanks broke through and got within a mile of the beach."

Patton's squeaky voice went up an octave. "I got on the roof of the local Fascist headquarters to see what was happening. It was dicey for a time. I saw a navy officer on the street holding a radio, and I yelled down to have his goddamn navy drop some shells on the German tanks! Well, pretty soon the cruiser *Boise* began giving those tanks hell! The *Boise*'s guns knocked out at least six Kraut tanks. After that shellacking, those Nazi bastards retreated."

"How's Omar Bradley doing?"

"Brad is a solid second in command, but not aggressive enough for my liking."

"Nobody is as aggressive as you."

Patton laughed. "That's true."

"What's happening now?"

"We're moving inland with strong opposition from the Germans and lesser resistance from the Italians. We've linked up with the Canadians on our right flank, so we have a solid front. Monty is moving on the coast road past Mount Etna toward Messina while I'm going west around Etna. I'll tell you, Ike; I'm going to beat Monty to Messina!"

"A little competition is good for the soul." Eisenhower laughed. "But remember we're allies, Georgie, so be careful with what you say. I don't want any nationalistic rhetoric demeaning our British cousins."

"Of course! I'm a diplomat at heart."

"I wish that were true," replied Eisenhower. "How's the air support been?"

"Spotty."

"Ted told me we're close to air dominance."

"That's bullshit! There've been periods when the only planes in the sky have been the enemies'. At least three American ships have been sunk, plus a handful of landing craft."

There was a crack of thunder as the guns from the nearby cruiser *Savannah* fired in support of Patton's troops on shore. The two generals got up and hurried to the bridge to take in the action.

In the far distance, several miles behind the beach, Eisenhower could see shells exploding. Cunningham's prophecy—that the navy's guns would be floating artillery for the grunts fighting on the ground—had proven accurate.

After lunch with Patton on the *Monrovia*, Eisenhower went back to the *Petard.* He sailed east, looking for Montgomery.

When they neared the HMS *Hilary* and Eisenhower learned it was the Canadian command ship, he decided to welcome them. This was the first battle Canadians were fighting under his command.

Arrangements were made for a DUKW to transport the general to the beach. The swimming truck brought Eisenhower ashore among a hundred naked Canadian soldiers bathing in pristine Mediterranean waters.

On the beach, Eisenhower found the most senior officer, an artillery captain. When he approached, the Canadian, a tall man with dark hair, saluted.

"General Eisenhower, how may I help you?"

"How did you recognize me?" Eisenhower asked.

"Sir, everyone in the free world knows who you are."

Eisenhower shook his head in disbelief. He still had a hard time believing he was famous. "I'm looking for the Canadian headquarters."

"It's pretty far inland. With all the supply traffic, it will take you an hour to get there."

He couldn't spend that much time ashore; he still needed to see Montgomery. "Captain, I wish to welcome you and your Canadian compatriots in arms to the Allied army. Canadians are a rugged and resourceful people. Its soldiers are a valuable addition to our grand alliance. Please pass along my welcome and good wishes to your commanding general."

"It'll be my pleasure, sir!" the officer responded, his face flushing with pride.

Eisenhower headed back to the DUKW to return to the *Petard.* On board, he learned Montgomery's chief of staff, General Freddy de Guingand, was visiting the *Hilary.* He decided to get a battle-status update from de Guingand and forgo the hunt for Montgomery.

Francis "Freddy" de Guingand was urbane and charming, a perfect right-hand man for the tactless Montgomery. Eisenhower had taken a liking to de Guingand from their very first meeting. When they saw each other, they warmly shook hands.

"Freddy, can you give me an update on what's happening in the British sector?"

"Of course."

"Can you start with the airborne assault?"

De Guingand grimaced. "That was a real cock-up. The pilots towing the gliders were inexperienced in nighttime attacks."

"Why weren't they properly trained?" asked Eisenhower, his anger boiling.

"The gliders arrived in Tunisia too late for adequate training."

Eisenhower grunted. *Another SNAFU, this one cost men's lives!*

De Guingand continued. "When the formations got close to the coast, they came under antiaircraft fire. Some of the pilots panicked and released the gliders without factoring in the high winds. Half of the gliders, sixty-five in total, crashed into the Mediterranean."

The news was sickening. *I took a gamble on the winds, and here's evidence my decision cost lives.*

Eisenhower thought of the loved ones who would be receiving telegrams of death. He felt the burden of command most when he tallied the cost in the lives of brave soldiers.

"Casualties?" he asked in a subdued tone.

"Over four hundred men confirmed dead."

Eisenhower sighed and tried to keep focused on the present. "What's Monty's feeling?"

"Of course, he's distressed by the airborne tragedy, but overall, he's quite pleased with what's been accomplished. Despite the heavy losses, the airborne mission was successful. We quickly captured Syracuse, then moved north and took Augusta. On the whole, Monty believes his Eighth Army has performed brilliantly."

When Eisenhower returned to Malta in the evening, he went directly to his dank, smelly tunnel office. He sat down and picked up a report lying on his desk.

The night of July 11, reinforcements from the Eighty-Second Airborne jumped into the Gela beachhead. Minutes before the paratroopers arrived, three German planes made a bombing run over the American fleet. Naval gunners on American warships misidentified the C-47s carrying the paratroopers as German planes. Twenty-three C-47s were shot out of the air. Hundreds of paratroopers are dead or missing. General Patton issued an order to expect the arrival of C-47s and for the gunners to hold their fire. Many of the ships claimed they never received Patton's order.

Eisenhower put down the report and lowered his head into his hands. *What an inexcusable fuckup!*

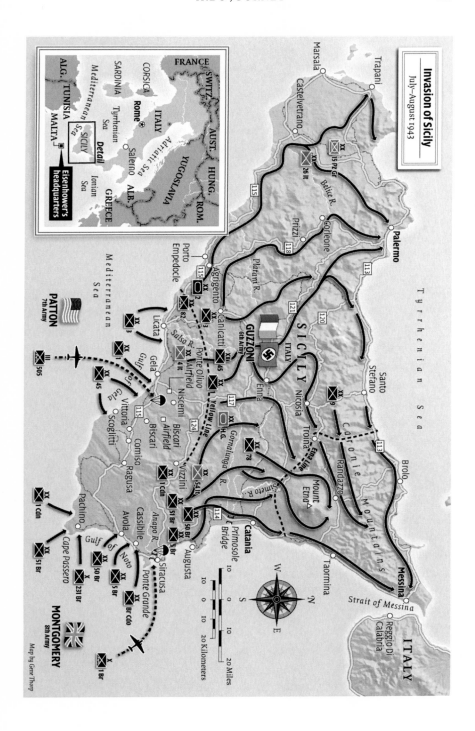

Invasion of Sicily
July–August 1943

Eisenhower's headquarters

Map by Gene Thorp

CHAPTER 46

Eisenhower was happy to decamp from the cold and gloomy Malta tunnel for his advance command post in Tunisia. Butcher had commandeered a large villa, La Maison Blanche, on the Gulf of Tunis in the exclusive enclave of Carthage. The house was modern with an integrally laid mosaic floor. A large terrace provided a vista of the crescent-shaped, sun-splashed gulf and the verdant hills of Cape Bon.

Alexander's temporary command post was also in Carthage. Tedder's was nearby in La Marsa, another upscale Tunis suburb. Only Cunningham continued on in Malta.

A week had passed since the Sicilian invasion, and Allied advances had slowed to a crawl. The Germans were fighting tenaciously in the mountainous terrain. The Italian army was losing strength as soldiers abandoned the fight and melted into the civilian population.

Midmorning Eisenhower received a surprise visitor. "Georgie, what are you doing in Tunisia?"

"Did you bless Monty stealing my road to Messina?" he thundered.

Eisenhower was so startled by the question that he could only utter, "What?"

Patton threw his hands up in utter frustration. "I thought so. When the Germans stonewalled Monty on the coastal road, he went to Alex and asked for the road on the west side of Mount Etna reserved for *my* army! Alex gave him the fucking road without consulting me or you! The American army is being screwed, and I'll not stand for it!"

"Georgie, calm down," said Eisenhower, simultaneously fighting to control his own temper. *The arrogant Montgomery acts like the Allied command exists only to support him!*

Patton took a deep breath but didn't calm down. "Alex gives Monty whatever the hell he wants! It was a fucking mistake to take that road away from me! Brad had to halt his attack against a weak German position, and by the time the Canucks took his place and attacked, the Krauts had brought up reinforcements. Now Monty's stymied on both sides of Mount Etna."

"I'll talk to Alex."

"No, Ike, I'll speak to Alex! He and Monty have disrespected the American army! My men must have a prominent role!"

"Georgie, I understand your frustration. Monty does get what he wants from Alex. They worked together to beat Rommel in the desert, and Alex implicitly trusts Monty."

"That's no reason to fuck me over!"

"No, it isn't." Eisenhower sighed. "What do you want to do now?"

"I want to move west and capture a port for supplies. I'll have Brad move through the mountainous center of the island toward Messina. Of course, I'll make sure the exalted Monty's left flank is not exposed." Patton paused. "I won't embarrass you when I speak to Alex."

Eisenhower nodded. "Okay, go ahead and meet with Alex—let him know your level of indignation. Get him to agree with a new plan for your army. I've no problem with you being forceful, but Alex is your commanding officer, so you cannot be disrespectful." Eisenhower pointed a finger at Patton. "Is that clear?"

"Yes, sir!"

A few hours later, Eisenhower received a note from Patton:

I met with Alex. He's approved my request to advance west. I'm satisfied with the outcome.

The next day, the commander in chief of the Canadian Army, General Andrew McNaughton, visited La Maison Blanche. Two days earlier, when McNaughton asked Eisenhower's permission to visit the Canadian soldiers fighting in Montgomery's army, Eisenhower told him he needed to get Alexander's approval.

After exchanging pleasantries, Eisenhower asked, "Have you spoken to Alex?"

"He said he had to check with Montgomery, and that little bastard responded he won't allow it—claims I'll be a distraction. It's outrageous! I'm the senior Canadian officer in Europe, and I can't see my men! Can you override Alexander? It's the height of discourtesy to deny me the right to visit my soldiers."

Eisenhower shook his head. Montgomery's arrogance knew no bounds. "Andy, I'll talk to Alex and try to persuade him to overrule Monty's objections."

"You're the commanding general. Can't you just tell Montgomery to go to hell?"

"It's not that simple. I have a dual role. I'm the senior American commander and the Allied commander in chief. If it was an American general, I'd overrule him in a heartbeat. When it's a British issue, I defer to the senior British commander. He has control over who visits the British sector."

"Ike, you have to back me on this. It's humiliating, not just for me but for Canada!"

"Andy, I'll support you, but at the end of the day, it's Alex's decision."

When McNaughton left, looking dejected, Eisenhower got up from his desk and walked out onto the terrace. Butcher was there using a pair of binoculars to scan the gulf. Eisenhower told him about the problem Montgomery was causing the Canadian general.

"We should send McNaughton to Patton," said Butcher. "He can give him a jeep and point him toward the British lines. Let Monty arrest him for trespassing on his precious territory!"

"Butch, I can't play that type of game. Canada didn't break ties with England the way we did. It's really an internal British matter."

Eisenhower began to pace back and forth on the terrace while Butcher returned to scanning the gulf. After a few minutes, Butcher exclaimed, "Alexander is in the water!"

Eisenhower took the binoculars from Butcher. Sure enough, Alexander was bobbing up and down in the blue gulf waters.

He handed the binoculars to Butcher and went inside the villa to put on swim trunks. It was time for some aquatic diplomacy.

From the villa's dock, Eisenhower jumped into the warm Tunisian waters and swam over to Alexander.

"Ike, this water is fabulously clear and warm! We don't have waters like this around England!" Alexander blurted out after wiping some water from his eyes.

"I just had a visit from McNaughton," Eisenhower said, getting straight to the point.

Alexander frowned. "The answer is no."

"That's unreasonable. He's the Canadian commander in chief. It's a gross insult to him and to the Canadians fighting and dying in Sicily!"

"Monty is firm on this. He doesn't have time to host visiting dignitaries."

"Goddamnit," Eisenhower growled, "McNaughton is not some politician; he's the senior Canadian general! The disrespect he's being shown is unseemly."

"There is a severe transport issue in the Eighth Army. When I went to Sicily, I had to thumb a ride on a lorry carrying rations to get to Monty's headquarters. I'm not going to impose on Monty the nuisance of having to look after McNaughton!"

"I'm worried this affront to the Canadian nation will get into the press. We'll look petty. It could affect Canadian public opinion, erode support for the war effort. This is a bigger issue than affronting, in a small way, Monty's monumental ego."

"Monty has no respect for McNaughton! When the Canadians first got to England in 1941, Monty helped with their training. He got to know McNaughton and formed a low opinion of him. He can't be bothered with him when he's in the midst of a battle."

Eisenhower was incensed by Montgomery's pettiness, and, as he and Alexander rode gentle waves, argued Montgomery shouldn't be allowed to insult Canada. Alexander wouldn't budge, and Eisenhower, disappointed, swam back to shore.

Goddamnit, holding an alliance together is a tricky business. I could have ordered Alexander to overrule Montgomery. But at what cost? Alex and Monty are two of the most senior British generals, and I'll probably be working with them for a long time. Alienating them over what they perceive as a strictly British matter is just stupid.

When he got back to his villa, Eisenhower found Butcher. "Send a message to McNaughton. Tell him I'm sorry. I did my best, but Alex wouldn't overrule Monty."

CHAPTER 47

On July 19, Eisenhower returned to hot and humid Algiers. He was in his office, awaiting word on the bombing of Rome, which Churchill and Roosevelt had approved. Concerned the attack might damage the Vatican or other historical treasures, Eisenhower had insisted the B-17 crews be specially trained and objectives limited to the most important rail marshaling yards. Despite Tedder's assurances the attack would be precise, Eisenhower was nervous. He knew bombers were blunt instruments of war.

In the late afternoon, Tedder called. "The attack on Rome was a great success!" he said enthusiastically. "Reconnaissance photos taken afterward show extensive damage to rail yards, which will disrupt rail traffic and delay military shipments to Sicily!"

"Ted, that's great news! Was there any damage to nonmilitary targets? Any civilian deaths?"

Tedder paused, and when he answered, his voice was softer. "From the photos, it appears the working-class district of San Lorenzo was inadvertently hit pretty hard. I'd guess a thousand or more civilians were killed."

"Goddamnit, Ted, you promised me the attack would have minimal impact on civilians other than those working in the rail yards!"

"Don't get on your high horse with me!" Tedder replied firmly. "We're at war with Italy! I'm not going to lose sleep over some noncombatant deaths. We didn't try to kill innocent people, like the Nazis have in England."

"What about religious sites?"

"The Basilica of San Lorenzo was heavily damaged."

"Any other collateral damage?"

"No, and the Vatican was never in danger. Look, Ike, the military value of attacking the rail yards justifies the accidental death of some civilians and the destruction of a church. War is a nasty business."

Eisenhower knew Tedder was right: he couldn't allow his compassion for the deaths of civilians to keep him from making the hard decisions necessary to win the war. "I'm not getting squeamish on you. I know it's impossible to avoid killing innocent people in war."

When he got off the phone, Eisenhower sought out Summersby at her desk in the hall of his office suite, where she was now working as a secretary in addition to her duties as a chauffeur. She answered, on Eisenhower's behalf, the hundred-plus letters he received monthly from Americans back home. She had proven adept at the job.

"Kay, I need some exercise. Alert the stable hands at Sailor's Delight we're coming out."

She gave him a shrewd look. It was unlike Eisenhower to go for an unexpected ride. But all she said was, "Of course, Ike."

Eisenhower was on his Arabian, galloping across the landscape, reflecting on the harshness of warfare. *Sherman said, "War is hell," and it truly is.* He grunted. *Tens of thousands of innocent people will likely die at the hands of my armies before the war is won.* He looked over at Summersby, so graceful on her horse. *I'm lucky to have her in my army family. What a beautiful counterweight she is to the ugliness of war.*

After an hour of vigorous riding, the two found their way to the quiet swale Summersby had discovered, a place where they wouldn't be observed by roving patrols.

Summersby pulled a blanket, a bottle of wine, a corkscrew, and two wineglasses from her saddlebag. After the two of them spread out the blanket and sat down, Eisenhower uncorked the wine and poured them each a glass.

"Kay, I feel bad I've been so wrapped up with the war, dealing with one crisis after another, that I haven't asked how you're coping with Dick's death."

Summersby took a sip of wine. "It's . . . been hard. The memories I have of my time with Dick are only happy ones. We talked about returning to the States after the war and having a family."

She began crying softly.

Eisenhower moved beside her and put his arm around her shoulder. After a few minutes, she pulled a handkerchief from her pocket and dabbed her tears.

Eisenhower removed his arm and sipped his wine as he thought about Kay. In the six weeks since Arnold's death, they had not been intimate. Yet their relationship had grown deeper. She had volunteered to be his ghostwriter and respond to the wide variety of letters he received, from mothers anxious about their sons, to citizens offering moral support to the commanding general. Summersby put aside the most moving letters—the ones from parents grieving the death of a loved one. Eisenhower responded personally to those.

He had assumed when the war ended, Kay would go off with Dick, and he would return to Mamie. But now, Arnold's death changed the equation. *Kay is available! Do I want to spend the rest of my life with her?*

The thought was tantalizing, but Eisenhower checked himself. He couldn't bring himself to be so cruel to Mamie. He had stretched his sense of morality to the breaking point, rationalizing a wartime relationship with Kay. *I can't allow my attraction to Kay to destroy my marriage to a wonderful and loyal woman.*

"Ike, you've drifted away," Summersby mumbled quietly, inserting her presence into his thoughts.

"I was thinking about you, Kay."

She looked surprised but pleased. "I hope they were nice thoughts."

"Of course. When I'm with you, I relax. The time we spend together helps me cope with the burdens of command. You're a godsend to me, Kay."

"Hearing that makes me happy."

Summersby reached out and squeezed his hand. Her touch never failed to excite him, and he felt a surge of electricity.

Eisenhower stared into her green eyes and felt an irresistible desire to make love to her again. He knew it was an immoral thought, but his willpower to resist the temptation was weak. He gently pulled her head toward him, and they kissed, softly at first, then passionately.

When they pulled apart, he said, "Kay, I've missed having you in my arms."

She gazed at him for a long time. "I've missed being in your arms, Ike."

That night, Summersby found her way to Eisenhower's bedroom.

The next day, Alexander, Tedder, and Cunningham were in Algiers to discuss post-Husky operations. While hard fighting continued in Sicily, a decision needed to be made on what to do next.

Eisenhower opened the meeting in the Paris conference room. "I propose invading Italy as quickly as possible once Sicily is in our hands. Does anyone disagree?"

When no one spoke up, Eisenhower said, "My preference is to invade as far up the Italian Peninsula as possible."

"From the navy's perspective, we need air cover for the landings," replied Cunningham.

"Ted, can you provide air cover as far north as Naples?" asked Eisenhower.

"No, Naples is too far," Tedder responded. "The Gulf of Salerno is as far north as we can go, and that's pushing the envelope. Our fighter planes will only have ten minutes to engage the enemy before having to return to bases in Sicily for refueling."

"ABC, what's the status of our landing craft?" asked Alexander.

"We're wearing out our landing craft supplying Patton's army. It's imperative the landing craft be repaired and serviced before Italy is invaded."

"How much time will that take?" asked Eisenhower.

"Thirty days from the time they're taken out of service in Sicily."

The meeting lasted for hours as the attendees explored various possibilities for invading Italy. Eisenhower ordered staff studies be made of every option.

CHAPTER 48

In Sicily, Patton fought his way northwest through difficult, mountainous terrain with spectacular speed and captured the ancient city of Palermo. Patton's mantra of constantly attacking paid huge dividends. In sharp contrast, Montgomery's more conservative approach of only attacking when he was fully prepared led to slow going against tenacious German resistance on both sides of Mount Etna.

Eisenhower was pleased Old Blood and Guts was proving himself on the battlefield. The American army that struggled in Tunisia had come of age!

By the end of July, Patton was driving toward Messina from the west, facing Germans holding strong defensive positions while Montgomery, with renewed vigor, was attacking along the east coast. The race to capture Messina was on between the two egotistical generals.

Eisenhower was having breakfast in his Carthage villa when he received a call from Smith in Algiers.

"Mussolini is out of power!"

"That's great news! What happened?"

"King Victor Emanuel announced Mussolini has resigned. He's being replaced by Field Marshal Pietro Badoglio, who issued a release saying the Italians are going to continue the war fighting with their German ally."

Eisenhower expressed his skepticism. "I don't believe for a second Il Duce would voluntarily give up power."

"There's a rumor Mussolini was arrested," Smith concurred. "There has been no public sighting of him."

Eisenhower was excited. Badoglio might claim to want to continue the war, but the Italian army's fervor for fighting was dwindling by the day. Was there a way to accelerate Italy's exit from the war?

Eisenhower quickly arranged a meeting with Harold Macmillan, who was in nearby Tunis.

Macmillan arrived in Carthage in high spirits, carrying a bottle of champagne. "The first of the tyrants has fallen!"

Eisenhower smiled. "It's the beginning of the end of Fascism in Italy!"

After Macmillan opened the champagne and they toasted to Mussolini's downfall, Eisenhower asked, "Do you think I could make a public statement encouraging the Italians to initiate peace discussions? I want the Italian people to pressure the King to negotiate for peace."

"That's a capital idea!"

"My concern is Roosevelt's unconditional surrender requirement leaves little room for negotiations. Could we structure a peace deal downplaying unconditional surrender?"

"After the Darlan matter, I'm afraid we're going to need approval from Churchill and Roosevelt for any peace overtures."

Eisenhower sighed. "I guess it was wishful thinking that we could take the initiative and get the peace train rolling without the inevitable delays of involving Washington and London."

The two men spent hours brainstorming ways to exploit Mussolini's downfall, concluding Eisenhower should make a public broadcast to the Italian people. They prepared a draft speech, emphasizing "unconditional surrender did not mean dishonorable obligations would be imposed," and sent it to Roosevelt and Churchill for approval. Attached were the peace terms Eisenhower proposed offering the Italians.

Days passed as cables flew back and forth among London, Washington, and Algiers on whether Eisenhower could broadcast a speech, and if so, what he could say. Finally, after Churchill revised the draft, Eisenhower received approval to make a propaganda speech along the lines he and Macmillan had proposed. He recorded the speech, and it was repeatedly broadcast into Italy.

Eisenhower's request for peace terms to offer the Italians, either the ones he proposed or others acceptable to Churchill and Roosevelt, went unanswered. He was deluged with contradictory cables from Washington and London on how to deal with Italy. By the beginning of August, the incessant messaging had worn him down.

While the interminable Italian debate consumed Eisenhower's time and attention, the battle continued to rage in Sicily. On August 2, he got out of Algiers and flew to Sicily.

Patton met him at an airfield outside of twenty-seven-hundred-year-old Palermo, Sicily's largest city.

"Welcome to American-controlled Sicily!" Patton said as he shook Eisenhower's hand.

"Georgie, you're doing a great job here."

At Patton's headquarters, the two generals studied a map of the German defensive line that ran from Mount Etna to the west coast.

"The Krauts are dug in on the high ground," Patton said. "The hill town of Troina is the anchor of their Etna Line. It's been hard going rooting those Nazi bastards out of their prepared positions. The frustrating thing is once we push them off a ridge, the sons of bitches fall back to the next ridge, and we have to do it all over again!"

"What progress are you making on the coastal road?"

"Slower than I would like. As they retreat, the Germans blow every bridge. A lot of the road is carved out of the sides of cliffs, and sometimes their demolitions cause the whole fucking roadbed to drop into the sea! You should pin some medals on our engineers, Ike. They've worked miracles in reconstructing the coastal road."

For lunch, Patton took his guest to the King of Sicily's palace. "Being a conquering general, I felt it appropriate to live in the King's palace!"

"We're liberating, not conquering," Eisenhower corrected.

"A distinction without meaning. I'm following in the footsteps of prior conquerors of this island—the Greeks, Romans, Arabs, Normans, Spaniards, and many others—and now the Americans!"

Eisenhower found Patton's fighting abilities admirable but his tendency to be pompous irritating. Patton led him into an enormous room. Its walls, arches, and ceiling were adorned with leopards, lions, peacocks, centaurs, and bowmen confronting one another among fruit and palm trees.

"This is the Ruggero Room. I thought you'd enjoy having lunch here. I had my chef prepare two famous Sicilian dishes for us."

Eisenhower turned his attention to his lunch of red prawns and ricotta-filled arancini. The food was delicious.

After lunch, Patton took Eisenhower to the Cappella Palatina, the royal chapel built by the Normans in the 1100s. Every square inch of the walls, ceiling, and floor was a dazzling work of art. The chapel's painted wooden honeycombed ceiling was Arabic, the wall mosaics inlaid with precious stones the work of Greek Byzantine artisans, and the intricately laid patterned marble floor the work of Norman stonemasons.

Eisenhower found the mosaics, which appeared to shimmer and oscillate, mesmerizing. "Georgie, this is a special place!"

"It truly is. I've never seen a more beautiful building."

For once, Patton displayed a bit of humility, lapsing into a respectful silence.

On August 6, Eisenhower was back in Algiers. He received a cable from Patton:

I've captured Troina and broken the Etna Line! I'm moving on Messina.

Two hours later, a cable arrived from Montgomery:

```
I've captured Catania! I'm advancing on Messina.
```

Eisenhower smiled. The end was near for the Germans in Sicily.

CHAPTER 49

Once again, Eisenhower approved an operation that could spectacularly fail. Operation Avalanche would land Mark Wayne Clark's Fifth Army on Italy's Gulf of Salerno beaches. The objective was to quickly move north and capture the port of Naples and the Foggia airfield complex.

Preparations for Overlord, the invasion of France in 1944, were draining resources from the Mediterranean. A lack of shipping, particularly landing craft, meant that only a weak invasion force of four divisions, two American and two British, could be landed at Salerno. In contrast, seven divisions had hit the Sicilian beaches. Eisenhower feared a powerful counterattack could drive the Allied soldiers into the sea.

Because there wasn't enough shipping to include Montgomery's army in the Salerno assault, Eisenhower was dividing his forces, violating the doctrine of concentration of force. Prior to Avalanche, Montgomery would cross the two-mile-wide Strait of Messina and attack the Italian toe in Calabria.

Montgomery had to attack before Clark, because Montgomery's landing craft were needed for Avalanche. Once in Italy, Montgomery would move three hundred miles up the Italian Peninsula to Salerno to support Clark. The separated Allied armies would be dangerously weak until they joined forces.

Napoleon had said Italy, like a boot, should be entered from the top. *Is it a bad omen I can't follow Napoleon's maxim?*

On August 7, Patton won the race to Messina, barely beating Montgomery. The Battle of Sicily had been won!

Eisenhower basked in the glow of victory until a disturbing report reached his desk from an army doctor in Sicily.

General Patton, in two separate incidents, slapped hospitalized GIs suffering from shell shock. Hospital staff and patients witnessed his outrageous conduct.

Eisenhower reared back in his chair, pushing the memo away with his hands. Striking an enlisted man was a court-martial offense. If Patton were a run-of-the-mill general, he would sack him!

But Georgie was a special general, a spirited warrior with an inherent feel for strategy and tactics who got the most out of his men. And there was a lot of war yet to be fought. *I don't want to lose Patton. I'll investigate the incidents. If they prove true, I'll give Patton a real jacking up!*

Two hours later, Smith came into his office.

"Quentin Reynolds of *Collier's* magazine and Demaree Bess of the *Saturday Evening Post* are here and want to see you. They just returned from Sicily and are hot on the Patton story."

Eisenhower knew and respected both reporters and was comfortable dealing with the press. "I'll talk to them. Bring them in."

Once Smith ushered in the two men, Reynolds took the lead.

"Ike, are you aware of allegations Patton slapped and cursed out two soldiers in army hospitals?"

"I first heard about the incidents a few hours ago."

"What are you going to do?"

"Investigate them, of course."

"We interviewed the medical personnel who witnessed the incidents," Reynolds said, "and they corroborated Patton's misconduct."

"Quentin, I'd like to hear their version of events."

Reynolds looked at his notebook. "On August 3, Patton approached Private Charles Kuhl, who was sitting on a stool in a field-hospital tent. Kuhl told Patton he wasn't wounded, but he just couldn't take it anymore. Whereupon Patton slapped Kuhl in the face with his gloves, grabbed him by the collar, dragged him to the tent entrance, and shoved him out while screaming he was 'a coward,' 'a gutless bastard,' and that 'he was going back to the front.' Five witnesses verified these facts."

"That's inexcusable conduct," said Eisenhower.

"Do you want to hear the second incident?" Reynolds asked.

"Yes."

"On August 10, Patton visited a different field hospital. He encountered Private Paul Bennett, who was sitting in a corner, shivering. He told Patton he wasn't wounded—that his nerves were shot, and he couldn't stand the shelling anymore. Patton slapped the soldier across the face, screaming he was 'a goddamn coward.' He then slapped Bennett a second time, knocking his helmet off. Patton continued to berate him and said, 'He should be put in front of a firing squad,'" Reynolds recounted. "Whereupon Patton pulled out a pistol and threatened to shoot Bennett. A doctor stepped in and prevented any further violence on Patton's part. Patton left the tent screaming to 'send the coward back to the front lines.'"

"That's disgusting, brutal behavior." Eisenhower's neck had turned red. "If my investigation verifies what you're saying, I'll discipline Patton severely. Such conduct is intolerable."

"Do you think Patton should be sent home in disgrace?" asked Bess.

"I don't. Patton is one of our best generals," replied Eisenhower. "Like Lincoln said of US Grant, he fights. Patton's invaluable to the Allied cause."

"Are you going to censor the story?" asked Reynolds.

"I'm not a big believer in censorship," Eisenhower said with a shake of his head. "I would ask you to not report it until I complete the investigation. At that point, I promise to meet with you and fully disclose what the investigation reveals."

Reynolds and Bess turned toward each other and had a brief,

whispered conversation. Reynolds turned back to Eisenhower. "We know you're a straight shooter. We'll sit on the story for now."

Not long after the reporters left Eisenhower's office, intelligence chief Ken Strong entered, smiling ear to ear. "We've had an Italian peace overture!"

Finally! thought Eisenhower. "Tell me about it."

"General Giuseppe Castellano, who is on the Italian army's general staff, saw the British ambassador in Madrid. Castellano is continuing to Lisbon as part of a diplomatic mission and wants us to send a representative to negotiate a peace deal. He said Badoglio wants peace but is afraid of the Germans, who have twelve divisions in Italy. Badoglio feels powerless to act until the Allies invade, at which time Italy will switch sides and join the fight against the Nazis."

Eisenhower was ecstatic. "Ken, prepare a cable for Churchill and Roosevelt. I want to send you and Beetle to negotiate with Castellano, and we need approved peace terms ASAP."

The next day, Eisenhower received a cable from Roosevelt:

```
You have approval to send representatives to meet with
Castellano in Lisbon. They should provide him the "short
terms" military surrender agreement you drafted. I'm in
conference with Churchill in Quebec City. We'll prepare
a "long terms" surrender agreement covering economic,
political, and financial terms that the Italians will have
to accept sight unseen and sign at a later date. You have
no authority to modify surrender terms.
```

Although disappointed he had no latitude within which to negotiate, Eisenhower took some solace that the "short terms" military surrender he had proposed had been accepted. Under the "short terms," the Italians were to surrender their armed forces, send their navy to Allied-controlled territory, cooperate with the Allies in facilitating an invasion of Italy, and aid the Allies in resisting the Germans.

Eisenhower called Strong and Smith into his office. "We've been

given no wiggle room to negotiate. The Italians must accept unconditional surrender."

Smith scowled. "If we've no room to negotiate, why in the hell are
you sending me to Portugal? I'm up to my eyeballs in work here!"

"I'm sending you with Ken because I want our meeting with
Castellano to include representatives of both Allied nations."

"When do we leave?" asked Strong.

"Tomorrow, and only pack civilian clothes."

Smith protested. "I don't have any civilian clothes!"

Eisenhower grinned. "You need to buy some in a hurry."

The next day, Eisenhower went into Smith's office to check out his
new wardrobe. He burst into laughter at the sight of Smith sitting at
his desk wearing a Tyrolean hat with a feather. "Beetle, you look ridiculous in that hat!"

"I didn't have time to be choosy," Smith said defensively.

"Get rid of the feather and you'll look a lot better."

As Smith lifted his arms to take off the hat, his suit coat opened,
revealing holsters with pistols under his armpits.

"Planning for a shoot-out with the bad guys?"

"Always good to be prepared for any eventuality."

CHAPTER 50

Eisenhower handwrote Patton a blistering letter:

There is no excuse for brutality, abuse of the sick,
nor exhibition of uncontrollable temper in front of
subordinates. . . . No letter I have been called upon to write
in my military career has caused me the mental anguish
of this one, not only because of my long and deep personal
friendship for you but because of my admiration for your
military qualities; but I assure you that the conduct such as
described in the accompanying report will not be tolerated in
this theater no matter who the offender may be.

He ordered Patton to submit a report on the incidents, and to apologize to the soldiers and medical personnel who witnessed his outbursts. Eisenhower decided to make it a personal, not an official, reprimand so Patton's formal record would remain clean. He gave the letter to his surgeon general, Frederick Blessé, to personally deliver. Blessé was tasked with conducting a thorough and impartial investigation.

In his response to Eisenhower, Patton acknowledged his actions were wrong, and apologized for causing grief to "you, a man to whom I owe everything."

Blessé's report corroborated the details Reynolds had provided.

Eisenhower had Smith set up the meeting with Bess and Reynolds. When the reporters entered his office, he handed them a copy of Blessé's report.

Bess was the first to finish. "Ike, are we free to run with the story?"

Eisenhower put his hands on his desk and stared at the reporters before speaking. "Patton has been disciplined and is appropriately remorseful. His deep emotions and calculated boldness make him a remarkable battlefield leader. The more he drives his men, the quicker victory is secured, which means fewer casualties for our brave fighting men. The American army is going to need Patton in the great battles to come." Eisenhower took a deep breath. "I ask you to keep this story secret; if not, we could lose Patton. The free world needs his military genius deployed on the battlefield. I'm asking you both, as American patriots, to suppress the story."

"What about the First Amendment?" asked Reynolds. "Patton's conduct was deplorable; the public has a right to know!"

"In peacetime I'd agree with you one hundred percent," replied Eisenhower. "But we're in a struggle with forces of evil that want to enslave the world's population!" Eisenhower waved his arm for emphasis. "If the Nazis prevail in Europe, Hitler will set his sights on the Western Hemisphere. To protect the homeland, we must secure victory in Europe!"

After an hour of contentious debate, Reynolds and Bess made a gentlemen's agreement to sit on the Patton story.

Eisenhower was so eager to be debriefed on the Castellano meeting that he met Smith and Strong at the airport on their return from Lisbon. He didn't waste time on pleasantries.

"Are the Italians ready to surrender?" Eisenhower asked.

"Castellano didn't have authority to discuss surrender," replied Smith.

"What in the hell is going on?" Eisenhower sputtered. The news was stupefying.

"Castellano stated his mission was to negotiate Italy's joining the Allies to fight the Nazis," explained Strong.

Smith added, "The Italians are more afraid of the Germans than they are of us. Italy is effectively an occupied country. The Nazis will overthrow the Badoglio government if they learn the Italians have surrendered."

"How many men do the Germans have in Italy?" asked Eisenhower.

"More than four hundred thousand," replied Strong.

"Goddamnit, Ken, that's a hell of a lot more than you previously estimated!" Eisenhower felt his blood pressure rising.

"Hitler is pouring troops into Italy," replied Strong. "He's determined to fight in Italy."

Eisenhower thought about Avalanche. It was a high-risk operation before the Germans built up their forces in Italy. *The possibility of a disaster has grown exponentially!*

He focused his mind on a peace deal. "How did Castellano react when he learned there was no flexibility to negotiate surrender terms?"

"At first, he was stunned it was a take-it-or-leave-it proposition," answered Smith. "After nine hours of conferencing with us, he seemed resigned they were the only terms the Italians were going to get."

"Do you think they'll surrender?" asked Eisenhower.

"I think so," replied Smith. "Their options are limited, and I sense there is not much fight left in the Italians, given the tremendous losses they've suffered in Africa and on the Russian front."

"When do we get an answer?" Eisenhower pressed.

"It will take a week for Castellano to make his return to Rome. He's traveling with a diplomatic delegation so as not to arouse German suspicions," replied Strong. "The Italians have until August 30 to signal acceptance of surrender terms. If it's a yes, there'll be a meeting in Sicily on August 31 to sign the short-terms surrender agreement."

With the battle for Sicily over, Eisenhower prepared efficiency reports on his American subordinates for Marshall. When it came to Omar Bradley, who had performed well in Tunisia and Sicily, Eisenhower was effusive in his praise, writing, "He has brains, a capacity for leadership, and a thorough understanding of modern warfare."

Eisenhower struggled with his rating for Patton, who had performed well in Tunisia and brilliantly in Sicily. Eisenhower first chose to address Patton's sterling qualities—his high energy, tactical skill, constant aggressiveness, and relentless pursuit of victory. He then described Patton's weaknesses "as an impulsive temper that sometimes led to abusive conduct of individual soldiers." He chose not to directly address the slapping incidents.

The next day, Eisenhower received a cable from Marshall:

Please recommend a general to lead US ground troops in the Overlord invasion.

It was a binary choice, Patton or Bradley. Before the slapping incident, Eisenhower would have recommended Patton. But his friend's loss of control in Sicily was troubling and could not be overlooked. So was Patton's loose tongue. In Tunisia, Patton openly criticized many senior generals, both British and American.

Eisenhower pensively twirled a pencil between his fingers. Bradley was Patton's intellectual equal. And unlike Patton, the Missourian had an even disposition and was a quietly solid leader. While Bradley lacked Patton's constant aggressiveness, he was less likely to fracture the alliance by attacking British leadership.

Eisenhower lit a cigarette and began pacing as he contemplated his choice. The answer came to him with clarity.

He sat down and prepared a cable to Marshall. After summarizing his thoughts, Eisenhower concluded, "The truth of the matter is that you should take Bradley."

On August 25, Smith entered Eisenhower's office with a puzzled expression. "A second Italian general, Giacomo Zanussi, appeared at the

British embassy in Lisbon to discuss a peace agreement, and he knows nothing about the Castellano mission!"

"What the hell are the Italians up to?" Eisenhower inquired, bewildered. "Did he have a letter of introduction from Badoglio?"

"No."

"This is bizarre."

"The British told Zanussi about the earlier meeting with Castellano and that there was nothing for them to discuss. They asked Zanussi to stay in Lisbon in the event circumstances change."

Two days later, Roosevelt's and Churchill's "long terms" arrived from Quebec City. Eisenhower put on his glasses and read the twelve-page document.

The Allies would be an occupying power, with total control over Italy's government, people, and economy. Italian merchant ships, fishing vessels, and the national bank would be under Allied control. Italy's newspapers, radio stations, and performing arts events would be subject to Allied censorship. The list of harsh conditions went on and on, page after page. When Eisenhower was done reading, he took a deep breath. *Clearly it would be best to get the short-term surrender agreement signed before the Italians see the "long terms."*

An hour later, a grim-faced Smith entered Eisenhower's office.

"The British ambassador in Lisbon is a fucking idiot! He gave Zanussi the long terms."

"What?" Eisenhower yelled. "If those severe terms get back to Rome, there'll be no peace deal!"

Smith got a cagey look in his eyes. "I have an idea how we can prevent that from happening."

"What is it?"

"How about I ask the British commander of Gibraltar to invite Zanussi for a tour of that famous military base? Then we make it so that Zanussi's return flight ends up in Algiers, where we can question him and prevent the transmission of the 'long terms' to Rome."

"He may have already sent the agreement to Rome."

"I don't think so. He told the British his mission was secret, and the Italian embassy had no knowledge of why he's in Lisbon. The only way Zanussi can get the long terms to Rome is to personally transport them."

"Okay, Beetle, execute your Machiavellian plan!"

Smith's gambit worked like a charm. The next evening, Zanussi and an aide, after enjoying a tour of Gibraltar, ended up in the Hotel Saint George's Paris conference room. There, Smith and Strong interrogated the general, and the information they extracted was disheartening: the "long terms" were sure to receive a hostile reception in Rome.

After being briefed on the results, Eisenhower met with Zanussi. An American officer who spoke Italian served as an interpreter.

He began the meeting trying to establish a measure of trust. "General Zanussi, you must be aware in Sicily, the Allies have treated civilians and captured Italian soldiers fairly."

Zanussi slowly nodded his head. "That is true, General Eisenhower."

"The 'long terms' in isolation appear harsh, and I'm worried if they're sent to Rome, the opportunity for peace will be lost. That would lead to more brave Italian soldiers losing their lives for no good reason. Your government must trust the Allies will act in good faith, like we have in Sicily, and that we will treat the Italian people fairly and with compassion."

Zanussi took his time before responding. "I trust you, General Eisenhower."

"Will you work with me in helping achieve peace?"

Another long pause ensued.

"Yes, General, because it's best for my people."

At Eisenhower's direction, Zanussi prepared a letter to the man who had sent him on the peace mission, General d'Armada Ambrosio, chief of Commando Supremo. In it he advocated acceptance of the "short terms" and urged Ambrosio to "believe in the good faith of the Allied governments." He did not attach the "long terms."

Zanussi gave his aide the letter. Smith arranged transport for the aide to Lisbon from where he could make his way to Rome.

CHAPTER 51

On August 29, Eisenhower flew to Catania, Sicily's second-largest city. As his plane turned over the Ionian Sea and made its landing approach, he marveled at the massive size of volcanic Mount Etna that towered behind Catania.

Montgomery met him at the airfield. "Ike, what a good fellow you are to pay me a visit!"

"I enjoy being in the field visiting my commanders."

The two got into an open car, and Montgomery's driver took off at hair-raising speed along the narrow, hilly coastal road. When they reached Taormina, a popular prewar European honeymoon destination, they stopped for lunch in a modern home built on a cliff high above the sea.

The two generals enjoyed the scenery from the large picture windows. Far below was a small harbor with fishing boats, where waves lapped against rock outcroppings. To the west was majestic snow-capped Mount Etna.

Eisenhower was impressed. "These are spectacular views, Monty!"

"When my staff heard Patton was living in a palace in Palermo, they found this house for me. Usually, I prefer to sleep in my caravan when I'm in the field. But this is such a beautiful spot, I decided to pamper myself and stay here."

Eisenhower heard a bark and looked down. A black-and-tan cocker spaniel was looking up at Montgomery, who bent down and scratched the dog's ears.

"Ike, this is Rommel."

Eisenhower bent down and petted the dog. "Is he named for the German general?"

"He is," replied Montgomery without elaboration.

During their lunch of Spaghettini alla Siracusana, Eisenhower said, "I'm surprised you haven't already crossed the Strait of Messina."

"I don't know why you'd think that," replied Montgomery in a clipped tone. "I'm embarking on a major continental campaign. I need my administrative tail nice and tidy before I start."

"I thought that because I've told you to move with utmost speed," Eisenhower said, arching an eyebrow.

"I'm moving as quickly as practicable."

"Well, can you speed up the process?" Eisenhower urged. "Ultra intelligence suggests the Germans are not going to defend the Italian toe."

"I'll cross when I'm ready," Montgomery snapped.

Eisenhower tried to control his temper. "Speed is of the essence! Your landing craft are needed for Avalanche. The sooner you cross, the quicker you'll get to Salerno."

"I will not be rushed! You—you Americans are always in a hurry!" Montgomery sputtered. "Meticulous preparations are key to a successful attack."

"Sometimes the need for speed trumps perfect preparations," Eisenhower said, his voice rising.

The English general glared at Eisenhower, setting down his fork and pushing away his plate. "You still have a lot to learn when it comes to combat. My experience trumps your inexperience. I'll cross when I deem fit."

Eisenhower's neck turned red, and his anger boiled up and over. He leaned forward and through clenched teeth snarled, "You can't talk to me that way! I'm your commanding officer!"

Montgomery's head snapped back like he had been slapped in the face. He appraised Eisenhower intently before responding. "I apologize if I offended you. I was only speaking the truth about our comparative experiences."

Eisenhower took a deep breath and sat back. His approach to

subordinate commanders was to give them a mission and allow them discretion to carry it out. Montgomery's arrogant exercise of that discretion was trying his patience. "I need a firm date for your crossing into Italy."

Montgomery was silent for a long time. "I'll cross in three days."

"Good."

From Sicily, Eisenhower flew to Mostaganem, a port city in northwest Algeria, for an Avalanche briefing with Clark, who met him at the airfield.

"Have the Eyeties agreed to surrender?" asked Clark.

"No, not yet."

Clark's face fell. "Our four divisions look mighty puny compared with the combined German and Italian forces we'll be facing."

"I know, Wayne; I know. My gut tells me the Italians will surrender before the invasion."

"Good God, I hope so."

At his headquarters, Clark took Eisenhower to his Map Room. There, he pointed to Salerno Bay.

"We're landing on a thirty-five-mile front. Two divisions of the British Tenth Corps will land north of the Sele River. One division of the American Sixth Corps will land south of the Sele River at Paestum. I'm holding the other US division as a floating reserve. A ranger force under Bill Darby and a commando unit under Bob Laycock will land on the Sorrento Peninsula and capture the mountain passes leading to Naples. We're dropping the Eighty-Second Airborne on the Naples plain to block an attack from the Italian garrison in the city."

After studying the map closely, Eisenhower asked, "There appears to be a gap around the Sele River between the British and the Americans. Is that a potential problem?"

"There's an eight-mile gap caused by sandbars at the mouth of the river. I want to avoid landing craft getting stuck on the sandbars. We'll close that gap once we're on land." Clark turned toward Eisenhower. "Is there any way to scrounge up more shipping so we could add another division to the assault?"

"The shipping limitations are real, Wayne. It's simply impossible to put more punch in the invasion. If you face strong opposition, you'll have to dig in and hold on until reinforcements arrive."

"This is a hell of a risky operation, Ike," Clark said, running a hand through his hair. "I'm getting more nervous by the day. I'm fearful we won't be strong enough to withstand a counterattack."

Eisenhower shared Clark's fears but knew it would be a mistake to show it. He needed to calm his friend's anxiety.

"The navy's big guns saved Patton's beachhead in Sicily. I'm counting on naval gun support to stop a counterattack against your beachhead. I'm confident you'll succeed, Wayne."

On August 30, Castellano sent a message requesting a meeting. The next day, Smith and Strong met him in a tent in an olive grove near Alexander's headquarters in Cassibile, Sicily. Eisenhower remained in Algiers, anxiously awaiting the outcome.

A cable came from Smith:

```
The Allies must agree to secure Rome from the Nazis for the
Italians to agree to surrender. I proposed to Castellano
dropping the Eighty-Second Airborne near Rome on the eve
of Avalanche, to help the Italian troops protect Badoglio's
government from the Nazis. Castellano believes such a
commitment would seal the deal.
```

Eisenhower threaded his fingers together as he thought things through. If he pulled the Eighty-Second away from Clark, his friend would be furious. But if the Italians didn't surrender and fought beside the Germans, the Axis forces near Salerno would outnumber Clark's men, and Avalanche would likely be a disaster. He had to get the Italians out of the war.

Eisenhower got up from his desk and walked to a wall map of Italy. Rome was 150 miles from Salerno. The Eighty-Second would be isolated deep behind German lines. If the Italian divisions around Rome were overwhelmed by the Germans, the soldiers of the Eighty-Second would end up either dead or in a Nazi prison camp. Agreeing to Smith's proposal was a huge gamble with the lives of crack paratroopers.

Eisenhower rubbed his lucky coins. Knowing what risks to take was an essential part of a commanding general's job. Thus far his gambles had paid dividends.

Eisenhower sent Smith a cable:

```
Offer the Eighty-Second to the Italians.
```

Castellano returned to Rome for consultations and was back in Cassibile on September 1. Eisenhower was in Algiers waiting to fly to Sicily to witness the surrender signing. A cable arrived from Smith:

```
Castellano still doesn't have authority to sign the
surrender document!
```

A furious Eisenhower fired off a reply to Smith:

```
Italy must surrender! Clark's troops are hitting the
Salerno beaches in eight days. Pressure Castellano to get
signing authority!
```

Time passed slowly for Eisenhower. At 9:00 p.m., Smith cabled:

```
Castellano has authority to sign! Be here at 11:00 a.m.
tomorrow for the signing ceremony.
```

As soon as Eisenhower touched down in Cassibile, Smith pulled him aside. "You won't believe the shenanigans we've gone through to force the Italians to surrender! Macmillan, Alex, and I hatched a plot right out of a Hollywood film!" He laughed. "We had Alex show up, announcing he'd come to meet the Italian general who signed the instrument of surrender. Macmillan replied that Castellano claimed he lacked authority to sign. Alex glared at Castellano and exclaimed he must be a spy and we needed to arrest him! He yelled that the Italians had engaged in perfidy, and the Allies would ruthlessly retaliate! Rome would be reduced to ruins!

"Castellano turned as white as a sheet. Macmillan, in his smooth diplomatic voice, told Castellano he must contact Rome and secure signing authority to avoid the destruction of Rome. Castellano agreed, saying there was no other choice."

"Thank God your amateur theatrics worked!" Eisenhower chuckled. "I love the creative ingenuity."

Smith led Eisenhower to the tent where Castellano was waiting. There, he shook hands with the diminutive Italian general, who was dressed in a civilian business suit.

"General Castellano, thank you for your contributions to securing peace. I'm happy our two great nations will no longer be at war."

After listening to the translation, Castellano responded, "General Eisenhower, we're ready to join the fight against the Nazis. I look forward to welcoming the Eighty-Second Airborne to Rome."

Quickly Smith and Castellano signed the "short terms." A bottle of scotch appeared, and there was a celebratory toast.

Eisenhower was on his way back to Algiers when Smith handed Castellano the draconian "long terms."

CHAPTER 52

On September 6, Smith and Castellano finalized the surrender arrangements. Badoglio and Eisenhower would simultaneously announce on the eve of the invasion Italy had surrendered. The ports of Taranto and Brindisi would be opened on D-Day to the Allied navy, and the Italian fleet would sail to Malta.

The next morning, General Maxwell Taylor of the Eighty-Second Airborne arrived at the Hotel Saint George for a hastily arranged meeting with Eisenhower.

"Max, what's on your mind?"

Taylor, a broad-shouldered man with dark, penetrating eyes, spoke with an urgent intensity. "I've spent the last three days in Sicily working out details of our Rome deployment with Castellano, and frankly I have reservations about Italian commitments."

"What's bothering you?"

"It's a complicated plan. Because of insufficient lift capacity, the drop is being spread over three days at two airfields twenty-five miles from Rome. Everything we've asked for Castellano cavalierly agrees to."

"Such as?"

"When I asked for six hundred trucks to transport my men from the airfields to Rome, Castellano immediately said yes without consulting anyone. Given the sorry state of the Italian army's trucks during the battle for Sicily, his quick answer raised a red flag."

"You're doubting his word?"

"My fear is the Italians are not organized and strong enough to make the plan work. I want to go to Rome tomorrow to make sure the promised arrangements are in place and make changes if they're not. If the Italians are lacking the ability to honor Castellano's promises, the attack should be called off."

"Do you have a plan on how you're going to get in and out of Italy?"

"If you approve it, Ike, I'm going to pose as a pilot who was captured by the Italian army after his plane was shot down. Castellano agreed to have two of his soldiers serve as my guards."

"Does Castellano know you doubt his word?"

"No, he thinks I just need to coordinate technical details of the drop."

"Okay, Max, do your inspection trip."

As Taylor stood to leave, Eisenhower held up his hand for him to wait. He took a pencil and wrote on a piece of paper "Situation Innocuous" and handed the paper to Taylor. "If you use this code phrase in a cable to me, I'll cancel the drop."

Early on September 8, Eisenhower left Algiers for his advance command post in Carthage. When he got there, he had a message to call Smith. Eisenhower immediately placed the call.

Beetle's voice thundered across the phone line. "That son of a bitch Badoglio wants the paratrooper movement canceled because the Italians can't guarantee the airfields! Badoglio won't announce the surrender because it would provoke the fucking Germans! And we received a cable from Taylor with the 'Situation Innocuous' phrase!"

Eisenhower absorbed the bombshell news. "Is Castellano still in Sicily?"

"Yes."

"Have him brought to Carthage. And cancel the airdrop on Rome."

"I could strangle Castellano for his false promises of cooperation!"

"He may not have intentionally lied. The Italian army is a disorganized mess."

Once Castellano got to Carthage, Eisenhower had him escorted by armed guards to a meeting room where the commanding general was flanked by Alexander and Cunningham, both of whom looked like they wanted to rip the little Italian to pieces.

"I've sent a message to Marshal Badoglio," Eisenhower said sternly. "I'm broadcasting the existence of the surrender agreement at six thirty p.m., as agreed. If the Italian government or any part of its armed forces fails to cooperate and honor all the commitments you negotiated on its behalf, I'll publish to the world Italy has broken its solemn agreement to surrender. Be assured Italy and its representatives who deceived us will pay a heavy price! I suggest you contact your government and persuade it to honor its obligations."

Castellano's hands were shaking. "I'll do my best, General Eisenhower," he said quietly.

Hours ticked by with no word from Badoglio. At precisely 6:30 p.m., Radio-Algiers broadcast Eisenhower's prerecorded message:

> *This is General Dwight D. Eisenhower, commander in chief of the Allied forces. The Italian government has surrendered its armed forces unconditionally. As Allied commander in chief, I have granted a military armistice. Hostilities between the Allies and Italy have terminated.*

Eisenhower waited for Badoglio to make his broadcast. After ten minutes with no word from Rome, he authorized Radio-Algiers to broadcast the text of Badoglio's announcement, which had been approved during the Cassibile negotiations. It announced the surrender and ordered Italian soldiers to cease all hostile acts against the Allies. Finally, at 7:45 p.m., Badoglio came on the radio and confirmed the Italian surrender and armistice.

The Nazis were undoubtedly moving on Rome and replacing the Italian defenders along the Salerno coast. When Clark's men hit the beaches at 3:30 a.m., they would be fighting Germans.

Eisenhower's stomach felt like a clenched fist as he rubbed his lucky coins. He had done everything possible for Avalanche to succeed, but he had an aching feeling it wasn't enough.

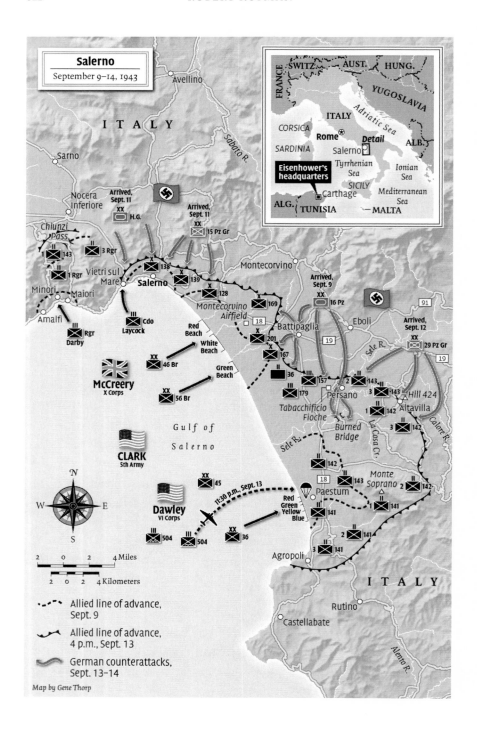

Salerno
September 9–14, 1943

ITALY

Avellino

Sabato R.

SWITZ. AUST. HUNG.

FRANCE

YUGOSLAVIA

Adriatic Sea

ITALY

CORSICA

Rome ⊕

Detail

ALB.

SARDINIA

Salerno

Tyrrhenian Sea

Ionian Sea

Eisenhower's headquarters

SICILY

Mediterranean Sea

ALG. TUNISIA

Carthage

MALTA

Sarno

Nocera Inferiore

Arrived, Sept. 11
XX H.G.

Arrived, Sept. 11
XX 15 Pz Gr

Chiunzi Pass

143
1 Rgr

3 Rgr

Vietri sul Mare

Salerno

Minori Maiori

Amalfi

Rgr Darby

Cdo Laycock

X 138

X 139

X 128

Montecorvino

Montecorvino Airfield

18

169

Arrived, Sept. 9
XX 16 Pz

Battipaglia

Eboli

91

Arrived, Sept. 12
XX 29 Pz Gr

19

19

Red Beach

White Beach

Green Beach

46 Br

56 Br

McCreery
X Corps

X 201

X 167

36

157

179

Persano

2

143

143

Hill 424

Altavilla

142

142

Sele R.

Calore R.

Tabacchificio Fioche

Burned Bridge

La Cosa Cr.

Sele R.

Gulf of Salerno

CLARK
5th Army

N
W   E
S

Dawley
VI Corps

45

11:30 p.m., Sept. 13

Red Green Yellow Blue

Paestum

142

18

143

Monte Soprano

2

142

141

141

504

504

36

Agropoli

141

141

ITALY

2   0   2   4 Miles

2   0   2   4 Kilometers

- - - ▶ Allied line of advance, Sept. 9

⌇⌇⌇ Allied line of advance, 4 p.m., Sept. 13

⌇⌇⌇ German counterattacks, Sept. 13–14

Rutino

Castellabate

Alento R.

Map by Gene Thorp

CHAPTER 53

In Carthage, Eisenhower received his first report from Clark:

Allied forces came ashore in calm seas but under deadly
artillery fire. The Germans have seized the Italian
positions in the hills surrounding the beaches. Casualties
are mounting quickly in the constricted beachhead.

Eisenhower rubbed his lucky coins. His stomach churned with anxiety. *Has my luck run out?*

In the late morning, Clark reported:

The Germans counterattacked with panzer tanks. Navy
warships approached close to the shore and pummeled the
German armor, forcing a retreat. The Americans and the
British have established beachheads, with the deepest
penetration three miles inland. Heavy fighting everywhere
along our lines.

A late-afternoon report was disturbing:

Closing the eight-mile gap between the British and American
forces proving more difficult than anticipated. Germans
fighting ferociously. Situation unsettled.

Eisenhower had thoughts of a looming disaster swirling in his mind when his intelligence chief, Strong, knocked on his open door.

"Ike, do you want an update on the Italians?"

"Sure, has the Italian army protected Rome?"

"No, the Nazis have control of Rome. Badoglio and the King have fled south. No orders were issued to resist the Germans. While some Italian units took the initiative and fought their former ally, most have allowed themselves to be disarmed by the Germans."

Eisenhower shook his head in disgust. "And the Italian navy?"

"They've honored their commitments, and their fleet is on the way to Malta."

"How fast have the Germans reacted with reinforcements?"

"Too fast. Within a few days, they'll have five divisions at Salerno."

"When in the hell is Montgomery going to get to Salerno?" asked Eisenhower.

"For someone whose only obstacle since landing on the mainland has been replacing blown bridges, he's moved with agonizing slowness. He's put no pressure on the Germans fleeing in front of him. In six days, Monty's only traveled forty-five miles."

Eisenhower left his office, furious with Montgomery's lack of progress. He went out on the terrace, lit a cigarette, and began pacing to work off his nervous energy.

He had repeatedly told Alexander to order Montgomery to go faster, all to no avail. Monty was marching to the beat of his own drum.

When Eisenhower returned to his office, there was a cable from Clark with some good news:

```
Darby's rangers and Laycock's commandos have captured the
mountain passes four thousand feet above the Sorrento
shoreline.
```

Eisenhower hoped this was a sign of propitious things to come.

Three days had passed, and Clark's reports were progressively more negative. The latest cable on September 12 caused Eisenhower's blood pressure to soar:

```
Have thrown in every reserve and barely holding on to
the beachheads. Relentless shelling by the Germans broken
only by their fierce counterattacks. The enemy is close to
reaching the shoreline, severing the Allied line. Darby and
Laycock are barely hanging on atop the Sorrento Peninsula.
Allied air cover spotty. Navy is losing ships to German air
attacks. Contemplating evacuating the beachheads.
```

Eisenhower gathered his subordinates in Maison Blanche's dining room, with tranquil views of the Gulf of Tunis, to address the crisis.

"ABC, can you get more naval firepower to Salerno?" asked Eisenhower.

"With the Italian navy neutralized in Malta, I can send two battleships and ten destroyers," replied Cunningham.

"Get them moving ASAP," Eisenhower ordered. "Ted, we need your bombers to stop attacking strategic targets and start pounding the Germans at Salerno."

"I'll begin attacking Salerno today with five hundred heavies," Tedder promised.

"What about air cover?" Eisenhower asked.

"We're building makeshift landing strips and bringing in planes from Sicily," replied Tedder. "Air cover is improving."

Eisenhower looked at Alexander. "Monty's moving like he's on holiday."

"To be fair, he's had to travel over difficult terrain that has worn down his equipment, particularly the trucks, faster than anticipated. I'll prod him to go faster."

Eisenhower exploded. "Goddamnit, do more than prod! Force that son of a bitch to hurry the hell up!"

Cunningham added his scorn. "That little bugger wouldn't get away with such insolent behavior in the Royal Navy! Monty does what he wants when he wants. I'd fire his bloody arse and put someone in charge who can get the job done!"

Alexander remained calm, as he usually did. "I'll get Monty

moving at top speed," he said before changing the subject. "Clark has requested the Eighty-Second Airborne be dropped tonight on the beachhead. There's a friendly-fire risk, given the proximity of the navy's warships."

"I'll authorize the jump," said Eisenhower. "Clark needs all the help he can get. And ABC, make damn sure the navy gunners know to hold their fire."

"What's happening with reinforcements?" asked Alexander.

"I shanghaied British landing craft moving through the Mediterranean on the way to India," Eisenhower replied as he lit a cigarette. "Those ships will ferry a portion of Patton's troops to Clark's rescue. I've ordered the Thirty-Fourth Division at Oran be sent to Salerno piecemeal as shipping becomes available."

"I pray reinforcements get there in time," said Tedder.

"Amen to that," replied Eisenhower fervently.

After the meeting ended, Eisenhower walked out on the terrace and stared at the blue water. He tossed down his cigarette and lit another from his fourth pack of the day.

The pressure on his shoulders was immense. Clark's army could be annihilated before sufficient reinforcements arrived.

Reinforcements, beginning with the Eighty-Second Airborne's successful night drop, solidified Clark's lines. Brave American and British troops repulsed near-constant German attacks with crucial help from the navy's guns. Tedder's bombers wreaked havoc with trains bringing German reinforcements to Salerno. And, although he was still days away, Montgomery had finally sped up.

Catastrophe had been avoided. Eisenhower's luck had held.

On September 15, Eisenhower boarded the HMS *Charybdis* in Tunis harbor. When the ship reached Salerno on September 17, a DUKW transported him to the beach. Allied planes roared overhead, bombing and strafing German positions while navy warships pummeled Nazi lines with twelve-inch shells. German artillery fire was hitting American lines, and a smoky haze hung over the battlefield. The shoreline was littered with broken and smashed landing craft, DUKWs, and tanks.

One of Clark's aides met him on the beach, hurrying him to a waiting jeep. As he drove Eisenhower toward a tobacco barn serving as Clark's headquarters, a German artillery shell exploded a hundred feet off the road, showering Eisenhower with dirt and pulverized pieces of rock. He felt a rush of adrenaline as he dusted himself off.

When Eisenhower arrived at Clark's headquarters, he saw the tobacco field had been turned into a field hospital. Soldiers lay on litters outside of tents, waiting to be operated on. A gruesome pile of sawed-off limbs reminded him of the horrors of war.

Eisenhower walked over to a surgeon in a bloodstained smock and asked, "Can I visit the patients recovering from their operations?"

The doctor looked up, and his eyes got wide. "General Eisenhower . . . I didn't expect to see you here." He pointed to a large white tent. "You can visit the patients in there."

"Thank you, Doctor."

The recovery tent was jammed full of men lying on cots. Eisenhower felt empathy for these soldiers who suffered wounds in the fight for freedom. They deserved the gratitude of their countrymen.

He stopped at the first cot. The soldier's head was covered in gauze with only one eye and half a mouth showing. He bent down and asked, "Where're you from, son?"

"Saint Louis."

"Are you a Cardinals fan?"

"Yes, sir," he replied with half a grin. "Love the Cards!"

"Me too," replied Eisenhower.

He spent an hour visiting every patient, asking about their hometowns and making small talk.

When he entered the headquarters barn, Clark greeted him warmly.

"Welcome to Italy, Ike!"

Eisenhower appraised his friend. Although Clark's eyes were bloodshot, he looked full of energy.

"It's good to see you, Wayne. When are you going to get out of this beachhead?"

"When that slow-footed bastard Montgomery gets here, I think the Hun will retreat."

Their discussion was interrupted when a German shell exploded and shrapnel rained down like hail on the roof.

When the noise abated, Eisenhower asked, "Any command issues, Wayne?"

"The Sixth Corps commander, Mike Dawley, has come up short. I want to relieve him."

The news startled Eisenhower. "I've known Mike for twenty years. He's had a good reputation up to now."

"He's not provided good leadership and has a defeatist attitude. Let's pay Dawley a visit, and you can evaluate him yourself."

They got into a jeep and drove two miles to a farmhouse that served as Dawley's headquarters. Along the way, they passed a field where stone-faced soldiers were busy burying their brothers-in-arms who had paid the ultimate price in the fight to rid the world of Nazis.

When they got to Dawley's headquarters, Eisenhower took his old friend, who looked haggard and worn down, aside for a quiet conversation.

"It's good to see you, Mike," said Eisenhower. "How's the battle going?"

"We're in a terrible position. The Kraut artillery on the hills makes the beachhead a living hell. Our boys are getting mauled. When they're not shelling us, the Germans attack. Our losses are appalling. I doubt we can hold on."

"Things are improving, Mike. Reinforcements are arriving, and Montgomery will get here soon. The navy's guns have held the German armor in check. The tide is turning."

"You're seeing the battle through rose-colored glasses," Dawley argued. "The Hun is kicking our ass!"

They talked for fifteen minutes, and nothing Eisenhower said altered Dawley's pessimism. As much as he appreciated Dawley's prior record and accomplishments, Eisenhower couldn't allow valiant US soldiers to be led by a man who didn't believe the battle could be won.

As they drove off, Eisenhower said, "Go ahead and relieve Dawley. He's spent."

That evening, Eisenhower sailed on *Charybdis* for Tunis. When he awoke the next morning, he received good news. Montgomery had finally gotten close to Salerno, and the Germans were retreating.

CHAPTER 54

By September 22, Clark and Montgomery had hooked up and turned north toward their objectives—Naples for Clark and the Foggia airfields for Montgomery. Their forces stretched across the Italian Peninsula, from the Tyrrhenian Sea to the Adriatic Sea.

The battle for Salerno had proven costly for Clark's army, which suffered fourteen thousand casualties. Montgomery's army, which had faced little opposition in reaching Salerno, lost six hundred men.

Smith came into Eisenhower's Algiers office with a smile on his face. "Cable from Churchill."

Eisenhower took the cable from Smith's hand and read:

I congratulate you on the victorious landing and deployment northward of our armies. As the Duke of Wellington said of the Battle of Waterloo, "It was a damn close-run thing," but your policy of running risks has been vindicated.

"It's a good feeling to have the PM's support," Eisenhower said, "although I could do without any more close shaves with disastrous defeats!"

"Oh, and you have some visitors."

"Who?"

"The M and M boys," Beetle said, a mischievous glint in his eyes. "Macmillan and Murphy."

Eisenhower groaned. "It must mean more French political problems!"

"Shall I tell them you're too busy to see them?"

"No, have them come in."

Once Smith escorted in the diplomats, Macmillan took the lead. "De Gaulle outmaneuvered Giraud. The copresidency of the FCNL is over."

Eisenhower sighed before wearily asking, "What happened?"

"You're aware that while the Battle of Salerno was raging, Giraud had a small French force liberate Corsica?"

"Yes. Giraud claims a great victory, although the Germans were already leaving Corsica when the French arrived," replied Eisenhower.

"Well, Giraud infiltrated agents into Corsica without de Gaulle's knowledge," Macmillan said. "They unwittingly helped the Communists seize control of the Resistance movement. In the uproar that ensued, de Gaulle took control of the FCNL. Giraud is still head of the army, but he's now answerable to the FCNL."

"Is there something you want me to do?" asked Eisenhower.

"The President wants you to minimize contact with de Gaulle because he can't be trusted," replied Murphy.

"It's hard to ignore de Gaulle as head of the FCNL; it's effectively the French government in exile," replied Eisenhower. "But I'll keep the President's advice in mind."

The British Tenth Corps absorbed Laycock's commandos and Darby's rangers as it slowly advanced over the Sorrento Peninsula toward Naples. The rugged, broken ground negated the mobility of tanks, and it was small infantry engagements that rooted out German defenders.

Pack mule trains moving supplies over trackless mountain terrain proved invaluable. Soldiers who knew how to handle a stubborn mule were in high demand.

Realizing more manpower was needed, Clark ordered the Eighty-Second Airborne to join the assault.

On September 27, Eisenhower received a cable from Clark that brought a smile to his face:

The Eighty-Second has broken through the German line and reached the Naples plain!

The next day, Clark cabled:

The British have broken through! The Germans are retreating toward Naples!

The Germans fought a delaying action as they systematically destroyed Naples harbor before abandoning the city. On October 1, Clark entered Naples.

Montgomery faced light opposition as he approached Foggia, which the Germans also abandoned. By October 1, the British occupied Foggia and the nearby airfields.

In little more than three weeks, despite the near-calamitous beginning, the immediate Avalanche goals had been achieved.

Eisenhower was on his way to Italy to visit Clark and Montgomery. As the plane approached Naples, he was pleased to see ships unloading cargo in the port the Nazis had demolished.

When Eisenhower deplaned, Clark was waiting for him. "Wayne, congratulations on capturing Naples!"

"It was a struggle, but our inexperienced troops are now veterans," Clark answered, a smile full of pride and confidence gracing his face.

"I'm impressed you got the port operating so quickly," Eisenhower said as they walked to a waiting jeep.

"All credit for that goes to the Corps of Engineers—they've worked miracles! The Germans sank every ship in the port, destroyed all the cranes, and demolished every warehouse. They were extremely thorough in their efforts to make the port useless for months. Our engineers constructed piers across the sunken vessels so we could access the waterfront, and amazingly, we were unloading supplies from our ships in just three days!"

When they got to the port, Eisenhower saw what Clark was talking about. Tanks, trucks, and jeeps were being unloaded from ships and driven across the engineers' hastily constructed piers. While the acronym "SNAFU" appropriately applied to many army operations, here was an example of brilliant work.

As they drove through Naples, there was rubble everywhere from destroyed buildings, mostly victims of Allied bombing but some from Nazi efforts to immobilize the city. Eisenhower grew pensive, thinking about the suffering inflicted on civilians.

Clark said, "The Germans destroyed the water, power, sewerage, and telephone facilities. But within days, the Corps of Engineers had all of the vital infrastructure restored."

"Truly impressive work," replied Eisenhower.

It began to rain. By the time they got to Clark's headquarters, it was a deluge. They shared a can of Spam as Clark discussed his plans.

"The Volturno River twenty miles north of Naples is our next objective. Intelligence reports the Germans are digging in and will oppose a crossing. Our meteorologist forecasts this heavy rain is going to continue for days. It complicates matters, of course, but we're moving forward with the offensive."

"I agree we can't let the weather slow us down." Eisenhower changed the subject. "Did you meet Monty at Salerno?"

"I did, and he gave me some advice. He told me when I get an order from Alexander I don't like, I should just ignore it—that's what *he* does!"

Eisenhower scowled. "That's exactly how Monty operates."

Then he sighed. His power over Montgomery was limited. The

English chose the generals of their armies, and Montgomery was Brooke's favorite general.

Eisenhower reconciled himself to living with an insufferable subordinate.

The next day, Eisenhower flew to Foggia in the rain.

Montgomery met the American general at the airfield. "You're a jolly good chap to visit me in weather like this."

"I enjoy being in the field no matter the weather."

"Did Clark tell you how I saved his bacon at Salerno?"

Eisenhower was astonished by the bravado. "With all due respect, the navy's guns and Tedder's planes saved the day at Salerno. You were rather late to the party."

"Of course, they helped stabilize the situation, but the Germans didn't retreat until I showed up!"

CHAPTER 55

October 17 was a sad day for Eisenhower. His close friend ABC was leaving for London to become First Sea Lord. The two men had gotten together to reminisce and say their farewells in Eisenhower's office in the Hotel Saint George.

"At the beginning of our relationship, Ike, when we were planning Torch, many senior British officers were openly contemptuous of the Americans. They put you down as an inexperienced novice to combat, sure to muck things up. It's been a transcendent experience to witness how you've used humility, intelligence, and a constant emphasis on teamwork to forge a truly unified headquarters."

Eisenhower choked up and tears filled his eyes. He hadn't expected such a tribute to his leadership. "ABC, I'm going to miss you both as a friend and as a man who can be counted on to control the seas. I'm sure you'll do a bang-up job running the British navy."

The friends traveled down to the port in separate cars.

When Summersby opened the door of the Cadillac for Eisenhower, she said, "I'm going to miss Admiral Cunningham! He's always treated me with dignity and respect. You can tell he cares about the little people."

"I'm going to miss him too," replied Eisenhower. "He's an old sea dog whom I can count on to deliver in the pinch."

At the port, Eisenhower had arranged for a ceremony to honor the admiral before he departed. Sailors, soldiers, and airmen from the United States and Great Britain formed an honor line that Cunningham inspected before walking up the gangplank of his flagship as the US Army Band played "Rule, Britannia."

At breakfast the next day, Butcher handed Eisenhower a newspaper article. "Read this! There's a grassroots movement among Republicans to nominate you for President in the 1944 election!"

"That's ridiculous!" Eisenhower scoffed.

He read the article through before grabbing a pencil and scribbling "Baloney!" across the top. "Why can't a simple soldier be left alone to carry out his orders? I'm upset the article said I'm a candidate—I ain't and won't!"

"You don't think you'd be a good President?"

"Hell no! I don't have patience to deal with politicians—except of course for Roosevelt and Churchill."

The latter part of October brought a string of VIP visitors to Algiers, including Navy Secretary Frank Knox, Secretary of the Treasury Henry Morgenthau, and Secretary of State Cordell Hull. All carried the same news: Roosevelt had chosen General Marshall to command Overlord, and Eisenhower would be recalled to Washington to replace Marshall as chief of staff.

Ambassador to the Soviet Union Averell Harriman was the latest VIP to visit Eisenhower's Algiers villa. Harriman, a wealthy Wall Street banker, had supported Roosevelt's New Deal politics and was a close confidant of the President's.

Eisenhower and Harriman were on the terrace enjoying a cocktail before dinner. "Ike, have you heard Marshall is getting the Overlord command, and you're going to replace him in Washington?"

"Yes, and it's a well-deserved honor for General Marshall. I'm resigned to my fate."

Harriman stared at Eisenhower. "You don't want to be chief of staff?"

"Not particularly. I'd prefer a field command."

"Well, it's not a completely done deal. Ernie King is vociferously opposed to breaking up what he sees as a winning team in Washington. King is trying hard to get FDR to change his mind."

"Thank you, Averell, for the insight."

Mickey came on the terrace, holding a document. "Ambassador Harriman, you received an urgent cable from Washington."

After Harriman read the cable, he said, "Please excuse me. I need to prepare a response."

Eisenhower was left alone on the terrace with his thoughts. He admired Marshall and was happy the man would get the chance to make his mark in history as a field commander. But he hated the thought of going back to a desk job in Washington. *For God's sake, I will technically be Marshall's boss, and how the hell is that going to work? Then there is MacArthur's monumental ego to manage.*

On top of that, a return to Washington meant ending his relationship with Summersby. Kay's ebullient presence buoyed his spirits in difficult times, and the war was far from over. . . . He would miss her effervescent spirit when he was chained to a desk in the Pentagon!

Then his thoughts moved to Mamie and resuming his old life with her. Eisenhower knew there would be challenges in their marriage. *Her anger with my bringing Kay to Africa would assuredly come out. It could be a rocky homecoming.*

By the end of October, Allied progress in Italy had slowed to a crawl. Clark and Montgomery's men were fighting under cold rainy skies against fierce German resistance. The mountainous Italian Peninsula was cut by many rivers, making it ideal terrain for defensive warfare. Every river crossing was contested by the Germans and earned with Allied blood. Rooting out Nazis from prepared positions on steep mountain ridges was proving a treacherous, high-casualty process. Cloud cover and heavy rain were taking away the Allies' greatest advantage—control of the air.

Eisenhower gave a heavy sigh and sat back in his office chair. He knew things were going to get worse. Seven divisions and most of his landing craft were being sent to England to train for Overlord. The Mediterranean had become a secondary theater.

He couldn't deny it—he was feeling blue. Abruptly he got up and walked out of his office and found Summersby at her desk. "Kay, alert the grooms at Sailor's Delight we're coming out this afternoon."

She smiled brightly. "Okay, Ike!"

Eisenhower returned her smile. He found their Sailor's Delight outings restorative; the physical exercise was a balm for his frayed nerves. When he was alone with Kay on the farm, he was able to relax—a near impossibility when he was at AFHQ or in the field.

A stiff breeze coming off the Mediterranean cooled the riders as Eisenhower and Summersby rode past a guard jeep parked in front of a towering cypress, the type of tree Van Gogh loved to paint. They continued until both their horses were well lathered.

Stopping in their private hollow, they shared a bottle of wine. After a while, Eisenhower grew silent and pensive. He swirled his wine before looking at Summersby.

"Kay, I may be going back to Washington soon."

"Then the rumors are true? You're going to become chief of staff?"

"It certainly looks that way."

She sipped her wine before asking in a tentative voice, "Would it be possible for you to take me with you to the States?"

Eisenhower steeled himself. He had to do what was right, even though the temptation to continue the relationship with Kay was strong, almost overwhelming. She was beautiful, fearless, smart, and competent. She liked and excelled at the activities he enjoyed, whether it was playing bridge or riding Arabians. And the sex between them was always exhilarating.

But bringing his mistress to America would humiliate Mamie and destroy their marriage. And he still loved his wife; they had gone through much together, including losing their first child and raising their beloved Johnny. It would be beyond cruel to flaunt Kay in her face, and he couldn't bring himself to visualize how it might affect her health. He had to do the right thing. And that was returning to being a faithful husband to Mamie and leaving the enchanting Summersby behind.

"Kay, we're having a wartime romance. I can't bring you back to America. I have to honor my life there and the commitments I've made."

She started crying softly, and Eisenhower moved closer and put his arm around her. He hated to hurt her, and he didn't want to end their relationship either. But if he was recalled to the States, that meant a return to his old life.

Summersby leaned her head on his shoulder and with a trembling hand wiped at her tears. "I'm sorry, Ike. I'm acting silly. I've always known about your life in the States, and I don't want to add to your burdens. That's something you cherish about me!" she said with a shaky and somewhat forced smile. She tilted her head back to look up at him. "Let's enjoy the time we have left."

Eisenhower didn't say a word. He lowered his head, and they kissed long and passionately.

The next day, Alexander visited Eisenhower in his Algiers office to discuss the dismal Italian campaign. He began the meeting lamenting his diminishing strength.

"Ike, we need to stop, or at least dramatically slow down, the transfer of troops and landing craft to England. This theater is being treated as a backwater."

Eisenhower demurred. "Marshall made it crystal clear there'd be no wiggling out of these transfers, and I agree with Overlord having priority. The quickest way to win this war is to invade France and drive the Nazis back into Germany from the west while the Russians push in from the east. We'll meet the Russian bear somewhere in Germany, and Hitler's Thousand Year Reich will be finished!"

"Can you at least get the transfer of landing craft delayed so I can do an amphibious move around the German line?"

"How much time do you need, Alex?"

"We need to retain at least sixty-eight LSTs until early January."

"Okay." Eisenhower nodded. "I'll try and hold on to the landing craft until the beginning of the year." He paused. "Look, Alex; I share your frustration with being in a nonpriority theater."

Alexander rubbed his forehead. "I'm under intense pressure from Churchill. He's obsessed with capturing Rome. The PM bombards me with cables that I don't bother you with."

"You're not alone! Churchill inundates me with cables on the urgency of capturing Rome too." Then Eisenhower had a disturbing thought. "If the PM is pressuring us, he's assuredly pressuring Roosevelt. Goddamnit, our grand alliance is fraying at the seams!"

CHAPTER 56

The calendar turned to November and word came from Washington that another summit of Allied leaders, this time including Soviet dictator Joseph Stalin, would be held in Tehran. A preliminary meeting between Roosevelt and Churchill would be held in Cairo. But first, Churchill and Roosevelt wanted to meet with Eisenhower as they passed through the Mediterranean.

On November 18, Eisenhower traveled to Malta to meet Churchill. After they enjoyed lunch in the Verdala Palace's fresco-ceilinged dining room, the Prime Minister lit a cigar and made his case.

"The tide has turned, Ike. Your great victories, coupled with the Red Army's success, has the Hun on the defensive! Opportunities abound in the Mediterranean. We could attack the Balkans from Italy, or we could go farther east and attack Greece. We need to strike Hitler another strong blow somewhere in the soft underbelly of Europe! It's a terrible mistake to withdraw seven divisions from your command when such opportunities are presented."

"As theater commander, I'd like all the resources I can get," Eisenhower said carefully, doing his best to be diplomatic, "but I've always believed in Overlord as the best way to end the war in the shortest time."

"Circumstances have changed!" The Prime Minister leaned forward and waved his cigar for emphasis. "Look at your success in Sicily and Italy. We need to be nimble, seize the moment, keep the

Mediterranean ablaze! Will you support me in arguing to keep your divisions?"

"No, I can't do that," Eisenhower said firmly. "Overlord deserves priority. If we hold on to those divisions, the invasion of France might be postponed."

Churchill sat back and sighed. "It wouldn't bother me if Overlord was delayed. I've concerns, fears really, about invading France. I've had nightmares of the English Channel turning red from the blood of our brave warriors with their corpses piling up on the beaches of Normandy."

Churchill's vision of a catastrophic defeat was sobering. Eisenhower thought of the Dieppe disaster and prayed Marshall could find a way to make Overlord a success.

A waiter entered the dining room with a bottle of whisky and two glasses. Churchill poured them each a generous portion. Eisenhower took his readily.

Churchill swirled his whisky. "I promised Brooke command of Overlord. But when it became evident American troops would out-number British forces, I deferred to the President to choose the commander."

"I've heard from multiple sources it's going to be General Marshall," replied Eisenhower.

"I don't believe Franklin's made a final decision." Churchill puffed on his cigar. "I've told the President both Marshall and you are accept-able to me for the Overlord command."

While it was pleasing to have Churchill's confidence, Eisenhower wasn't holding out much hope he would be put in charge of Overlord.

"Who is your favorite American Civil War general?" Churchill asked, unexpectedly changing the direction of the conversation.

"Robert E. Lee," replied Eisenhower without hesitation.

"Lee, a bold risk taker! Now I see why you want to roll the dice with an invasion of France. But remember, for all of Lee's brilliance, he gambled at Gettysburg with Pickett's Charge, and he suffered a disas-trous defeat."

"Your knowledge of American history is impressive."

"I love history—and remember, I'm half-American!"

Eisenhower flew from Malta to Oran to meet with Roosevelt. The President was arriving the next day at Mers el-Kebir, the French naval base.

The next morning, a cold breeze was blowing off the snow-capped Atlas Mountains as the USS *Iowa* anchored in the sheltered bay. Eisenhower shivered as he watched a small boat containing the President lowered into the water and rowed to the dock. Two Secret Service agents lifted Roosevelt out of the boat and into Eisenhower's car.

As they drove to an airfield for a flight to Tunis, the President said, "I so enjoy getting out of Washington! All the political infighting becomes tiresome." He put a cigarette into his holder and lit it. "A few days ago, the US Navy almost sank the *Iowa*."

A startled Eisenhower uttered, "What?"

"The convoy was conducting drills, and a destroyer accidentally launched a torpedo right at the *Iowa*. Alarms sounded, and one of the sailors screamed, 'This ain't no drill!'"

"Holy cow!" exclaimed Eisenhower. *The President was almost killed by friendly fire!*

"The captain sped up and heeled the ship hard to port to evade the torpedo. I told my attendant to wheel me to the starboard rail. I wanted to see the torpedo."

"Did you see it?"

"No, the torpedo hit the ship's wake and detonated a few hundred feet astern. It added a little spice to the trip."

Once they were aboard the plane and settled in, the President asked, "What did Winston want to discuss with you in Malta?"

"He's convinced we should exploit opportunities in the Mediterranean, even if it means postponing Overlord."

"Winston is an old imperialist! While he wants to win the war, he also wants to preserve the British Empire. His motives in pursuing a Mediterranean strategy are not entirely pure."

"I believe in Overlord, sir, and I refused his request to ask for a delay in the transfer of troops to England."

"I'm glad you were firm with Winston. Overlord is not going to be delayed."

Upon landing in Tunis, Eisenhower exited the plane and looked around for Summersby. She was going to drive the President to Carthage, where Roosevelt and his entourage would stay. Eisenhower spotted her in a heated argument with Secret Service agent Mike Reilly.

He turned his attention back to the President. Eisenhower waited until Roosevelt had been lifted into the back seat before sliding in beside him. He was surprised when a male soldier got into the driver's seat.

When the car started moving, Roosevelt asked, "Where's your pretty English driver Winston's told me so much about?"

"She was supposed to drive you. I saw her having an argument with the Secret Service. I assume they wouldn't let her drive you."

Roosevelt frowned. "Those boys are overly protective. I'll make it clear to them that I want your driver at the wheel. She drove Churchill; she can drive me!"

When they got to Maison Blanche, the President said, "I want to meet that driver of yours. Could you ask her to come into the villa?"

"Of course."

He found Summersby outside the villa. She followed Eisenhower into the house. Looking out a window at the Gulf of Tunis, FDR was flanked by his two sons, Franklin Jr., a naval officer, and Elliott, an air reconnaissance officer. They had been given temporary leaves to see their father.

"Mr. President, this is Kay Summersby."

Roosevelt smiled before he reached out and shook Summersby's hand. "Winston has talked very favorably about you. I was looking forward to your driving me. What happened?"

"The Secret Service wouldn't let me!" replied Summersby, her eyes flashing fire.

Roosevelt laughed heartily. "That's what Ike suspected. Would you like to drive me from now on?"

"It would be a tremendous privilege, sir!" she said, her eyes regaining their sparkle.

"Very well, it's settled. You'll be my driver for the rest of my stay in Tunisia. I'll let the boys know."

As they were leaving the villa, Eisenhower asked Summersby, "Why did Reilly refuse to allow you to drive the President?"

"He said no woman has ever driven the President, and none would as long as he's in charge—certainly, no Limey woman!"

The next day, Summersby, with Telek sitting beside her, drove Eisenhower and the President to see the Tunisian battlefields. Reilly had arranged for a twenty-vehicle convoy to accompany and protect the President.

As Summersby drove over rolling brown hills and past olive groves and wheat fields, Eisenhower pointed out where Bradley had broken through German lines to capture Bizerte. When they reached Hill 609, Eisenhower described the many bloody assaults it took to capture the high ground.

As they drove on, the President said, "Ike, I'm sure you've heard rumors I'm going to name Marshall to command Overlord."

"General Marshall would be an excellent choice."

"You and I know Henry Halleck was Lincoln's chief of staff, but few Americans know Halleck's name. Marshall has performed superbly, and I believe he's earned the opportunity for his name to go down in history as the commander of Overlord."

"I couldn't agree more, Mr. President."

"Of course, it can be dangerous to monkey around with a winning team."

Suddenly Telek flung himself at Roosevelt. Eisenhower deftly leaned forward and caught him before he landed in the President's lap.

"I'm sorry, sir; Telek likes to take flying leaps!"

Roosevelt laughed. "Here, let me have him. I love dogs."

Eisenhower handed him the dog, and Telek immediately began licking the President's face.

After a few minutes of playing with Telek, Roosevelt pointed to a grove of palm trees. "Ike, that looks like a good place for our picnic." He called out to Summersby. "Child, could you pull over and park the car by those trees?"

Summersby turned off the road for the unscheduled stop. The

vehicles in front of the Presidential car continued down the road, un-aware they'd lost their precious cargo.

In a minute, Reilly ran up, red-faced from exertion. He leaned in through Summersby's open window. "Mr. President, we have a secure spot picked out for lunch a few miles farther on!"

As Reilly spoke, Secret Service agents from the back end of the convoy spread out in a protective arc. The President scanned the agents, who had drawn weapons.

"I feel safe here, Mike," Roosevelt said. "It's fun to improvise once in a while."

Summersby got out of the car and started walking away to have lunch with the other drivers. Roosevelt asked, "Child, won't you stay and have lunch with an old man?"

"I'd love to!"

Eisenhower got out of the car to retrieve the picnic lunch from the trunk. Summersby took his place sitting beside the President. Eisenhower stood outside the car and handed food in through an open window while the President chatted with Summersby.

On the way back to Carthage, Roosevelt asked Eisenhower, "Do you think the Americans and the Germans fought over the same ground the Romans and Carthaginians did during the Battle of Zama in 202 BC? Where Hannibal used elephants to attack the Roman Legions?"

"I don't believe the exact ground has ever been identified," Eisenhower replied, "but it would have to be in this area."

For the rest of the drive, the President and the general discussed the finer points of the Second Punic War.

CHAPTER 57

After the President left for his meeting with Churchill in Cairo, Eisenhower returned to Algiers. On his desk was a letter from Mamie:

I'm much happier not sharing an apartment with Ruth. I'm spending more time with my other girlfriends. We're having such fun playing mah-jongg. We pool our coupon books so we can have a nice meal after we play. Remember you have all my love. I can't wait till we're reunited!

He had just picked up a pen to write a reply when Smith rushed into his office with a sour face. "The shit has hit the fan!"

"What's happened, Beetle?"

"Drew Pearson broke the Patton-slapping story on his national radio broadcast! He sensationalized and embellished the story with false facts, making Patton look like a crazy person! All hell's broken loose. Newspapers and congressmen are calling for Patton's scalp."

"Christ on a mountain!" Eisenhower yelled. His effort to keep a lid on the Patton story had blown up in his face.

A cable soon arrived from Marshall, who had joined the President in Cairo. He requested an explanation of the Patton matter.

Eisenhower prepared a response detailing the incidents and defended his actions in trying to save Patton for future battles against the Nazis. Would Marshall be angry he tried to protect his friend?

He wouldn't have to wait long to find out. Tomorrow he would be in Cairo to make a presentation to the Combined Chiefs on the Italian campaign.

That night at 10:00, Eisenhower boarded the plane for Cairo. He invited Summersby and four other staffers to come along. For the staffers, the trip would be a vacation, as they would have no duties to perform in Egypt.

On board the plane, Eisenhower had trouble falling asleep, worried about Marshall's reaction to the Patton saga. Eventually he dozed off, awakening as the sun was rising. Looking outside his window, he spied a group of pyramids backlit in shades of yellow and gold. It was an awe-inspiring sight for a poor boy from Abilene fascinated with the history of ancient civilizations.

He exited the plane into a furnace of suffocating heat. Two cars were waiting, and soon Eisenhower and his traveling party were ensconced in a large villa. He quickly left for the Mena House Hotel in Giza, site of the Cairo conference.

The opulent Mena House Hotel was built facing one of the Seven Wonders of the World, the Great Pyramid of Giza. It was the place to stay for the rich and famous who wanted to visit the pyramids and the Sphinx. The British army had taken over the hotel, evacuated its guests, and turned it into an armed compound.

After clearing a security checkpoint, Eisenhower walked up marble steps flanked by large flowerpots of chrysanthemums and entered the hotel lobby. An aide to Marshall was waiting for him. "Sir, the chief would like to see you. Please follow me."

He was led to an outside patio. Marshall was standing there next to a huge eucalyptus tree, looking at the Great Pyramid. He turned as Eisenhower approached.

Marshall gave him a steely stare. "It was a mistake for you to hide this Patton affair from me. It's quickly snowballed into a national scandal that I'll have to deal with when I get back to Washington."

Eisenhower accepted the reprimand that he knew he deserved.

"Sir, it was an error in judgment on my part. I promise in the future to fully and transparently communicate with you."

Marshall's stare lost none of its intensity as he said, "I'm concerned about Patton's lack of control. A commanding general must keep his senses about him at all times."

"His conduct in Sicily was an aberration. While Patton can be quick to anger, these are the only two incidents of physical abuse that I'm aware of. Patton's our best field general and would provide invaluable service commanding an army in France under men with steady hands, like yourself and Bradley."

Marshall was silent for a minute, absorbing Eisenhower's recommendation. Then he looked at his watch. "Your Italy presentation is in an hour."

After Marshall left, Eisenhower stayed on the patio, studying the immense pyramid that gleamed in the sunlight. After a few minutes, a familiar voice called, "Ike!"

He turned and saw a smiling Churchill walking toward him. He looked like a tourist on a grand tour with his white suit, black bow tie, and broad-brimmed white hat. "Amazing, isn't it?"

"It's breathtaking," replied Eisenhower.

"Ike, would you reconsider your position on losing seven divisions to Overlord?"

Eisenhower sighed. The PM was relentless in pursuing his objectives. "I'm sorry, but I believe Overlord must have priority."

Before the men could continue the discussion, one of Churchill's secretaries hurried up. "General Brooke needs to see you."

Eisenhower followed Churchill into the hotel. He found the dining room, where a white-robed waiter served him a nourishing breakfast.

At the appointed time, Eisenhower entered the Combined Chiefs conference room. In attendance were England's and the United States' most senior military leaders together with guests Mountbatten, who was on his way to Burma to assume command of Allied forces in Southeast Asia, and Tedder, who had responsibility for the conference's air defense.

As Eisenhower sat down, Marshall asked, "General Eisenhower, will you update us on the Italian campaign?"

"After capturing Naples, we've pushed the Germans fifty miles north to their Winter Line, a series of mountains blocking the road to Rome. We're bringing up supplies for a winter offensive."

Brooke asked, "If you lose seven divisions to Overlord, will you be strong enough to take Rome?"

Marshall interjected, "Removing those seven divisions to England is not open for debate!"

"Why the hell not?" Brooke glowered at Marshall.

"Because at the Quebec conference, Churchill signed a memorandum agreeing to the transfer of those divisions for Overlord," Marshall shot back. "It's the paramount operation of the war, and nothing can be allowed to weaken or delay it."

"Circumstances have changed! Can't you see that?" Brooke hollered. "Our great Allied war effort shouldn't be governed by an out-of-date document!"

"Nothing has changed," Marshall forcibly retorted. "We made a promise to Stalin we'd open a second front in France in the spring of 1944. It was agreed at Quebec that Overlord had priority in 1944, and Italy—indeed, the entire Mediterranean—would become a secondary theater."

"It's a mistake in war not to take advantage of changed circumstances," Brooke argued. He turned his attention back to Eisenhower. "What's your ultimate objective in Italy?"

"After the capture of Rome, I want to reach the Po Valley. From that region, our armies would pose threats in multiple directions to Hitler's empire. The French Riviera, Yugoslavia, and even Austria would be threatened."

While Brooke scribbled a note on a pad, Marshall said, "The Po Valley is a long way from Berlin. I don't care if we ever get there. We're going to defeat Hitler by invading France!"

Brooke's face turned red. "You refuse to allow yourself to see the Mediterranean opportunities!"

The contentious meeting continued with Eisenhower winning his request to hold on to landing craft until January. Marshall rejected all of Brooke's other efforts to strengthen Mediterranean operations at the expense of Overlord.

After the meeting concluded, Eisenhower met Mountbatten for a drink in the hotel lobby.

"I thought Brookie was going to have a heart attack in the meeting today," Mountbatten said.

"It was like a prizefight between two heavyweights," joked Eisenhower.

"I agree with Marshall—France must be invaded to get to Germany!" said Mountbatten. "I'm sad I won't be there for the big show, but my assignment in Burma precludes it."

"Dickie, we're in the same boat. I won't be in England either for Overlord."

They had just finished their drinks when Eisenhower saw Marshall approaching.

"May I have a word with you?"

Nodding, Eisenhower followed Marshall to a quiet part of the lobby.

"You look exhausted and worn out. I want you to take a few days off."

"I need to focus on Italy. I don't need a break."

"It's an order, not a suggestion," Marshall said firmly. "Do some sightseeing in Egypt."

It was useless to argue with the chief. "Sir, thank you. I'm sure a little rest will do me good."

As Marshall headed off, Eisenhower stood in the lobby, wondering what to do with his time off. When he saw Tedder walk by smoking his pipe, he called out, "Ted, do you have a minute?"

"Of course."

"I've been ordered to take a few days off. You've spent years in Egypt—what do you suggest I do?"

"You must fly to Luxor and tour the temple ruins and visit the Valley of the Kings. Both are truly extraordinary experiences!" Tedder enthused. "You can use my personal plane. I'll assign Major Walter Bryan Emery, one of the world's leading Egyptologists, to be your personal tour guide."

"That's most generous of you. Can I bring along a few people from my staff?"

"Of course. And for today, I suggest you walk around the pyramids and the Sphinx. Tomorrow Emery will explain the significance of what you've seen."

CHAPTER 58

Eisenhower asked his staff and Elliott Roosevelt, who had traveled to Cairo with his father and shared Eisenhower's passion for history, to tour Luxor with him. All eagerly accepted the invitation. The next morning, their little party met Emery at the airfield to fly south in Tedder's C-47.

Once the plane ascended, Emery, who wore thick, black horn-rimmed glasses, began to educate his fellow passengers. He spoke with the passion of a professor for his favorite subject when he introduced his new charges to Egyptian history.

"Around 3100 BC, a unified kingdom was formed in Egypt, which led to a series of dynasties over the next three thousand years. Historians break up the long history into Old, Middle, and New Kingdoms. The three pyramids at Giza, which you visited on your own yesterday, were built during the Old Kingdom forty-five hundred years ago."

"What was the purpose of the pyramids?" asked Summersby.

"The Egyptians believed in an afterlife, which is why they mummified bodies of the deceased pharaohs and built elaborate tombs to aid their Kings' journey to the afterworld. The pyramids were filled with great treasures the pharaohs would need in the afterlife, as well as items for their everyday needs, like food and clothes."

"And the significance of the Sphinx?" asked Roosevelt.

"An animal body with a human face is a sign of divinity, signifying that Khafre, the pharaoh whose face is carved on the Great Sphinx, is a god. It was likely built as a guardian for the Giza pyramids."

In two hours, the plane landed at a dusty airfield. After a short drive, the group arrived in Luxor. The modern city had been built next to the ruins of an ancient Egyptian temple.

Emery found a spot in the shade where he gathered his travelers. "Luxor is the modern name for the ancient city of Thebes. During the New Kingdom period, from 1570 BC to 1077 BC, Thebes was the most important religious site in Egypt. Many pharaohs engaged in building projects here at Luxor Temple and at Karnak Temple, two miles north. The Egyptians worshipped many gods, but one became preeminent— Amun-Ra, the King of gods. His consort was the goddess Mut, and their son was the god Khonsu. The Luxor and Karnak Temples were dedicated to these three gods who make up the Theban triad."

Emery led his group into the sun. He halted them in front of a large obelisk. "Ramesses the Great built this entrance to the temple more than three thousand years ago to honor himself. He erected two obelisks to mark the entrance of the temple."

Emery pointed to a seventy-five-foot obelisk. "This monument was carved from a single piece of red granite. The hieroglyphics carved into the stone tell stories about the great feats of Ramesses the Great."

"There's only one obelisk here. What happened to the other?" asked Roosevelt.

"When Turkey controlled Egypt, they gave it to the French. That obelisk is now in the Place de la Concorde in Paris." Emery then pointed to two huge seated pharaohs flanking the entrance to the Luxor Temple. "These are statues of Ramesses the Great."

"How tall are those statues?" asked Summersby.

"Almost fifty feet high! Ramesses believed in a colossal building style. The entrance facades depict Ramesses at the Battle of Kadesh, where he won a great victory against the Hittites in Syria."

Next, Emery led the group through the entrance into a courtyard filled with large pillars. "Ramesses built this courtyard. There are seventy-four pillars carved with scenes of Ramesses making offerings to the gods."

Eisenhower observed more large statutes. "Are those also Ramesses?"

Emery smiled. "Yes, the man had a healthy ego."

As the tour continued, Eisenhower absorbed the information dispensed by the scholarly Emery like an awestruck tourist. What he was observing and learning was thrilling and took him completely away from wartime stress.

That night, Emery's tourists dined together at their Luxor hotel. Kay was the first to excuse herself, with the others soon following. An hour later, Eisenhower slipped into Kay's unlocked hotel room.

The next morning, the travelers crossed by boat to the West Bank of the Nile. They drove through a fertile farming area, then into barren desert. Soon they turned onto a dirt trail that ran over a series of hills. The trail ended above two empty-looking ravines.

Emery gathered his small flock. "Below us is the Valley of the Kings, one of the most magnificent archaeological sites in the world! Here the pharaohs of the New Kingdom were buried in underground tombs. Why?"

Roosevelt answered simply, "Grave robbers."

"Precisely! The great riches the pharaohs took with them for the afterlife attracted grave robbers, who stripped the pyramids of their precious objects. During the Old Kingdom, over one hundred pyramids were built, and all of them were plundered by grave robbers."

"But these tombs were robbed too," Roosevelt added.

"Sadly, yes." Emery nodded his head. "Only the tomb of Tutankhamun was discovered largely intact with its precious artifacts."

The group spent the morning exploring the 450-foot-long tomb of Seti I. Its eleven chambers were decorated with exquisite bas-reliefs and vibrant, colorful paintings. In one, a solar barque was used to transport the pharaoh on an adventure to rebirth. The vivid artwork contained good snakes, dangerous snakes, a celestial cow, a hippopotamus constellation, and magic spells.

The fantastical netherworld the Egyptians had created for Seti I's afterlife fascinated Eisenhower. *How lucky I am to experience it through the eyes of an expert!*

During a lunch break, Eisenhower asked Emery, "What do you do for Tedder?"

"I analyze air-reconnaissance photos. During the fight with Rommel, my knowledge of the desert proved quite useful in identifying Nazi tanks that were camouflaged to blend into the desert landscape."

After lunch, Emery asked Eisenhower if he had seen enough of ancient Egypt.

"Absolutely not. This is a once-in-a-lifetime experience. I want to see as much as possible."

The group stayed in the Valley of the Kings until nightfall, exploring more of the magnificent tombs. Eisenhower loved every minute.

CHAPTER 59

On his return to Algiers, Eisenhower received a cable from Jimmy Doolittle, commander of the newly created Fifteenth Air Force. Doolittle's headquarters was in the Italian city of Bari.

Eisenhower put on his glasses and read the disturbing note:

On the night of December 2, the Germans bombed Bari and its harbor. Seventeen cargo ships were destroyed, and more than a thousand sailors, soldiers, and civilians killed.

Late in the morning, Doolittle called. "Ike, it was like Pearl Harbor—we were taken totally by surprise," Doolittle said, his voice cracking.

"Didn't radar give you warning?"

"The radar station was being repaired and was nonoperational. The reason I'm calling is one of the cargo vessels destroyed was filled with mustard gas."

Eisenhower felt a sense of dread. The army was stockpiling poison gas bombs and artillery shells for swift retaliation if Hitler ever used nerve gas. "Did any of the gas escape?"

"Unfortunately, yes."

Eisenhower rubbed his forehead. *More innocents exposed to the horrors of war.*

Doolittle continued. "Hospitals are overflowing with victims from the bombing. Early reports show quite a few people with symptoms of gas poisoning. There are sure to be fatalities. My question is, should we impose censorship about the mustard gas?"

"Yes, censor the news. I can't allow word of such a calamity to be made public."

That evening, as Summersby deftly navigated the Cadillac through steep, twisting streets, Eisenhower questioned for the hundredth time if he was making the right decision leaving her behind. As much as he cared for Kay and hated the thought of severing their relationship, he always came to the same conclusion. It was a romance forged in the crucible of war that had to end when he returned to the States. Going back to Mamie was the right thing to do. She was a loving and loyal wife who didn't deserve to be discarded.

But returning to his old life with Mamie was unlikely to be smooth going. They had been apart for eighteen months, and Mamie was sure to vent her anger over Summersby. Eisenhower feared his hair-trigger temper would explode and do untoward damage to their marriage.

He prayed for the strength to weather his homecoming.

Two days later, Eisenhower flew to Tunis to prepare for the President's return from the Tehran conference. FDR wanted to visit Malta and Sicily before returning to Washington.

As Eisenhower deplaned, he saw Elliott Roosevelt. He walked over and asked, "How was Tehran?"

"Full of Big Three power brokering. Father seemed to hit it off with Uncle Joe."

"Did you meet Stalin?"

"I did. He's rather short in stature, but there is a dynamic quality about him that makes him seem larger than life. I attended a banquet he hosted. At one point, Stalin toasted to putting fifty thousand Nazi war criminals in front of firing squads. Winston took great offense and declared no Nazi would be executed without a fair trial. Father proposed a compromise—that only forty-nine thousand Nazi war criminals be put before firing squads! Stalin laughed, but Winston was peevish. He didn't think joking about mass executions was funny."

Eisenhower felt a bit hollow inside after hearing the tale. He had heard stories of Soviet purges with wholesale killings and didn't think Stalin was necessarily joking. "Was Churchill able to delay Overlord?"

"No, Stalin said a second front in France was imperative, and he opposed any new Mediterranean operations that would weaken or delay Overlord."

"Good."

"Stalin asked who would command Overlord, and when Father told him no decision had been made, he was dismissive. Father promised him a decision would be made in a few days, so you'll know your fate soon."

"It'll be Marshall, not me. He richly deserves it." Eisenhower lit a cigarette. "Sounds like Churchill had a tough conference."

"He was visibly disappointed Stalin rejected his Mediterranean stratagems. Father thinks Winston wants to invade through the Balkans so the Western Allies can reach Eastern Europe before the Russians and limit Stalin's postwar influence."

"Churchill's strategy may be a good political move," Eisenhower assessed, "but from a military perspective, invading France will end the war sooner than prying Nazis out of Balkan Mountain passes."

After a few minutes, they parted ways, and Eisenhower walked to his car. Summersby gave him a welcoming smile as she opened the back door. "Did Elliott have any insight into who will get the Overlord command?"

"No, only that a decision is imminent. I'm resigned to sitting behind a desk in the Pentagon."

The next morning, December 7, Eisenhower received a cryptic cable from Marshall:

In view of the impending appointment of a British officer
as your successor in the Mediterranean, please recommend
steps for an effective transfer of command.

It was a bit puzzling, as there was no mention of his next assignment. Probably that was because chief of staff was a Presidential appointment. When he picked FDR up in two hours, the President would likely tell him of his Pentagon appointment.

Eisenhower was waiting at the airfield when the President's plane landed. Two Secret Service agents carried the President off the plane and deposited him in the back seat of the Cadillac. As Summersby began driving, Roosevelt abruptly said, "Well, Ike, you're going to command Overlord."

Eisenhower was stunned. *My fate has changed! I am going to command the most important campaign in the war!*

As his veins pulsed with excitement, Eisenhower told himself to get a grip. He had to show the President a steady hand. "I'm surprised but honored to command Overlord."

"I was going to give the command to Marshall, but when push came to shove, I simply couldn't spare him. I don't think I could sleep at night if I didn't have him by my side in Washington. Your appointment will be kept confidential until I get back to Washington and make a public announcement."

"When does the appointment take effect?"

"January 1. You'll have time to hand over the Italian campaign to whomever Winston chooses as your successor."

As the ride continued and Eisenhower chatted with the President, a thought floated in the back of his mind: *my relationship with Kay doesn't have to end.*

That evening, before the predinner cocktail hour with the President at La Maison Blanche, Eisenhower walked onto the terrace. The sun was setting, and yellow, red, and pink hues peeked through the clouds.

It had been two years since Pearl Harbor. He had risen from obscurity to worldwide fame, survived brutal on-the-job training as the

Allied commander, learned from his missteps, and earned the respect of his British subordinates—except for Monty. He was proud to have created an integrated Allied headquarters and successfully managed three invasions. Now Roosevelt had entrusted him with the most important command of the war, and he couldn't help but think about Mamie's reaction. She would swell with pride when the President announced his name as Supreme Allied Commander. He wished he could see her face when she found out the news.

While he cherished the opportunity to command Overlord, he was beginning to have nagging doubts about its chances of success. There hadn't been a successful invasion across the English Channel since 1066. Hitler, a supreme risk taker, lacked the courage to cross the channel to invade England. Eisenhower was chagrined when he remembered how naively gung ho he was to invade France in 1942 when the Allies were woefully unprepared for such an enormous undertaking. Brooke had been right: Sledgehammer would have been a disaster! *Will Churchill's grim image of the English Channel running red with the blood of Allied soldiers become a reality?*

Summersby came up beside him and laid her hand over his on the railing. "You look somber. I thought you'd be dancing a jig getting the Overlord assignment."

"Overlord will be the riskiest endeavor of the war. Churchill fears it will be a colossal failure. If it's a disaster, we could lose the war." Eisenhower stared at the darkening gulf. "I'd be known as the man who lost the greatest conflict in human history."

"You're a great general," Summersby protested, her eyes ablaze. "You swept the Nazis out of Africa and Sicily and knocked Italy out of the war! With your leadership, Overlord will be a smashing success!"

"Thank you, Kay," Eisenhower said, some of the tension leaving his body. "I'll be returning to England, and you'll come with me."

She squeezed his hand. "I'm thrilled our time together will continue. I've been crying myself to sleep thinking of losing you."

He smiled at her. "When we're together, I feel a tranquility, a peace of mind that allows me to relax and forget the war. I'm happy you'll be with me for Overlord."

As they turned to walk into the villa, Eisenhower reached into his pocket and rubbed his lucky coins. He was an optimist at heart, always believing America with its millions of soldiers and vast industrial capacity would power the Allies to victory. So right here, right now, he vowed to overcome every obstacle and challenge the Nazis and strong-willed bosses and subordinates could throw at him. Hitler's Fortress Europe would be breached, and the subjugated people liberated. The evil Nazi empire would be destroyed!

For the sake of the world, Overlord has to succeed. Failure is not an option.

AUTHOR'S NOTE

This novel covers many significant events of the first two years of America's involvement in World War II. All the military operations and political happenings described occurred. The descriptions and interpretations of these events are the author's.

While this is a work of fiction, every character in the book was a real person in history. The thoughts, characterizations, and dialogue of the individuals are fictional.

Historians differ on whether there was a romantic relationship between Eisenhower and Summersby. Kay Summersby wrote two books about her time with Eisenhower. In her second book, written after Eisenhower's death in 1969, she claimed there was a love affair. For the writing of this book, the author, guided by the intuitive insight of his wife, concluded there was a wartime romance.

The military cables and memoranda are either originals (noted by quotation marks), paraphrases of the originals, or fictional ones that capture the essence of the information being conveyed. The quote from Patton's letter of reprimand and his response to Eisenhower; the quote from Patton's letter to his soldiers before going into battle in Tunisia; Cunningham's order to "Sink, burn, and destroy"; and Churchill's congratulatory cable on the Salerno battle are original. The Mincemeat letters are paraphrases of excerpts of the originals. Montgomery's demand for the Fortress is an edited version of the original.

The letters between Mamie and Eisenhower are fictional. John, their son, published Eisenhower's wartime letters to Mamie in the book *Letters to Mamie*. Those letters are under copyright protection. No wartime letters from Mamie have been made public.

In my book *General Meade: A Novel of the Civil War*, I wrote an afterword describing what happened to the major players after the Civil War. I do not do that here because all the major characters in this novel appear in the upcoming sequel, *Victory in Europe: A Novel of World War II.* That novel covers the remainder of Eisenhower's wartime adventures, including D-Day, the struggle for France, the Battle of the Bulge, and the ultimate victory in Germany.

ACKNOWLEDGMENTS

I want to thank my editors, Barbara Henderson, Elizabeth Zack, Jane Steele, Jaye Whitney Debber, Emilie Sandoz-Voyer, and Leighton Wingate, for their professional guidance. Their efforts greatly enhanced the quality of the book.

Lastly, I must thank my extraordinary wife, Rosa, for her editorial insights and her understanding and patience with how much time and effort are needed to research and write a historical novel.

ABOUT THE AUTHOR

Robert Kofman is a retired labor and employment law attorney living in Miami, Florida. He is also the author of *General Meade: A Novel of the Civil War.*